White Dolphin

Gill Lewis

OXFORD
UNIVERSITY PRESS

OXFORD
UNIVERSITY PRESS

Great Clarendon Street, Oxford OX2 6DP
Oxford University Press is a department of the University of Oxford.
It furthers the University's objective of excellence in research, scholarship,
and education by publishing worldwide in

Oxford New York

Auckland Cape Town Dar es Salaam Hong Kong Karachi
Kuala Lumpur Madrid Melbourne Mexico City Nairobi
New Delhi Shanghai Taipei Toronto

With offices in

Argentina Austria Brazil Chile Czech Republic France Greece
Guatemala Hungary Italy Japan Poland Portugal Singapore
South Korea Switzerland Thailand Turkey Ukraine Vietnam

Oxford is a registered trade mark of Oxford University Press
in the UK and in certain other countries

First published 2012
First published in this paperback edition 2013

British Library Cataloguing in Publication Data
Data available

ISBN: 978-0-19-275621-3
3 5 7 9 10 8 6 4 2

Printed in Great Britain

Paper used in the production of this book is a natural, recyclable product made from wood grown in sustainable forests. The manufacturing process conforms to the environmental regulations of the country of origin.

Praise for White Dolphin:

'A passionate and lyrical story about the power of the sea and its creatures.'

Guardian

'A beautifully told, nail-biting tale, that will inspire and empower anyone who reads it.'

Kate Humble

'A lyrical, emotive, engrossing adventure.'

Sunday Times

'Packs a powerful emotional message into an exciting plot.'

Daily Mail

'A wonderful story. Utterly Captivating. The interplay with the natural world is magical.'

Nicholas Crane, presenter of BBC's Coast

'An addictive page-turner.'

Bliss

'An uplifting and beautifully told tale . . . with much to appeal to fans of Lauren St John and Michael Morpurgo.'

Bookseller

'Gracefully written and intense—you can almost feel the salty air brushing your face.'

Telegraph

Praise for Gill Lewis' first novel, Sky Hawk:

'Opens your eyes, touches your heart, and is so engaging it almost turns the pages for you.'

Michael Morpurgo

'Rich in atmosphere and full of heart, Sky Hawk is an intense and touching story . . . A book to treasure.'

Lovereading4kids.com

'A heart-soaring read.'

The Big Issue

'An edge-of-your-seat wildlife adventure that tells a very human story of friendship, discovery and an incredible journey. I loved it!'

Kate Humble

'A truly moving and inspiring tale of wildlife, friendship and growing up.'

TBK Magazine

'This beautifully written, captivating book should be on everyone's bookcase. Breathtaking. Poignant. Unforgettable.'

Virginia McKenna, Founder of the Born Free Foundation

'The reader is held spellbound by the intensity of the writing and the optimism in the message. This is a book for everyone from 8 to 80+!'

The School Librarian

For

Mum and Dad

and for

the *Nerys-Jane*

'A book to be kept for life.'

NAZIA, AGE 11

'This is one of the best books I have ever read . . . I give it 10 out of 10.'

ZAK, AGE 11

'A heart-touching story.'

LYDIA, AGE 11

'It was as if the characters were alive and walking around you.'

HARRY, AGE 11

'Extremely inspiring.'

EMMA, AGE 10

'Gill Lewis is a great writer . . . Five stars!'

ASHWIN, AGE 11

'A brilliant, outstanding book.'

MICHELLE, AGE 10

Prologue

Each night it is the same. I stand here on the shoreline, curling my toes into cool wet sand. Above, the moon is bright, bright white. It spills light, like a trail of milk upon the water. The dolphin is here again, her pearl-white body curving through the midnight sea. She twists and turns beyond the breaking waves, willing me to follow. But the ocean is vast and black, and I don't know what lies beyond this shore. So I just stand and watch her swim away.

Each night I have this dream. Each night the white dolphin waits for me. But where she goes, I am too afraid to follow.

Chapter 1

I rip another page from the book.

I tear it out, right out.

The paper is tissue thin and edged with gold. It flutters in my hand like a tiny bird, desperate to escape. I let it go and watch it fly up into the clear blue sky.

I rip out another, and another. The pages soar and tumble across cow-scattered fields into the haze above the silver-blue sea.

'Oi, Kara!'

I look down. Jake's pink face is squinting up at me against the glare of sun. Ethan's standing next to him trying to find finger-holds in the granite blocks of the wall. He jumps to pull me off, but I pull my legs up out of reach.

The wall's too high.

Chapter 1

I'm safe up here.

'Kara-two-planks,' yells Jake. 'Teacher's looking for you.'

I run my finger along the rough leather binding of the book. It's heavy in my lap. The hard edges dig into my skin. I rip out another page and set it free, soaring upwards, skywards.

'You're in big trouble, Kara-two-planks,' shouts Jake. 'That Bible is school property. You'll be sent to hell for that.'

'She won't get there, though,' calls Ethan. 'She won't be able to read the signs.'

Jake laughs. 'Learnt to spell your name yet, Kara? K-a-r-a W-o-o-d. Kara-thick-as-two-planks-of-wood.'

I've heard all this before, a thousand times. I turn my back on them and look down to the footpath on the far side of the wall. It runs one way to the coast path along the cliffs, and the other, down steps tangled with nettles and bindweed to the harbour in the town below.

'What I want to know,' says Ethan, 'is Kara Wood as thick as her dad?'

'My mum says,' confides Jake, 'that Kara's dad lost his last job because he couldn't write his own name.'

Ethan sniggers.

I spin round and glare at them. 'Shut-up about my dad.'

But Jake's not finished. 'I heard your mum had to write his name for him. Isn't that right, Kara?'

My eyes burn hot with tears.

'Who writes his name for him now, Kara?'

I blink hard and turn back to the sea. The waves out there are tipped with white. I feel the hot sun on my face. I mustn't cry. I won't let them see me cry. If I ignore them they'll go away like they always do. The sea breeze is damp and salty. It catches the white cotton of my shirt and billows it out like a spinnaker sail. I close my eyes and imagine I am sailing across an endless sea, a wide blue ocean, with nothing else around me but the sun and wind and sky.

'Oi, Kara!'

Jake's still there.

'It's a shame about the Merry Mermaid,' he shouts.

If Jake knows about the Merry Mermaid, then everyone does.

I turn round to look at him.

A few other children from class are watching us from a distance. Chloe and Ella are both looking this way from under the deep shade of the horse-chestnut tree. Adam has stopped his game, his football clutched against his chest.

'Still,' Jake says, 'it never was much of a pub. It'll make a great holiday home for someone, a rich Londoner probably. I heard the food was terrible.'

Jake knows my dad works in the kitchens of the Merry

Mermaid. He knows he'll have no job and no money to live on when it closes at the end of the summer. Jake would love it if we had to move from Cornwall.

'Maybe your dad can come back and work for mine on our trawlers?' says Jake. 'Tell him we'll be fishing for shellfish when the dredging ban is lifted in ten days' time. My dad's even bought new gear to rake every corner of the seabed out there. He can't wait.'

I just glare at him.

Jake laughs. 'I'll ask him if you can come too.'

I tighten my grip on the Bible's hard leather binding.

Beyond, I see Mrs Carter striding towards us. I could try and hide the book, but Jake and Ethan would tell her anyway.

'Have you seen the advert at the boatyard, Kara?' says Jake. He's looking at me now and grinning. Ethan's grinning too. They know something I don't. It's in Jake's voice and he's bursting to tell me.

Mrs Carter's halfway across the playground. Her face is set and grim.

'The *Moana*'s up for sale,' Jake shouts out. He's jubilant now.

I scramble to my feet. 'Liar!'

It can't be true. I'm sure it can't.

But Jake is smug. He pulls his trump card. 'My dad's going to buy her and chop her up for firewood,' he shouts. 'Cos he says that's all she's good for.'

I hurl the book at him. The Bible's hard edge slams into Jake's nose and he drops like a stone, both hands clutched across his face.

Mrs Carter is running now. 'Kara!'

I glance down at Jake, moaning in the dirt below me.

'Kara, come down, now!' Mrs Carter yells.

But I turn away from them all and jump, leaving Jake Evans bleeding through his fat fingers, turning the dust-dry ground blood red.

Chapter 2

I run and run, down the nettled footpath, along cobbled lanes and back alleyways to the sea front. I have to find Dad.

I have to.

The town is busy, clogged with traffic and the sound of drills and diggers working on the new road into the harbour. Beyond the orange cones and construction fences sits the Merry Mermaid, her roof green with weathered thatch. The air is thick with the smell of beer and chips. The tables sprawled across the pavement are packed with people eating lunch in summer sunshine. The Merry Mermaid scowls down at them from her faded painted sign above the door. I slip through into the darkness and let my eyes adjust from the glare outside.

'You OK, Kara?' Ted is polishing a glass in his hand, turning its rim round and round with a cloth.

'I'm fine,' I say. 'Where's Dad?'

'He took the day off,' he says. He holds the glass up to the light, inspecting it for smudges. 'Is everything all right, Kara? He didn't seem himself today.'

I look around, as if I expect Dad still to be here.

Ted puts the glass down and leans on the bar towards me. 'You sure you're OK?'

'Yes,' I say, 'I'm fine.'

I back out of the pub. The sun is bright. It glares off the whitewashed houses. I start running away from the harbour and up the hill to the new estate on the other side of town. A stitch stabs into my side, but I keep running past front gardens and driveways, past scraps of green with paddling pools and tricycles and on to the end house, where a caravan sits on bricks upon the grass.

I slow down and push open the front gate. Aunt Bev is hanging overalls and oilskins on a washing line strung between the garage and the caravan. Uncle Tom must be back from sea.

Aunt Bev pulls back the legs of the overalls to look at me and rests her hand on her swollen belly. She holds two wooden clothes-pegs in her teeth. They stick out like warthog tusks.

Chapter 2

I try the handle of the caravan door. Flakes of red rust crumble from the door frame, but the door is locked. 'Where's Dad?' I say.

Aunt Bev takes the pegs out of her mouth. 'You should be at school,' she says.

I hammer on the caravan door.

'Your dad went out,' she says.

I try the door again.

'I said he went *out*.' Aunt Bev pegs a pair of trousers to the line. She doesn't take her eyes off me.

I duck under the line and try to dash past into the kitchen, but she puts her hand across the door.

'You in trouble, Kara?' she says.

'Forgotten something, Auntie Bev,' I say. 'That's all.'

'Well, be quick, Uncle Tom's asleep. Don't wake him.' She lifts a hand from the doorway, and lets me pass.

I feel her watching me climb the stairs and slip into the room I share with Daisy. Daisy's sitting on her bed among her dolls, reading Teddy-cat one of her fairy books. She stuffs something behind her back as I come in. I hear it rustle in her hand. A tell-tale marshmallow lies upon her princess-pink duvet.

'You're off school,' I say. 'You're meant to be ill.'

Daisy's mouth is full. She looks at the open door and then at me.

I smile. 'Don't worry. I won't tell.'

A blob of sticky dribble slides down her chin. 'I feel sick now,' she says.

'I'm not surprised,' I say. I wipe the sugar dust from the bed and sit down beside her. 'Daisy, have you seen my dad?'

Daisy nods. 'Uncle Jim's gone fishing,' she says. 'He took his sea rods, them long ones.' Her hair bounces as she nods. It's light and frizzy, a sign the good weather's set to stay. I've seen it go tight and curly before the storms blow in.

'How long ago?'

'Not long,' she says. 'Just after Mum had her coffee.'

'Thanks, Daisy.' I reach under my camp bed for my swimming bag, mask and flippers. Daisy's toys are scattered on my bed. A pink marshmallow is pressed into my pillow. I can't complain, really. It's her room after all. And they'll need my space when the baby comes.

'Are you going with him?' Daisy says.

I nod. 'Please don't tell.'

Daisy draws her fingers across her heart and presses them against her lips.

I change into T-shirt and shorts, and it's not until I hear a car door slam and voices on the drive outside that I realize a car has pulled up outside the house. Jake's dad's big black pickup is parked across the drive. I back away from the window. I don't want Jake's dad to see me here.

I hear him talking to Aunt Bev in the kitchen.

'Jim's not up there, Dougie.' Aunt Bev's voice is high and tight. 'I'll get him to call when he gets back.'

'It's his girl I want to see.'

'Kara?' Aunt Bev says. I hear her hesitate and stumble on the words. 'She's at school.'

Through the crack in the bedroom door, I see Aunt Bev below me in the hallway. She's blocking the doorway to the kitchen. The back of her neck is bright scarlet and she twists a tea towel round and round her hands.

Dougie Evans leans his hand on the door frame. 'I know she's up there, Bev.'

Aunt Bev takes a step back. Her voice is quiet, almost a whisper. 'What d'you want with her?'

'Just a word, that's all.'

'What's she done?'

Dougie Evans is in the hallway now, at the foot of the stairs, his sea boots on Aunt Bev's clean carpet. 'She broke Jake's nose, that's what she's done.'

I close the door and press myself against it.

Feet sound on the stairs, loud and heavy.

White Dolphin

Daisy stares wide-eyed at me, the duvet pulled up around her chin. 'He's coming up,' she whispers.

I push the camp bed up against the door and cross the room to the window. The garage roof below is flat, but it's still a long way down.

'Kara!' It's Aunt Bev calling now. Her voice is sing-song, almost casual, but I can hear the tremor in it. 'Dougie Evans wants to see you.'

I throw my bag down to the garden and swing my legs out of the window.

Knuckles rap against the door. It flies open and jams against the camp bed.

'Go,' mouths Daisy.

I drop onto the roof, twisting as I land. From there I jump down to soft grass. I turn and see Dougie Evans red-faced and leaning from the window. But he can't stop me now.

No one can.

I grab my bag and run.

Chapter 3

'Wait,' I yell. 'Wait.'

I see *Moana* before I see Dad. She looks small compared to other boats in the harbour. With her terracotta sails and open wooden deck, she stands out from the moulded whiteness of the modern yachts. I scramble down steps and run along the pontoon, my feet thudding on the boards. *Moana* is drifting slowly out towards the narrow gap between the high harbour walls. I see Dad sitting at the tiller.

'Dad,' I shout. 'Wait for me.'

Dad pushes the tiller across and *Moana*'s sails flap loose as she turns back into the wind. She drifts towards me, her painted hull throwing rippled patterns of pale blue upon the water. She could have sailed out from one of the old photos of this harbour a hundred years ago.

I steady myself as she bumps against the pontoon, grab the mooring rope and pull her in. 'Take me with you,' I say.

Dad shades his eyes against the sun to look at me. 'Why aren't you at school?'

'I can't stay at school,' I say. 'Not today, of all days, Dad.'

Dad just sits there, one hand on the tiller, watching me. I wonder if he remembers today, if it means something to him too. *Moana*'s sails flap and ruffle above our heads. She's impatient to be off.

'Let me come, Dad,' I say. I want to ask him if it's true about *Moana*, if he's really going to sell her. But something stops me, because I want to sail her one last time, not knowing if it's true. It's safe not knowing. It leaves a small space inside for hope.

Dad rubs the stubble on his chin. 'All right,' he sighs. 'Get in.'

I climb on board, pull my life jacket on and push *Moana* away. The water here behind the long arms of the harbour walls is deep and green and still. Rainbow ripples of oil spread out across its surface. Dad sets the mainsail and I pull in the jib. I watch the triangle of sail above me pull taut, and catch the wind, and we slide under the shadow of the harbour and out to sea.

Chapter 3

The sea is alive out in the bay. A steady offshore breeze is blowing, kicking up small waves, flecked with tips of white. Salt spray flies over *Moana*'s bow as she dips and rises out towards the headland. I sit and watch the harbour town and the pale strip of golden sand slip far into the distance. The school and Aunt Bev's house are soon lost among the sprawl of roads and houses that rise above the harbour. The yachts and trawlers and the long white roof of the fish market seem far away now too, another world away, almost.

And it is just us, again.

Moana, Dad, and me.

I sit beside Dad, but he doesn't look at me. His eyes are focused on the distant horizon, looking beyond there somehow, to another place that I can't see. He could almost be sailing in a different boat, on some different sea. I close my eyes and try to think back to how it used to be.

Beyond the headland, the wind is strong and cold. It blows in from the west, gusting dark ruffles on the water. I wish now that I'd thought to grab a jumper and put on jeans instead. I wrap my arms around my knees and watch goosepimples rise on my arms and legs.

'You OK, Kara?'

I look up and see Dad watching me now. I nod, but my teeth still chatter.

'Get your blanket if you're cold,' he says.

I slide forwards on the seats and open the small locker under the foredeck. Three blankets are neatly folded where they always are, strapped to the low shelf above the tool kit and the flares. I pull my blanket out and wrap it round me. It's deep turquoise, like the summer sea, woven through with strips of silver ribbon.

I curl up against *Moana*'s curves and bury my head in the thick folds of blanket, breathing in the salty mustiness of it. The ocean rushes beneath us, a constant stream of white noise. Waves slap against *Moana*'s hull, like a heartbeat. I touch the painted wood to feel it pulse against my hand. Somewhere under the thick layers of paint are the pencil drawings of leaping dolphins that Mum drew for me. I try to trace the outline of them with my fingers now. I can almost smell the sawdust and steamed wood of the boatshed where Mum and Dad rebuilt *Moana*. If I close my eyes, I can still see Dad curving steamed planks of wood to make *Moana*'s hull, Mum laying white caulk between the boards to make her water-tight, and me sitting in the dirt, floating paper boats across wide puddle seas.

Mum, Dad, and me.

Those pencil dolphins are still there beneath the paint, etched into *Moana*'s hull. I try to picture them in my mind.

Chapter 3

I never thought I would forget, but somehow, now, it seems however hard I try, I just can't see them any more.

And it must be like this that I fall asleep, cradled in *Moana*'s hull. Because when I wake the wind has dropped and *Moana* is still. Her sails are down and she is rocking gently, anchored in the shelter of the cove where we keep our lobster pots. Threads of hot sweet coffee steam drift my way from Dad's red tin cup. The sun is warm on my back, and the sea is turquoise blue, rippled with silver light. Somewhere above a seagull cries. But otherwise, all is quiet and still.

Dad is leaning over the side, pulling on rope. It coils in the boat, dripping weed and seawater. He hoists a lobster pot in and places it on the floor. I can see a tangle of legs and antennae of a lobster inside. It's a big one and will fetch a good price at market. I know we need the money.

Dad opens the trap and runs his hand along the armoured shell of the lobster's back. He draws it out and its claws slash through the air. Its red antennae flick backwards and forwards. Dad turns it over, and in the soft protected curve of its belly lie hundreds of tiny eggs bunched together, glistening black in the sunlight.

'She's berried,' I say. 'We can't sell her. Look at all those eggs.'

Dad looks up. He's just noticed I'm awake. 'We'll take her and release her in the marine reserve,' he says.

'Not much point,' I say. I scowl at him. 'Jake says his dad is going to pull his dredging chains across every last corner of the reserve when the dredging ban is lifted.'

Dad places the lobster in a large black bucket and covers it with a towel. His face is tight in a frown, running deep creases across his face. He knows there's nothing we can do to stop Dougie Evans from destroying the reef.

'Keep out of Jake's way,' he says. 'He's got a nose for trouble like his dad.'

I stifle a laugh. I picture Jake lying in the dirt, blood pouring down his face. 'Not any more he hasn't.'

Dad looks up. I try to hide my smile, but I can tell Dad's seen already.

'You in trouble, Kara?' says Dad.

I lift the towel and peer in at the lobster. She glares at me with her small black eyes. 'She needs seawater in there,' I say.

'What else has Jake been saying?' says Dad.

I cover the bucket with the towel and sit back so I can look Dad in the eye. I ask the question that has filled my mind all this way. 'Is *Moana* up for sale?'

Chapter 3

But Dad turns away. I watch as he ties a chunk of mackerel flesh bait for the lobster pot, and throws it back into the water. The coil of rope unwinds and disappears into the wavering shafts of light.

'It's true, isn't it?' I say. 'You're selling her. You're selling *Moana*.'

I want him to tell me that it's not true, because Dad never lies to me.

But he doesn't say that.

He turns to look at me. 'Yes,' he says. 'It's true.'

And that's all he says. But it's like the breath has been punched right out of me.

'But you can't,' I say. It comes out in barely a whisper.

'We've got no choice, Kara,' he says. 'I owe more money than I'll ever earn. We can't even afford her mooring fee.'

I twist the end of my blanket round and round in my hand. 'What about Mum?' I mumble the words.

Dad flicks the last drops of his coffee out to sea and screws on the thermos cap tight. 'There's no other way.'

'What about Mum?' I say it louder this time, to make sure that he can hear me.

'Mum's gone,' he says. He looks right at me. 'She's been gone a year today. D'you think I don't know that? She's gone, Kara. It's just us now.'

I stare at him. Dad hasn't talked about Mum for months. 'Mum would never sell *Moana*,' I say. 'She belongs to all of us. We built her together. How will you tell Mum you sold our boat when she comes back? She'll come back, I know she will.'

Dad watches me, like he's trying to decide just what to say.

'She'll send a sign,' I say. My eyes are blurred with tears. I blink and push them back. I think of the dove feather I found the day Mum disappeared. I think of the cowrie shell, pure white; the one I found by candlelight, the night we floated candles for her out to sea. 'Like she did before, she'll send a sign.'

Dad holds me by my shoulders, but his hands are trembling. 'Let it go, Kara,' he says. 'There are no signs. There never were.'

I push Dad's hands away.

The silence is thick between us.

The wind is still. The water flat, like glass.

'Kara,' Dad says. He kneels down in front of me. 'Look at me.'

I close my eyes tight.

'Kara . . . '

I cover my ears because I don't want to listen.

I fold my head into my lap to block him out.
I don't want to hear what he's going to say.
I don't want to hear it.
But it's no use.
I hear him say it, anyway.
'Mum is *never* coming back.'

Chapter 4

Dad has never said those words before. I stand up and back away from him.

'You've given up,' I say. 'You've given up.'

'Kara . . . '

I pull off my life jacket and reach into my bag for my face-mask and fins.

'Kara, sit down,' says Dad.

I push my feet into my fins, pull on my face-mask and stand up on *Moana*'s side, holding on to the metal shrouds that support her mast. The water below is crystal clear.

'Kara, come down . . . ' Dad reaches out his hand.

But I don't take it.

I let go and dive into the water, down into bright blueness shot with sunlight. I turn and watch a trail of silver bubbles spiral upwards. I see Dad through the rippled surface leaning out, looking down. I kick my fins hard and pull through the water and swim away from him towards the shore.

I count the seconds in my head before I can burst above the water. I count the seconds before I let myself breathe. My heart is pounding fast, too fast. I can't relax. My lungs burn. My ribs ache. I can't find the quiet space in my head that lets my heart slow down and my mind go clear. I'm too angry for that. I have to breathe. I burst upwards and gulp the air.

I'm halfway between Dad and the shore. I can hear Dad call my name, but I keep swimming until my hands touch the soft sand of the cove. I pull my fins and mask off and walk barefoot up through the rocks to the clifftop path. My T-shirt flaps wet and cold against me, and my shorts cling to my legs, but I keep walking and don't look back.

It's only when I reach the stile that turns inland, that I double back and crawl through the long grasses. *Moana*'s sails are up, and Dad is sailing from the small cove. I watch him sail towards the marine reserve, the stretch of seabed that lies between the shore and Gull Rock, the small island out beyond the headland. *Moana*'s sails cast long shadows in the early evening sun.

I sit up and brush the sand and sea salt from my clothes, and look around. A fresh breeze ripples through the grasses. There's no one else up here, just me. I don't want to go back to Aunt Bev's house. I can't face her and Uncle Tom. I don't want to face Dad now either.

Beyond this cove there is another smaller cove, too narrow for most boats to enter. The water is deep and crystal clear. It shelves up to a strip of sandy beach. I head there now, away from the coast path, towards the green wall of gorse that lines these cliffs. The gorse spikes snag my T-shirt as I scramble between the bushes to the cliff edge. Below the crumbly topsoil and twisted roots of gorse, a ledge of hard dark rock cuts through the softer green-grey layers of slate, and curves down to the cove. I climb down, finding all the footholds and handholds I know so well, counting the layers of folded rock. Millions and millions of years squashed together. Like explorers going back in time, Mum used to say.

The small beach is covered by the high tide. I edge my way to the flat rocks that jut out beyond the cove into the sea. Sometimes grey seals haul out on these rocks and lie basking in the sun. I press my back into a hollow curve of a rock worn eggshell-smooth by wind and waves.

Mum used to sit here with me and we'd watch for

dolphins. I used to think she had special powers, as if she could feel them somehow, or hear them calling through the water. Sometimes we'd wait for hours. But she always knew they'd come. They would rise up like magical creatures from another world, the sunlight shining from their backs, the sound of their breaths bursting above the water. They would leap and somersault in the water, just for us, it seemed. It made me feel as if we'd been chosen somehow, as if they wanted to give us a glimpse of their world too.

I haven't been back here since then. Not since Mum left. I wrap my arms around my knees and stare out across the gold, flat sea. The sun's rim touches the horizon, bleeding light into the water. I've been waiting for a sign from Mum all day, but it's too late now. The sun has almost set.

Maybe Dad is right and there are no signs to look for.

Maybe I have to accept Mum is never coming back.

I watch the last rays of sunshine flare like beacons across the sky.

And then I see it.

I see a flash of white leap from the water.

The light shines on its smooth curved body, before it plunges back into the sea.

I scramble to my feet and stand at the ocean's edge, watching the spread of golden ripples.

White Dolphin

This is the sign I have been waiting for.

I just know it is.

It has to be.

The dolphin leaps into the air again. It's white, pure white. It twists and somersaults before diving under water, sending up plumes of golden spray.

I see other dolphins too, their grey streamlined bodies and dorsal fins curving through the water. There must be at least fifty dolphins, a huge pod of them. I've never seen so many at one time. Their bursts of breath blast through the stillness.

But it's the white dolphin I'm looking for. Then I see it again, much smaller than the rest. Its pale body is tinged with pink and gold in the fading light. A much larger dolphin swims close by its side. Mother and calf, they break the surface together in perfect time. I watch them swim side by side, out into the open sea. I wrap my arms around me and feel warm despite the chill night air. I feel so close to Mum somehow, as if she's right here beside me, as if she sent the dolphins. I can almost see Mum's face, her big wide smile. I can't help wondering if, wherever she is right now, she is thinking of me too.

Chapter 4

I watch the dolphins until I can no longer see their fins trail dark lines upon the water. The sea has darkened under a star-scattered indigo sky. The silhouettes of two oystercatchers skim across the surface, their short pointed wings beating fast and hard. But that is all.

I know Dad will expect me home by now. I scramble up the cliff to the coast path that runs between the cliff edge and the fields. The air is fresh and damp with dew. It clings in a pale mist above the wheat fields that run inland. The in-between light of dusk holds everything in a strange stillness, like time's drawn breath.

And it feels to me as if *everything* is about to change.

Chapter 5

The tarmac of the coast road is still warm from the day's sun. It's more than two miles home from here and I hope Dad's not waiting for me. He has a late shift at the pub today, so maybe I can slip back without him noticing.

I haven't walked far along the road before a car pulls up, its headlights glaring in my eyes.

The passenger window slides down. 'KARA! Is that you?'

It's Aunt Bev. She leans across from the driver's side. She's furious. I wish I'd walked across the fields back home instead.

'What's wrong?' I say.

'Just get in the car, Kara,' she snaps, 'now.'

I climb in the back seat next to Daisy. She's in her

dressing gown and slippers, munching a family pack of crisps. She's usually in bed by now.

Aunt Bev twists round to glare at me. 'What's wrong?' She spits the words out.

I glance at Daisy. She points at me and draws her hand across her throat. I'm as good as dead.

'What's wrong?' shouts Aunt Bev again. 'The coastguard and the police are out looking for you, that's what's wrong. Your dad's in a right state. He's gone with them too.' She slams the car in gear and we lurch forward. 'You've got some questions to answer when we get back. I can tell you that, my girl.'

I say nothing. I strap my seat belt up and say nothing.

We drive back home in silence and in darkness. Daisy takes my hand in hers and squeezes it. I squeeze hers back.

'I told them you'd be OK,' she whispers. 'But they wouldn't listen.'

'That's enough from you, Daisy,' snaps Aunt Bev. 'You should've been in bed an hour ago.'

Back at the house, I sit in the kitchen and wait for Dad. I can hear Uncle Tom phoning the police and coastguard to say that I've been found. Aunt Bev is heating up a pan of milk for Daisy's bedtime drink. Daisy's been told to go upstairs, but she's sitting at the kitchen table, twirling a curl of golden hair round and round her finger.

She leans across so our heads are close together. 'What happened?'

The question catches me off guard.

'The white dolphin came,' I whisper.

Daisy's eyes open wide. She's the only one who knows the dreams I have.

'It's bedtime for you, Daisy,' says Aunt Bev. She pours the warm milk into a mug and points up at the stairs.

I stand up to go too, but Aunt Bev signals me to stay. I don't want to be here, just her and me. I watch Daisy cup her hands around her mug and leave the room. She gives a small smile before disappearing around the door and up the stairs.

Aunt Bev pours herself a mug of tea and leans against the oven. 'Well?' she says.

I stare at my hands and say nothing.

'I heard you bust Jake Evans's nose today.'

I look up at her. She's glaring at me, daring me to challenge her.

I don't deny it.

'The only person with a proper job in this house is employed by Jake's dad,' she snaps. 'Do you want Uncle Tom to lose his job as well? Do you?'

Chapter 5

I shake my head. 'No, Auntie Bev,' I say. 'I'm sorry.'

She sighs and rubs her hand across her swollen belly. 'God knows this year's been hard for you, Kara, but you're not the only one who's struggling. We can't go on like this. It's time we had some straight talking in this family . . . '

But she doesn't finish, because Dad bursts through the door.

He pushes past the table and pulls me into him. He wraps his arms around me, so I'm buried in his thick wool jumper. It smells of wood-smoke and engine oil. I feel his warm breath in my hair, and I feel five years old again.

'I'm sorry, Kara,' he says, 'I'm so sorry.'

Aunt Bev's voice cuts through. 'It's Kara who should be sorry. She's had us all worried sick.'

But Dad holds me by my shoulders. 'I'm sorry,' he says, 'what I said about Mum. I shouldn't have.' His eyes are red, so that I could almost think he's been crying, but I've never seen him cry before.

I smile at him. 'It's going to be OK, Dad. She sent a sign. I saw a dolphin, a white dolphin. Mum sent it for us.'

Dad pushes back my hair. He looks right in my eyes but I can't tell what he's thinking any more.

'Mum's still here for us, Dad,' I say. 'I know she is.'

Aunt Bev thumps her mug down, slopping tea across the table. 'Your mother stopped being here for you the day she left.'

Uncle Tom lays a hand upon her arm. 'That's enough, Bev.'

Aunt Bev's not finished. 'But it's true. And we were left to pick up the pieces. It can't go on like this, Jim. How long are you going to wait for her? Another year? Five years? Ten years?'

'Leave it, Bev.' Uncle Tom tries to steer her away. 'Not now, not tonight.'

Aunt Bev pulls away and glares at Dad. 'Kay should never have left. Her responsibilities were *here.*' She raps her finger hard on the table to make her point.

Dad sits down and puts his head in his hands. 'We've been through this before, Bev. She had her reasons.'

'Going halfway around the world on some hippie dolphin-saving trip?' she snaps. 'Was that a good enough reason to leave a husband and child?'

I scowl at Aunt Bev. 'Mum's a marine biologist,' I shout. 'She's stopping people catching wild dolphins. You *know* that.'

But Aunt Bev ignores me and sits down next to Dad. 'You've got to face it, Jim. If your own sister can't tell you, then who can? You've just got to accept that Kay isn't coming back.'

Dad shoots her a look. 'We don't know that, Bev. We just don't know.'

Aunt Bev throws her hands up in the air. 'Exactly. That's always been the problem. We don't know anything. A year on and still the only thing we *do* know is that she landed in the Solomon Islands, checked into her hotel room and vanished.'

Dad shakes his head. 'I should have gone and looked for her at the time.'

'You couldn't afford the bus fare to the airport, let alone the plane ticket,' Aunt Bev snorts. 'The authorities there couldn't find her. Not even the private detective hired by the families of the others that disappeared could find her. The case is closed.'

Dad frowns. 'People don't just disappear.'

Aunt Bev sits back and looks at Dad. 'You can't bury your head in the sand for ever, for Kara's sake at least. You've got all Kay's debts to pay. Thousands for that trip and all that fancy diving stuff she bought. But I bet you haven't told Kara that, have you, Jim?'

Dad stands up. His chair knocks back against the wall. 'I'm going out.'

Uncle Tom shifts aside to let him pass.

'That's right,' Aunt Bev shouts after Dad. 'Walk away like you always do.'

I stand up too. 'Mum wouldn't leave us. I know she'll come back. She sent the dolphin.'

Dad stops, his hand on the door.

Aunt Bev glares at Dad's back. 'You've got no house, Jim Wood; no job to speak of, and soon no boat.' She takes a deep breath and turns to me. 'So there'll be no more talk of dolphins in this house, Kara. Is that understood?'

She folds her arms.

She's said her piece.

She's done.

But I don't care. The white dolphin is a sign that Mum's out there somewhere, and I'll wait for her, however long it takes. I want Dad to know this too. Mum will come back. I know she will. We'll live on *Moana*, the three of us, and sleep under canvas stretched across the boom. We'll sail away together one day like she always said we would.

Mum, Dad, and me.

The phone rings through the silence.

Uncle Tom answers it and passes it to Dad. 'It's for you, Jim.'

Dad takes the phone and I hear him pacing in the

hallway. I hear his voice, soft and quiet. He walks back into the kitchen and puts the phone down on the receiver. He opens the back door, leans against the door frame and lets the cool night air rush in.

Aunt Bev's got her head on one side. 'Well . . . who was that?'

Dad's shoulders are slumped. 'It's an offer for *Moana*,' he says. 'A man wants to view her this weekend.'

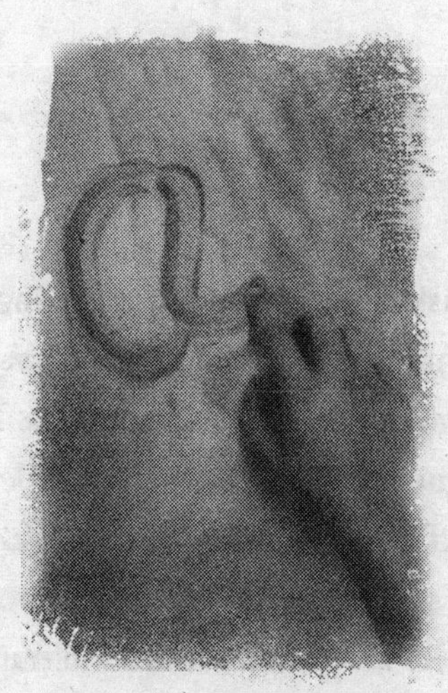

Chapter 6

I cut Daisy's toast in triangles and push the plate to her side of the table.

She pulls off the crust and looks at me. 'Aren't you having any breakfast?'

'Not hungry,' I say.

Aunt Bev looks at me across the top of her magazine. 'You're not having a day off school. The head teacher wants to see you about what you did to Jake Evans's nose.'

I frown. I don't want to go to school at all.

'I sent a big box of chocolates to Jake with your name on,' she says. 'Cost me nearly ten pounds it did. Let's just hope it keeps his dad happy too.'

I get up from the table and grab my schoolbag. 'I'll be waiting outside,' I tell Daisy.

Chapter 6

Outside the sky is clear and blue. A rag of pale grey cloud stretches along the distant horizon above the sea. All I want to do is go out on *Moana*, but Dad left early to cook breakfasts for guests staying at the pub. I lean against the caravan and scuff the dry ground with my feet and wait for Daisy. I wish I was back at the primary school with her too. I felt safe there. It wasn't just words and numbers like it is now in senior school. Mum was still here last year too.

'I'm coming,' calls Daisy.

I watch her walk down the path with her schoolbag across her shoulder and a larger bag dragging along the ground. 'What've you got in there?' I ask.

'Fairy dress and wings and wand and a present for Lauren,' she grins. 'It's her party after school.'

I roll my eyes. 'I forgot,' I say. 'Come on, I'll carry it.'

I walk Daisy through the mothers and pushchairs at the school gates of the primary school and give her a hug. 'I'll be back here after school,' I say.

Daisy reaches into her bag and pulls a scrunched-up piece of paper from the pocket. 'I did this for you,' she says, 'for good luck when you see Mrs Carter.'

I flatten the paper out and smile. A white wax crayon dolphin is swimming in an ink blue sea. 'Thanks, Daisy,' I say. 'It's just what I need.'

I mean it too. I'm going to need all the luck I can get.

I have to miss double art on Friday mornings to have extra sessions with Mrs Baker, my learning support teacher. I wish I could miss maths or ICT instead. Art is the only lesson I enjoy. It's not that I mind Mrs Baker. At least I don't get laughed at in her lessons. She says my dyslexia is just a different way of thinking. I remember her saying it often runs in families and I reckon that's why Dad can't read or write. Mum once tried to get him to see someone about it but he wouldn't go, said it was too late for him to learn.

The only spare classroom is a Portakabin at the far end of the playground, now used as a store. I sit at one of the tables, a tray of sand in front of me. We're doing Mrs Baker's new technique today. *Multi sensory development*, she calls it.

I call it a waste of time.

I pull the tray towards me and pick up a handful of sand, letting the grains run through my fingers. It's the coarse gritty sand from the car park end of the beach, not the fine white powder sand near the rock pools towards the headland.

Mrs Baker pulls up her chair and pats the sand down flat. 'Let's try the "*au*" sound, as in "sauce".'

Chapter 6

My fingers hover above the sand and I start to trace the outline of an '*a*'. I know this one. It's the shape of Gull Rock from the shore, one rounded side and one steep, a dark cave circled in the centre. I start the top loop of the '*a*' where the rocks are stained white with centuries of seabird mess. Gannets nest on the seaward side. I've watched them twist in the air and dive for fish, like white missiles into the water. Dad and I have seen puffins, too, scoot along above the waves. I curl my finger down to the base where grey seals haul out on the flat rocks and have their pups on the narrow pebble beach that faces the mainland shore. Submerged rocks and underwater caves and arches spread out into the sea. A wrecked warship has become part of the reef. I run my fingers across in wave patterns in the sand. Mum once showed me a photo she'd taken of a cuckoo wrasse, a fish with bright blue and orange markings, swimming through a rusted porthole and another of pink and white feather-stars living along the old gun-barrels. The whole reef spreads out from Gull Rock to the shore, an underwater safari park, a hidden wilderness.

'Kara!'

I look up. I didn't hear Mrs Carter come into the room. She smiles briefly at Mrs Baker and pulls up a chair beside me. She slides the Bible and some of the ripped pages on the table.

'I think Kara and I need a talk,' she says.

Mrs Baker's eyes flit between us. She gathers up her papers and shoulders her saggy carpet-bag. 'There's no lesson next Friday, Kara, as it's the last day of term, so if I don't see you before then, have a lovely summer.'

I watch her walk out towards the car park at the back of the school.

A cloud shadow slides across the playground, darkening the room.

Mrs Carter leans forward in her chair. 'I hear you've been making great improvements with your writing,' she says. Her smile is a thin hard line.

I stare at the tray of sand and run my fingers through the coarse grains. We both know we're not here to talk about my dyslexia today.

'I know this year's been hard for you, Kara.'

I look up. Mrs Carter is watching me. She takes her glasses off and folds them neatly on the table.

'It's all right to be angry.' Her voice is soft, controlled. 'I understand.'

I trace a circle in the sand, round and round and round. I want this to be over with.

'But you can't take your anger out on other children and school property.'

I let silence sit between us.

Mrs Carter leans closer. 'You broke Jake Evans's nose,' she says. 'How do you feel about that now?'

I dot two eyes and trace the outline of a smile in my circle. 'His dad's going to destroy the reef,' I say. 'He's going to pull his dredging chains across it and rip it up when the ban is lifted.'

'There is never an excuse for violence, Kara.'

I stare hard at the sand. Mrs Carter sits back in her seat and folds her arms. I think she wants this to be over with as much as me.

'But why rip up the Bible, Kara? Tell me that.'

I want to say it's because she told us God will answer all our prayers. Well, I've been praying for news of Mum for a whole year now and I haven't heard a thing. But I don't tell her that. Instead, I shrug my shoulders and scrunch the sand up in my hands.

The school bell rings marking the end of the second lesson. The next lesson is maths, before the break. I glance up at Mrs Carter.

'How can we resolve this, Kara?' she says. 'You tell me.'

I run my finger along the hard edge of the Bible. Resolve what? Mum not coming back? Dredging the reef? I know she doesn't mean those things at all. I lift the corner of a tissue-thin ripped page. 'I could help mend it,' I say.

Mrs Carter sits back in her chair and nods. 'It would be a good start,' she says. 'You can help me repair it on Monday after school. It'll give you the weekend to think things through. But you know I'll have to speak to your father about all this.'

I let the sand trickle through my fingers and watch it pile up in a little mountain in the tray.

'And you're to apologize to Jake as well,' she says.

I stare at my hands, flecked with tiny crystal grains.

Mrs Carter stands up and tucks the Bible under her arm. 'You can go now.'

I stand up and walk away but I feel her eyes burn in my back. Maybe she can read my mind. I'll help her stick the pages in her Bible.

But I won't say sorry to Jake Evans.

I'd rather die.

Chapter 7

I stand in silence in the corridor outside the maths room. Through the end windows I see the bright sunlit playground and far beyond that, the sea. I could walk out of here; just keep walking on and on. There's no one here to stop me, no one here to see. But I don't do that. Instead, I put my hand on the door and push it open. Everyone in my class knows I've had to see Mrs Carter about breaking Jake Evans's nose. I know they'll all stop and turn and stare when I walk in.

I keep my head down as I walk across the classroom. I stop at the place where I usually sit. But there's someone else already there, in my seat.

'Find another seat, Kara,' says Mr Wilcox above the silence. 'Be quick.'

I spin round and sit down at a spare desk by the window and spread my maths books out in front of me. I glance sideways at the new boy in the class sitting next to Chloe. He's wearing black jeans and a white shirt. But it's his face I notice more. The muscles in his neck stand out in straight tight lines, pulling the left side of his face down and sideways. It looks like his face has dropped on one side. His left arm is twisted up against his chest and writhes around as if he can't keep it still at all.

He sees me staring, so I look away.

At break, Chloe and Ella stay behind with him to talk to Mr Wilcox. I guess they've been given the job of showing him around today. They've hardly talked to me at all. No one's mentioned Jake's nose either. I don't think anyone would dare in front of Jake and Ethan.

It's not until the morning lessons have finished, that I can join Chloe and Ella in the lunch queue. I grab a tray and slide it along behind Chloe.

'Where's that new boy?' I ask.

Chloe looks over her shoulder. 'Felix?' she says. 'He's only doing mornings. He's just getting to know the school before he joins after the summer.'

'It's hardly worth it,' I say. 'There's only a week left before we break up.'

Chapter 7

Chloe pours two glasses of water, one for her and one for Ella. 'Mrs Carter said the school might need to make changes before he comes, like put in ramps and hand rails and stuff. He can't walk that well.'

'What's he like?' I say.

Chloe shrugs her shoulders and looks at Ella. 'Dunno. Didn't say much did he?'

'Couldn't wait to go,' Ella says. 'Don't blame him though.'

Beyond Ella, I see Jake sitting at the table. He's stopped mid-mouthful to watch us talking. Chloe and Ella have seen him watching too.

I take a plate from the stack. 'Daisy can't wait till Lauren's party,' I say. 'You got many coming?'

Chloe puts her plate out for chips. 'About fifteen. Mum's dreading it. Dad's just got back from sea and he's dead tired. Mum wants us to help.'

Chloe's dad works with Uncle Tom on Dougie Evans's boats too. He's come home to fifteen Daisys, high on fizzy drinks and birthday cake.

'I don't mind helping too,' I say. 'I've got to bring Daisy along, anyway.'

Chloe glances across at Jake and then at Ella. 'We'll be fine,' she says. The words come out too quickly. 'It'll be a bit crowded in our house. We won't need any help.'

Ella stares down at her tray.

'All right,' I say. I feel my eyes smart with tears. Chloe and Ella have always let me join in with them before.

'Chips or jacket?'

I look up. The dinner lady is holding out a scoop of chips in one hand and a baked potato on a fork in the other.

'Chips,' I say.

She empties her scoop of chips on my plate and I pick up the ones that scatter across my tray.

Chloe slides a chocolate brownie on her tray and turns to me. 'I've got to pick up Lauren and her other friends from school, so I'll take Daisy too,' she says.

I nod and pretend to concentrate on the plates of pudding and the bowl of fruit in front of me. 'Tell her I'll pick her up at half five.'

I watch Chloe walk away. She sits down next to Ella on the long table by the window. Jake and Ethan are at the table too. Jake glares at me. His face is a blue black mess of bruise. A bright white plaster sits across his nose.

I grab an apple and walk across the hall feeling Jake's eyes on me all the way. The table is full. If Chloe moved up I could sit next to her, but her back is turned to me and her elbows are spread either side of her tray. The other tables have older children from Years Eight and Nine. I take my tray and sit at an empty table by the door.

I try to force my lunch down, but my mouth is dry and the chips stick in my throat. I push them to the side, hide them under my knife and fork and take a bite of apple. It's Friday at least. No school for two whole days, and then only one more week until the summer holidays begin.

'Having fun?' Jake puts his empty tray down on the table and sits opposite me. Ethan leans against the door frame and smirks.

I look across at Jake. Close up, one eye is bloodshot red. The edges of the bruise are sickly yellow.

'You don't think you can make up for this with a box of chocolates do you?' The corner of Jake's mouth curls up as he speaks.

'It wasn't me who sent them,' I say.

I wait for him to go, but he sits there, staring at me.

'You know why my dad hates you so much?' he says.

I stare down at the half-eaten apple on my plate. I know the reason why. I've heard all this before.

Jake leans across the table. 'Aaron's dead because of your mum.'

I grip the edges of my tray. The fork rattles against the

china plate. 'Your brother didn't have a life jacket on when he was found,' I say.

Jake snorts. 'My dad says you're going pay for this.' He lowers his voice so not even Ethan can hear. 'Soon you and your dad will have *nothing* left.'

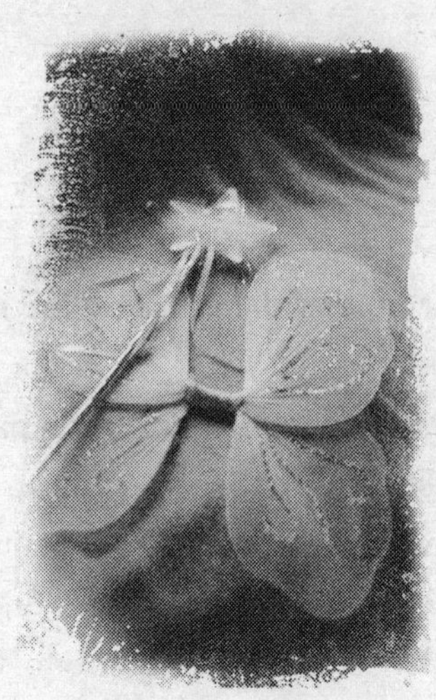

Chapter 8

I slip my hand through Daisy's. 'Good party?' I say. Her fairy tutu rustles as we swing arms, and she skips along beside me.

Daisy nods and smiles up at me. 'Why didn't you come too?'

I glance back at the house. Lauren's waving from the door, but there's no sign of Chloe or Ella.

'I had to get some shopping for your mum,' I lie.

Daisy runs ahead and pulls me by the hand. 'Will you play with me at home?'

I shake my head. 'I'm going out.'

'Where?'

'Just out.'

She stops and pulls away from me. 'You're going to look for the white dolphin aren't you?'

I hold my hand out. 'Come on, Daisy,' I say. 'I told Aunt Bev I'd get you home.'

It's not entirely true, but I want to go back to the cove and I can't take Daisy with me.

'I want to come with you,' she says. She juts her chin out and just stands there, like she's not going anywhere. A gust of wind blows her long blonde curls across her face. Her fairy wings flutter. She clutches her wand and party bag in one hand and folds her arms across her chest.

'Come *on,* Daisy,' I say. I'm not in the mood to fight. '*Please.*'

She shakes her head. She looks like the sugar plum fairy. Sugar-plump and squashed into a ballet dress, about to have a tantrum.

I sit back on a low wall behind me and rest my head in my hands. I feel we could be here a while.

'I'll buy you an ice-cream at Zagni's,' I say. I jangle some coins in my pocket. I hope I've got enough to buy one. Maybe Daisy won't feel like one after all that party food. But I know Daisy. She never turns down an ice-cream. I wait and watch.

Daisy twirls her wand round and round. She puts her hands on her hips and looks at me. 'It has to be mint choc chip,' she says.

'Done,' I say. 'Mint choc chip it is.'

I get up from the wall, ready to go.

'And a flake,' says Daisy.

I shake my head. 'Haven't got enough money for that.'

'Chocolate sauce, then?'

I nod. 'You've got yourself a deal.'

Daisy flashes her smile at me and takes my hand. Her hand is small and soft and warm, like putty. She skips along beside me, her tiara bouncing on her curls. And I can't help smiling too, because Daisy manages to wrap *everyone* round her little finger.

Zagni's is warm inside. Too warm. Condensation clings to the windows. We stand in the ice-cream and pizza queue and wait. The queue is long and snakes around the chairs and tables by the racks of postcards, shell necklaces, and key rings. We edge forward and I see Jake and Ethan at one of the tables. I want to leave and go back outside, but Daisy has my hand held tightly in hers. I hide behind the man in front of me and keep my head down, out of sight.

Jake and Ethan haven't seen me. They're watching a boy and a tall fair-haired woman arguing at one of the tables by the window. I can't hear what they're saying, but the woman slams her hands on the table and stands up. Her chair knocks backwards to the floor and she stoops to pick it up. The boy glares at her as she storms past us and out through the door. It's only now that I can clearly see his face.

'He's the new boy,' I whisper to Daisy. 'He was in my class today.'

Felix gulps his drink and leans back in his chair. He wipes his sleeve across his face, leaving a trail of orange juice on his chin.

Daisy tugs my arm. 'What's wrong with him?'

'I don't know, Daisy.' I pull her arm. 'Come on, it's rude to stare.'

I hear Jake explode with laughter and look up. But it's not me they're laughing at this time. It's Felix. Ethan pulls his arm up against his chest and pulls a leery grin. Felix's face darkens. He looks across at me as if I'm in with them too, so I turn away.

We shuffle forwards in the queue.

But Jake and Ethan aren't done. I hear them laugh again.

I look round to see Ethan let a trail of saliva dribble down his chin.

Daisy hangs back on my hand. I try to pull her forward but she breaks free.

'Stop it,' she yells. 'Just stop it.' She stands in front of Jake and Ethan, hand on hip, wand raised like Tinkerbell in front of Captain Hook and Smee. She points at Felix. 'He can't help it,' she says. Her wings bristle and her face glows bright red.

Jake and Ethan snigger. But people in the café are turning in their seats to look at them. Jake stands up, sees me and scowls. 'Come on, Ethan,' he says. He shoves past me and mutters under his breath but loud enough for me to hear. 'It's just for spastics and losers in here.'

Daisy grips my hand again, tighter this time. I can feel her nails dig in my palm.

I put an arm round her and glance back at Felix. He's staring at the table, spinning the salt cellar round and round with his good hand.

We reach the counter, about to order, but Mrs Zagni has an ice-cream ready for Daisy. Two scoops of mint choc chip, dripping with chocolate sauce and a chocolate flake.

'This one's on the house, Daisy Varcoe,' she smiles. 'That's a big thing you did back there. You're what the world needs right now.'

Daisy beams and takes the ice-cream.

'Come on, Daisy.' I take her wand and party bag. 'Let's get out of here.'

'I just want to say hello,' she says.

I wait for her by the café door and smile. Daisy wants the

whole world to be her friend. She stops in front of Felix's table, puffs out her chest and grins.

But something happens. Something's said that I can't hear. Daisy's face falls. Tinkerbell's little light has been snuffed out. She drops her ice-cream. The cone shatters and splatters mint choc chip across the hard tiled floor. Daisy runs right past me, through the open café door, her cheeks burning crimson and streaked with tears.

CHAPTER 9

I find Daisy by the harbour. She's sitting between a pile of lobster pots, sobbing and puffing, catching her breath.

'What is it, Daisy? What happened?'

She pulls her wings off and throws them in the dirt. She tries to snap her wand, but the plastic just bends and she throws that in the mud and oil too.

'Did you hear what he said?' Her eyes are big and full of tears.

I kneel down and put my arms around her. 'What, Daisy?'

She shakes her head and buries her head in my chest.

I lift her chin up. 'Come on, Daisy, you can tell me.'

'He said . . . ' A sob catches in her throat and she gulps it back. 'He said . . . he didn't put out an advert for a fat fairy godmother.'

'You're kidding!' I say.

Daisy shakes her head. 'That's what he said.'

I try to hide my smile. 'Forget it, Daisy. He was rude, that's all.'

She looks at me with her big round eyes. 'I'm not fat, am I?'

'Course not,' I say, and I smile this time. 'You're just right the way you are. And it was a brave thing you did back there.'

She looks at me but she's not convinced. Her face is tear-stained and smudged in dirt. Her whole body shudders with big sobs as she breathes.

I lift her to her feet. 'Come on. Let's see if we can find that white dolphin.'

Her face lights up a little and she smiles. 'Really?'

I nod. I can't take her to the secret cove. The cliffs are too steep to climb and we won't get back home in time for Aunt Bev.

'Let's go down to the beach,' I say. 'Maybe we'll see it there.'

I take Daisy's hand and we walk along the beach to the rock pools on the far side. I look out into the sea, but there's no sign of any dolphins in the bay.

'Let's go to the Blue Pool,' I say. 'Let's see what we can find.'

Chapter 9

The tide is still low enough for us to pick our way along the slabs of rock and patches of pale sand towards the headland. The rock pools here are deep and hidden. Some are two metre narrow crevices holding mini underwater worlds. But there is one rock pool bigger than the rest. It's a mini universe.

The Blue Pool is a tidal pool, flanked on three sides by massive slabs of slate. Some fifty years ago, a concrete ledge was built across to keep the water in. It's now a huge deep rock pool, big enough to swim in. The walls inside are lined with anemones and kelp, and sometimes fish become trapped between the tides.

At high tide, the sea reaches just over the ledge and then the Blue Pool looks like one of the posh swimming pools I've seen in magazines, that go on and on and look like they're part of the sea. It can be packed with people here in high summer. But today, it's just Daisy and me.

I take my shoes and socks off and roll my trousers up. I sit down and dip my feet in the cold seawater. I stare down through the sunbright surface hoping to see a jellyfish or maybe a large fish trapped inside. 'What can you see, Daisy?'

'The Bird Lady,' she says in a hushed whisper.

'What?' I say. I look up. Daisy's pointing along the

rocky shore. I didn't see her before. She was hidden in the shadows. But now I see an old lady sitting by the boulders at the water's edge, her long grey hair and black shawl lifted by the breeze. I watch her tear chunks from a loaf of bread and throw them up into the sky. The gulls wheel and dive to catch them, and squabble on the rocks for fallen crumbs.

'It's Miss Penluna,' I say. 'I thought she'd moved away.'

'She's a witch,' says Daisy.

'Daisy!' I laugh, because if Miss Penluna had a broomstick I'd think she was one too.

Daisy frowns at me and folds her arms. 'She *is* a witch. Tommy Ansty said when the cows on his dad's farm got big warts, the vet couldn't cure them, but the Bird Lady did. She put a spell on them. Tommy said the warts dropped off the next day.'

'Well, watch out,' I say. 'She's coming this way. She might put a spell on you too.'

Daisy tries to pull me up. 'Come on, let's go.'

'Don't be silly, Daisy,' I say. 'There's no such thing as witches.' Despite my words, I press myself in to the rock shadows as she passes. Daisy clings on to me and we watch her shuffle past and climb the steps, worn smooth by people's feet over the years, up to the path along the headland. Her long shawl trails a wet line across the rocks where it's dragged in rock pools on the way. She's almost made it to the top, when we see her fall. She stumbles forward. Her stick clatters to the ground and slithers down the rocks. All we see is the top of her shawl above the long grasses.

She doesn't move.

I look at Daisy, and Daisy looks at me.

'We'd better check if she's OK,' I say.

Daisy nods and follows me across the rocks. By the time we reach Miss Penluna, she is sitting up and rubbing both her knees. A small bloodstain has soaked through the ribbing on her woollen tights.

I pick up her stick. 'Are you OK?'

Miss Penluna looks up and smiles. 'I think so, thank you, dear.'

I hold out my hand. She takes mine in hers and I help her to her feet. Her arm feels thin and bony beneath her shawl. She's so light it's as if she's made out of nothing at all. Her bird-like eyes dart across my face.

'You're Kay Wood's child, aren't you?'

The question takes me by surprise. No one talks about Mum any more.

I nod.

Daisy clutches my hand tight in hers.

'She used to bring me birds,' Miss Penluna says. She cups her hands as if she's holding one. 'Funny little black and white birds, like penguins. Lost, they were. They couldn't find their rabbit holes in the storm.'

I hear Daisy stifle a giggle. She holds her hand across her mouth and I see the corner of her eyes crinkle in a smile.

But Miss Penluna hasn't noticed. She leans into us, eyes wide, and whispers. 'I kept them in my drainpipes for the night.'

Daisy is shuddering beside me now, and I cough to hide her helpless giggles. 'Are you sure you'll be all right?' I say.

Miss Penluna nods and pulls her shawl straight around her shoulders. She takes her stick from me. 'I'll be just fine now, thank you.'

She's about to walk away but she turns and faces me, her head cocked to one side.

'How is your mother?' she asks. 'I haven't seen her since I've been away.'

I shrug my shoulders. It's such a simple question but I don't know the answer any more. 'I don't know where she is,' I say.

Chapter 9

Miss Penluna's eyes search my face and I feel careless somehow, like a small child who's lost a precious toy. I thought everyone in this town must have heard about Mum. It was front page news last year. Four members of the whale and dolphin charity she worked for just disappeared in the Solomon Islands, including her. They were helping local people to stop dolphins from being caught for sealife theme parks around the world. One theme park in Dubai wanted twenty dolphins and another park in the Caribbean wanted some too. Mum wanted to find out who was behind it all. She said someone was making a load of money. *Blood money* she called it.

Miss Penluna prods me in the chest with her stick. 'I'll ask the angels to look for her,' she says. 'Maybe they can help.'

I nod and glance at Daisy. 'Thank you.' I can't think of anything else to say.

I watch her climb the last few steps and amble slowly along the coast path back to town.

Daisy turns to me wide eyed. 'Maybe she can find your mum.'

'Don't be silly, Daisy,' I say. 'It's rubbish all that stuff. She's bonkers. You saw that for yourself.'

A gap opens in the clouds and Miss Penluna is lit up in

a golden shaft of light, as if it's shining right down from the heavens. I try to push the thought out of my head. It's a stupid thought, I know. But I can't help wondering. I can't help thinking that maybe Daisy could be right.

Maybe Miss Penluna can really talk to angels after all.

Chapter 10

The smell of bacon threads up the stairs and into the room I share with Daisy. She's still asleep, her golden curls spread out across the pillow. I pull my dressing gown on and climb downstairs to the kitchen. Uncle Tom is sitting at the table. He's in his oilskin trousers and his fishing boots are by the back door. I guess he's going back out to sea today. Aunt Bev is standing at the cooker, frying bacon. She rests her other hand on her belly. Her stomach is huge now. The baby is due in six weeks' time.

'Is Daisy up yet?' she says. She waggles the spatula at me. 'I'm taking her to Plymouth with me for the day. I don't want to miss the bus.'

'I'll go and see,' I say.

I go back up to the bedroom and wake Daisy. She follows

me dreamily down the stairs, half asleep, clutching Teddy-cat to her chest. Dad is in the kitchen now too, pouring himself a coffee.

'You look smart,' I say.

Dad looks up. His hair is brushed and he's wearing his only suit. On Saturday mornings he's usually tinkering about with *Moana* at the harbour dressed in his old jumper and jeans.

Dad frowns. He nods his head at a light blue folder on the table. 'I'm seeing the man who wants to buy *Moana*,' he says.

'Don't sign anything till you've let me check the small print,' says Uncle Tom. 'You want a good price for her.'

I sit down and glare at Dad. Daisy sits down next to me and plops Teddy-cat on the table.

'Can you move that,' Aunt Bev says. 'Can't you see breakfast's ready.'

Daisy pulls Teddy-cat on her lap and Dad puts his folder on the chair beside him.

Uncle Tom takes Daisy's plate of bacon and fried eggs and starts cutting up the bacon for her. 'Good party last night, Daisy?'

Daisy nods her head and looks at me. 'Me and Kara saw the Bird Lady,' she says.

Chapter 10

Uncle Tom frowns. 'The Bird Lady?'

I nod. 'Miss Penluna.'

'Miss Penluna?' Aunt Bev snorts. She drops another piece of bacon in the pan. 'That mad old witch? I'm surprised they let her out.'

'Out of where?' I say.

Uncle Tom coughs and glares at Aunt Bev. 'She's not been well,' he says.

Daisy leans across the table and whispers, 'She says she can talk to angels.'

'See what I mean?' says Aunt Bev. The bacon spits and fizzles as she turns the heat up. 'She's not changed. Did you know Muriel from the post office once went to see her?'

Uncle Tom shakes his head and takes a glug of coffee.

Aunt Bev lowers her voice. 'Muriel wanted to speak to her husband, Ernie, across the other side.'

'The other side of where?' asks Daisy.

'Of the grave,' says Aunt Bev.

I glance at Daisy. Her eyes are wide, wide open.

Aunt Bev looks around to check she's got all our attention. 'Miss Penluna told Muriel she had to bring something of Ernie's to show the angels,' she whispers. 'Well, Muriel took his pension book along. And do you know what that mad old witch said Ernie's message was?'

Uncle Tom shakes his head.

The clock on the wall ticks through the silence.

Aunt Bev folds her arms across her stomach for greater effect. 'She said Ernie wanted to tell Muriel to stop sticking her big nose in everybody's business.'

Dad splutters in his coffee.

Uncle Tom hides behind his copy of the *Fishing News*, but I hear him mutter, 'Maybe Miss Penluna's not so mad after all.'

'That's not even funny,' snaps Aunt Bev. 'You should have seen the state of Miss Penluna's house when they took her away. Filthy it was. Muriel said there was bird muck everywhere. There were six crows in her living room, for goodness' sake. I'm surprised they didn't burn the house down after she'd gone.'

Daisy giggles. 'She told us she kept penguins in her drainpipes. She said they couldn't find their rabbit holes in the storm.'

Aunt Bev shoves a bit of bacon in her mouth. 'See what I mean? Completely mad.'

I wash up the dishes while Aunt Bev gets Daisy ready for their trip to Plymouth. They bustle out of the door with bags and coats, and I wave to Daisy as Uncle Tom drives them away to the bus stop on the top road out of town.

Chapter 10

I sit down next to Dad in deep still silence. It's our space now, for a little while at least.

'Fancy Miss Penluna remembering that,' says Dad.

'What?' I say.

'About the birds,' he says. 'Mum *did* once take birds to her. Manx shearwater, they were. Little black and white birds that nest in rabbit holes on islands out at sea. And they did look a bit like penguins. Mum found a couple of fledglings that were exhausted after storms had blown them inland.' Dad takes a sip of coffee and chuckles. 'Miss Penluna kept them in old pieces of drainpipe for the night before she let them go the next day.'

I smile. 'Maybe Uncle Tom's right,' I say. 'Maybe Miss Penluna's not as mad as everybody thinks after all.'

Dad glances at the clock, lifts the folder from his lap and puts it on the table. He sighs and runs his hands along the folder's tatty edge. 'I'll have to go soon.'

I know what's inside the folder. I've seen it countless times before. Dad's shown me the photos of *Moana* when Mum and Dad found her rotting in a creek, photos of her being rebuilt, and the drawings and sketches of her design and a small square patch of sail cloth.

Dad takes one photo out. 'I thought we'd keep this one,' he says.

I look at it and trace my finger across the top edge. It's the day we launched *Moana*, the first time she had sailed for more than a hundred years. She's supported in a winch frame, about to be lowered into the water. Mum had said our boat needed a new name for a new life. She said it had to be a name to connect us all. So she'd chosen *Moana*, a name from her homeland of New Zealand. In Maori, it means Ocean.

I tuck the photo in the folder. 'Keep it in there,' I say. I get up and stare out of the kitchen window and catch a glimpse of sea between the houses. I remember Mum once saying that if we looked after *Moana*, she'd look after us. I can't help feeling that we've let her down.

'I'm coming with you, Dad,' I say. 'We can't just sell her to anybody. We owe her that at least.'

Dad nods. 'I'll wait for you outside.'

I get changed into my T-shirt and jeans and pull on my pale blue jumper. It's the only one without a hole. I walk with Dad across the town and up the steep hill to the row of new houses high along the cliff top.

The houses are hidden behind high walls and gated driveways. Big 4x4s and shiny cars sit outside the double garages. Dust blows our way from the building site for new houses on the other side of the road.

'Some people have all the luck,' I say. 'I bet *Moana* will be just a toy to them.'

'Mr Andersen sounds OK,' says Dad.

'Is he the man who wants to buy her?'

Dad nods. 'He says he's done a lot of sailing in the past. He owns a software company now in London. He says he's lived there fifteen years too long, that's why he wants to move down here. And he's got a son too, about your age.'

'Great!' I mutter. I thought someone would buy *Moana* and take her away. But it will be worse, somehow, seeing someone else sailing her in the bay.

'This is the one,' says Dad.

We stop outside a gravelled drive at the end of the lane. Dad rings the bell on an intercom set into the wall and the gates glide open automatically. A man stands in the doorway of the house in faded jeans and a T-shirt. I just stare at him. I had imagined Mr Andersen in a suit and tie.

'Mr Wood,' he smiles, holding out his hand to Dad.

Dad shakes his. 'Meet my daughter, Kara.'

Mr Andersen turns to me. 'Pleased to meet you, Kara.'

I dig my hands deep in my pockets and scrunch the gravel beneath my feet.

'Well come on in,' Mr Andersen says. 'I'll find my son. You'll have to meet him.'

I stand with Dad in the hallway and watch Mr Andersen walk away. The room is huge. The walls are white. The floor is sun-bleached wood. On a table beside the sweeping staircase sails a model tall-ship enveloped in a dome of glass. I press my nose against it and let my breath mist on the glass. I imagine pirates sailing through thick fog towards this ship. I want to watch my tiny pirates swing from the rigging. I want them to make the captain of this ship walk the plank into the painted sea.

'Great, isn't it?'

I look round. I hadn't heard Mr Andersen return.

He looks through the misted glass too. 'It's a replica of the *America*, the schooner that won the very first America's Cup around the Isle of Wight in 1851.'

I straighten up and try to wipe the misted breath with my sleeve. I look around for his son, but he's not in the hallway.

'Come with me,' he says, 'I've found him at last. It'll be good for him to make some friends in this town.'

Dad and I follow Mr Andersen along the corridor and through a door into a bright and sun-filled room. Huge curved windows, floor to ceiling, fill one side. All I can see is sea, the vast expanse of the Atlantic. White leather sofas face the view.

'Kara, meet my son,' says Mr Andersen.

I turn round. A boy is sitting at a table, his back to the windows, staring at a big computer screen. I can only see the top of his head above the leather padding of his chair. He swivels round and frowns.

I scowl.

I can't believe it's him.

I fold my arms across my chest and I know I can't hide the dislike on my face.

'We've already met before,' I say.

Chapter 11

It's Felix.

The new boy from school.

The boy who was rude to Daisy.

A ceiling fan whirrs above us in the silence.

Mr Andersen looks at Felix, eyebrows raised.

'We met at the school,' says Felix. His voice is strangely nasal as if he's got a bad cold, and his words are slurred.

Mr Andersen's eyes flit between me and Felix. He rubs his hand along the bottom of his chin. 'Why don't you show Kara what you've been doing on the computer, Felix? I'll ask Mum to bring some lemonade. Would you like that, Kara?'

I nod and stare up at the whirling fan blades.

'Kara!' Dad gives me one of his sideways glares.

Chapter 11

'Thank you, Mr Andersen.' I pronounce each word and glare back at Dad. 'That would be very nice.'

Mr Andersen smiles briefly. 'Good,' he says. 'Well, Jim, let's go and find somewhere quiet to talk about your lovely boat.'

I watch them walk away. I feel cheated somehow, left behind. I want to stop Mr Andersen from buying *Moana*. I turn back to Felix but he's facing his computer again, his good hand tapping on the keys. I stand behind his chair and watch. The chair is large and padded with soft white leather like the sofas. Computer consoles are set into the armrests. I've seen gaming chairs like this in magazines and in the big gaming shops in Plymouth.

The only sound is the tapping of the computer keys and the whirring fan blades.

'Daisy was only trying to help, you know,' I say. My voice sounds loud and echoes in the room.

Felix stops tapping on the keyboard. His fingers hover above the keys. 'Well, I'm sorry if I offended her, but you can tell your sister I don't need her help.'

'You can tell her you're sorry, yourself,' I say. 'Anyway, she's my cousin, not my sister.'

'Whatever,' says Felix. He starts tapping on the keys again. 'Look, if other people get their kicks from laughing at me, it's their problem, not mine. It's no big deal.'

A blank screen comes up on the computer. Felix hammers the keys and slams his hand down on the desk. 'But what *is* a big deal is *this.*' He runs his hand through his hair. 'There's no broadband here. How can you *live* like this?'

I dig my hands deep in my pockets. 'What are you trying to do?'

Felix rolls his eyes. 'Obvious, isn't it? I'm trying to log on the internet to play this game. But I can't connect. I'll have to play offline.'

A warrior in combat gear flashes on the screen. It revolves slowly round and round, surrounded by a choice of weapons. His clothes transform through military green, to desert colours to Polar white.

'At last,' breathes Felix. 'Stealth Warriors,' he says. 'Have you played it before?'

I shake my head.

'Going up different levels gives you different levels of camouflage,' he says. 'I'm on level ten. At level ten, you can blend in with any background.'

I rub my eyes. The computer screens at school always give me blinding headaches.

'What did you think to school?' I ask.

'Not much,' he says. He doesn't take his eyes off the

screen and taps the keyboard. His warrior appears against a city scene. 'Look, watch this,' he says. Six enemy warriors run down a road towards him. Felix presses something on his console and his warrior starts to blend in with the background of bricks on the wall behind him. When the enemy arrive, all that remains is his shadow on the ground. 'Cool, isn't it?'

I shrug my shoulders. But as I watch the screen his warrior turns bright red. The biggest enemy warrior shoots him dead.

'Professor Lexus!' cries Felix. He flops back in his chair. 'I should have known. My warrior turns red with anger when he sees him. I'll have to start again now.'

I don't want to watch Felix play his computer game. I can't stop thinking about what Dad and Mr Andersen are talking about right now. Does he want to buy our boat? I walk over to the windows and look out at the sea. The sun pours in, and despite the fans it's hot in here. I pull my jumper off and leave it on the floor. A fulmar glides past, angling its outstretched stubby wings to ride the wind. The sea glitters in the sunlight. It looks calm, but the base of Gull Rock is white with plumes of spray. A sailing boat is leaning in the wind. It dips up and down through waves. It's rougher than it looks out there today.

Footsteps tap on the floor. I turn to see a woman walking over with a tray of drinks. I recognize her from the café. It's Mrs Andersen, the woman Felix was arguing with.

'You must be Kara,' she says.

I nod.

'Felix isn't letting you play, I see,' she says.

Either Felix hasn't heard or is ignoring her.

Mrs Andersen smiles but says loud enough for him to hear. 'He always has to be in the control seat.'

'I'm not that interested in computer games anyway,' I say.

'Good for you,' she says. 'Hear that, Felix? You could take a break from it.'

Felix gets up from his chair and walks over to us. His steps are short and jerky. I notice his bare toes hit the floor before his heels. He picks up a glass of lemonade in his good hand and glares at his mother. 'If we were back in London, I'd be out somewhere with my mates.' He glugs back his drink and crams a biscuit from the tray into his mouth. I guess this was what they were arguing about in the café yesterday.

I pick up my drink and look back out of the window.

'Amazing isn't it?' says Mrs Andersen. 'We bought this place for the view.'

Chapter 11

I sip my drink. It's fresh lemonade from real lemons, not the fizzy bottled stuff.

'We saw dolphins two nights ago,' says Mrs Andersen, 'right from this very window.'

I look across the wide sweep of the bay. 'I saw them too.'

Mrs Andersen smiles. 'They're such clever animals. We saw them at a water park in Florida. Do you remember, Felix? All those tricks they did?'

'Amazing,' says Felix. He doesn't try to hide the sarcasm in his voice. 'Just how exciting can it get, watching yet another dolphin jump through a hoop?'

I wonder how he thinks the dolphins must feel, jumping hoop after hoop every day in a small pool, but I don't trust myself to speak. Instead I stare into my drink. All I want to do is find Dad and leave, but I don't even know where he is right now.

Mrs Andersen ignores him and turns to me. 'So have you and your dad always lived here?'

I nod. I wish she'd stop trying to be so friendly. 'Dad's a fisherman,' I say. Even as I say it, I think how stupid that sounds. How will he catch fish without his boat?

'And your mum?' says Mrs Andersen. 'What does she do?'

I swallow hard. It feels as though the ground has dropped

away from me. I tighten my hands around my glass and stumble on my words. 'Away,' I say, 'Mum's away right now. She's . . . ' But my voice trails off. I don't know what to say.

Mrs Andersen swirls the ice in her lemonade round and round. It clinks against the glass. She looks as relieved as I feel when we hear Dad's voice and see him and Mr Andersen come through the door.

Mr Andersen smiles. 'Well, Kara, you've got a very clever dad. The *Moana*'s a wonderful boat. There's real craftsmanship there.'

I had wanted to say something to stop him buying *Moana*, but I lose my moment, because I've never heard anyone talk about Dad like that before.

Mrs Andersen puts her head on one side. 'Well, Matt?'

Mr Andersen grins and looks at Dad. 'Can I tell them, Jim?'

I look at Dad, but can't read his face. Surely he hasn't agreed to sell *Moana*?

Felix is frowning too.

Mr Andersen smiles. 'Jim, here, has offered to take us out tomorrow for a trial run in *Moana*.'

Felix finishes his drink and puts his glass down on the table. 'I'm busy.'

'Not all day,' says Mr Andersen.

Chapter 11

I notice him frown at Felix.

'What's the weather going to be like?' asks Mrs Andersen.

Dad looks out to sea. The waves are capped with white horses, and I see the topmost branches of a tree in the next garden sway in the wind.

'It'll be a bit lively out there today,' says Dad. 'But the wind's meant to die down tomorrow, so we should be OK.'

Mrs Andersen glances at Felix and then her husband. 'I think it's best if you just go, Matt. Felix doesn't want to anyway.'

Mr Andersen shoves his hands deep in his pockets. 'Fine,' he says, 'fine.' A frown creases on his face. But I can't help smiling deep inside. He's the only one of them interested in *Moana*. Maybe he won't buy her after all.

Mr Andersen leads Dad and me back into the hall. He opens the door and the cool outside air rushes through.

'Wait a sec,' I say. 'I've left my jumper.' I turn and run back to the room. I hope I can slip in without Felix noticing, but he's standing by the windows looking out to sea. I cross the room to fetch my jumper. He doesn't even turn to look at me.

'What's out there?' he says.

I look beyond him to the wide blue sea.

'There's nothing there,' he says. 'Nothing until you get to America, and that's where I'm going one day.'

I tie my jumper round my waist and start walking to the door.

'No offence,' says Felix, 'but it's a dump round here. There's nothing to do.'

I stop and turn. 'So go back to London,' I say.

Felix rolls his eyes. 'According to Dad, I need some good sea air, and according to Mum, London's becoming far too dangerous.'

'It can't be that bad?'

'Of course it isn't,' says Felix. 'And I actually have a life back there.'

'So, make them go back,' I say.

Felix presses his head against the glass and stares through his reflection, out to the sea. 'Believe me, I intend to.'

I spin on my heels and walk towards the door. I feel a surge of hope inside because maybe Mr Andersen won't buy *Moana* if Felix can make them all go back to London.

I stop by the door and turn. 'You're right not to go sailing tomorrow. It's far too rough. It can get pretty wild out there.'

Felix snorts a laugh. 'It doesn't bother me,' he says. 'I just can't see the point going up and down in a stupid boat.' He walks away in his short jerky steps to sit in his control chair and starts tapping at the keyboard.

I smile because he hasn't fooled me. 'It's no game out there,' I say. 'When the wind is screaming in your face and the waves are coming over the sides, there are no second chances. You can't just die and start again.'

Felix's fingers hammer the keys, but I know he's listening.

'Just how brave are you,' I say, 'when the real world is out of your control?'

Felix's fingers stop tapping.

I shut the door and smile, leaving Felix and deep silence in the room.

Chapter 12

'I've put a flask of coffee on the side to take and some saffron buns as well,' says Aunt Bev. 'Let's hope it makes Mr Andersen want to buy *Moana*.'

Dad's fishing tackle, spare life jacket, and a bucket of bait are piled by the kitchen door. I squash the flask inside the canvas bag with the rest of the picnic and place the yellow buns on top. Dad's already packed some pasties, crisps, and a large bottle of lemonade and paper cups.

'He'll be expecting sushi, not pasties,' I say.

Dad looks up. 'What's that?'

'Nothing.' I slide down against the door frame and push my foot against the corner of the bag. I hear the crack of the plastic cups and feel my foot press against the soft bag of pasties. I want the meat and onions to split through the bag and stick against the thermos and the crisps. I pick a currant from one of the buns and roll it in my fingers.

'Leave that.' Aunt Bev glares at me above her magazine. 'Mr Andersen won't want half-eaten buns.'

Daisy is cutting pictures out from magazines and catalogues, and sticking them on paper. She stops cutting, scissors in mid-air, and frowns. 'His son's the one from the café, isn't he?'

I nod. 'He's the new boy in our school.'

Daisy's frown deepens. 'There's something wrong with him, isn't there?'

'You're right there,' I say, 'he's rude and I don't like him.'

Dad turns the cold tap and watches water swirl into an old plastic bottle. 'Mr Andersen told me Felix has cerebral palsy,' he says.

Aunt Bev looks up and sucks air sharply through her teeth. 'I've just been reading about that in my *Pregnancy* magazine. It happens if a baby doesn't get enough oxygen to the brain before it's born.' She covers her belly with her hand and holds up the magazine. 'There's a story in here about a girl with it. She can't walk or talk. Stuck in a wheelchair she is, for life.'

'That boy's not in a wheelchair,' says Daisy.

Dad turns off the tap and caps the bottle.

'I think it affects some worse than others.'

Aunt Bev closes the magazine and shakes her head. 'I pity his poor parents.'

'Me too,' I say. It's the first time Aunt Bev and I have agreed on something. 'I don't know how they can stand him.'

'Kara!' Aunt Bev frowns at me. 'You shouldn't say that. He's . . . ' She pauses as if she can't find the words she's looking for. 'You should feel sorry for him, is all I'm saying. He's not like you or me.'

I pick the picnic bag up and walk out of the door. 'Doesn't seem to stop him being rude,' I say.

Dad's standing inside *Moana*, pulling the mainsail up the mast. 'We'll have to put a reef in,' he says. 'It's a bit fresh out there.'

I look out through the gap in the harbour walls. The sea beyond is lumpy and flecked with white. 'It's not that bad,' I say. 'We've been out in worse with full sails.'

Dad runs a fold along the bottom of the sail to make the mainsail smaller. 'We're not racing,' he says. 'We're giving Mr Andersen a gentle trip out.'

'We should charge him for it,' I say. 'He's got enough money.'

Chapter 12

I heave the picnic bag and swimming bag and spare towels into the boat and push them into the locker under the foredeck. I tie the bucket with the bait around the mast base to stop it rolling across the deck as we sail. I want it to be just me today. Just me and Dad. I don't want anyone else on our boat.

'Here's Mr Andersen,' says Dad.

I look up to see Mr Andersen walking along the pontoon followed by Mrs Andersen and Felix. I'm surprised they've come along to see him off. The wooden boards of the pontoon bounce with their footsteps and I see Felix stumble to his knees. His mother tries to help him up but he brushes her away.

'All set?' says Mr Andersen. He puts his bag beside the boat.

Dad nods. 'It should be fun out there today.'

Mr Andersen glances back at Felix. 'I hope it's still OK with you, but Felix has changed his mind. He'd like to come along too. I've borrowed a life jacket for him.'

'That's fine with me,' says Dad.

Felix glares at me and looks away.

I climb out on to the pontoon to take Mr Andersen's bag.

Mrs Andersen's scarf flaps across her face and she pulls it

free. 'I really don't think this is a great idea, Matt,' she says. 'It's too windy today.'

'It's fine,' says Mr Andersen. 'What d'you think, Jim?'

Dad looks up at the flag on the chandlery. It's flying full out, rippling in the wind. The top branches in the tree beyond are swaying. 'It's a force five, I reckon,' he says. 'But I checked the weather report and it's going to settle down later.'

I dig my hands into my pockets and take a sly glance at Felix. 'Looks like a force six or seven to me,' I say.

Mrs Andersen wraps her coat around her and folds her arms. 'I don't think you should go, Felix.'

Mr Andersen turns to her. 'But, Sarah . . .'

She lowers her head next to his, but I can still hear them. The wind is blowing this way.

'Anything could happen out there,' she says. 'What if you capsize, what then?'

Mr Andersen runs his hands through his hair. 'Nothing's going to happen, Sarah.'

'Look, Matt, buy the damn boat if you must,' she snaps. I glance at Dad and I know he can hear them too. 'But don't expect either of us to step foot in it.'

'I want to go, Mum.' Felix is grim faced, staring at the water. 'I'll be fine.'

CHAPTER 12

I pull my life jacket on, zip it up and pull the Velcro cords tight. I can't imagine Felix enjoying this trip.

Mrs Andersen glares at Felix. 'What's changed your mind?'

Felix doesn't take his eyes off the water. 'I want to go.'

Mrs Andersen spins round to her husband. 'Have you got your mobile on you at least?'

'Yes, Sarah,' he says. He puts his arms out to hug her but she walks away. The thud of her footsteps on the wooden boards jars through the bare soles of my feet.

I watch Mr Andersen fasten Felix's life jacket and help him into the boat. Felix struggles to swing his left leg over. One leg is stiff and locked straight out and his arm is bent and curled. *Moana* sways underneath him and his dad catches him as he tumbles forward.

'You might find it easier to sit up at the front,' says Dad. 'There's more space and there's a handhold.'

Felix pulls himself up on the seat and grips the brass handle with his good hand. His knuckles turn white and I feel a twinge of guilt run through me. I hadn't actually thought how hard this could be for him.

I untie the mooring rope and push *Moana* away from the pontoon. Dad sets her sails and we slide out between the harbour walls.

The first wave hits us side on and I see Felix lurch sideways. He stares down at the floor and presses himself against the side, bracing himself for the next wave. He doesn't look up until we are far out in the bay. It's less choppy, but an ocean swell rolls in from the Atlantic in grey green hills of waves. Mr Andersen is leaning back, smiling, the sun shining on his face. He holds the jib sheet in his hand, keen to help Dad sail *Moana.* But Felix is looking at his feet again.

And he's a sickly shade of green.

I slide over beside him. 'It helps if you look out of the boat,' I say.

Felix looks up briefly and scowls at me. 'I'm not interested in the view.'

I lean back and stare out to sea. 'What I mean is, if you fix your eyes on the horizon, you won't feel so sick.'

Felix nods and looks out beyond the boat.

'We'll check our lobster pots, if that's OK by you, Mr Andersen,' shouts Dad, 'then we'll go on to Gull Rock where we can stop for lunch.'

'That's fine by us,' Mr Andersen shouts back. He lets the jib out a little as Dad turns away from the wind. 'How many pots do you and your dad have, Kara?'

'About twenty.'

Chapter 12

'Do you catch much?'

'Enough,' I say. I turn my back on him, fold my arms on *Moana's* side and look out to sea. I want to see the dolphins again. I want to see them leaping through our bow waves. *Moana's* wake runs in lace ribbons out behind us. The sunlight sparkles in the sea like stars. Soon we won't have this. We won't have any of this, any more.

We round the headland and pass along the rugged coastline of rocky inlets and deep shelving coves. Bright orange buoys of crab and lobster pots bob on the water marking the lobster pots beneath. A man in his boat waves to us. I see the initials TL on his buoys. It's Ted from the Merry Mermaid checking his pots. I remember painting Dad's initials on our buoys. I painted flowers on them too, big white ones. Dad said he never heard the last of it down the pub. They called him the flower pot man for months. They teased him too, because Mum made him use traditional withy pots made from willow, not the modern metal and mesh nylon ones.

Dad spills some wind from the sails and we slow down towards the mouth of the rocky inlet where we keep our lobster pots. Two ravens croak from the clifftop. Waves slap against the rocks and gulls wheel and scream in a tight circle above the cove. I crane my neck to look, because there must be something there to pull the gulls and ravens in. A buoy with painted flowers bobs loose on the water like a small child's lost balloon. It trails a blue rope in a long line out behind it.

Suddenly I feel sick deep inside, because something here feels so wrong.

A roar of engines cuts through the air, and a puff of black smoke drifts up into the sky. An orange ribbed inflatable bursts from our cove. It rears over a wave and smacks down into the water sending up spumes of flying spray.

It passes close and slews in a tight arc around us. *Moana* rocks in its wake, and I have to put my arm out not to fall. I see Dougie Evans at the wheel, a grim smile on his face. Jake holds up his hand, his finger and thumb out in a loser sign.

But my heart is thumping in my chest because Jake's words repeat over and over again in my head.

'*Soon, you and your dad will have nothing left.*'

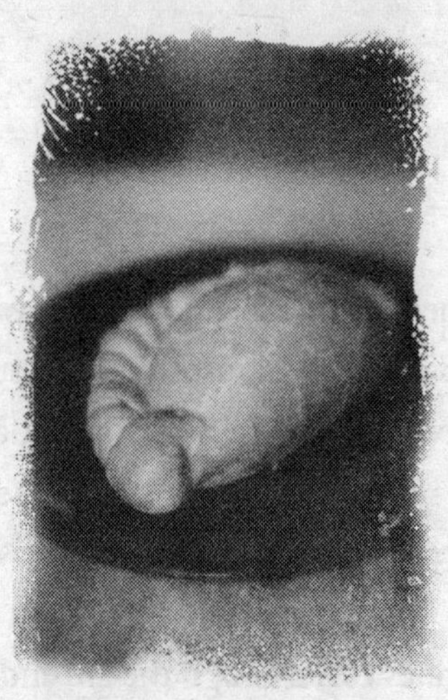

Chapter 13

The small inlet is empty of our buoys, almost.

Two more orange buoys float against the rocks, trailing cut ropes across the water. I see our initials on them, and the flowers. There's one buoy floating in the water near us. Dad hauls it in and pulls up the rope. But I can see it's coming up too quickly. Dad pulls on the rope, hand over hand, not coiling it but spilling it in a tangled mess inside the boat. The lobster pot comes up over the side, a wreck of smashed-up wicker. The door has been wrenched off, and the curved funnel of the trap has been cut apart. It's useless now.

Dad just stares at the mangled mess in his hands. 'That's all of them gone, Kara,' he says.

I stare out to the orange rib inflatable disappearing into the distance, spumes of white spray flying in its wake.

Mr Andersen is sitting forward, his face a tight frown. 'What happened here?'

'Let's call the police, Dad,' I say.

Dad shakes his head. 'No point. There's no proof is there? It's his word against mine.'

'But, Dad . . .'

Dad shoves the remains of the pot on the seat next to me. He forces a smile to his face and turns to Mr Andersen. 'Let's go for lunch, shall we?'

He pushes the tiller over hard, the boom swings out and the sail snaps tight. *Moana* lurches forward.

I sit back and watch the cove recede into the jumble of boulders along the coastline. An empty Coke can bobs in a slick of engine oil. I hate Jake Evans. I hate him for everything he is. My eyes burn hot with tears, and this time I can't stop them fall.

I glance at Dad, but his eyes are focused out to sea, a deep frown line on his face. He's sailing *Moana* roughly through the water. She jars against the waves, each one slamming into us as we roll and pitch.

Felix is staring at his feet, his face a deeper shade of green. Each wave thumps the boat against his back. I try and warn Dad, but it's too late. Felix lurches forward, vomits, and whacks his head against the deck.

Chapter 13

'Felix!' yells Mr Andersen.

Dad turns *Moana* into the wind and lets her sails flap loose.

'Take the tiller, Kara,' orders Dad. 'Keep up into the wind.'

I sit at the stern and watch Mr Andersen wipe Felix's face with a towel. Dad empties the bait bucket, fills it with seawater and helps clean up Felix too. Felix is a deathly shade of white. His whole body shakes and he looks like he'll be sick again. Mr Andersen props him up and pulls a water bottle from his bag. Dad fetches the first aid kit from the locker and kneels down to clean a cut on Felix's face.

'I think we should head back,' says Dad.

Mr Andersen rinses the towel in the sea and wrings it out. 'You're right.' He hangs the towel across the seat beside him. 'Sorry, Felix, Mum was right on this one. I shouldn't have let you come today.'

Felix leans back against the seat and glares at me. 'I'm fine,' he says. 'Let's go on.'

Mr Andersen crouches next to him. 'You don't look great. I think it's best if we go back.'

Felix takes a swig of water from his bottle. 'I said I'm fine.'

Mr Andersen looks at Dad and shrugs his shoulders.

'If you're sure,' says Dad. 'We can stop off at Gull Rock and head back after that.'

Felix nods and fixes his eyes out to sea.

I watch a dark patch of wind-ruffled water sweep towards us. *Moana*'s sails flap in the passing gust.

'The wind's not so strong now,' says Dad. 'We'll let *Moana* have full sails.'

I lean forward, in line with Felix, as Dad and Mr Andersen take the reefs out of the sails. 'You don't have to go on, you know. You've proved your point.'

Felix takes another swig from the water bottle and doesn't even look at me.

Dad slides around to the back of *Moana* and gives me a gentle shove. 'Go up the front, Kara. I thought Felix could have a go at sailing. Would you like that, Felix? It'll take your mind off seasickness if you can concentrate on something else.'

Felix nods. He looks slightly better, a paler shade of green now.

I sit up at the front of the boat with Mr Andersen, but can't help looking back at Dad and Felix. A pang of jealousy runs through me and I try to push it away. Dad taught me to sail like this, sitting with him by the tiller, allowing me to test the wind and feel it in the sails. Felix can't control the mainsail and the tiller with only one good arm. It takes two hands for that. But I watch Dad show him how to adjust the mainsail, when to pull it in and how to spill air if we heel over too far.

Moana slices through the water on a course set for Gull Rock. We're running fast and smooth. Mr Andersen and I have to lean right out to balance her. I run my hands in the bow waves that furl along *Moana*'s sides. Her sails above us are curved and taut like birds' wings. We're racing through the water. It feels as if we're flying, almost.

I look back again to see Dad and Felix, big grins stuck on both their faces. That pang of jealousy hasn't gone away. It's not because of Dad, this time. It's because of Felix. For someone who's never sailed before, he's good at sailing.

He's far too good.

I don't want to admit it, but Felix Andersen is a born natural.

Dad takes over near Gull Rock and guides *Moana* into the crescent-shaped cove that faces the mainland shore. It's sheltered here. The waves that heave against the seaward cliffs of Gull Rock swirl round here in foam-topped eddies. Mr Andersen drops the anchor and Dad lets down the sails.

Felix's eyes are shining and the colour is back in his face. 'That was *so* cool.'

Dad sits back and grins. 'That was some sailing, Felix. Don't you think so, Kara?'

I shrug my shoulders. 'It was OK.'

Mr Andersen can't take the smile off his face. He punches Felix on the shoulder. 'I told you you'd like it.'

Dad pulls the picnic bag out from the locker. 'You could enter the regatta race with sailing like that.'

Felix just sits there with a massive grin.

'What race is that?' asks Mr Andersen.

'It's the one held every summer on the last day of August,' says Dad. 'Any sailing boat can enter. It's a race from the harbour around Gull Rock and back.'

I pull my knees up to my chest. I don't want Dad to be telling them any of this. It's *our* boat, *our* race. I look out at the shelving pebble bay and the sheer cliffs of Gull Rock and feel an ache deep in my chest. This is our special place. It could be the last time we ever come out here.

'Pasty, anyone?' says Dad.

The smell of cooked meat and onions drifts across the boat.

He holds one of the squashed pasties out to Felix. 'Are you up to this?'

Felix nods. 'I'm starving.'

Dad pours out lemonade into plastic cups, balancing them on the wooden seats.

Mr Andersen takes a mouthful of pasty and leans back with his feet up on the seats. He pulls his hat over his eyes and smiles. 'I have to say, this has to be the best meal I've had in years.'

I don't touch my pasty. I can't imagine watching someone else sail *Moana* in the regatta race. I want to forget about Felix and his dad. I want to forget about Jake Evans too. All I want is to escape.

'Can I have a quick swim, Dad?' I say.

Dad nods, and I reach into the locker for my mask and snorkel. I peel my shorts and T-shirt off to my swimming costume underneath.

Mr Andersen looks at Felix. 'Why don't you go too? You could do with cleaning yourself off a bit.'

Felix's shorts are patterned with crusted sea salt and flecks of dried vomit. He looks down at them and shrugs his shoulders. 'OK.'

I stare down at my feet. I want to swim by myself, not have Felix tagging along.

'Is that OK, Kara?' says Mr Andersen.

'There can be strong currents out there,' I say.

'You're only swimming to the rocks,' says Dad.

'Felix is a good swimmer,' says Mr Andersen.

'And it's cold too,' I say.

Dad finds a spare face-mask. 'Here, Felix. You should see a lot today, the water's crystal clear.'

I curl my toes over *Moana*'s side and look down. My reflection is rippled like the water. When I was small, I used to think it was a magic mirror, a secret entrance to another world below.

I take a deep breath of air.

And dive.

Cold water rushes through my hair and across my skin. I twist and look up to the surface, a dolphin's eye view of *Moana*'s shadowed hull. Shafts of sunlight filter through the water, reaching into deep, deep blue. I swim towards the rocks that lie submerged beneath the cliffs. Purple jewel anemones line the narrow crevices. Small silver sand eels flit between the rippling strands of seaweed. I spread my arms and soar above this world, above a landscape of mountains, valleys and vast grasslands of green kelp.

When I come up for air, Felix is right behind me. I didn't think he'd be able to swim so fast. I hadn't really thought he could swim at all. I push my hair from my eyes and tread water beside him.

Chapter 13

Felix lifts the corner of his face-mask to drain some water that's leaked inside. 'Can't see a thing,' he says.

His mask is steamed up and blurry. 'Spit in it,' I say.

Felix frowns at me. 'What?'

'Spit in it. It stops the mask from steaming up.'

Felix pulls his mask off and spits inside, rubbing the saliva with his thumb. He struggles to pull the strap over his head again. I almost help him, but see Dad and Mr Andersen watching, so I swim away, towards a submerged shelf of rock lined with fine white sand.

Felix joins me and we drift side by side, arms outstretched, our fingertips almost touching. I stare down, hypnotized. Nothing is still. The sea floor is a changing pattern of swaying seaweed and shifting sand. A silver river of tiny fish thread through the kelp, each fish no longer than my thumb. But there is something else moving through the water too, a creature I've heard about but never seen before.

It's here now, right now.

I catch a fleeting glimpse of zebra stripe between the kelp and then it's gone.

I nudge Felix in the side and point.

He bursts up to the surface and I take a gasp of breath too.

I shake the water from my hair. 'Did you see it?' I say.

Felix pushes his mask up from his face. 'See what?'

'Down there in the kelp, you must've seen it.'

'What, Kara?'

'Stealth Killers,' I say and can't help grinning. 'Level ten.'

Chapter 14

I float beside him, looking down. I see it again, this time a flash of dark against the pale sand, but it's changing all the time.

Felix bursts up again from the water and I lift my head up too.

'I still can't see anything down there,' he says.

I sweep my wet hair from my face and look at Felix. 'That's because you aren't looking right,' I say. 'I'll point. Just keep looking at the sand.'

I dive under to skim the pale sand floor. Scraps of seaweed and a crab shell-case rock back and forth. I can't see the animal I'm looking for at first. Its camouflage is far too good. But then I see it watching me from the sand below me. Only the horseshoe-shaped black pupils of its eyes give it away. The speckled pattern of its body perfectly matches the sand beneath. I reach out to touch it, but it rises upwards, away from me, and stops mid-water, changing colour in an instant to bright red. It looks like a small deflated beach ball with long tentacles at one end. Its body is fringed by a rim of fins that ripple along each side. The tentacles stick straight out in front of it, like a sword.

I burst upwards to catch a breath of air.

Felix takes a breath too. 'What *is* that?'

'Cuttlefish,' I say.

Felix frowns. 'What old ladies feed to budgies?'

I roll my eyes. 'That's the cuttlebone, its skeleton inside.'

'I want another look,' says Felix.

We float on the surface, faces down, slowly spinning with the current. We are skydivers looking at a world far, far below.

The red cuttlefish is still there, watching us, watching it. It's a strange feeling, being observed like this. Another cuttlefish swims into view, a pale brown one with a perfect white square patch on its back. I remember Mum telling me that males and females come to breed and lay their eggs on kelp in the spring and summer. The red cuttlefish is changing colour again. Its head and tentacles are still bright red, but its body now has zebra stripes of black and white. The stripes begin to ripple across its body in moving patterns. The brown cuttlefish is changing too. Bands of dark colour sweep across its body.

I see Felix beside me take a breath and dive down. He reaches out his hand. His fingers almost touch the tentacles of the red cuttlefish, but both cuttlefish propel backwards and he is left groping in a billowing black cloud of ink. Felix bursts upwards again for air. I keep looking under water, but when the ink clears both cuttlefish have disappeared. They could be anywhere by now, perfectly camouflaged against the pale sand or dark grey rock.

Mr Andersen helps to haul us out of the water. He wraps Felix in a big beach towel and Dad wraps my blanket round me too.

'What did you two see over there?' says Mr Andersen. 'You were there for ages.'

'Cuttlefish,' I say.

Mr Andersen turns to Felix, 'Cuttlefish?'

Felix nods. He can't stop his teeth from chattering. 'They were amazing, Dad. You've got to go and look. Just don't try and touch one, like I did.'

'I think we should take a look,' says Dad. 'I've not seen them before, myself.'

Dad and Mr Andersen strip off their T-shirts and jump into the water with the face-masks and snorkels.

I sink down out of the wind and take a bite of pasty.

Felix takes a bite from his pasty too and stares out to sea, his face lit up in golden light.

'I've not seen anything like that before,' he says.

I look at him and nod. 'It's not just there,' I say. 'It goes on and on. There's a whole coral reef down there and I'm going to see all that someday.' I finish my pasty and shake the crumbs from my blanket. 'Mum said when I'm sixteen I can learn to scuba dive. She said she'd take me out to see the reef. If it's still there, that is.'

Felix slides down beside me and leans against *Moana*'s curved hull. 'Why wouldn't it be?'

'The dredging ban is lifted in a week's time,' I say. 'Then dredgers from up and down the coast will come and haul their metal rakes across the seabed for scallops. It's not just scallops they'll be ripping out, but everything else, all those things you've seen today. There'll be nothing left.'

Felix stuffs the end crust of his pasty in his mouth and sucks his fingers. 'So stop them,' he says.

I glare at him. 'Easy for you to say. What can *I* do? Just sit out here in a rubber dinghy and turn their trawlers away?'

Felix rubs his towel in his hair. 'I don't know,' he says. 'But if it meant that much to me, I wouldn't give up without a fight.'

I pull broken pieces of wicker from the tattered lobster pot and look at Felix. 'You don't know Dougie Evans. No one can stop him. No one.'

'Who's he?'

'The man you saw who wrecked our lobster pots,' I say. 'That's him.'

'So why's he got it in for you?'

I flick the pieces out into the water. I don't know how much Felix knows about me and Dad. 'Mum got the dredging ban put in place for a ten year study of the reef,' I say. I sit up on one of the seats and stare out to sea. 'But she never got to finish her research. Time ran out. Her funding ran out too. That's why the ban is being lifted. She never got to show her final results.'

'So Dougie Evans wasn't happy about the ban?' says Felix.

I nod. 'He said Mum was a greenie foreigner who couldn't tell him what to do. But all the local fishermen were on her side, especially when she found out Dougie Evans was trying to sell his fish as line-caught fish.'

'What difference does that make?' says Felix.

'It's more expensive, but people will pay more because it's dolphin friendly. Hundreds of dolphins drown in fishing nets each year.'

'So he hates you because your mum found out he was a cheat?' says Felix.

'It wasn't just that,' I say. 'Dougie had another son too. Aaron. He was seventeen when he was swept off one of Dougie's trawlers in a bad storm. Dougie blamed Mum, saying that if he'd been able to fish closer to the shore where the reef is, his son would be alive today.'

Felix gives a small laugh. 'And my mum thought London was dangerous! She thought we'd moved to a safe sleepy fishing town. I think she's in for a shock.'

CHAPTER 15

Dad lets Felix take the tiller as a light breeze takes us home. The golden sunlight of afternoon slants across the bay. I stare down into the water hoping to see the white dolphin. Once or twice I almost imagine something white rushing beneath our bow waves, twisting in our wake. I want it to be her. I want to see her because maybe then it means we'll keep *Moana*. But instead, all I see are cloud reflections skimming across the water.

Mrs Andersen is waiting for us on the harbour wall, twisting her scarf around her hands. She waves as we slide through the gap into the deep-water moorings. Mr Andersen waves back and Felix grins and gives the thumbs up. His face has caught the sun and his hair is salt-crusted and windswept. He looks a different boy to the one we took out this morning.

The tide is too low to take *Moana* to her mooring site at the pontoon, so Dad takes her alongside the trawlers and the lifeboat.

'We'll help you take down the sails and sort her out,' says Mr Andersen.

Dad smiles. 'We'll be just fine. You go on home. Kara and I will wait for the tide to come in and take her to her mooring.'

Mr Andersen puts out his hand and pumps Dad's hand up and down. 'Well, thanks, Jim. It's been great. I'll be in touch.'

Felix stands up and steadies himself on *Moana*'s side. His dad helps him out onto the rough steps cut into the harbour wall. Felix opens his mouth as if he's about to say something, but then turns, grasps the rusty hand rail and lifts one foot to the next step. I watch Mr Andersen sling his bag over his shoulder and climb up behind Felix, up to the top, to Mrs Andersen peering anxiously down.

I tidy up *Moana* and wipe the salt spray from her decks. Dad helps me stuff the wrecked lobster pot in a spare canvas bag.

He slings it on the floor and sighs. 'It's not as if we're going to be using them much longer.'

I wipe up crumbs from the seats and tip them out into

the harbour water. I look down to see small fish dart up and take the crumbs. 'D'you think Mr Andersen will buy her?'

'We'll have to see,' Dad says. 'He's going to have a chat with his wife and ring me later.'

We have to wait another hour for the tide to creep in. I hear it sucking across the mud, filling in the lugworm holes. Two oystercatchers run up and down the shoreline, stopping to probe their orange bills deep into the mud. I help paddle *Moana* across to her mooring, watching the oar swirl through the still water.

'It was a good trip today,' I say. '*Moana* sailed well.'

Dad smiles. 'She never lets us down, does she?'

I shake my head, but can't help feeling that's exactly what we're doing to her.

We walk back to Aunt Bev's through the town in early evening, tired and sunburnt. I flop down on the sofa. Daisy's watching a game show on TV and Aunt Bev is knitting bootees for the baby. I hardly move until the phone rings. I strain my ears to hear who Dad is talking to.

I hear Dad say goodbye and put the phone back. I don't want to know. I don't want to hear what he's got to say. Aunt Bev puts her knitting down and glances at the door.

Dad walks in, sits down next to me and runs his hands through his hair.

Aunt Bev mutes the volume. 'Well?' she says.

Dad shakes his head and frowns. 'Mr Andersen doesn't want to buy her.'

I sit up. 'What?'

Aunt Bev glares at him. 'I said you should've dropped the price.'

'It's not that,' says Dad. 'Mr Andersen seemed keen at the time, but he said something about listening to Felix, and "doing the right thing".'

'They're going back to London,' I say. 'That's what they're going to do.'

Aunt Bev snatches up her knitting. 'Let's hope you find another buyer soon, Jim. It's the only way you'll pay those debts.' She shakes her head and turns the volume back up.

But I can't take the grin off my face.

Maybe it *was* the white dolphin I saw beneath the bow waves. Mr Andersen has changed his mind. He doesn't want to buy *Moana*.

Moana's still our boat.

She's ours for now, at least.

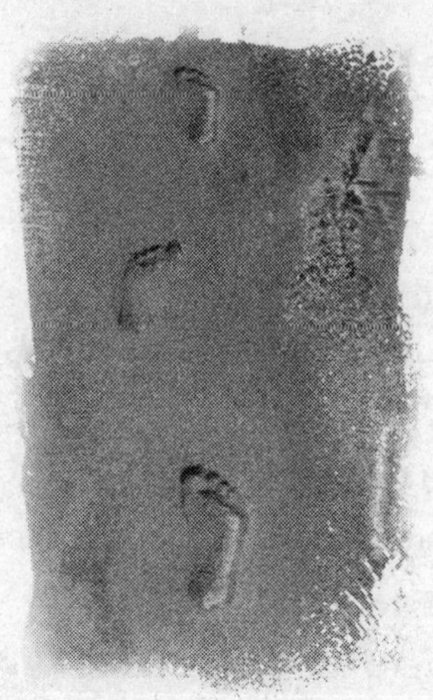

Chapter 16

I sit in Mrs Carter's office after school while she watches me press sticky tape across the last of the ripped pages of the Bible. Some of the pages were never found. Lost at sea. Presumed drowned.

I close the Bible and push it across the table. 'I'm sorry,' I mutter.

School finished half an hour ago. Through the office window, I can see some of my class in the play park beyond the school gates. Jake is sitting next to Ethan, twirling round and round on the preschool swings.

Mrs Carter leans forward, elbows on the table. 'Kara, did you know that I asked your father to come and see me today?'

I nod. Dad said she wanted to see him about me breaking Jake Evans's nose.

'And you know that while I have every sympathy for your situation, I cannot accept violence in the school?'

I nod again.

'I've told your father that if this happens again, we will have no choice but to exclude you.'

Part of me wants to laugh. It hardly seems a punishment. I'd do anything not to have to come to school.

Mrs Carter opens the Bible at one of the ripped pages. Her voice is suddenly soft and measured. 'Your father and I spoke about this too.'

I frown and look down at the Bible. I've already said that I was sorry. I don't like to think about them talking about me, discussing me behind my back.

Mrs Carter pulls her chair closer to the table. 'Can I tell you a story, Kara?'

All I want to do is go.

'It's about a man,' she says, 'who dreams he is walking with God along a beach.'

I stare at my hands. I'm in no mood for one of Mrs Carter's Bible stories.

'The man looks back at the path they have taken and he sees that in one place there is only one set of footprints. He's angry at God and says, "You left me when I most needed you. See, there is only one set of footprints in the sand." '

Chapter 16

I pick at a loose corner of sticky tape holding the page together. A memory of Mum flashes through me, the time she carried me out of the sea after I'd stepped on a weaver fish. I'd wrapped my arms around her neck, pain throbbing through my foot. I'd clung to her and watched her bare footprints trail out behind us. I look up at Mrs Carter. I already know the ending to her story.

She smiles at me. 'God said to the man, "I never left you. Those footsteps you see are mine. They are when I carried you." '

I close the Bible and slide it over to Mrs Carter.

'God never leaves us, Kara.'

'What if you don't believe in God?' I say. The words have tumbled out before I could stop them. I know Mum doesn't believe in Him.

I think Mrs Carter is going to give one of her assembly speeches, but she doesn't. She gets up from her seat and puts the Bible back on the shelf next to the atlas and the dictionary. She sits back down on the table edge. 'You know, Kara,' she says. 'When you love someone, they never really leave you, ever. Some part of them always stays with you deep down inside.'

I nod and shift in my seat. I feel hot and stuffy all at once. I don't want her talking to me about all this. I just want to go.

'You can go home now.' Mrs Carter is smiling at me. 'It was good to talk today, Kara.'

I almost run out of her office and grab my coat from my locker. I don't want to go out through the front gates and everyone in the park. I feel too churned up inside. Instead of heading out of the main doors, I walk along the corridor to the staff car park on the other side of school. If I take the top road out of town, I can swing back along the coastal footpath without anyone, especially Jake and Ethan, seeing me.

It's not just that. I want to give myself an excuse to go back to the cove, to look for the dolphins again. Dad's not expecting me home for at least another hour, so I still have time to spare. Maybe I'll have time to go and see *Moana*. I can't believe she's ours still. Felix wasn't at school today, so I guess I'm right, and he's going back to London after all. I'm glad he's not buying *Moana*, but part of me wanted to see him at school today, because when he saw the cuttlefish and the reef, it seemed to mean something to him too.

The road from the school winds up the hill under a tunnel of branches throwing zebra stripes of deep shadow on the tarmac. Beyond the tunnel of trees, I catch glimpses of the sea in gaps and gateways between the high banks of the hedgerows. Goose-grass and bindweed scramble over stunted wind-bent hazel. I climb the stile to the wheat fields and run along the stubbly footpath to the cliffs. Above, the sky is clear and blue. A breeze carries the coconut smell of gorse from the bushes along the clifftop and a single seagull hangs in mid-air, angling its wings to catch the updraught from the sea.

I scramble through the gorse and look down. The water in the cove below glitters in the sunlight. I have to shade my eyes against the flashes of reflected glare. But I see something else moving through the water. The blue-grey body of a dolphin twists and turns in the shallows. I can hear it calling, its high-pitched whistles. It surges forward in a spray of surf, trying to beach itself on the sand. I can't believe it's really here, as if it's me it's waiting for.

I scramble down the cliff and jump the last few feet to the small beach uncovered by the ebbing tide. I run through the maze of boulders. My feet slap on the soft wet sand. Pooled water and pale boulders reflect bright white light. I don't stop. A flock of seagulls lifts into the air and a raven croaks and hops down from a boulder in the shallow waves. Another raven flaps up and flies away. Its wingtips almost brush my head.

And that's when I see it.

Even though the boulder is snagged with weed, it's too smooth and white to be a rock here. It's not a rock at all.

White Dolphin

It's a dolphin.

It's the white dolphin lying beached upon the shore. Small waves run in and furl around her. But the sand is wet and hard. The tide mark of scum and seaweed curls around her tail flukes. The tide has turned and is ebbing out to sea.

The other dolphin in the water rushes at the shore again. I was stupid to think it was me she was waiting for. She's not waiting for me at all. She's trying to reach her calf beside me on the sand.

I've never seen a dolphin so close up before. I've seen them in the distance and in books, but I've never been right next to one. I guess the white dolphin must be young but I can tell she's not newborn. She's maybe one of last year's calves. I follow the curve of her back and dorsal fin to her tail flukes. She's not really white at all. Her body is pale pink and her fins and tail are tinged with blue. Deep scratches, dark with blood, line her back. Her blowhole is clear of the water, but I cannot hear or see her breathe.

I take a step towards her. Her eye is partly open. The lids are dry and crusted with salt. The eye beneath looks dull and lifeless, like frosted glass. She doesn't blink or move.

I crouch down beside her in the sand. Strands of thick seaweed are wrapped around her lower jaw. Only as I look closer, it's not weed at all. It's fine mesh fishing net. Fine mesh nylon wrapped so tightly, it has cut deep into the skin behind her dolphin smile. Her tongue is blue-black and swollen. Shreds of nylon twist around her peg-like teeth. Flies buzz up from the wound and I see peck marks from the ravens around her jaw.

I sink down onto my knees and feel bile rising up inside me. I can see how she came to be like this. I can see her drowning, tangled in dark waters, thrashing in a fishing net trying to escape.

I close my eyes and try to push those thoughts away.

But the image of the dolphin drowning haunts me.

I splash water on my face and open my eyes.

The sun is bright white in the sky. A line of sweat trickles down my back beneath my shirt.

I don't want to be here any more.

I stand up to leave. But I want to touch the dolphin once before I go.

I wet my fingers and reach out to trace them in an arc across her face.

Chapter 17

'PFWHOOOSH!!'

I fall back into the water.

A blast of wet breath fills the air.

It stinks of fish.

The dolphin draws in a breath, a whistling sucking through her blowhole, then the blowhole snaps shut again.

The dolphin's eye is wide open now. She is watching me.

I slap the water with my hand. 'You're alive,' I shout. 'You're alive.'

The dolphin's tail flukes flap the shallow water.

I get up and kneel down beside her, so my face is close to hers. I look into her small pale pink eye. She blinks and she looks back as if she's working out just who I am, and what I'm going to do.

Chapter 17

But my mind is blank. All these years I've secretly dreamed of rescuing a dolphin and now I don't know what to do. I put my hands on her side and try to roll her back to sea, but she might as well be one of the boulders on the shore. She's much too heavy on land. She breathes again, a sudden burst of air, and I wonder if I've hurt her doing this.

I reach out to touch the white dolphin's face again. Her skin is dry and hard, like sun-baked rubber. I remember I have to keep her wet and shaded from the sun. All the things Mum taught me start flooding back to me now. I know she could dehydrate out here. I jump up and run across the beach from boulder to boulder, pulling armfuls of wet seaweed from the rocks. I lay these across her body, careful to keep her blowhole open and uncovered.

I dig hollows in the sand beneath her fins to take the pressure off the bones inside. Tiny sand hoppers flip around the scooped-out sand. I brush my hair back from my eyes and see the white dolphin is still watching me.

I force myself to look at the wound in her mouth. The fishing net has cut deep into the skin. I try to gently pull the green mesh, unwinding it from around the teeth. Strands of fresh blood thread into the wet sand. The dolphin flinches as I pull and slaps her tail. Her tongue is a swollen mess. Her mouth is bruised, a bloody mass of skin and muscle.

I can even see the white of jawbone shining through. She can't catch fish like this. Even if I wait with her until the tide turns and comes back in, I don't see how she can survive.

I scoop water with my hand and let it trail across her wounds. I don't know what to do. I just don't know what to do.

The mother has slipped back with the tide and is too far out to hear her call. The white dolphin's eyes close. I wait to hear her breathe. I count the seconds in my head, but the breath doesn't come. I don't know how long she can last like this.

'Wake up,' I shout. I tap my fingers on her side. She blasts air out through her blowhole. She opens her eye again and looks at me. She mustn't sleep. Dolphins don't sleep. I know that if she falls asleep she'll die. I remember Mum telling me that every dolphin breath is a conscious thought. People don't have to think to breathe, but dolphins must remember to take each one. Dolphins suffering in captivity can choose not to breathe. They can choose to die.

And I don't want her to die.

I soak my coat in seawater and squeeze it out across her back. I keep talking to her all the time. I tell her that she will swim with her mother across the sea again.

She watches me closely as I clean sand from around her

eyes and mouth. I look into her small pale eye and have the strangest feeling I am looking at myself. I wonder if she sees her own reflection in my world too.

I feel I'm keeping her alive, somehow.

I know I must get help, but I can't leave her here all alone.

The ravens croak above me on the clifftop.

I press my head against hers and close my eyes.

I don't know what to do.

I just don't know what to do.

'KARA!'

I look up and fall backwards in the wet sand.

Someone is stumbling up through the shallow waves towards me in a wetsuit and fluorescent life jacket.

I can't believe it.

He's silhouetted against the sun, but I know just who it is.

'How did *you* get here?' I say.

Chapter 18

Felix stops in the shallow water and stares up at the sheer cliffs behind me. 'I could ask you the same thing,' he says. 'I told Dad it was you here on the beach.'

Beyond Felix, I see his dad swimming in from a small sailing dinghy anchored in the cove.

Felix sinks onto his knees beside the dolphin. 'What happened here?'

I kneel down beside him. 'She's been caught in fishing net.'

'Is she alive?'

I nod. 'Only just.'

I hear Felix's dad's feet slap on the sand behind us. He crouches down beside the white dolphin. 'There's another dolphin in the water going crazy,' he says. 'It almost caught my leg with its tail. I guess this must be its calf.'

'We must get help,' I say. 'The Marine Life Rescue will help with this.'

Felix's dad pulls his mobile from a waterproof pouch around his waist. He taps the keys and frowns. 'No network. It must be these cliffs.'

'Can't we push her to the water?' asks Felix.

I shake my head. 'She needs a vet, anyway.'

Felix's dad stands up and looks out towards the sailing dinghy. 'Listen, I'll sail back and get some help. You two stay here with the dolphin.'

'Go to the chandlery and ask for Carl,' I say. 'I think he works part time there.'

I watch Felix's dad climb in the dinghy and guide it out of the narrow cove. It's not like the sailing dinghies at the sailing club. Felix's dad sits deep inside the centre of the boat like a racing driver in a car, instead of sitting at the stern next to the tiller.

I scoop some water from the trench around the dolphin's body and pour it through the layers of seaweed protecting her from the sun. 'I thought you were going back to London.'

Felix frowns. 'What made you think that?'

'You weren't at school today and your dad didn't want

to buy *Moana*. He said he was going to listen to what you wanted instead.'

Felix helps scoop more water and runs his wet hand along the dolphin's skin. 'Dad *did* listen to me,' he says. 'That sailing yesterday was the coolest thing I've ever done, but I can't sail a boat like *Moana* by myself. I like to be the one in control, remember?'

'So?' I say.

Felix sits back in the sand and grins. 'So Dad borrowed a sailing dinghy from someone he knows through the cerebral palsy charity. I couldn't believe it when they brought it over today. That's why I didn't come into school. Dad and I decided to try it out in the bay. It's designed for the Paralympics. The seat is low down in the cockpit and I can control the sails and tiller with a central joystick with just one arm.'

'So you're really going to learn to sail?' I say.

Felix grins. 'Not just that. I'm going to win the regatta race around Gull Rock in five weeks' time.'

I flick water at him. 'You'll be in second place. *Moana*'s going to win it this year. She always does.'

Felix flicks water back at me and laughs. 'I wouldn't bet on that, if I were you.'

* * *

Chapter 18

We hear the rescue boat before we see it. The orange rib inflatable slews in a narrow arc into the cove with the dolphin mother arching through its bow waves. Dad and Mr Andersen are sitting in the boat with two Marine Life Rescue volunteers. One I recognize as Carl, one of Mum's marine biology students from last year, and the other, Greg, one of the local crab potters and scallop divers.

Carl switches off the engine, drops a shallow anchor in the water and jumps out of the boat. He runs up the sun-bright sand towards us. I haven't seen him since the night we floated candles out to sea for Mum. He used to make amazing sand sculptures of mermaids and sea monsters just for me.

I pull him down beside me. 'You have to save her, Carl,' I say.

Carl kneels down and pulls some weed away from the dolphin's head and whistles softly. 'She's albino. I've never seen an albino dolphin before.'

'She's badly injured,' I say. 'She needs a vet.'

'We've called the vet, but she's out on another emergency right now,' he says. He shines a small pocket torch inside her mouth. 'You're right. These wounds are nasty.'

'But how long will the vet be?' I don't think the dolphin will last much longer here.

'She said she'd radio us when she's on her way,' he says.

Dad crouches down beside me. 'Mr Andersen told me you were here. You know you're not meant to come here on your own.'

'I'm sorry, Dad,' I say. 'But if I hadn't come . . .'

Dad sighs and shakes his head. 'You can't just go running off. I have to know where you are.'

'I will, Dad, next time . . .'

'Hold this,' says Carl. He passes me the end of a tape measure. 'You stand at the head end, Kara. You don't want to be in the way of her tail.'

We measure the dolphin from beak to tail flukes. Carl reaches into the black bag for a clipboard and a pen. 'A hundred and sixty centimetres,' he says. 'She can't be much more than a year old. She may even still be feeding from her mother.'

Felix points towards the water. 'Her mother's out there, waiting for her.'

Carl nods and writes notes on his clipboard. 'We saw her as we came in.'

Greg crouches down to examine the white dolphin too. He presses his hand against her flanks. When he takes it away, it leaves a dented handprint in her skin. He shakes his head. 'Not a good sign. She's very dehydrated.'

Chapter 18

Carl looks at his watch. 'Her breathing rate is up too. Ten breaths a minute. It should be about four or five.' He sits back on his heels and rubs his chin.

I wet my fingers and trace water across the white dolphin's face. She blinks and watches me. 'What are we going to do, Carl?'

Carl runs his hands through his hair. 'Let's give her some fluids by stomach tube while we wait for the vet to get here.'

Greg nods. 'It'll make her feel better. But I don't think there'll be much the vet can do.'

I feel my mouth go dry. 'What d'you mean, not much she can do?'

Carl looks at Greg and then at me. He talks softly to try to break the news, but it makes no difference, the words are still the same. 'These wounds are bad, Kara. She can't catch fish like this and I doubt she could suckle from her mother. She would die if we let her back to sea.'

He reaches in the bag and pulls out a long clear tube.

'You mean the vet will put her down?' I say.

Carl looks up and nods. 'I'm sorry, Kara. I don't think she'll have a choice.'

I stand up and back away from him. 'But her mother's waiting for her.'

Dad wraps his arms around me. 'I know it's hard, but Carl's right. It'd be cruel to put her back into the sea.'

I push Dad's hands away and glare at Carl.

Carl crouches down next to the white dolphin's head and looks up at me. 'You've done really well, Kara. Both you and Felix, you've done everything right.'

I scowl at him. 'It's made no difference.'

'It has to her,' he says. 'She's suffered less because of you.'

I watch Carl measure the stomach tube against the dolphin's side, and slide it into her mouth. She shakes her head as it passes over her swollen tongue.

'You're hurting her,' I say.

Carl doesn't speak or take his eyes off the dolphin until the tube is pushed in place. He stands up and holds the bag of fluids high. I watch the level sink lower in the bag as the fluids pass through into her. I just stand and stare at him. I can't believe it's come to this, that there is nothing else they can do.

Carl glances at Greg. 'Why don't you take these guys back to the harbour? You can pick the vet up from there too when she arrives.'

'I'm not leaving,' I say.

Felix sits back and digs his hand deep in the sand. 'I'm staying too.'

Chapter 18

Carl presses his head against the bag of fluids. 'You won't want to stay.'

'Come on, Kara,' says Dad. He tucks his hand under my arm. 'I think it's for the best.'

'You too, Felix,' says Mr Andersen. 'You've done all you can do.'

I pull away from Dad and kneel down beside the white dolphin and stroke her head. She watches me so closely, that I can't help thinking she wants our help. I know she doesn't want to die.

I look up at Carl. 'There must be *something* we can do.'

Felix kneels down beside her too. 'Why can't we take her to a rescue centre, where they can look after her until she's better? They do it in America.'

'We don't have Sea Life centres here,' says Carl. 'Even if we did, they might not take her because wild animals can pass on diseases to the captive ones.'

'What about a swimming pool?' says Felix. 'Or one of those small inflatable pools you can buy?'

I nod. 'Felix is right. There's got to be something like that we could use.'

Carl drops the bag of fluids lower and sighs. 'Look, kids, it's no use. Even if we could use someone's swimming pool, it wouldn't be right for a dolphin. For a start a swimming pool is full of chemicals and has fresh water, not salt water. The water would need to be changed and filtered to get rid of waste. Forget it. We don't have salt-water pools in this country. We don't have anything like that.'

I jump up to my feet. 'But we do, Carl.' I almost shout the words out. 'We have something *exactly* like that.'

Chapter 19

'The Blue Pool?' says Carl.

I nod. 'You know: the tidal pool out towards the headland. It's perfect. The sea washes over it and cleans it out twice a day.'

'I don't know,' says Carl. 'I mean, if the weather gets up, there can be big waves crashing over there. We can't have rescuers putting their own lives at risk.'

I look up at the clear blue sky. 'The forecast is good for this week,' I say. 'Please, Carl, we have to chance it.'

Carl looks at Greg and he shrugs his shoulders.

'Seems like it'd be worth a go to me,' says Mr Andersen.

'We've got to try,' says Felix.

Carl sighs. He gently slides the stomach tube out of the dolphin. It slithers out smeared with blood and slime.

'I'll radio the vet, see what she thinks.'

I watch Carl walk down the sloping beach to the rescue boat. I pick up scoopfuls of dry sand and let it trickle through my fingers. Carl speaks into the radio. I try to read his face, but all I see is him nod and frown. Felix crosses the fingers of his good hand and holds them up to me. I smile, but I don't feel much hope inside. Carl is walking back towards us, his face grim and serious.

I jump up and brush the sand from my clothes. 'What did she say?'

Carl shakes his head. 'The vet thinks the stress of moving the dolphin may be too much.'

'It's her only chance,' Felix blurts out.

'I know,' says Carl, 'and the vet can't get to us for at least another hour. Considering the injuries, she thinks it might be worth trying your plan and taking the dolphin to the tidal pool so she can assess it there.'

'Thank you, Carl,' I grin. 'She'll get better now. I know she will.'

Carl shakes his head. 'She's very sick. Don't get your hopes up too much.'

Carl fetches a tarpaulin from the rescue boat and I help to

slide the edges to the dolphin's sides.

'When we roll her on,' instructs Carl, 'watch out for her tail. Keep away from her blowhole too. Their breath can carry some nasty diseases.'

We all line up and put our hands on the dolphin's back.

'This is the risky part,' says Carl. 'Her lungs have been crushed by the weight of her own body. She could find it difficult to breathe.'

Carl nods the signal and we all push and tilt her to one side. Greg slides the tarpaulin under her and we roll her the other way and pull the sheet out straight beneath her. The dolphin lashes her tail against the sand. Already she seems stronger since the fluids. Her flippers and her tail have lost their deep blue colour, and gained a tinge of pink. Carl rubs Vaseline around her blowhole and spreads sun-block on her body as Greg wipes the tarpaulin clear of grit and sand.

I take a corner of the tarpaulin with Dad. The dolphin is much heavier than I thought she would be, and we struggle with her to the water's edge. Greg pulls the rescue boat close up to the shore and we heave her in. She takes up most of the space inside the boat and the rest of us have to sit out on the rubber sides. I pull on a spare life jacket and cling on as Carl fires up the engines and takes the boat out of the cove into the wind and waves and sea.

The mother dolphin follows us, almost pressed against the boat, lifting her head above the water to see her calf. She whistles and clicks to her and slaps her tail down hard. I wonder what it is she is trying to say and if she understands what we are trying to do.

'She's injured too,' I say.

Carl shades his eyes against the sun. A deep V-shaped notch is cut into the base of her dorsal fin. The edges are raw and congealed with blood. 'I don't think it's as bad as it looks,' he says. 'It's superficial. It should heal OK.'

He slows down as we enter the harbour walls. 'I can't take her to the tidal pool,' he says. 'There are too many rocks at low tide. We'll have to take her across land from here.'

The mother dolphin follows us, her dorsal fin curving through the water as if she's on a tow-rope right behind. She's still with us, despite the smell of oil and diesel in the harbour, and the outboard engine roar that must echo under water between the walls.

The tide is low, and I feel the underside of the boat scrape on the mud and stones. Carl pulls up at the bottom of the slipway where the concrete is barnacled and green with weed and algae.

'I'll get my pickup truck,' says Greg. 'We'll drive her across to the Blue Pool.'

Chapter 19

Carl nods. He wets a cloth and lets the water trickle across the white dolphin's back. The mother dolphin surfaces in the deeper water and blasts a breath of air. The white dolphin copies her, the *pfwhooosh* of their breaths calling each other, letting each other know they are still there.

'How will she know where we're taking her calf?' I ask Carl.

He shrugs his shoulders. 'That's why this might not be a good idea. The separation stress could be too much for her.'

I see Greg's truck reversing down the slipway. Two other Marine Life rescue volunteers jog alongside. Greg slams his driver's door and unhooks the tailgate of the pickup. 'The vet's waiting at the tidal pool for us,' he says. 'There are other volunteers there too.'

'Good,' nods Carl. 'Let's get her there.'

Carl helps Felix climb out of the boat and I join Felix on the slipway. We stand back to let the rescue volunteers lift the white dolphin up into the truck. She lies on foam mattresses sandwiched between Greg's crab pots and folded nets.

Carl turns to Dad and Mr Andersen, and nods in our direction. 'I think you should take these kids home,' he says. 'They both need to get warm and dry.'

'I'm fine,' I say. I tuck my hands under my armpits to

warm them up and hide the blueness of my fingers. My feet are numb with cold.

'I'm fine too,' says Felix.

Mr Andersen puts his arm around Felix. 'Look at you. You're shivering. You're freezing cold.'

I put my foot on the tow bar. I want to climb up beside the white dolphin and go with her to the tidal pool. 'I've got to come with you, Carl,' I say.

Carl puts his hand across to stop me. 'Not this time,' he says. 'The vet will need time to assess her and make her decision.'

'I have to come.'

Carl hauls himself up beside the white dolphin. 'I'll ring your dad tonight. I'll let you know what happens.'

Greg revs the truck and the white dolphin thrashes her tail and blasts air through her blowhole.

I hold on to the tailgate. 'Don't let her die, Carl. Please don't let the vet put her down.'

Carl looks down and shakes his head. 'It won't be up to me, Kara.'

I put my hands on the dolphin's face and look into her eye. But she looks beyond me to her mother and the blue curve of the horizon far beyond the harbour walls.

Carl pulls on my hands. 'Let go, Kara.'

Chapter 19

I lift my hands and watch the truck drive up the slipway and disappear into the traffic along the harbour road.

I hate it. I hate them taking her away from her mother like this. I feel as if I'm betraying her somehow.

It feels worse than letting her take her chances in the sea.

Chapter 20

Daisy spreads a white bun thickly with jam. 'Are we going to see the dolphin?'

I put my fingers to my lips. Aunt Bev is making a pot of tea. 'We'll have to go now,' I whisper, 'before school.'

Daisy nods and bolts down her roll.

Last night she sat wide-eyed while I told her all about the dolphin. She'd scowled when I told her Felix had been there to help too. I told her that he was all right really, that he'd been angry the day we'd met him in the café. But it didn't seem to matter what I said about Felix. Daisy's made her mind up about him already.

I sling my schoolbag over my shoulder and wait for Daisy by the door.

Aunt Bev narrows her eyes at me. 'You're off early.'

Chapter 20

'Got some homework to hand in,' I say.

She stares hard at me and Daisy. 'You're not planning on seeing that dolphin, are you?'

I shrug my shoulders. 'What dolphin?' I glance at Daisy, but she's turned bright red and is staring at the floor.

Aunt Bev folds her arms. 'The one Jim was talking about on the phone, after you two had gone to bed.'

'What did he say?'

'I don't know,' says Aunt Bev. 'I didn't hear all of it.'

'I just want to know if it's all right,' I say.

'You're both going straight to school. You've been in enough trouble as it is and I don't want Daisy in trouble too.' She grabs her handbag and the door keys. 'In fact, I'll walk you there myself.'

There's no point arguing with her. Dad's on an early shift at work so I can't ask him.

All the way to school I try to catch glimpses of the headland, but the tidal pool is tucked away below the cliffs and out of sight. Greg's pickup truck is parked in the headland car park, so all I can do is hope that means that Greg and Carl are there and that the dolphin is still alive.

* * *

I can't concentrate on anything all day. Felix has been moved to the top group in maths and English, so I only get a chance to meet up with him at break.

He's talking to two girls from our year at the tuck shop, but he breaks away from them when he sees me. I sit down next to him on one of the wooden benches in the playground. 'How's the dolphin?'

Felix fumbles with a chocolate wrapper and tears the corner with his teeth. 'Carl rang to say she's still alive,' he says. 'They need volunteers to support her on a raft until she can balance on her own in the water. Dad's doing a two hour shift before he picks me up at lunch.'

'I could meet you there later, when I come out of school,' I say. 'Maybe Carl will let us help too.'

'Yeah, that'd be cool,' says Felix. He snaps the chocolate and offers me some. 'At my last school you could get expelled for eating chocolate.'

I stuff two chunks of chocolate in my mouth. 'No way!'

Felix grins. 'Chocolate was forbidden. We were only allowed cereal bars and carrot sticks for snacks.' He shoves the rest of the bar in his mouth, and speaks through a mouthful of chocolate. 'I think I could get to like it here.'

* * *

Chapter 20

After lunch I watch the hands on the clock above the teacher's desk turn slowly round and round and round. I'm jealous that Felix will be at the Blue Pool already. When the end of school bell rings, I'm first out of the gates. I run to Daisy's school and grab her when I see her. I almost pull her down the road. I can't wait to see the dolphin.

'Come on.' I sling her bag across my shoulder. 'We've got to run.'

The tide is too high to walk along the sand to the Blue Pool, so I run with Daisy along the coast road. The headland car park is now full of cars, but Greg's pickup has gone. There are lots of people too, strung out along the coast path. A crowd has gathered on the cliff above the tidal pool. I guess news has spread quickly about the dolphin. I push my way through the people to the stone steps down to the pool, but a line of police tape is stretched across the path and a policewoman puts her arm across to stop me from going through.

'No one's allowed,' she says, 'I'm sorry.'

I glance down to the rocks. Two dome tents stand on the ledge of flat rocks above the pool. I can see rucksacks and sleeping bags piled up inside. A white cover stands on poles, stretched across the pool to shelter the dolphin from the sun. Only her tail sticks out beyond the cover. She lies supported on a flotation raft between two long yellow cushions of air. A woman I've not seen before crouches next to a small gas stove and pours steaming water from a kettle into two mugs. Behind her, towels and wetsuits are draped across the rocks to dry.

'I have to go down there,' I say.

The policewoman shakes her head and smiles. 'I can't let you I'm afraid.'

'Carl!' I yell. 'Carl, it's me.'

She tries to gently push me back, but I see Carl's head pop out from under the white cover.

He speaks to someone in the pool and runs up the stone steps towards me. His feet leave dark wet prints on the pale rock. He ducks under the police tape and pulls Daisy and me away from the crowd.

My words tumble out. 'How is she?'

Carl sits us down on the grassy verge. 'She's holding her own for now,' he says. 'But she can't swim. Her muscles have been damaged from all that time she spent pressed against the sand.'

'Why can't we see her?' Daisy says.

Carl glances back at the crowd. 'The vet said the dolphin could pass some diseases on to people. But it's for the dolphin's protection too. We've got volunteers camped here for shifts in the water, but we don't want lots of people trying to touch her. She needs peace and quiet.'

'But *we* can see her, can't we?' I say. 'It was me who found her. We can help look after her.'

Carl shakes his head and sighs. He runs his hands through his hair. 'Kara, I don't know how to tell you this, but it's not good news.'

My hands feel clammy and cold. Daisy clutches my arm. 'What?' I say.

'The vet has taken advice from some experts in America. Even if we can make her better, she won't survive in the wild without other dolphins. She's far too young.'

I point towards the harbour. 'But her mother's waiting for her,' I say.

Carl frowns. 'Lots of boats went out to ride alongside her. We haven't seen her for several hours now. We think she's been scared away.'

'She'll come back though,' I say. 'Won't she?'

Carl shrugs his shoulders. 'She last saw her calf in the harbour. She doesn't even know her calf is here.'

'We can't give up now, Carl. We'll look for her.'

Carl peels his wetsuit gloves off and rubs his eyes. His chin is covered in fine stubble. He looks exhausted. I guess he's been up all night. 'Felix and his dad are sailing in the bay looking for her right now,' he says. 'But she could be miles away. She might have even rejoined her pod.'

I stand up and kick the ground. 'So how long do we give the mother to come back? A week? Two weeks? A year?'

Carl breathes out softly through his teeth. 'Tomorrow. The vet says we'll give her until tomorrow.'

'Tomorrow?' I shout. 'You can't do that. She'll come back, I know she will.' Heads start to turn our way, but I don't care.

Carl leans forward and lowers his voice. 'It's not fair to put her calf through this if we can't release her to the wild. It's not up to me, Kara. Many stranded whales and dolphins die or need to be put down. It's not easy, but it's just the way it is.'

I glare at him. 'At least let me see her.'

'I can't, Kara,' he says. 'I'm sorry. I just can't.'

He squeezes my shoulder but I pull away from him. I storm across the car park and sink down behind a stone wall, out of sight.

Daisy slides down and puts her arms around me. 'What are you going to do?'

I push my palms against my eyes and shake my head. 'I don't know, Daisy,' I say. 'I just don't know.' I feel so helpless sitting here. There's absolutely nothing I can do.

Chapter 20

I watch a jackdaw strut up and down beside us, its beady blue eyes on a crust of bread beside my feet. I pick the bread up and roll it between my finger and thumb into a small ball of dough. 'I wish Mum was here,' I say. 'She'd tell me what to do.'

The jackdaw hops forward. It turns its head from side to side, watching me all the time.

I hold the bread out on the flat of my hand.

I wonder if it will dare. I wonder if it will dare to put its trust in me.

Daisy slips her hand in mine. 'Maybe there's a way you *can* ask her.'

I turn to Daisy and nod.

I was thinking exactly the same thing.

Chapter 21

I run along the seafront with Daisy, clutching the only thing I have of Mum's in my hand. A small blue memory stick, moulded in the shape of a dolphin. Mum brought it back from a conference about sea life and I always wanted it for my own. I took it from her room the day before she left, just because I liked it. I never told her and I feel guilty about it still. After she disappeared, I threaded it onto a necklace made of shells. It now hangs below the pure white cowrie shell I found. The other shells are top shells, the purple stripes worn away to show the pearliness beneath, and between each of these a periwinkle, sunshine yellow. It's all I've got. She never kept *things*. She didn't even want a wedding ring from Dad. She had her diving kit and camera, and that was all. The computer wasn't even hers. It belonged to the research centre. The only *thing* she kept was her old battered green rucksack. The rips were patched with different fabrics from different lands. Each patch of cloth told a different story, she used to say. But that rucksack is now gone. It went with her too.

I know I haven't got long. Aunt Bev gave me money to get fish and chips for supper and will expect us back in half an hour. I leave Daisy in the queue. It's a long one that snakes around the corner and along the harbour road. It'll buy me some time, at least. I turn up past the chandlery and jog up the steep hill out of the other side of town. My legs ache and my lungs hurt to breathe but I don't stop until I reach the row of whitewashed cottages overlooking the sea.

Miss Penluna's cottage stands at the end, along a shared gravel pathway. The stones scrunch under my feet as I walk past the other doorways. Buckets and spades and body-boards lie outside in the small front gardens. Window boxes bright with geraniums sit on the slate window ledges. No one *real* lives in these cottages any more. They're all holiday rentals now.

All except the end house. Miss Penluna's cottage is a pale off-white grey. Beneath the flaking whitewash, the stones are dry and crumbly. The windows are smeared with wind-blown sea salt from past winter storms and the curtains behind are drawn tight shut. In the tangle of weeds and grasses in front of the cottage stands a lone bird-feeder filled with seed. It's the only clue that someone lives in here at all.

I stand in front of the door. My heart is banging in my chest. I can feel it pulse through me and against the memory stick I have clutched in my hand.

I knock on the door.

Something scrabbles against the other side. Then all is still. I knock again. Maybe Miss Penluna has gone out to feed the gulls again.

I slowly turn the handle of the door. It creaks and the door pushes inwards. A blade of sunlight cuts through the darkness to a flagstone floor.

'Hello?' I call.

The cottage is silent. I take a step inside and almost gag. A sharp stench fills my nose and mouth, and stings my eyes. It smells of the cliffs at Gull Rock when the cliffs are covered with birds at breeding time.

'Shut the door!'

A flurry of feathers beats against my face and the door slams shut. In the gloom I see the small figure of Miss Penluna standing in front of me.

'You can't take him,' she says. 'He's not well.'

Chapter 21

'Take who?' I say.

She peers at me closely. 'You from the council?'

'I'm Kara. We met on the beach.'

I hear the scrape of claws on the flagstones beside me and watch a jackdaw hop away towards another door.

'You can't stay,' Miss Penluna says. She shakes her head and points with her stick to the door. 'You've got to go.'

'I need your help,' I say.

'Off you go.' She opens the door and tries to prod me out.

'*Please*,' I say. 'I need your help.'

She stops still, the end of her stick against my chest.

'I've got something to show the angels.'

Miss Penluna peers outside, then grasps my arms in her bony hand and shuts the door. 'You can't stay long.'

I follow her into the kitchen. The floor is strewn with newspaper and empty china plates. The jackdaw flaps and hops on the table and watches me with its bright blue eyes.

'So what do you want to know?' she says.

I twirl the shell necklace round and round my hand. 'Can you really talk to angels?'

Miss Penluna pushes a chair out from under the table with her stick and sits down. 'They think I'm mad down in the village.'

I pull out another chair and sit opposite her at the table. The white tablecloth is splattered with patterns of spilt tea and jackdaw droppings.

She reaches out a bony finger and gently strokes the bird across its beak. 'I've always heard them singing in my head. My mother told me they were angels.' She sits back and shakes her head. 'I don't hear them so much any more.'

I slide the necklace and dolphin memory stick across the table. 'This belongs to my mother,' I say.

Miss Penluna turns it over in her hand. Her fingers are long and thin. Claw-like, almost. She pulls the memory stick apart and peers at the metal USB drive inside. 'What's this?' she says.

'A memory stick,' I say.

She holds it close up to her eyes. 'Whose memories?'

'It's not like that,' I say. 'It's for a computer.' I wonder if Miss Penluna has even seen a computer before.

She clips it shut and brushes it aside to the edge of the table. Maybe it's not good enough to show her. She's not interested in it at all. The jackdaw tries to peck at it, so I put it in my lap and wait.

Miss Penluna leans forward on the table. 'What is it you *really* want to know?'

Chapter 21

My mouth goes dry. My mind is blank. I close my eyes and try to think.

The jackdaw's feet tip-tap on the table.

'I want to know what happened,' I say. 'I want to know what happened the night Mum disappeared.'

When I open my eyes, Miss Penluna is still watching me. She pushes her wispy hair from her face. 'The question is, are you ready?'

I grip the memory stick tightly in my hand and nod. I'm about to know what happened. I'm about to know the truth. I feel I am standing on a cliff edge, looking down, and I feel I am about to fall.

'You must listen to the dolphins,' says Miss Penluna.

I shake my head and stare at her. I thought I'd hear an answer, a definite answer. 'I don't know what you mean,' I say.

Miss Penluna shrugs her shoulders. 'They are angels of the sea.'

I sit back. I feel cheated somehow, as if I've used up my magic question and now other questions are flooding in my head too. How can I save the white dolphin? How can I stop the dredgers ripping up the bay? Will I ever see Mum again?

Miss Penluna leans forward and grasps both my hands

in hers. I notice her eyes are pale, pale blue, just like the jackdaw.

'You will hear her if you listen,' she says. 'You must listen to the dolphins.'

Chapter 22

By the time I reach the chip shop, I can see Daisy through the window handing money to the man behind the counter. I lean on the railings, catch my breath and look down into the dark green harbour water. It's almost low tide. Mooring ropes lie long and draped with weed. I was stupid to build my hopes up and think I would find some answers. I don't even know how to save the white dolphin. Aunt Bev is right. Miss Penluna is mad. She's as mad as they come. Mum never believed in talking dolphins, not with human voices anyway.

Daisy hands me the bag, hot with packets of fish and chips. 'What did the Bird Lady say?'

'Later,' I say. 'Come on, let's get home.'

'Don't look now,' says Daisy. She nudges me in the ribs.

I look beyond her to see Felix and his dad walking towards us on the pavement. They're both wearing wetsuits and life jackets. Their legs are caked in mud.

Felix and his dad stop beside us. I wrinkle my nose. Their wetsuits smell of rotten seaweed.

'We got caught out by the tide,' smiles Mr Andersen. 'I guess we've got a lot to learn.'

Daisy pulls my arm, trying to hide behind me. I elbow her away and turn to Felix. 'Did you see the mother dolphin?'

Felix shakes his head. 'We went past Gull Rock and further up the coast, but we didn't see any sign of her.'

I twist the necklace through my fingers. The mother dolphin could be anywhere by now. 'She must be somewhere out there.'

'We saw grey seals,' says Felix, 'and a basking shark, a huge one . . . '

'She wouldn't leave her calf,' I say. I twist the silk thread of the necklace round and round and round. Daisy grabs my arm again. She yanks it back and the silk breaks, scattering shells across the ground. 'DAISY!' I yell. I scrabble on the floor to save the shells, but some bounce over the harbour edge. I look down to see the cowrie shell plop into the water, spreading green ripples in circle patterns of light.

I spin round to look for the memory stick but that's gone

too. I didn't even see it drop into the water. I look inside the bag with the fish and chips to see if it fell in there.

Daisy holds out three periwinkles and a top shell in her hand. 'I'm sorry, Kara.' Her eyes are welling with tears.

I scoop them from her hand. They're all that's left.

'Is this yours?' Felix is crouching down, his hands in the gutter. 'I thought this dropped too.'

He straightens up and holds out the blue dolphin memory stick in his hand.

'Thanks,' I say. I curl my fingers around it and slide it in my pocket.

He frowns at me. 'I thought you weren't into computers.'

'I'm not.' I hold it tightly in my hand. 'It's Mum's.'

'What's on it?'

I shrug my shoulders. 'I think it's empty.' I don't want to tell him that I tried looking on the school computer, but I couldn't read the log-in signs. I showed Carl once too, but he said it was password locked.

'I could take a look,' says Felix. 'If there's something on there, I'll find it.'

I run my finger along the curved dolphin shape in my pocket. I've always wondered if there was anything on there, some photos of Mum, a diary? I've always wanted to know. 'Maybe,' I say.

'I'll look after it,' he says, 'promise.'

I press the memory stick deeper into my pocket. 'It's all I have.'

'Up to you,' Felix says. 'But let me know if you change your mind.'

I watch him follow his dad along the seafront. I know I won't find out any other way.

'Wait,' I call after him.

He turns back to me.

I hold the memory stick out to him. 'I want you to,' I say. 'I want you to look.'

Felix nods and I place it in his outstretched hand.

Maybe that's exactly what it is.

Memories.

Someone's memories, waiting to be unlocked.

We're late home with the fish and chips. Aunt Bev is in her dressing gown stretched out on the sofa, watching a talent show on TV. Her stomach's so big now, that I wonder that she doesn't burst.

Daisy pulls plates out from the cupboard. 'I'm sorry about your necklace.'

I scatter forks across the table. 'Doesn't matter.'

Chapter 22

'What did she say?' says Daisy. 'What did the Bird Lady say?'

I thump the ketchup in the middle of the table. 'She said the dolphins were the angels of the sea.'

Daisy stops, plate in hand. 'Real angels?'

'Don't be silly, Daisy,' I snap. I rip open the grease-spotted paper of the fish and chip packets. 'They're just dolphins. Animals, like us.'

Dad sits down at the table and yawns. Dark rings sit under his eyes. He's doing as many hours as he can at the pub. I hardly see him these days at all. He picks up a fat chip and takes a bite.

Aunt Bev and Daisy sit down too.

'Tom's home tomorrow,' Aunt Bev says. 'Let's hope they've had a good catch this time.'

I see Daisy's eyes light up. 'He said he'd take me to see a film.'

I shake salt onto my chips. I don't want to see what tomorrow brings. I turn to Dad. 'Can we go sailing before school?'

Dad shakes his head. 'I'm on three shifts.'

'But we have to look for the mother dolphin,' I say. 'We have to find her. Her calf will be put down if we don't.'

Dad wipes his mouth with a tissue. 'Look, Kara, Carl's

been out there looking today and so have Mr Andersen and Felix.'

'But we know the bay better than any of them. We'll find her.'

Dad puts the tissue down and pushes his plate away. 'I haven't got time tomorrow.'

I stab a chip with my fork. 'You've never got time any more.'

Dad glares at me. 'That's not fair, Kara. I have to earn some money.'

'But we have to find her, Dad.'

Dad gets up and chucks the chip paper in the bin. 'It's the ocean, for God's sake, Kara. She could be anywhere. How would we know where to look?'

I push my plate away. 'You've given up, like everyone else.'

Aunt Bev rests her hand on my arm. 'Listen to your father, Kara.'

I push my chair back and ignore Aunt Bev. 'You've given up,' I yell at Dad, 'like you've given up on Mum.' I storm up to the room I share with Daisy. I lie down on the camp bed fully clothed and pull the covers over my head. Dad comes in the room and whispers my name, but I pretend to be asleep. I hear the bang of the front door as he leaves the house and the blare of the TV in the room below.

Chapter 22

When Daisy comes into the bedroom I wait for her to put the light out and settle down in bed. When I hear her steady breathing, I fold the covers back and look up through the window at the darkening sky.

'Kara?'

I hold my breath. I thought she was asleep.

'I know you're awake,' she whispers.

I let my breath out slowly and turn on my side.

'Where is she?' Daisy asks. 'Where do you think she is?'

I feel silent tears fall down my face and soak into my pillow. 'I don't know,' I say. 'I just don't know.'

Chapter 23

The sun is bright, bright white.

The sea is turquoise blue.

I sit on the shoreline scooping sand to make a moat around my castle. It's the perfect castle. Three tall turrets and a drawbridge made from driftwood. I've decorated it with shells and seaweed. A cowrie shell reflects the sunlight from the turret nearest the sea. I fold my arms around my knees and gaze at it. Nothing can knock my castle down. But I don't hear the wave. It swirls into the moat and floods the castle walls. The turret nearest the sea is the first to fall. It slumps into the waves and disappears. The cowrie shell rolls along the hard wet sand, towards the sea. I try to scoop it up, but it slips through my fingers and tumbles into foaming surf.

Chapter 23

'Come on in, Kara.'

Mum is standing in the water, smiling. The wind blows back her hair. I can even see the freckles on her face, and the sunlight in her grey-green eyes. She's wearing the T-shirt and cut off jeans she always wears. A wave furls around her legs and rushes up the sand towards me.

Mum shades her eyes against the sun. 'Come *on*, Kara,' she smiles. 'I'm waiting for you.'

It's bright, bright white, that sun.

The waves are sliding on the shore, in and out, in and out.

But I want to find that cowrie shell. I search through seaweed heaped upon the sand, but all I find are beer can rings and plastic bottle tops.

I look back out to sea.

But Mum has gone.

The moon is shining through the window, bright, bright white.

Daisy is breathing softly in her bed, in and out, in and out.

But I just stare at the bright white moon.

I saw Mum's face. I heard her voice.

I'm waiting for you.

It felt so real.

White Dolphin

I reach under my camp bed for my swimming bag. Daisy snuffles in her sleep and turns on her side. The hands of her fairy clock point way past midnight. I grab my thick fleece, tiptoe down the stairs and slip out into the night.

I have to find the dolphin.

I have to find a way to talk to Mum.

The night is still. I stand at the water's edge, scrunching my toes into the soft damp sand. There are no waves. The high tide is slack, about to turn. The sea lies slick and black, like oil. I pull on my mask and fins and step into the water. I slide my feet forward until I stand waist deep. The cold water presses against my skin but I feel strangely far away, as if my body isn't mine at all.

I dive under, wrapped in darkness. I feel I can dive further and deeper tonight, as if I am part of the ocean, as if it's part of me. I run my hands along the rippled sand beneath me and listen to the deep still silence. I hold my breath. The seconds stretch like hours. My heartbeat slows. My mind drifts, clear and light. Bright stars swirl through the water. Something is swimming with me, by my side. A dolphin. Her body glows bright white, shining in the darkness. A trail of spinning stars spiral from her fins and tail flukes.

Chapter 23

She looks not of this world.

An underwater angel, almost.

I take a breath and she surfaces beside me.

'Pfwhooosh!'

I see the smooth dark curve of the dolphin's back and the deep notch in her dorsal fin, silhouetted in the moonlight. I knew the white dolphin's mother would return. I knew she would come back here to the bay. She dives under again, leaving a tumbling trail of phosphorescent swirls of light. I dive too, and watch the bright stars trail from my fingertips. A million tiny plankton, lighting up an underwater sky.

We surface again and she swims around me. I hear her clicks and whistles and feel her sonar pulse right through me, reading me. Her small dark eyes twinkle in the moonlight. I can hardly breathe. She is close, so close. I reach my hand out and she lets me touch the smooth warm skin of her face.

She dives again and circles. I know she is looking for her calf here in the shallow water. If she follows me along the shoreline to the Blue Pool I can lead her there.

I keep close to the line of dark rocks that runs out towards the headland, leaving the orange lights of town behind. The ebbing tide swirls around my legs and I can feel its pull towards the open sea. I shouldn't be out here. Dad would kill me if he knew. I can almost hear his voice *. . . what d'you think you're doing, Kara . . . hypothermia . . . no life jacket . . . on your own too!* I shut him out and swim on, grasping on the barnacled rocks that graze my skin.

The sound of a car alarm and the rumble of a distant lorry carry out across the sea, reaching far into the night. But they belong to another world almost, not mine.

Everything seems further at night. I think I've passed the Blue Pool when I see a light up ahead and two dome tents reflected in the moonlight.

Even at high tide, the water below the tidal pool is shallow and strewn with rocks. But now the tide is on the ebb, I can see the concrete rim of the pool above the water. I don't know if the mother dolphin can swim close enough to see her calf.

'Pfwhooosh!' The mother dolphin surfaces and lifts her head above the water.

I cling on to a rock and listen in the silence.

Then I hear another, 'Pfwhooosh,' reply.

The mother dolphin slaps her tail, the sound echoing out across the water. She opens her beak and a stream of whistles and clicks call out into the night.

I hear voices from the pool too, human voices.

Chapter 23

'Hey, Greg.' It's Carl's voice. He must be on a night shift. 'Something's out there.'

I back away into rock shadows. I don't want Carl to see me here. He's silhouetted on the poolside looking down into the water.

'There's another dolphin,' calls Carl. 'Get my torch. Let's see if it's the mother.'

A beam of torchlight scans the water and finds the dolphin. It follows the curve of her back to the deep notch in her dorsal fin.

'It's her all right,' says Greg.

'Kara was right.' Carl's voice is almost a whisper.

I strain my ears to hear the rest.

'She knew the mother dolphin would never stop looking until she found her calf.'

Chapter 24

'Wake up, Kara! Wake up!'

I feel small fingers poking at my eyelids.

'Wake up! You've missed breakfast. It's time for school.'

I open my eyes and push the hands away. Daisy's sitting on my camp bed staring at me.

'You've been asleep for ages,' she says.

I push myself up. My head is fogged with sleep and my legs ache with cold, deep into the bone. My mind swirls with last night's dream.

Daisy reaches out her hand. 'Why's your hair wet?'

I run my hand across my hair and see the dark patch on my pillow. My clothes lie in a wet heap on the floor. I was really there last night. I really saw the dolphin. It wasn't just a dream.

Chapter 24

I swing my legs out of bed. 'The mother dolphin is back. I saw her, last night.'

'You *saw* her?' Daisy's eyes are open wide.

I hold both her hands in mine. 'Don't tell your mum, Daisy, please don't tell.'

I pull my school clothes on and grab my bag and race down to the kitchen.

Aunt Bev is frying bacon on the stove. She tuts when she sees me. 'You'll have to take a bacon sarnie with you on the way to school.'

I take a slice of bread from the open packet on the table.

Uncle Tom is sitting at the table. He's in his shirt and oilskin trousers, the braces straps hang loose around his waist. He's unshaven and tired. He slumps forward and puts his head in his hands.

'Put the kettle on, Kara,' says Aunt Bev. 'Make your uncle a coffee.'

I fill the kettle with cold water from the tap. Daisy tries to climb on Uncle Tom's knee but he pulls her off. 'Get ready for school, Daisy. Don't be late.'

He says it roughly, not like Uncle Tom at all. I pour boiling water in the mug and watch the powdered coffee swirl around. Aunt Bev is watching him. This is when he brings the money home, his share from selling all the fish they've caught at sea.

Uncle Tom sits back and opens his hands. His palms are bare. 'There's nothing, Bev,' he says. 'French and Spanish boats were working the same area. We spent more on fuel than what we caught. Dougie Evans blames me. He says if I can't find the fish for him, he'll find another skipper for his boat.'

'He can't do that, Tom. We've got bills to pay, and the baby's due soon.' Aunt Bev glances in my direction. 'We've extra mouths to feed too.'

'I know that, Bev, I know.'

'Tom, we *need* the money.'

Uncle Tom slams his hands on the table. 'What d'you think I'm trying to do?'

Daisy grabs my arm and leans into me. Her eyes flit between her mum and dad.

Aunt Bev shoves a piece of bacon in my bread and pushes it in my hand. 'Go on, both of you. It's time you went to school.'

I take Daisy's hand and we run along the seafront. Instead of heading up the hill, I lead her along the coast road.

Daisy grips my hand tightly in hers. 'We're not going to school, are we?'

I shake my head. 'We're going to see the dolphin.'

Chapter 24

* * *

The vet's car and Greg's pickup are among the few cars in the headland car park. I'm relieved to see no one else on the path above the pool. Carl is sitting outside one of the tents, wrapped in a sleeping bag. He waves for us to come on down. Felix and his dad are down there too.

Daisy and I slip under the police tape and clamber down the steps.

The rocks are deep purple in early morning shadow. The sea is pale blue. A thin mist hangs above the water. It's cool now but it's going to be a hot day later, I can feel it. A notched dorsal fin slices through the water's surface beyond the tidal pool.

Carl looks at us and grins. 'We've got good news. The mother dolphin did come back.'

'We know,' beams Daisy.

I nudge her in the ribs. 'We always thought she would.'

A mobile phone rings from inside the tent. 'That's mine,' says Carl. He crawls in the tent to answer it.

Felix's dad glances at his watch and frowns at us. 'Shouldn't you both be on your way to school?'

'We just wanted to see the white dolphin,' I say.

'Me too,' says Felix. 'We can give you a lift in, can't we, Dad?'

Felix's dad nods. 'Well, we'd better not be long. We'll be late as it is.'

I turn to Daisy but she's already walked away from us, across the rocks to the pool's edge.

'She's still mad at me, isn't she?' says Felix.

I smile. 'She hasn't worn her fairy outfit since.'

I follow Felix. He walks slowly across the uneven surface, holding onto boulders with his good arm to stop himself from falling on the rocks.

'Did you find anything on the memory stick?' I ask.

Felix shakes his head. 'It's password locked. I've tried your name and "*Moand*", and lots of others, but I haven't cracked it yet. Is there anything you can think of that your mum would use?'

I shrug my shoulders. It could be anything from her favourite food to the Latin name for starfish.

I duck under the white cover and crouch down next to Daisy. Beside me in a bucket are the remains of a dark brown liquid. Straggly pieces of gut entrails stick like cooked spaghetti on the bucket's sides. I wrinkle my nose. It stinks of fish. Greg is in the water supporting the flotation raft. In front of the dolphin stands a woman, holding up a funnel attached to a long tube that passes into the dolphin's mouth.

The woman smiles at me. 'So you must be Kara. I've

heard all about you from Carl. I'm Sam, the vet, by the way.'

I smile back and look at the white dolphin. I lean forward so I can look into her eye. She blinks and looks back at me. I wonder if she recognizes me, if she remembers who I am. 'Will she get better now?' I ask.

Sam nods. 'She's got a fighting chance. Once she can balance in the water and feed herself, we can set her free.'

Daisy pushes back her curls of hair. 'Can we help look after her?'

Sam laughs. 'I don't think you'd like this job.' She points to the thick brown liquid in the funnel. 'It's dolphin baby food! Puréed fish and antibiotics! When the swelling in her mouth goes down, we try her with whole fish.'

Daisy takes her shoes and socks off and dangles her feet from the pool edge. 'What's her name?'

Sam shrugs her shoulders and smiles. 'She hasn't got a name.'

'She has to have a name,' says Daisy.

'I'm sure she has a dolphin name,' says Sam. 'Every dolphin has its own signature whistle, a name they call themselves.'

'We have to find her a name,' says Daisy. She slides knee deep into the water and reaches out to stroke the dolphin.

Sam shakes her head. 'We mustn't get her used to human contact. It's really hard, I know. But it's best for her.'

I jump when a flurry of black wings rushes past me. A jackdaw tips the bucket and flaps off with a piece of fish tail in its mouth. I watch it fly up above the Blue Pool, and see a figure walking slowly along the clifftop path.

'The Bird Lady,' whispers Daisy.

Felix shades his eyes against the sun to look at her. 'The Bird Lady? Who's she?'

I glare at Daisy and nudge her in the ribs. I don't want her to say anything about me going to see Miss Penluna.

'I know her,' says Sam. 'She sometimes brings sick birds to the surgery.'

Daisy clings on to my sleeve. 'She says dolphins are the angels of the seas.'

Sam smiles. 'Angels?' she says. 'Yes, maybe they are.'

The white dolphin glows pearly pink in the early morning light.

'Then that's what we'll call her,' says Daisy, a big grin on her face. 'We'll call her Angel.'

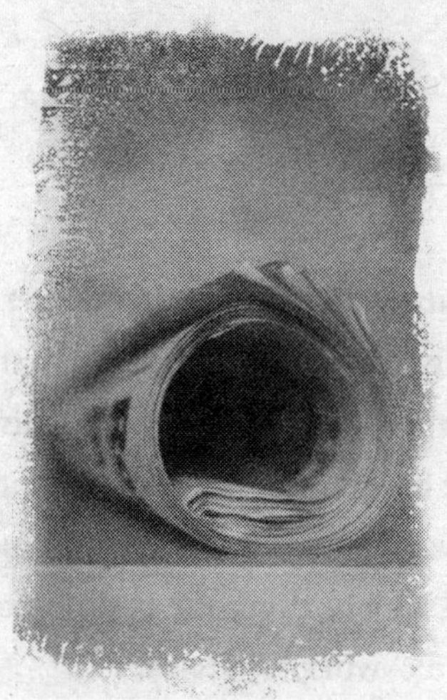

Chapter 25

'Angel?' says Carl.

Daisy nods. 'She's got to have a name.'

Carl stares at his mobile phone in his hand. 'That's just what the man said to me. He said she had to have a name.'

'What man?' I say.

Carl frowns and puts his phone in his back pocket. 'A journalist from the local paper. There's been loads of interest in the dolphin, especially since we put her story on the Marine Life Rescue website,' he says. 'There are newspapers and TV and environmental groups who want to come and see her. I've got to find a venue for a press conference for Saturday. I've rung up the town hall but they say, "no". They say it's too short notice.'

'No surprise there,' says Greg. 'Dougie Evans is on the committee.'

I fold my arms and lean back against the rocks. 'We'll soon have coach-loads of people coming here to our bay. Everyone will want to see her. She'll become like a side show in a theme park.'

'People love to see dolphins,' says Carl. 'It gives us a chance to tell them about what the Marine Life Rescue team do, and the dangers facing our sea life too.'

Felix slaps the water with his hand. 'But that's it,' he shouts. 'That's exactly what we need her for. We need to use her to tell them about the reef.'

I shake my head. 'And make her something for people to stare at? People should be interested in the reef without putting a dolphin on display.'

Felix rolls his eyes. 'It's not the same is it? I mean, what d'you think people want to read about, "Save the Sea Squirt" or "Save the Dolphin"?'

I scowl at him. 'OK, so how do you suggest we do it?'

'Use the internet,' says Felix. He's grinning from ear to ear. 'Websites, social networking sites, blogs, and Twitter, get people involved.'

I shake my head. 'It wouldn't work.'

Felix throws his hand up. '*Why* not, Kara? I can't believe

you don't want to give it a go. We could get an online petition for people to sign to stop the dredging of the reef.'

'It's no use,' I say. 'You can put up all the stupid blogs you like. You can get a million people to sign the petition, but nothing will work. Nothing will work unless we can convince the trawler owners to save the reef.'

I turn my back on Felix and flick small stones across the flat rocks.

'Come on,' says Felix's dad. 'It's time I got you all to school.'

We sit in silence on the way to school. I hold my bag tightly against my chest and stare out of the car window. I can't believe Felix and Carl want to use Angel like some circus act for the newspapers and TV to come and gawp at.

By the time we've dropped Daisy off, we're late for lessons. I watch Felix walk along the corridor to his maths class. His steps are short and jerky. It's all right for him; he could use it as an excuse for being late. I would if it were me. I know I'll be told off for being late again. It's almost the end of term. So instead of climbing the stairs, I walk out of the side door into the playground and sink down against the thick trunk of the horse-chestnut tree.

I curl up in the fork of tree roots, hidden from the school, and rest my head on my schoolbag. My eyes ache with lack of sleep and my thoughts spin out like threads of cloud across the blue, blue sky. The shade beneath this tree is cool and still. Somewhere above, a blackbird sings. A breeze sifts through the dense leaf cover, and draws me into sleep.

'There you are,' says Felix.

I open my eyes and sit up.

Felix is standing in front of me, frowning. 'I've been looking everywhere for you.'

I get up and brush grass and dirt from my skirt. 'What time is it?'

'It's the end of break,' he says and frowns. 'Mrs Carter wants to see us both.'

I guess we're in trouble for being late this morning, but I've gone past caring. There's only two more days left. Two more days and I can forget all about school. I follow Felix along the corridor to Mrs Carter's office. He knocks and pushes open the door. Inside the room, Chloe and Ella and several others from our year sit on cushioned chairs around the table. I glance at Mrs Carter. I wonder what they're doing here as well.

'Come on in, Kara,' she says. Her smile unnerves me.

Felix sits down next to Chloe.

Chapter 25

Mrs Carter points at a seat for me to sit down, but I don't take it. I stand beside the door. 'Felix has been telling us about the dolphin you both helped to save.'

I glance at Felix.

'We'd all like to offer our help too,' she says.

Ella's smiling. Chloe is fiddling with her bracelet, but looks up at me through her fringe.

I don't want this to be happening. I can't believe Felix has been telling everyone at school.

'What do you think, Kara?' Mrs Carter is still smiling at me, waiting.

'There are plenty of helpers at the moment,' I say. 'And it's a bit crowded down at the Blue Pool. No one's allowed to touch her anyway.'

I see Ella's face fall.

'Felix suggested a way maybe the whole school can be involved,' Mrs Carter says.

I shake my head. Angel's our dolphin. We found her. Now Felix wants everyone to have a piece of her too.

I take a couple of back steps to the door and glare at Felix. 'Thank you, but we don't need any help.'

Felix glares back at me. 'You're wrong, Kara,' he says. 'If we want to save the reef, we need all the help we can get.'

'We're fine just as we are,' I say.

Mrs Carter opens her arms wide. 'Felix is right, Kara,' she says. 'We all want to protect the bay too. None of us want the dredging ban to be lifted. I've offered Carl the school hall for the conference he needs. There'll be everyone from the press and politicians to the trawler men here. It's our chance to show everyone how much we all care about our bay.'

'We're going to make posters and put them up all around the hall,' says Chloe.

'Come on, Kara,' pleads Ella. 'It's important to us all.'

Chloe nods. 'It's our bay too, Kara.'

I look around them all. 'D'you really think it could work?'

Felix pushes himself forward on his seat. 'It has to work, Kara,' he says. 'The ban is lifted in less than one week's time. It's the only thing left that we can do.'

Chapter 26

I make sure I get to the school just after lunch on Saturday. I thought I'd be early, but I'm not the first one here.

I hold the main doors open for Greg. He's carrying a big cardboard box in his arms. I can see rolled-up posters and bits of dried seaweed sticking out of the top. 'Back at school already, Kara?' he says with a grin. 'On the first day of the holidays? You must be keen.'

I laugh and follow him into the school hall. I wouldn't miss this for the world.

I can't believe how much we've managed to do in so little time. We stopped lessons for the last two days and did a school project on the reef instead. Our year made a huge mural of the coral reef along one side of the hall. Year Eights made a timeline of our town with fishing boats and nets and shoals of tin-foil fish. Only Jake and Ethan didn't get involved. Jake didn't even come in to school at all on the last day.

'What d'you think?' says Chloe.

She's pinning up the last photo on a display board just inside the doors. There are the first photos Carl took on the day we found her, to new photos Chloe took today.

'It's great,' I say. I stare into the photo Chloe took this morning of Angel swimming on her own in circles in the Blue Pool.

'She's eating by herself too,' says Chloe.

I look at another photo, a close-up of Angel's mouth. The deep wound has almost healed. Apart from a line of thick scar tissue that dips down at the corner of her dolphin smile, there's no sign that she's had an injury at all.

Felix's dad walks past with a stack of chairs. 'Hey, Kara, can you give us a hand?'

Felix's mum is here too, putting chairs out in rows. The chairs almost fill the hall from front to back.

'How many d'you think will come?' I ask.

Felix's dad shrugs his shoulders. 'We'll find out soon enough,' he says.

Felix hands me small postcards with a photo of Angel on the front. 'Can you help with these?'

Chapter 26

I turn one over in my hand. 'What are these for?' I say.

'I made them yesterday,' Felix says. 'I thought we'd put them on all the seats. They're for people to sign on the other side and put in the petition box to stop the dredging.'

I turn one over and see the black lettering on the other side. 'They're great, Felix,' I say, 'really great.'

Felix looks at me and grins. 'I hoped you'd like them.'

I walk up and down the rows putting cards on the chairs. At the back of the hall, Carl is setting up the laptop for the big screen up on the stage. It's less than two hours until the meeting and less than two days until the trawlers can dredge the reef.

More children and parents join us and help stick pictures on the wall and put a display of different shells and seaweeds on a table. When the last picture has gone up, Greg walks in from the kitchens with a tray of drinks.

I take a glass of orange squash and flop down next to Felix. 'We're done,' I say. 'There's nothing more we can do now.'

The doors open and swing shut and Mrs Carter walks through. She unrolls a long sheet of paper. 'I've just come across this on the internet,' she says.

Ella helps to pin it to the board then stands in front of it and reads the words out loud. ' "To the dolphin alone, beyond all other, nature has granted what all good philosophers seek; friendship with no advantage."'

Mrs Carter nods. 'Plutarch, an ancient Greek philosopher, wrote that, two thousand years ago. It's important for today too. Friendship, for friendship's sake, and not because we think there's something else we can gain. It's amazing how dolphins have an effect on people.'

'The Maoris in New Zealand believe dolphins carry the spirits of their ancestors,' I say. I stop and look around. Everyone is quiet, listening.

Mrs Carter smiles. 'I wonder what the Maori name for dolphin is.'

I stare into a picture of a dolphin above Mrs Carter's head. I try to remember. I know Mum told me once. I remember the name sounds like dolphin breaths bursting above the water.

'What is it then?' says Felix.

His question's so direct. I turn to look at him.

He leans forward and stares at me. 'Well?'

'It's "te . . . pu-whee",' I say.

'Are you sure?'

'I think so.'

'How d'you spell it?'

'I don't know,' I say. 'Does it matter?'

Chapter 26

Felix runs his hand through his hair. He looks at me and then at the clock. 'I've got to go,' he says. 'It's worth a try.'

'What?' I say.

'Tell you later.'

He gets up and pulls his dad away.

'Carl's giving his talk in an hour,' I call after him.

But Felix and his dad have gone. The doors of the hall swing and slam shut behind them.

I help Greg and Mrs Carter clear away the cups and take them to the sink in the kitchens.

'Goodness, look out there,' says Mrs Carter.

I stand on tiptoe to look out of the high windows. I can't believe my eyes. 'We won't fit them all in,' I say.

Greg shakes his head. 'Some will have to stand.'

The car park is already full of cars, and some are lined up along the road. A long queue of people curls around the playground.

'Does Carl know?' I say.

'He's gone to get changed,' says Greg. 'I don't think he'll know what's hit him.'

I look out along the row of people. There are lots of tourists in bright shorts and beach gear. But I see lots of people I know from the town too.

'That's Mr Cooke, our local politician,' says Mrs Carter.

'That's got to be good,' I say. 'Maybe he can pass a law to stop the dredging.'

Greg frowns. 'That's up to politicians up in London,' he says. 'Most of them wouldn't know a cod from a mackerel if one hit them in the face.'

Then I see who Mr Cooke is talking to. I see Dougie Evans. I see them smiling, sharing a joke. I don't want Mr Cooke to be on Dougie's side. I remember what Felix said about not giving up without a fight. There's less than two days until the dredging ban is lifted. Less than two days before the trawlers can haul their chains across the reef. We might never get this chance again.

This is it.

It has to work.

This is our one big chance to save the bay.

Chapter 27

I push my way through the crowd of people milling in the entrance and take a seat next to Dad and Daisy at the front. The room is packed. People are lined up along the the walls. I see a group of fishermen a few rows from the front. Dougie Evans is leaning back in his chair, arms folded across his chest, a smug smile on his face.

'Dougie met some of the trawler owners at the pub at lunch time,' whispers Dad. 'He told them all to protest about the petition for the dredging ban, told them it's their livelihoods being taken away.'

I turn round to look at the sea of faces in the room. 'I bet loads here will sign the petition to protect the bay.'

Dad shakes his head. 'It will only be a voluntary ban for

now. You know it won't mean a thing if the fishermen don't agree.'

The room is hot despite the open doors and windows. The murmur of voices hushes as a journalist and cameraman walk up through the aisle and take a stand in a corner at the front. The local radio is here too, about to broadcast the meeting live.

'Where's Felix?' I whisper. 'He should be here by now.' I glance back over my shoulder at the crowded room. Maybe Felix can't push his way through. I get up to go and look but Dad pulls me back down.

'Carl's about to talk,' whispers Dad.

I watch Carl climb up the steps onto the stage and turn to face all the people.

Silence falls across the hall. Chair legs scuffle and a baby cries somewhere at the back. I watch Carl. He looks so different in a suit and tie. His hair is brushed and he wears thin gold-rimmed glasses. He shifts from foot to foot. He looks pale too. I can hear the rustle of paper in his shaking hands.

I cross both fingers for him.

It doesn't start well. The microphone doesn't work and he's so quietly spoken that I guess people halfway back can't hear him speak at all. Sunlight slants through the windows and someone has to pull the curtains and switch the lights out to see the screen behind him. People listen when he shows pictures of Angel. There are gasps at the deep wounds in her mouth, and sighs at her taking her first fish.

But then Carl starts to talk about the bay and the project to save the coral reef. He shows graphs and pie-charts on the screen, and talks about the different sorts of rock under the sea. He uses the Latin names of different sea animals and plants and holds up fragments of coral in his hand. I know the people at the back can't see. No one's really listening. All they want to hear about is Angel.

When Carl has finished speaking, the lights come on and he asks for questions from the hall. Someone asks where they'll release the dolphin. Someone else asks if the white dolphin will change colour. But no one is interested in the reef. It's out of sight, out of mind. Then Dougie Evans stands up. He walks up on the stage next to Carl, his cap in hand. He faces everyone, and I notice he's wearing his oldest clothes. They look worn and shabby.

'It's good to see so many here today,' he says, 'tourists and locals too.'

His voice booms out across the hall. An easy smile sits on his face, but he doesn't fool me.

He opens his arms wide. 'I hope you're all having a lovely time. But this lovely town of ours in't just for sandcastles and holidays. We've been fishing from this port for hundreds of years. It's our livelihood. When tourists go home, we've still got to make a living.'

Everyone is listening now. It's hard not to. There's something about Dougie Evans which holds people. I glance across the room and see Jake looking smug.

'There's plenty of reef round this coastline,' Dougie goes on. 'There's plenty for everyone. We dredge for scallops in our bay like the farmers plough their fields.'

The room is silent. I look around and see all eyes fixed on Dougie.

He puts his fist against his chest. 'Fishing is the heart of this town,' he shouts out. 'Always has been. So if you still want the freshest scallops on your plate, then support us too. Support the fishermen. Don't sign the petition for the ban.'

The murmur of voices rises and a ripple of applause flows back across the people. It's not just some of the fishermen who are clapping, but tourists too. Dougie Evans takes a quick bow and steps down to take his seat again.

'Say something, Carl,' I mutter under my breath. But Carl just stands there, shuffling his feet while Dougie grins, victorious.

Chapter 27

'STOP!'

Heads turn to the shout from the back of the hall. Dougie Evans squints to see who's calling. I turn too. Chairs scrape and feet shuffle as people clear a space for Felix to get through the aisle.

He stops in front of me, the dolphin memory stick clutched in one hand. 'Kara, I've found something, something important.'

'What?' I say.

Voices are rising in the room. It's hot and stuffy. There's nothing to keep people here now. I see people at the back of the hall get up to leave.

Felix glances at them too. 'You've got to buy me some time. Stop them going. Get up on stage and say something, anything you want about the bay. Two minutes, that's all I need. Tell them they're about to see what they could lose.'

I shake my head. 'I can't.'

Felix glares at me. 'Just do it.'

I watch him walk back down the aisle.

I've never stood in front of a crowd like this before. I see more people at the back of the hall stand up to leave. I don't know what Felix has found, but I can't lose this chance. I climb up the steps and face the audience. I don't even know what I'm going to say. The sea of faces stares back at me. I feel sick and dizzy. I see Jake's mouth curled in laughter. Dougie Evans is watching me too. His eyes bore right through me. I look around the walls of the hall, at the mural of traditional fishermen, fishing boats and nets and barrels of salted fish.

'Dougie Evans is right,' I say. My voice comes out much louder than I expect. The hall is silent, listening. A few people sit back down in their chairs. 'Fishing *is* the heart of this town.' I look around. This is my one big chance. 'The boat my mum and dad rebuilt together, fished from this harbour a hundred years ago. Back then, she would have come home full of pilchard and herring, so full the fish would be spilling over her sides back into the sea.' I swallow hard. The back of my throat is dry, like sawdust. I look around and fix my eye on Dougie Evans. 'But she can't do that any more. We've taken all the fish from our seas. Dougie Evans's trawlers have to go further and deeper to find fish, and even then they sometimes come back empty. Now we're dredging our bay for scallops, tearing up the reef. I wonder, will we still be fishing here at *all* in another hundred years?' I glance across the hall. There's no sign of Felix, but I remember what he wanted me to say. 'You're about to see what we could lose.'

I stand there in the silence and look around the hall. I

don't know what's meant to happen now. I climb down the steps and sit next to Dad.

The hall lights go out.

The whole room holds its breath.

A clear voice cuts through the silence. I have to grab the edges of my seat. My head spins and I feel myself tip forward.

I hear Mum, speaking through the darkness.

CHAPTER 28

'*Let me take you on a journey through our last great wilderness, a place of mountains and deep valleys. Yet it doesn't lie in some distant land, but here, below the surface of our cold Atlantic sea.*'

Dad takes hold of my hand. The room is silent. The huge screen on the stage is dark at first. A faint greenish glow in the centre of the screen becomes brighter and brighter and we are rising up, towards the sun shining through the surface of the water. Bright green kelp fronds reach upwards to the rippling mirror screen of light. A seal swims up to the camera, his nose almost touching the lens. It's as if he's watching everyone in the hall. His big dog eyes are chocolate brown. He snorts a breath. Silver bubbles spiral upwards and he twists away, flippers pressed together, his grey body sliding through the water. And we're twisting through the water too; down, down, down through shafts of rippling sunlight, past rocks jewelled with pink and green anemones, down past coral mounds and feather-stars and sea-fans.

This must have been the last film Mum made here in the bay.

Her voice guides us into dark green waters full of rocks encrusted with soft pink corals and yellow sponges. A cuckoo wrasse hovers in mid-water, bright blue and yellow, lit by torchlight. A purple sea-slug threads its way through reddish seaweed. Beneath all this, the rocky bed is alive with corals and urchins. A velvet swimming crab scuttles by. Everything is alive in here.

But suddenly, a tearing sound rips through the hall. The image on the screen changes and fills with metal chains and billowing mud and sand. When the mud settles all that's left is a gravelly sea bed, littered with broken sea-fans. The silence in the hall is still and deep.

Mum's voice speaks out one last time.

'*Unless we protect our oceans, there will be nothing left but wasteland.*

'*We are not farmers of the sea. We never sow, we only reap.*'

The lights come on. No one speaks. We've all been brought

back from another world, the images still vivid in our minds. Mum's voice is still ringing in my head. Carl climbs back on the stage. He clutches his notes in his hand and is about to speak, but a ripple of applause starts at the back of the room and rolls forward like a wave. I look across to see some of the fishermen nodding. Others are just staring at the screen, transfixed. Only Dougie Evans is sitting hands folded tight across his chest. Jake is glaring at me from across the room. I turn away. I don't want to spoil this moment. I heard Mum's voice again. I want to hold it deep inside. Hold it and keep it there for ever.

'I'm sorry I couldn't warn you,' says Felix. 'I didn't have time.'

I roll my jeans up and dip my feet into the pool. Angel glides past on her side, her small eye watching me. I stretch my leg out and she lets my toes brush against her smooth warm body.

'How did you find out?' I say.

Felix sits beside me on the rocks and holds out the memory stick. '*Tepuhi*,' he says. 'I should have thought of it before. The Maori name for dolphin. It's the password. The one your mum used for the memory stick.'

I take it from him and curl my fingers around the moulded plastic dolphin. It seems strange to think that it holds a memory of Mum, a snapshot of the past, as if it holds part of her inside it too. 'Was there anything else on there?'

'Not much else,' he mumbles.

I want to ask him what he means by 'not much else' but Carl sits down beside us.

'I'm glad that's over,' he says. His tie hangs loose around his neck and his pressed trousers are now crumpled. He runs his hands through his hair. 'I couldn't have done it without you.'

'D'you think it'll make a difference?' I ask.

'There were loads of signatures for the voluntary ban on dredging,' he says. 'I counted hundreds of names.'

'What about the fishermen?' I say.

'I don't know,' Carl says. 'I guess we'll find out soon enough.'

Angel swims past us again and slaps the water with her tail. I reach out to run my hand along her head and the bumpy scar across her jaw.

Carl frowns. 'She's becoming too dependent on us,' he says, 'and we're worried for her mother too. There were lots of boats out on the bay today. She could get injured by their propellers.' He stands up to wipe the water from his trousers, then crouches down beside me and Felix. 'I shouldn't be telling you this, because no one else must know . . . '

I feel my heart sink because I know just what he's going to say. 'You're going to let her go, aren't you?'

Carl nods. 'Sam thinks she's ready. But we don't want lots of people around when we release her.'

Angel lifts her head above the water. It's as if she's listening to us too. I want her to go back into the wild, but I feel torn apart inside. I know that once she's gone, it could be the last time I see her.

'When?' I say.

'Tomorrow,' says Carl, 'we release her on the beach, at dawn.'

Chapter 29

I'm the first on the beach. I wrap my arms around me and wish I'd brought my coat. The Milky Way is a river of stars across the sky. I remember Mum telling me the Maori story of Tama-rereti and how he scattered tiny pebbles into the sky to light up his way, and how the Sky God put Tama-rereti's canoe up in the sky as the Milky Way to show how all the stars were made. I dig my toes into the cool sand and listen to the line of breaking surf. I want to see the mother dolphin. I strain my ears for the sound of a dolphin blowhole opening out on the water.

'Kara, is that you?'

I turn.

Dad is walking towards me, silhouetted against the street

lights. 'I heard you leave the house. What are you doing out here?'

'Carl's releasing Angel at dawn.' I can't stop my teeth from chattering. A cool wind is blowing off the shore.

Dad takes off his fleece and slips it over me. The sleeves are far too long and the fleece comes down to just above my knees. Dad hugs me tight against him and we watch the dawn spread across the eastern sky, a pale strip of light fading out the stars. A flock of sanderlings skims low across the beach and settles further along the shoreline.

'Here's Carl,' says Dad.

A pickup drives towards us, its headlights reflecting in the wet sand.

'I hope Felix and his dad get here in time,' I say.

The pickup stops beside us and Carl and Greg jump down followed by Felix's dad and Sam. I lean over the back of the pickup to see Felix sitting by Angel's head. Angel is wrapped in wet towels on the yellow flotation raft.

Carl scans the water. 'Any sign of the mother dolphin?'

I shake my head. 'I hope she's not waiting by the pool.'

I take a front corner of the raft with Dad and we all help lift Angel down.

She's heavy, a solid mass of bone and muscle. I rest one

hand on her head as we carry her to the water. Her breaths are short and shallow, her eyes wide open.

'Not too deep,' says Carl. 'Let's wait for her to get used to the water. We don't want her swimming off too early.'

We float Angel out into the waves until we're waist deep in water. The waves are breaking further out, running to the shoreline in steps of broken surf. Angel is strangely calm, as if she's waiting too. I feel her clicks and whistle pass right through me, invisible pulses of sound spreading out through the dark waters of the bay.

The sun's rim rises above the hills behind us, turning the sea to liquid gold.

I feel Angel's body tense. She's still and silent, listening.

Maybe I can feel the vibrations of whistles through the water too, because I sense her mother near us.

'Pfwhooosh!' She surfaces close by.

'Just watch her,' says Carl. 'She could turn aggressive if she wants her calf.'

Angel flaps her tail, desperate to swim.

Carl and Greg deflate the two long cushions of the raft and let it slip beneath her. I run my hands along her back one last time as she surges forward to meet her mother. They swim side by side, their bodies touching, and slide together beneath the sea.

White Dolphin

Two plumes of warm breath rise in the chill dawn air.

I watch the space where they had been, and feel a strange emptiness deep inside.

It's not for what I've lost.

But for what I hope will be.

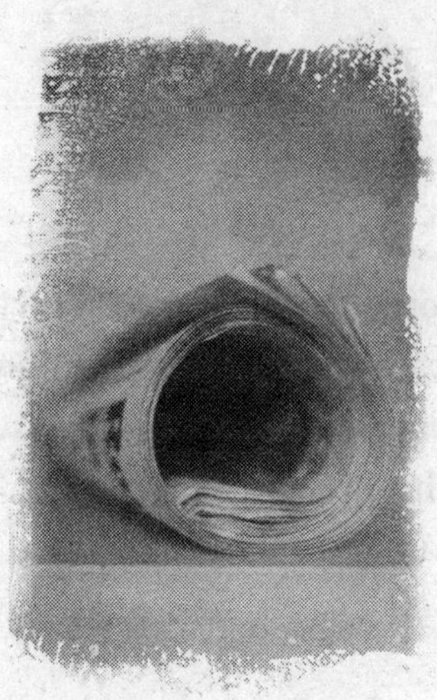

Chapter 30

Carl offers us a lift home in the pickup truck. My shorts are soaking wet and I'm freezing cold. I sit in the back with Dad and Felix. We bump along the rippled sand and turn up the slipway to the coast road. The newsagent is open early. The shopkeeper is already putting the papers on the display racks outside. Dad raps on the window for Carl to stop and he jumps out to buy Aunt Bev some bread and a local paper.

I snatch the paper from his hands. On the front is a huge picture of Angel. I flick to the inside pages and see a double spread with photos of Carl and Dougie and the school hall. Daisy and I are pictured too.

'What does it say?' I ask. I push the paper into Felix's hand.

Felix holds up the paper. '"*Save our Seas: Locals and tourists filled the school hall yesterday to give their support to the marine reserve* . . ."'

Felix is silent for a moment while he skim-reads the article. He breaks out in a huge grin. 'We've done it. Listen here . . . "*Local fishermen signed the petition for the voluntary ban on fishing and dredging the area, while a law to ensure the bay gets statutory protection is put through parliament. The petition was signed by over six hundred people in less than two hours.*"'

'So the fishermen are on our side,' I say. 'They've promised not to dredge the bay until a new law is passed to protect the reef.' I can't help grinning. I never dreamed it would happen like this. We've saved Angel and we've saved the bay.

'We've got to remember this moment,' Felix says. 'It doesn't get much better than this.'

I nod, because he's right and nothing can take away this feeling.

Nothing.

Not even Dougie Evans's jeep parked in Aunt Bev and Uncle Tom's drive.

Carl pulls up outside the house. We can hear raised voices

coming through the open kitchen window. Uncle Tom and Dougie Evans are doing the shouting. Aunt Bev is standing with her back to us, pressed against the kitchen sink.

'Do you want us to come in with you?' says Felix's dad.

Dad shakes his head and looks grim. 'It's OK,' he says. 'I guess Dougie Evans has seen the paper too.'

Dad and I jump down from the pickup. I wave at Felix as they turn the corner and disappear out of sight.

I follow Dad up the path towards the door. I try hard not to step on the cracks in the paving stones, but Dougie Evans flings the door open and stops in front of us. I see he has the same paper in his hand.

He chucks it on the ground. 'Means nothing, this,' he snarls. 'It's not worth the paper it's written on.' He kicks it with his foot, and the pages scatter into the air.

Dad stands back to let him through and he glares at me as he passes. I think he'll walk right past, but he stops and turns back to face me.

'Saving bloody dolphins like your mum, eh?' His face is pressed close up to mine. Sweat glistens on his forehead. 'Look what happened to her.'

'Go home, Dougie.' Dad pushes himself in front of me. 'Just go home.' Dad's voice is calm, but his hands are clenched.

I try to slip in front of Dad. I want him to be safe, but Dad just holds me back.

'No one tells me what to do,' Dougie shouts. 'No one.'

He turns away and storms down the path to his jeep. He spits on the pavement, climbs in and roars away.

And we are left in dust and silence.

Dad puts his arms around me. 'Ignore it,' he says.

I lean into Dad and walk into the house with him. But I can't help thinking Dougie Evans would rip up the whole sea and everything in it if he could.

Aunt Bev is standing at the sink, her hand across her belly. Uncle Tom goes to put his arm around her but she shrugs him off. 'You didn't listen to me, did you?'

Uncle Tom sits down at the table and puts his head in his hands.

'What happened?' Dad asks.

Aunt Bev shakes her head and stares at her husband. 'I told him not to sign that petition, but he wouldn't listen.'

Dad looks between them. 'Bev, what happened?'

'He's lost his job. Dougie fired him just now.'

Dad pulls up a chair next to Uncle Tom. 'He can't just do that,' he says.

'Of course he can,' snaps Aunt Bev. 'He's Dougie Evans. He does what he likes. You should've known that, Tom.'

Chapter 30

Uncle Tom gets up. He grabs his jacket and walks to the door.

'Where are you going now?' snaps Aunt Bev.

'Out,' he says. 'I need fresh air.'

He pushes past us and I hear the front door slam shut.

'We need the money, Tom,' she calls after him through the open window. 'What are we going to do without money?'

I back away to the door too. Aunt Bev's in no fine mood. I expect the shouting to start at me and Dad, but she sinks into a chair. She pushes back thin strands of hair from her face and stares up at the ceiling.

'What am I going to do, Jim?' she says. 'We got no money for the rent this month.'

Dad takes Aunt Bev's hand in his. 'Things will work out, Bev. You'll see.'

But Aunt Bev shakes her head. She doesn't even wipe away the tears that fall and soak dark drops into the T-shirt stretched across her bulging belly.

'We can't keep you and Kara too,' she says. 'God knows how we'll keep ourselves.'

Dad nods and sits with her, still holding her hand. 'You've been good to us, Bev,' he says. 'I'm sorry.'

I back out of the door and turn to head up the stairs. But Daisy's sitting on the bottom stair, Teddy-cat clutched to her chest. Her face is puffy and her eyes are red with tears.

'I don't want you to go,' she says. She wraps her arms around me.

I hug her tight. 'Come on, Daisy,' I say. I put my arm round her and we climb the stairs up to her bedroom. I sit next to her on the bed and hug her into me. 'Carl released Angel this morning,' I say.

'I wish I could have come,' she says.

I stroke her hair. I feel bad that I didn't take her. But I couldn't have asked Aunt Bev. She'd never have let me go either. 'She found her mother. She was waiting for her in the bay.'

Daisy smiles and picks at the fluff balls on Teddy-cat's fur.

'We saved the reef too,' I say. 'There's a picture of you and me in the paper. We're famous, Daisy.'

Daisy frowns. 'Dougie Evans is mad at that.'

'I know,' I say. I can't help smiling. 'But we've got the other fishermen on our side. They're not going to dredge the reef.'

Daisy shakes her head. 'Dad said he wouldn't do it, that's why Dougie Evans started shouting.'

'Uncle Tom said *he wouldn't do* what?'

Daisy looks at me. Her bottom lip trembles. 'I heard them

in the kitchen, and Dougie Evans is going to do it anyway.'

I feel my heart pump in my ears. I search her face. 'Do what?' I say.

Daisy hugs Teddy-cat tight into her chest. 'Dougie Evans said he's going fishing on the midnight tide. He's going to rip out every coral in the bay.'

CHAPTER 31

'It didn't make any difference, did it?' I say.

I turn the brittle skeleton of the pink sea-fan over and over in my hand. A small piece comes away and falls onto the wet sand. Every day, more sea-fans and corals are washed up on the shoreline. It's been nearly a month since the local fishermen signed the voluntary ban. But since then, more and more trawlers from other fishing towns up and down the coast have come to dredge the bay. It seems they don't care about the ban, or the bay.

Felix flings a pebble into the waves. 'Dad heard the local fishermen complaining because they're not getting as many lobsters and crabs in their pots. And the fish market in town won't buy the scallops,' he says. 'At least they still support the voluntary ban. The trawlers that come here have to take their catch elsewhere.'

I shake my head. 'For now,' I say. I know Uncle Tom managed to get work on another boat. He'll be out there soon too. And he's not the only local fisherman to go out on the trawlers. Dad heard them say it wasn't fair that other fishermen were taking their share of shellfish instead. I stare out to sea. At least it's been too rough to work these past few days. The high waves have washed up broken reef. I don't want to imagine what it looks like now. It must look like a ghost reef, like the pictures of torn down rainforest, only under water, out of sight.

Felix pulls his hood up over his head. We're the only ones on the beach today. The clouds are low and heavy. They scud across the headland and the hills behind. Cold rain blasts in from the sea, horizontal.

'We saved Angel, though,' says Felix. 'It counts for something.'

'I know,' I say. 'I wish we could see her again.'

We've looked for the dolphins every day, but we haven't seen them since Angel was released. Carl asked us to record any sightings of dolphins or whales. He took us out one day in the Marine Life Rescue boat and we saw basking sharks, their sail-like black dorsal fins cruising through the water and their huge white mouths gaping open, filtering plankton from the sea. We saw grey seals too, their fish-fattened bodies stretched out on warm rocks, sleeping in the sun.

'I don't reckon we'll see much out there today,' says Felix. 'Come on. Let's get some food in town.'

I stand up and wipe the sand from my hands. 'Don't you ever stop eating?'

Felix grins. 'Lunch was two hours ago. I'm starving.'

We walk through the streets in town, but the cafés are packed. Through the mist of condensation on the windows, I see families crowded around tables. Bags, coats, and umbrellas lie scattered around chairs.

'We could get some chips from the take-away and eat them in *Moana* under the cover,' I say. 'There's not much room, but we'd be dry.'

'It'll do for now,' Felix grins. 'We'll have more room when I get my yacht for my solo trip around the world.'

I laugh. 'So you're still up for the regatta race next week?'

'Yep,' he says. 'Dad and I got round Gull Rock and back in under an hour and thirty minutes last time.'

'Not bad,' I say. But secretly, I'm impressed. The fastest time Dad and I raced *Moana* was in one hour and forty-five, but I'm not telling Felix that. He and his dad have been out sailing nearly every day. I've watched them from the shore. I've watched, wanting to be out there too with Dad in *Moana*, like it used to be. But now, even on his days off work, he finds something else to do. He's just not interested any more. It's as if he's turned his back on her. Maybe it's because he can't face losing her. Maybe that's the way he feels about me.

Felix and I take our chips from the counter. I slip mine inside my coat to keep dry and we turn down Rope Walk, a quicker way to the harbour. Rain hammers on the rooftops and water pours out of gutters and across our path. The cobbles shine wet, the moss between them damp and slippery. Felix picks his way slowly down, but I hurry ahead, keen to get out of the rain. I hear him shout. I turn and see him stumble to the ground and his knees hit the hard stone cobbles. His chips scatter into the rivulets of water.

I run back and kneel down beside him. 'Sorry, I shouldn't have rushed on.'

I offer my hand to help him up, but he pushes me away and swears under his breath. I try to scoop up some of his chips, but even the ones still in the packet have turned to mush. The seagulls are pacing up and down behind us, ready for an easy meal.

Felix pushes himself up and thumps his hand against the wall. 'I *hate* being like this sometimes.'

His jeans are ripped at the knees. Dark red bloodstains spread across the frayed denim.

He leans against the wall and kicks the chip packet towards the seagulls. 'Out on the water, I can do anything anyone else can do. It's like my boat is part of me.' He thumps the wall again. 'Out there, I'm free.'

I nod, because I know just what he means. *Moana* feels part of me. She keeps us safe, a protective shell around Mum and Dad and me.

The wind gusts up from the harbour walls and whips my hair across my face. I wrap my coat tightly around me and feel my packet of chips burn warm against my skin. The smell of vinegar and salty chips wafts up around my collar. 'Come on,' I say. 'I've got loads in here. You can share mine.' I'm starving too, and can't wait to eat them under *Moana*'s cover spread across the boom.

The harbour walls are empty. A few gulls march along the wall beside the waste bins hoping for scraps of food. I look down along the line of pleasure yachts to see *Moana*. But her cover's been drawn back and there are two people sitting inside. Even from here I can see who they are. It's Ethan, and Jake Evans.

Chapter 31

I leave Felix on the harbour wall and climb down the ladder set into the granite blocks. I run along the pontoon, my feet thudding on the boards.

I stare at them in the boat. Crisp packets and a drink can lie scattered inside. 'Get out,' I yell.

Jake and Ethan exchange glances. Ethan puts his feet up on the seats.

I climb inside *Moana*. 'Get out of my boat.'

Jake leans forward and smirks at me. 'I think you'll find she's not your boat.'

I scowl at him. 'What d'you mean?'

Jake just smiles. 'Take a look.'

I look around *Moana*. Everything's the same. I open up the cubby under the foredeck. The flares and toolbox are still there, but our blankets have gone, and so have Dad's fishing tackle and the red tin cups.

I look up at Jake and he's still grinning. 'Didn't your dad tell you? My dad bought her last weekend.' He looks at the chip packet sticking out of the top of my coat. 'Your dad was in a hurry to sell her. Cheap as chips, she was.'

I just stare at him. It can't be true.

But Jake's mouth forms in a thin hard line. He holds up the keys to the locker under the foredeck. 'So I think it's for me to say, get out of *my* boat.'

I back out of *Moana* and climb the ladder. I shove the chips in Felix's hand. 'I've got to go,' I say. I run all the way to Aunt Bev's house and don't stop until I burst through the door. Aunt Bev's ironing shirts, watching the TV.

I stand in front of her. 'Where's Dad?' I say.

Aunt Bev tries to look round me. 'He went out.'

I switch the TV off. 'Where?' I say.

She up-ends the iron and puts her hand on her hip. 'What's this about, Kara?'

'He's sold her, hasn't he?' I try to blink back the tears. 'He's sold *Moana*.'

Aunt Bev stoops to pull the plug of the iron from the wall. 'Sit down, Kara.'

I don't sit down. 'He's sold *Moana* to Dougie Evans.'

Aunt Bev reaches out to touch my arm but I step away. 'He said he couldn't bring himself to tell you.'

I just stare at her in blank silence.

'Don't be angry at him, Kara. He's trying to get his life back. God knows, he needs to.'

'Where is he?' I say.

Aunt Bev fiddles with a button on a shirt. 'He's gone to Exeter for the day.'

'Exeter!' Dad didn't mention this to me. 'Why Exeter?'

Aunt Bev takes a deep breath. I watch her fold the shirt,

running long straight creases down the sleeves and seams. She lets her breath out slowly and lays the shirt on the pile next to her.

'I shouldn't be telling you this,' she says. She smooths the front of the shirt and straightens the collar. 'But he's gone for a job interview. Don't ask what. He wouldn't even tell me. But he told me he was doing this for you.'

I storm past her out of the room. She calls after me, but I run up the stairs to Daisy's bedroom, glad she's out at Lauren's today.

I curl up under my duvet and lie in empty silence.

I can't believe we've lost her.

Moana isn't ours.

That shell around Mum and Dad and me has broken.

It feels as if nothing can protect us any more.

Chapter 32

I sit with Felix on the wooden boards of the roundabout in the park. Rainwater soaks through my jeans and the cold metal of the bars of the roundabout burn into my skin. It feels like a winter storm, although it's summer, still. The skies are low and heavy and the sea is a shifting mass of grey and green. All the fishing boats have run for home, all except Dougie Evans's. His trawlers are still out there on the high seas.

It's been a week now since I found out Dad sold *Moana*. I can hardly bring myself to speak to him. It's not as if he speaks to me these days anyway. I've lost Mum and now I've lost *Moana*. It feels as if I'm losing Dad now too. He hasn't even mentioned his trip to Exeter, and I'm not going to ask him. It's not as if I can do anything. The baby's due any day, and Dad and I will have to find somewhere else to live.

I push the roundabout round with my feet. 'Are you still sailing in the regatta race tomorrow?'

'If it's not cancelled,' says Felix. His hood is pulled over his head and the storm collar of his coat is drawn across the lower half of his face so only his eyes are showing.

'I hope you win,' I say. 'You deserve to.'

He pushes back his hood. 'I asked Dad if you could sail with me tomorrow instead of him, but he says I'm not ready yet.'

'Thanks,' I smile. 'But I reckon your dad wants to do this with you too.'

I push faster with my feet and the hills and sea spin all around us.

'You know that sailing coach Dad got for me?' says Felix.

I nod. 'I saw you with him out on the water.'

Felix holds on to the roundabout with his good arm and leans out over the spinning concrete. 'He wants to put me in the junior training squad for the Paralympics sailing team.'

I slam my foot down. The roundabout scrapes to a halt. 'You're kidding! Why didn't you tell me before? That's fantastic, Felix. Brilliant.' I mean it too.

He pulls the storm collar from his face and looks right at me. 'One of the race categories is for a disabled and an able-bodied sailor. Would you do it with me?'

The question takes me by surprise. I've never sailed any other boat except *Moana.*

'We'd make a great team,' he says. 'We wouldn't argue . . . much.' He's grinning now. 'And we'd do all our training here, in the bay. We'll train in my boat.'

I stare at the ground. I'd love the chance to sail again, especially to race with Felix, but for all I know, Dad's got a job in Exeter. Soon we'll be far away from here. I shake my head. 'I don't know, Felix,' I say. 'I don't think it would work.'

'But, Kara . . . '

'Just leave it,' I snap.

I stand up and walk away from him to the park fence. The town is sprawled out beneath me. The houses are darkened by the rain and the harbour is full of boats sheltering from the storm.

In the distance I see Dougie Evans's trawlers rear up on the horizon. Maybe it would be better to be far away from here. I don't think I could bear to see Dougie Evans sailing *Moana* in the bay. Felix leans on the fence next to me and we watch the trawlers come back across the heaving sea, like wolves returning from their hunt. Their prows rise over waves and slice down, sending up plumes of spray. A flock of seagulls trails in their wake, bright against the slate-grey sky. I guess the trawlers have come back with full nets this time.

'I'm sorry I snapped,' I say.

'Just think about it,' says Felix. 'Promise me?'

I nod and stuff my hands deep in my pockets. 'I'd better go. Aunt Bev wants me back for lunch.'

I walk with Felix across the play park. The wind whistles through the top bars of the climbing frame, like a gale through a mast. Big puddles spread across the tarmac and rain shines off the seesaw and the swings. Outside the gate we almost bump into Adam and his brother Joe running down the road, their footsteps slapping on the wet pavement.

Adam stops in front of us, his hands on his knees, panting. 'Have you seen it?'

'What?' I say.

'The great white shark,' says Adam. 'Dad's heard that Dougie Evans has caught a great white shark in his nets.'

I shake my head. Joe pulls Adam's arm and they set off towards the harbour. I can't believe Dougie Evans has caught a great white shark. We don't get them in these waters. He's probably caught a basking shark. I know they can get to forty feet in length. But there's a doubt in my mind because we sometimes get leather-backed turtles washed up here from more tropical seas.

'Shall we take a look?' I ask Felix.

Felix shrugs his shoulders. 'Can you face seeing Jake again?'

'It won't be for long,' I say. 'I bet loads of other people are down there too.'

By the time Felix and I reach the harbour, a small crowd has gathered on the quayside beside one of Dougie Evans's trawlers. We walk past the fish market. I glance through the clear plastic flaps of the entrance into the cool bright space inside. Yellow crates, full of fish, lie in rows along the concrete floor. Two of the fishermen inside are grinning widely. It's been a good trip for Dougie Evans and his men.

I look around for Felix, but Jake is suddenly beside me. 'Hey, Kara,' he says. 'Ever seen a great white shark before?' He looks smug, but there's something else, something more than boasting in his voice.

I look beyond him to the crowd of people.

I can see something lying on the ground half hidden behind rows of legs.

Chapter 32

I try to push my way through, but Chloe's suddenly next to me, pulling me away.

I can hear Jake's voice again. 'Come and see what my dad's caught in his nets.'

Chloe pulls me harder. 'Don't look,' she says. Her eyes are red with tears. 'Come away, Kara.'

And suddenly I don't want to be here, because I know it's not a great white shark that Jake Evans wants me to see.

I want to turn away, but I can't. I catch glimpses of it, smooth and grey between the legs of people crowded round.

I see Felix on the far side of the crowd. He looks sick and pale.

Overhead, a gull screams.

I push my way through, following Jake. There is no great white shark or basking shark. On the bloodied concrete lies the still grey body of a dolphin. Its eye looks unseeing into the leaden sky. I follow the smooth curve of its back to the dorsal fin, to a deep notch at the base.

I fall forward on my knees and taste the sharp acid of bile in my mouth.

Angel's mother is dead.

Chapter 33

I run. I don't stop running until I reach the cove and sink down in the soft white sand. Thin trails of bright blood trickle down my arms into the water. I didn't feel the gorse and brambles cut my skin, I just had to get here. I had to get away. I lie down and let the water swirl around me, soaking through my jeans. I rest my head upon the sand and close my eyes. And it floods over me again, that she is dead. Her staring eye and broken face stay fixed inside my mind and I can't wash them out, however hard I try. It feels like part of me has gone, as if the part that kept Mum close has gone now too.

I press my forehead on the wet sand and dig my fingers in. I want to push my way into the sand and let it cover me and lie here for ever. It's sheltered here. The running furl of surf and the soft patter of rain are the only sounds.

I lie like this and let the water swirl up around my jeans and shirt, scouring a small trench of sand around me. A small white pebble washes up the beach past my fingers. I watch the flecks of crystal catch the light. I turn to face the sea and watch it roll back down into the sheen of rain-spattered water, my cheek pressed into the sand. The waves rise and fall like folds of grey-green silk.

'Pfwhooosh!'

I sit up.

I hear it again, that burst of dolphin breath. Angel is here, her white dorsal fin curving through the water. She's come back here to find her mother, back to this cove where I first found her. But her mother isn't here this time. Just me.

I wade out into the water. It rises over my waist and chest, and I can feel it pull on the heavy material of my jeans. I can see her again, not far from me. Her eye is pale pinkish grey. Her skin is the colour of pearl. She sends a series of whistles and clicks and I sense she's calling to her mother. I reach out to touch her, but she slides away and disappears under water. I wade further out. The waves swell under me and lift me up, out of my depth.

'KARA!'

I turn to see Felix and his dad standing at the clifftop.

'Kara, get out of there,' Felix's dad yells. He's waving both his arms at me.

Felix starts to slide forward on the ledge of dark grey rock. I know he won't be able to balance or find a safe way down. I turn and wade out of the water and up the beach, my feet heavy in the soft sand. I look once behind me. The cove is empty. Angel has gone.

When I reach the clifftop, Felix's dad pulls me up and wraps his coat around me. I feel cold. A deep, deep cold right through my bones. My hands are blue, and my fingers are blanched white.

'We've got to get you back, Kara,' he says.

I look back down into the cove. 'We can't leave her. She needs us now. We're all she's got.'

'I've got to get you home,' says Felix's dad. 'Your dad's worried sick. He's out there looking too.'

Felix's dad guides me to the track beyond a field gate. I can hardly put one foot in front of the other and I can see Felix is struggling with the deep mud.

'Wait here, both of you,' Felix's dad says. 'I'll get the car and pick you up.'

I slide down against the stone wall, out of the cold blast of wind, and watch Felix's dad jog away from us along the track. I press my back into the long grasses and fold my arms around my knees.

Felix slides down beside me and pulls his hood over his head. 'People in town are mad at Dougie Evans for what he's done.'

'Won't change anything,' I say. I pull a piece of grass and wrap it round and round my hand. Dad was right. If we can't get all the fishermen on our side, then we can't save the reef. I don't think there's anything anyone can say or do to make someone like Dougie Evans change his mind. I wonder just how much he has to lose before he sees there will be nothing left.

I strip the wet seed heads from the grasses and flick them in the air. Mr Andersen's car headlights find us through the drizzle.

Felix pushes himself to his feet and reaches deep into his pocket. 'I'm not sure I should show you this,' he says. He looks around at his dad's car bumping along the track. 'I told my dad I wouldn't. But I thought if I were you I'd want to know.'

'What?' I say.

Felix pulls out a white envelope and holds it in his hand. 'There was something else on that memory stick,' he says. 'Dad looked into it. He's got some contacts.'

'What, Felix?'

Felix stands in front of me and stuffs the envelope in my hand. 'Hide it. Don't let Dad see.'

I feel my heart thud against my chest. 'Why didn't you tell me this before?'

'It might help you understand, that's all.'

The car pulls up beside us and Felix's dad gets out. 'Come on then, you two.'

I slip the envelope under my jumper and slide in the back seat next to Felix. 'Understand what?' I whisper.

Felix's dad twists round in his seat. 'What are you two talking about?' he says.

'Nothing,' says Felix. He frowns and turns away.

We sit in silence as we bump along the rutted track. I hold the envelope tight against my chest and feel the corners press deep into my skin.

It holds something to do with Mum.

A missing key to where she is, maybe.

CHAPTER 34

I stare at the photograph for the hundredth time. The shock of seeing Mum jolts through me once again. She's crouched down beside her diving gear, her hair tucked back behind her ears, a look of deep concentration on her face. I've seen her check her diving gear before, running through the list of safety checks in her head. It's pointless trying to talk to her like this. She can block out the outside world, absorbed in every detail of her work. Palm trees line the backdrop of a foreign port. The stern of a container ship fills the left half of the view and the right half shows a busy port with ships and cranes along docksides stretching into the distance. Rucksacks and boxes are piled up by Mum. I see her rucksack with them too. Shadows slant deep and long so it must be early morning or late at night, I can't tell. I can almost imagine her face turn to look at me.

'Kara!'

I stuff the photo back under my pillow, where I slept on it all night. I don't want anyone to know. I've stayed in Daisy's bedroom all morning, hiding from Aunt Bev. She's been cleaning the house like mad, clearing out the cupboards and changing all the sheets.

'Kara,' Aunt Bev shouts again, 'Felix is here. He wants to know if you're going to the regatta.'

I climb down the stairs into the kitchen. I can hear cartoons blaring from the sitting room and guess Daisy's trying to avoid her mum too.

Aunt Bev is leaning on her mop, beads of sweat pricked on her forehead. All the surfaces are cleared away and tidy and I notice the oven's sparkling clean. Even the windows have had a polish.

I tiptoe across the floor to Felix standing on the doormat and pull him into the hallway. 'I didn't think you were going to the regatta,' I say. 'Didn't you hear the race is cancelled? There's a storm coming.'

Felix shrugs his shoulders. 'I know, but I thought I'd see what was happening in town. Want to come?'

I nod. 'I'll get my shoes.'

Chapter 34

I pull my sandals from the shoe rack in the hall. 'I'm going into town with Felix,' I yell.

Aunt Bev leans against the doorframe and watches me strap up my shoes. She stretches and rubs the small of her back. 'Take Daisy with you, Kara. I've too much to do today.' She pulls some money from the tin above the microwave. 'Here's ten pounds to get a hot dog each.'

I stuff the money in my pocket and walk with Felix along the coast road. Daisy runs ahead of us scattering gulls up into the sky.

'Did you look at it?' says Felix.

I nod.

'It was taken at Honiara,' he says, 'a port on the Solomon Island of Guadalcanal. It was taken just before sunset on the night your mother disappeared.'

We walk in silence for a while. I'm glad Felix's told me the facts, just plain and simple.

'How did you get it?' I say.

'There was a folder on the memory stick marked Honiara. There were lists of addresses: hotels, car rentals, and diving centres. A colleague of Dad's who's done some business out there made a few enquiries for him. He found this photo in the archives of a local paper.'

I stop and turn to Felix. 'So why haven't we seen this before, from the investigation at the time?'

Felix shrugs his shoulders. 'Dad's colleague says the story wasn't run. It was bad publicity. Bad for tourism.'

I lean on the railings and stare out to sea. The photo's proof that Mum went out diving that last night, but it doesn't tell what happened. There's no clue to where or why she went.

Despite the warm and humid air, the beach is empty. The sea is a pale pearly green. A deep ocean swell lifts its polished surface into smooth ripples, like antique glass. Yet no one is in the water. It is calm, too calm. Everything is still. The flag above the chandlery hangs limp and loose. Even the seagulls have left the air and are lined up on roofs and chimney pots and along the sea wall. It feels as if the whole sky is pressing down on us. The storm's eye is above us now. This is the calm before the storm, and we are given time to think and breathe. Yet we are being watched, it seems.

Daisy runs back and pulls my arm. 'Come on,' she says. 'Let's go into town.'

We walk through the narrow streets under bunting hung between the shops and houses. Dad is outside the Merry Mermaid clearing plates. He waves and smiles to us as we pass and I give a small wave back. In the square outside the town hall are several stalls and games. The mayor is in the stocks waiting for wet sponges. There's a coconut shy and a strongman game. A brass band is playing too and a team of majorettes are twirling batons and marching up and down. I buy hot dogs and sit with Felix and Daisy on one of the benches in the square. I look across at Felix. I don't feel in the mood for this and I can tell he feels the same way too. I let Daisy have the change from the money for the hot dogs and watch her run off to play a game of hook the duck and spend her money on the stalls.

It's only when she's run out of money that she comes back and flops beside us, a fluffy duck and a packet of fudge in her hands.

'Let's get you home,' I say.

We walk towards the sea front along the road above the harbour. A small breeze lifts the edges of my shirt.

'Feel that?' I say.

Felix nods.

I look across to the flag above the chandlery. Its edges curl and ripple in the breeze. A new wind is blowing from the west. Dark clouds unfurl across the milk-white sky. A shiver runs down my spine and goosepimples prickle along my arms and legs, because out across the ocean a storm is coming, and we lie directly in its path.

We turn down a narrow stepped street between old cottages to the harbour.

'Hey, Two Planks!'

I glance behind. It's Jake and Ethan coming down the steps behind us.

Daisy takes hold of my hand and holds it tight.

'Hey, Kara,' shouts Jake. 'Did you hear I'm moving house?'

We keep walking, but Jake and Ethan catch us up. Felix is struggling with the steps. The handrail stops halfway down the slope.

'Dad's buying one of them posh houses up on the hill that look over the bay,' says Jake. 'Massive garden. He said he'd get me a quad bike too.'

I ignore Jake.

'Dad says he'll call it Shell House,' says Jake. 'Know why, don't you? It's from the profits of the scallops from the bay.'

I want to keep walking but Felix is at the top of a run of steps. I know he doesn't want me to help him, so I wait beside him while he makes his own way slowly down. His face is lined with concentration trying to balance on the steps.

'Shame the regatta's cancelled,' says Jake. 'It's just I thought you'd like to see me sail *Moana* in the race.'

'You can't even sail,' I say.

Chapter 34

'Ethan and me have sailed before,' laughs Jake. 'It's not that hard.'

'You've done a couple weeks' dinghy sailing with school,' I say. 'That's all.'

'Can't be that hard if he can do it.' Jake jerks his head in Felix's direction. 'He can hardly walk.'

Ethan explodes with laughter.

I feel Felix tense up beside me.

'We'll race you,' says Jake, 'us in *Moana* and you two in the loser boat. We'll even give you a head start.'

I turn to face Jake. 'There's no regatta today,' I say. 'There's a storm coming.'

Jake throws his head back and laughs. 'As if I'm scared of that!'

I turn away. It's not worth arguing any more.

Jake strides off. 'Come on, Ethan. Fancy a sail around Gull Rock?'

I watch them disappear around the corner of the end house of the street.

'They wouldn't,' I say. 'Would they?'

As we reach the harbour, big drops of rain slide from the sky and hit the pavement, spotting the pale cement dark grey. I feel the heavy drops land in my hair and on my clothes. The sky is almost black, and beyond the harbour the sea heaves in big green swells. There are no white horses out there yet, just the rolling curves of waves.

'I don't believe it.' I point down to the pontoon. Jake and Ethan are in *Moana.* They've pulled back the tarpaulin from her boom and I can see them rigging up the mainsail.

'They're crazy,' says Felix.

'Dougie Evans would have a fit if he knew Jake was going out to sea,' I say. 'Come on, we have to stop them. Not just for their sake, but *Moana's*. They'll wreck her if they try.'

I climb down the ladder while Daisy follows Felix down the ramp. By the time I reach *Moana,* Jake and Ethan have the mainsail up and the jib. They've not even reefed the sails. A gust of wind catches the sail and swings the boom out over the water.

'Don't be stupid, Jake,' I yell.

But Jake just laughs and holds his hand out to feel the wind. 'A summer breeze, that's all,' he says.

But there's something more than bragging in Jake's eyes. There's fear too, as if he's gone too far and can't find his way back.

I pull *Moana* closer and her fenders bump against the pontoon.

'Don't do it, Jake,' I say. 'Your dad's lost Aaron. He doesn't want to lose you too.'

Chapter 34

Jake just stares at me. Heavy drops of rain slide from the sky and pit the water's surface. The drops fall faster, thick and heavy, and soon there is a screen of rain between us. I can't make out his face any more. He unties *Moana* and pushes off with a paddle. Ethan's at the tiller. *Moana* slides across the water and thumps into a small cruiser moored against the other pontoon. Jake pushes off again, and this time Ethan points *Moana*'s bow to the harbour opening. She scrapes against the harbour wall and I hear the scars tear in her side. Jake looks back once before *Moana* slips out of the harbour, the tip of her mast showing above the harbour wall. And it's only now I realize too, that Jake and Ethan have no life jackets at all.

'We've got to stop them,' I say. I look around the harbour, but the walls are empty. The rain has driven everyone away.

'We'll take my boat,' says Felix. He leans down and starts untying the cover.

'Don't go,' says Daisy.

I look at her. She's freezing cold and wet through. I kneel down beside her and hold her hands in mine. 'Be brave, Daisy. Go and find my dad. He's in the Merry Mermaid. Tell him what's happened. Tell him to call the coastguard.'

'Please don't go, Kara,' she begs. Her eyes are big and full of tears.

'I have to,' I say.

'You'll disappear. You won't come back.'

I put my arms around her and wonder if this is how Mum felt when she left. 'I'll be careful,' I say. 'I'll come back, I promise you.'

Daisy pulls away from me. 'I'm coming with you.'

'You can't, Daisy,' I plead. 'It's too dangerous for you.'

Felix looks up from what he's doing. 'Daisy,' he says, 'someone has to call the coastguard. We might need help out there.'

Daisy looks at him and I see her bottom lip tremble.

'Right now, I need that fairy godmother, Daisy . . . ' says Felix, '. . . she might be the one to save us.'

A flicker of a smile crosses Daisy's face. She nods and wipes the tears from her face. 'I'll go.'

I watch her run along the pontoon. I shouldn't let her out of my sight, I know. What if she falls in the water or gets knocked down crossing a road? I try to push the thoughts from my mind and help Felix into his boat.

Felix starts pulling up the mainsail. 'Put a life jacket on,' he yells. 'I've got two here.'

'Hang on,' I yell. I run down the pontoon, clamber into one of the sightseeing boats and lift up one of the bench seats. I pull out two more life jackets, one for Jake and one for Ethan, and run back to Felix. We have to stop them before they get beyond the protection of the headland. Maybe we can make them turn round. I pull my life jacket on, climb in and help Felix with his.

'Let's go,' yells Felix.

I cast off and push the dinghy away. Felix guides us through the narrow gap between the harbour walls, out into the open sea, and out into the grey-green ocean swell.

Chapter 35

The swell rolls in and slumps against the harbour walls. I can feel the power of the waves in the recoil that jars against the dinghy's hull. Jake and Ethan have put a lot of distance between us. *Moana*'s sails are full and she is leaning heavily across the water.

Felix has put a reef in our sails, but she heels over and I sit out to balance her. I'm glad of the long centre-board in his boat and know at least we have less chance of capsizing. I glance at Felix, but his face is tightened in a knot of concentration. The headland is veiled in a sweeping curtain of rain. Gull Rock lies out at sea, pale grey against a darker sky. Beyond the headland the water is flecked with white horses. There are ocean currents and strong winds out there. It's no place for any small boat and I wonder how long the lifeboat will take to get out here too.

'We must put another reef in,' yells Felix, 'before we hit those waves.'

He turns up into the wind and I press myself against the mast and reef the mainsail, spreading my feet to balance against the rolling swell. I know Felix is right. We'll go slower but we can't risk the bigger sail.

I sit back down in the centre line seat behind Felix as he reefs the jib sail. The wind is stronger, the swell bigger all the time.

We plough into the breaking waves beyond the headland. The first wave runs across the boat and I take a sharp intake of breath as the water floods across my legs and around my waist. We don't have wetsuits or warm gear. It suddenly seems so stupid to have followed Jake out here. I turn to look back, but the land is screened from view behind the rain. Ahead, *Moana* lurches through the waves. I see her buck and jar and slew sideways as the waves knock her off course. We're catching up, despite smaller sails.

Jake and Ethan are struggling. The jib sail is flying loose and I can see Ethan putting all his weight on the tiller. *Moana* dips and pushes on beyond Gull Rock. They will have to turn her to pass round the other side. I hope they know to sail far beyond Gull Rock before they make the turn. If they try to make the turn too soon, the wind and waves will push them too close to the rocks.

Maybe it's because they're scared to go too far out into the sea, or maybe they misjudge the turn, but Ethan swings *Moana* across the wind and we see her turn sharply around the rock. Jake is leaning far out on *Moana*'s side, the rope to the mainsail in his hands. I don't have time to yell to Jake. The wind fills the other side of the sail and pushes it across. The boom swings over, a blur through the air, and I know Jake doesn't stand a chance. His head flies back as he is knocked in a high arc across the sea, his arms flailing above the foaming surf before he disappears beneath the waves.

'Jake,' I scream.

Felix has seen it happen too. He sails towards *Moana*, sailing close behind the cliffs. The sea is in white chaos. The spray from exploding waves showers us like heavy rain. The recoil from the cliff base swamps us with foaming green water and pearl-white surf. The dinghy lurches side to side, her sails almost slap the water.

I push wet hair from my eyes to look for Jake. I hold the mast and rise up on my knees to get a better view. 'He's gone,' I yell. 'He's gone.'

'We've got to move,' shouts Felix.

We're too close to Gull Rock. If the long centre-board

breaks beneath us we won't stand a chance. I lean out to balance the dinghy as Felix steers towards Ethan and *Moana.* I look back one more time towards Gull Rock. I want to wake up from this nightmare. I can't believe that Jake has gone.

Then I see his head and arms splash above the water. Another waves sweeps over and he disappears again.

'He's there,' I yell. The waves heave and crest into peaks, curling over near the rocks. Jake's head rises above the water. He claws at the air but sinks under again.

'I see him,' Felix yells.

He swings the dinghy towards Jake. The air is filled with flying sea foam. We ride down one wave into the deep trough and rise up the other side. I look down into the water and see Jake again suspended below us, his shirt billowing around him and his arms outspread as if he's underwater flying.

He's rising towards us through the water. I reach out and grab Jake's shirt as a wave rolls him up and we fall in a mass of tangled arms and legs inside the boat. For one brief moment I thought I saw a flash of white beneath the waves, something beneath Jake pushing him up towards the air. I look again, but all I see is the white swirl of sea foam in the water.

'Let's get out of here,' Felix yells.

Ethan is clinging to *Moana*'s mast as another wave rolls over her. The sky is black with cloud. There is no horizon. Sea and sky are one. Felix brings the dinghy up on *Moana*'s seaward side. I help Jake pull a life jacket on. He's a dead weight. Blood is pouring through his hair and down his forehead. I grab the other life jacket and scramble across, to join Ethan in *Moana*.

'Get back to shore,' I scream to Felix. 'Get Jake back. I'll bring Ethan in *Moana*.'

Another wave lifts us and crunches the two boats together. I give the dinghy a shove.

'Just go,' I yell.

Felix pushes the central joystick of his dinghy across and sails away, running with the wind towards the harbour. A gust of wind hits my back and scuds across the ocean. I watch Felix and Jake dissolve into the grainy curtain of rain.

I feel sick and heavy inside. I don't know if I will ever see them again.

Chapter 36

'Kara!'

Ethan stumbles over to me and clings on to my arm. His face is white. His whole body shakes. He pulls his life jacket on and fumbles with the straps.

Moana heaves and falls over the waves. She's taking on water fast, heeling far over in the water. Another wave spills in the boat and Ethan and I slip and flounder together while sea foam swirls all around us.

My mind is white with fear. I have to think. I try to think.

A tangle of rope and loose sail spreads across the foredeck into the water. I see now why *Moana*'s heeling in the water. Jake and Ethan have opened the spinnaker sail. It twists under the boat, an underwater parachute, pulling us towards the rocks.

'Help me with this,' I yell. But Ethan doesn't move. He just stands holding the mast, as if he's holding the boat into the sea. I pull and pull on the rope, but the sail is heavy, weighed down into the water. The yawning cliff caves thunder with the breaking waves.

'Ethan,' I scream. 'The knife. In the locker.'

Ethan stumbles forward, and pulls stuff from the locker. He finds the short-bladed knife from the tool box and leans out towards me. I take it in my hands and saw across the spinnaker rope. It cuts loose and the sail billows away, a monster jellyfish escaping back to sea.

The waves are white-capped mountains now, vast moving ranges, rising higher and higher. The wind is screaming past and the air is filled with flying foam. We're being pushed towards the breaking surf. Our only hope now is to sail away. I pull on the mainsail and slide back to the tiller, pulling Ethan with me.

'Stay back here with me,' I yell.

The sail fills with wind, pulls taut and I feel *Moana* surge forward.

'KARA!' Ethan yells.

I look past him to a wall of dark green water, rising up and up. A freak wave, higher than all the rest.

Everything slows down.

Chapter 36

Moana ploughs up into the wave. She rises up the wave's steep side. But the wave is changing. A crest of foam brims at its peak. *Moana* struggles forward, but the wave is curving inwards and begins to break. She can't make it now. *Moana*'s prow twists in the air and the wave curls over us, folding us in a blanket of green surf. And this moment stays freeze-framed in my mind. *Moana*, on her side, and a thousand tonnes of water stretched out across us, about to push us down.

I grab Ethan and pull him under one of the seats. *Moana* rolls and everything goes dark. Seawater rushes in and fills the space we're lying in. The water thunders all around, and through the roar of wind and waves there is a tearing crack, like a gunshot. I can feel it split the water.

Moana spins back up, and Ethan and I burst up for air. *Moana*'s mast is down, ripped apart by rocks beneath the boat. Its jagged end is broken like a stick. But the sail ropes are still attached and anchor *Moana* to the rocks. The sea is boiling all around us. *Moana*'s hull protects us from the full force of the waves. But each wave thumps against her and pushes her towards the cliff. I feel her keel grinding on the rocks below.

'Flares,' I yell. 'There's a flare in the front locker.'

I scramble forward and reach into the locker. I pull the

flare from the clips and try to read the instructions but *Moana* is heaving in the churning sea. The flare is soaked. I only hope it works. I've never had to use one before. A wave crashes over *Moana*, and I fall back against the hard seat. I pull the tag and hold it skywards. At first nothing happens, but then a blast of light explodes from the flare. I watch its trail spiral upwards, and hold there above us, a bright red beacon burning in the darkened skies.

Another wave crushes us against the rocks. One of the metal stays that held the mast rips from the wood and flies close past Ethan's head.

'Get down,' I yell.

Ethan lurches towards me and we crouch low under the seats. The sound of splintering wood and tearing metal rips through screaming wind. I feel the hull grind against the rocks below us and know *Moana*'s keel is being wrenched away. It's all that's holding us from being thrown against the cliffs.

Ethan and I push further under the seat as wave after wave after wave thumps against us. There is nothing we can do now, nowhere for us to go. Ethan takes my hand and I hold his tightly in mine. The waves thud and thud and thud against *Moana*, and I can't tell if it's the waves, or the hammering of my heart.

Chapter 36

But there's another hammering too, a thudding high above the waves. A beam of light shines down and hits the boat.

'HELICOPTER!' Ethan yells.

We scramble out and wave our hands. The beam holds us fast, and above us a helicopter sways in the gale.

'We're too close to the cliff,' yells Ethan.

A man drops down towards us, silhouetted by the light. He drops down on a wire, his feet whizzing past above our heads. I duck, but Ethan lunges at his boots. He swings back again and drops into the boat. He loops a harness over Ethan and grabs me as a wave swamps over us. We plunge off the side into the foaming sea. Water rushes into my mouth and nose. The wire pulls tight and I feel the lightness of air as the wave passes over and we rise up above the water. The wind catches us and spins us round and round and round as we lift up into the sky. I look down and see *Moana* far below.

I want to lift her with us too, take her away from here. But as I watch, a wave folds over, lifts her and explodes against the cliff. In the spinning kaleidoscope of sea and spray, all that's left of her is twisted metal and flying fragments of splintered wood.

Chapter 37

'Have you got the others?' I yell.

The winch-man is trying to get me to lie down on a stretcher, but I sit back up. 'Have you got them? Have you got Felix and Jake? They went in the other boat.'

He speaks into his mouthpiece and holds the headphones tight to his head so he can hear.

'Where were they heading?'

'To the harbour,' I shout. I feel a pit of fear rise in me, because he'd have told me if they'd been found.

He speaks again into the mouthpiece and then the helicopter changes direction, veering sideways.

'We'll take you to the town and get an ambulance for both of you. Then we'll go back out to look for your friends,' he shouts.

Chapter 37

I've lost *Moana*, but it feels nothing to losing Felix and even Jake. Ethan doesn't say anything. He's lying on the stretcher under blankets, eyes closed tight. I wrap my blanket around me and look out beyond the open doorway to the sea below. It's a heaving mass of grey-green surf. I want to see the white sails of Felix's dinghy skimming across the waves below. But rain sweeps across the sky and we are folded in a cloak of cloud, and it's impossible to see anything out there at all.

My ears pop as we descend onto the playing field outside the town. The sky is black. The streetlights glow dull orange, and cars have their headlights on, even though it's only early evening. The blue light of an ambulance flashes along the top road, coming this way. The winch-man helps us out, guiding us under the turning helicopter blades to the cars parked on the road.

I see Dad running through the rain.

'Kara!' He folds his arms around me and pulls me in. I feel his warm breath in my hair. He holds me tightly to him. His whole body shakes and when I look up at him, his face is crumpled into sobs.

'Kara!'

A hand holds me by the shoulder and I turn to see Felix's mum.

'Where's Felix?' Her hair is plastered to her face and her mascara has run into long black streaks.

Felix's dad and Dougie Evans are there too.

Dougie Evans crouches down beside me. His eyes are wild with fear. 'Where's my boy, Kara? Where's my boy?'

The last time I saw Jake, he was stretched across the dinghy coughing seawater out of his lungs.

'They're in Felix's dinghy,' I say, 'on their way to harbour.'

Lightning flashes across the sky. Felix's mum grasps my arm.

'They could be back by now,' I say. It's a wild impossible thought, but maybe they could. Maybe Felix has got them safely in. 'Let's go there,' I say.

And it's as if they've been jolted out of sleep.

'Come on,' says Felix's dad, 'in my car.'

Dad wraps me in his coat. 'You need a doctor, Kara.'

'I'm fine,' I say. I pull away and start running after Felix's mum and dad, and we all crowd in the car, Dad, Dougie Evans, and me along the back seat.

Felix's dad pulls up on the pavement by the harbour and we spill out and run to the harbour's edge. The flags above the chandlery are flapping hard and the mast lines of the yachts are screaming in the tearing winds. I scan the harbour. All the fishing boats are in, lined up in the deep-water moorings. The yachts and motor boats are secure against the pontoon. I see the space where *Moana* had once been, and it hits me all over again, that she is gone. I won't see her again.

But there is no dinghy in the harbour, no sign of Felix or Jake.

A plume of spray rises over the wall and scatters across a figure looking out to sea. Her black cloak and long hair are flying in the wind. I clamber up on the higher stone ledge next to Miss Penluna. She reaches for my hand, but doesn't take her eyes off the sea.

Felix's mum and dad and Dougie Evans join us, leaning on the granite wall staring out into the waves. Lightning flashes and a crack of thunder tears the air apart. The tide is high, pushed up further by the wind and waves. People are lined up all along the wall to watch the storm. It draws people, this sort of power, to see what it can do. Massive waves curl and cross over each other. Foam and spray are flying past.

The helicopter clatters past above our heads.

'They'll find them,' Dad shouts.

But I wonder how, because we can't see anything through the driving rain.

The waves roll in, one after another, massive mountains of moving water, spray flying from the tops like wind-blown snow. I doubt *Moana* could have sailed in this.

Dougie stands right up on the wall. 'MY BOY!' he yells. But the gale flings the words back in his face. 'WHERE'S MY BOY!'

He runs his hands over his head. His eyes are red and wild. He clutches on Dad's arm. 'I've lost them, Jim. I've lost both my boys.'

Dad puts his arm around him. 'Come on. Let's go back and wait for news.'

I turn to look at Miss Penluna. She's standing sentry-like, looking out to sea.

Dougie Evans pulls her round to face him. 'I want him back.'

Miss Penluna stares into his eyes.

'He's all that's left,' he sobs.

Miss Penluna pulls her shawl around her. 'What is he coming back to, Dougie? What world are you leaving him?'

Dougie Evans searches her face and I hear Miss Penluna's words despite the wind and rain. 'He's in the company of angels now.'

Dougie's knees buckle and he stumbles to the ground.

A wave slams against the wall, soaking us with freezing spray.

'Come on,' says Dad. He pulls my arm.

I look back into the storm one more time.

CHAPTER 37

And it feels my heart has skipped a beat, because I saw something, out there, I'm sure I did.

I strain my eyes into the grey veil of rain.

There it is again.

A sail.

A mast and sail rising up behind a wave, and then I see the white hull of Felix's dinghy rear up into sight.

'I SEE THEM!' I yell.

Felix's mum and dad clamber up beside me and Dougie pulls himself to his feet.

Dougie grabs my shoulder. 'Where?'

'There!' I look but the boat has disappeared behind a wall of surf.

It rises up again.

'It's them,' shouts Felix's dad, 'it's them.'

The boat is so small against these waves. I see Felix in his cockpit seat and Jake slumped in the seat behind.

They are running with the wind. It's on their backs, driving them towards us. They are faster than the waves, outrunning them. The dinghy's bow is well out of the water, and they are skimming across the surface. They dip and ride up another wave. But closer in, the waves are breaking, pounding on the harbour wall. The helicopter clatters through the rain above them. But Felix can't stop now or turn into the wind. They only have one choice and it looks as if he's chosen it without a second thought. He's heading for the narrow gap between the harbour walls. It seems impossible to aim for in the raging sea.

I glance at Dad but his eyes are fixed on Felix. Beyond Dad, the crowds along the sea wall are frozen still, just watching. There is nothing anyone can do.

The dinghy is hidden again behind a huge wave. It rides up the back but the wave is changing, beginning to curl. I want them to miss this wave, let it break without them, but they are past the point of no return and they slide down the breaking wave, faster and faster, surfing with it, a curling wall of water chasing them in. Too fast, I think, they can't make the narrow gap. The wave is pushing them sideways along the line of breaking surf. Felix throws his weight on the side of the boat. The dinghy's bows swing as the wave crashes over them. I see her mast go down, and all of her is lost in the white foam of the running sea.

The wave explodes against the wall and I look away. I don't want to see them break against the granite blocks. A foaming wall of surf surges between the harbour walls in a strange and muffled silence. The whole harbour has held its breath, it seems. I clutch Dad and press my head into his chest. But Dad pulls me away.

Chapter 37

'Kara, look!'

I look down into the harbour. Through the foaming wall of surf shoots the dinghy. Its sails are shredded and the mast is a wreck of twisted metal. It slews in an arc and comes to rest, rocking gently in the sheltered water. Two figures are slumped inside, motionless.

'FELIX!' I scream.

He leans back in his seat and looks up at me. He gives the thumbs up, and grins. And this time it's a wave of shouts and cheers that explodes all along the harbour walls.

Chapter 38

I open my eyes. Through the window, the sky is bright, bright blue. A slight breeze lifts the checked curtain edge bringing in the salt smell of the sea.

'You've been asleep for ages, Kara.'

I turn my head. Daisy is sitting legs crossed on her bed, watching me. My neck is stiff and my body feels heavy. The memories of the day before wash over me.

'What time is it?' I say.

'It's four o'clock,' she says. 'You've missed breakfast and lunch and you've almost missed tea.'

I push myself up on my elbows. 'It's that late already?'

Daisy nods her head. But her eyes are shining bright and she's grinning from ear to ear. She climbs down from her bed and takes my arm. 'You've got to come with me, Kara,' she says. 'You've got to come and see.'

I swing my legs over the side of the camp bed. My whole body aches and my mouth feels dry and sore. I pull a T-shirt on and jeans.

'Come on, there's someone who wants to see you,' says Daisy. 'She arrived late last night.'

'Who?' I say.

'Surprise,' says Daisy. She's at the door, impatient for me to follow. 'She's been waiting for you all day.'

'I'm coming,' I say. I stand up and the room spins around me. My head's so thick and heavy, I can hardly think.

Daisy takes my arm again and leads me into her mum and dad's bedroom. Uncle Tom is sitting on the side of the bed, and Aunt Bev is propped up on cushions, her back against the headboard.

Daisy squeezes my hand and grins. 'I've got a sister.'

And then I see the baby wrapped up in Aunt Bev's arms. She's so small. Eyes closed, lips pouting. Aunt Bev's face is soft and dreamlike. Her hair is loose and tumbles round her shoulders. Her hand is cupped around the baby's head.

Mum must have held me like this once.

'She's beautiful,' I say.

Aunt Bev looks up. 'Kara,' she says, and pats the duvet.

I sit down beside her and just stare at the small baby wrapped in pink.

'Daisy told us what you did yesterday,' says Aunt Bev.

I wait for the telling off. I know I shouldn't have left Daisy alone to find Dad.

'You were very brave,' Aunt Bev says. I see tears well in her eyes. 'But, Kara, you could have *died*.'

I reach out to touch the tiny hand that's curled around the blanket edge.

'You are your mother's child,' says Uncle Tom. 'It's what she would have done.'

I look at them and see something between sorrow and pity in their eyes. The baby's hand grasps my finger and she squeezes it in her sleep.

'What's she called?' I ask.

Daisy sits down next to me and takes my other hand. She smiles one of her biggest smiles at me. 'I chose it,' she says. 'We've called her Mo, short for Moana. But she'll be just Mo to us.'

I feel my eyes burn hot with tears. 'Hello, Mo,' I say.

I didn't hear Dad come into the room, but when I look up I see him standing in the doorway.

'Come on,' he says. 'Let's give them some time alone. Uncle Tom's going out to sea next week. Dougie Evans gave him back his old job and a pay rise too.'

I look at Uncle Tom, but he's only got eyes for Daisy and Mo.

Dad slips his arm through mine and I walk with him down the stairs and out into the sunshine. The storm has cleared the air. The colours are brighter, sharper. A car door slams and Dougie Evans walks up the path, his face hidden behind a huge bunch of flowers. He stops when he sees Dad and me.

'I brought these,' he says. 'For Bev and the baby.'

'Go on up,' says Dad.

But Dougie Evans doesn't move. He scrunches the cellophane of the bouquet in his hand.

'How's Jake?' Dad says.

Dougie Evans stares at the floor. 'He'll be just fine,' he says. 'A few stitches on his face, that's all. Might remind him how stupid he was to go out to sea like that.'

I try to edge round him, but he's not finished.

He turns to me. 'If it weren't for you, my boy would be dead.'

I look at Dad and then at Dougie. 'It wasn't just me,' I mumble.

Dougie scrunches his face into a frown. 'Jake said a funny thing too. He said the white dolphin saved him. He said it lifted him up, out of the water.'

I watch Dougie Evans wrestle with his thoughts. He twists his hands round and round the stems of the bouquet of flowers. His face is pulled into a tight knot. Pieces of flower stem fall to the floor, but Dougie doesn't seem to notice.

'The truth was staring me in the face all the time,' he says. 'I just chose not to see it.'

Dad puts his hand on Dougie's shoulder. 'It's all right, Doug,' he says.

But Dougie wants to get this off his chest. 'It made me think, it did, that and what Miss Penluna said. If we go on ripping up the sea bed, hauling out all the fish, there'll be nothing left worth saving. There'll be nothing left for Jake.' He clutches the flowers to his chest. 'I want you to know, I've signed the petition to stop the dredging. Not just that, but I've signed up to test out new ways of fishing to stop dolphins drowning in our nets too.'

I glance at Dad. I can't believe Dougie Evans has changed his mind.

Dad smiles. 'Good on you, Dougie.'

We turn to walk away, but Dougie calls Dad back and puts out his hand.

'There's a job on one of my trawlers, Jim,' he says. 'It's yours if you want it.'

Dad takes Dougie's hand and shakes it. 'Thanks,' he

says. 'But I've got a job lined up already.'

I follow Dad down the path and out onto the coast road along the seafront.

'I don't want to move from here,' I say.

Dad smiles and puts his arm around me. 'We don't have to,' he says. 'I didn't find out until yesterday. I didn't want to disappoint you if I didn't get it.'

I stop and pull him round to face me. 'Get what?' I say.

Dad grins like I've not seen him grin for a long, long time. 'I've been accepted on a boat-building course at the boatyard,' he says. 'I've been assessed and I'll even have help with my dyslexia. It starts next month.'

I wrap my arms around and hug him tight. 'That's brilliant, Dad,' I say.

Dad ruffles my hair. 'I know. I think so too.'

We walk along the road to the far end of the beach and take the path that curls up the hill. I look out to sea, hoping to see a white dorsal fin. I can't get Angel from my mind. She haunts my thoughts now, not my dreams. She's alone out there, without her mother, and I don't know how she will survive all on her own.

'This way,' says Dad.

I follow him along the sandy coast path that runs along the bottom of the campsite fields. 'Where are we going?'

'Can't tell you,' he smiles. 'It's a surprise.'

We pass one field of tents to another field of static caravans. The field slopes down to the dunes that back the beach. Beyond the dunes, the sea is calm and silvery blue. It's hard to believe it was a mass of churning green and white last night.

'There,' says Dad.

The end caravan faces the sea. Bunting hangs across from the caravan to a line of gorse hedge and dry stone wall. A table is laid with plates and glasses, and a bright pink dolphin windsock is twirling in the breeze. I see shadows in the windows of the caravan.

The door bursts open and Felix tumbles out followed by his mum and dad and Miss Penluna. Carl and Greg and Sam the vet are here, and Chloe and Ella too.

Dad wraps his arms around me and pulls me close. 'Welcome home, Kara,' he says.

'Home?' I say. I frown and look at him.

'It's not much, I know, but it's a home for us, for now.'

The windows of the caravan face the sea. I'll see and hear the ocean every day. 'It's perfect, Dad,' I say, and hug him tight, 'the best.'

Felix pokes me in the ribs. 'What kept you?'

I grin. 'Where's your medal?'

Chapter 38

Felix frowns. 'Medal?'

'You won the regatta race remember?'

Felix laughs. 'Yeah, that's right. First the regatta race, next the Olympics.'

'Come on,' says Felix's dad, 'you must all be starving and we've enough food in the caravan to feed an army.'

I smile and look back out across the fields along the stretch of headland. The sunlight slants, golden yellow. It's the first day of September and the chill of autumn is in the air. I want a moment by myself, just me, before I join them.

'Come on,' calls Chloe.

'I won't be long,' I say.

I leave them sitting in the sunshine and take the path through the dunes. My toes dig into the cool soft sand. The sea is turquoise, woven through with strands of silver. I climb up on the highest dune and sit sheltered by the dune grass, and stare out to sea.

'Kara?'

I turn. I hadn't heard Dad follow me. A stream of sand trickles down the dune as he sits beside me. I draw my knees up and fold my arms around them.

'We mustn't be too long,' he says. 'They've been waiting for you for ages, especially Felix.'

I look back at the small white caravan strung with

bunting, and the people round the table. I see Felix stretched out on the lounger in the sun. 'We've got some good friends, haven't we?'

Dad nods. 'If Mum were here, she'd be so proud of you,' he says. He scoops up a handful of sand and lets it run through his fingers. 'You did what she couldn't do. You made Dougie Evans change his mind.'

'Dougie Evans was right about one thing,' I say.

Dad turns to me, his eyes crinkled in a smile. 'I never thought I'd ever hear you say that.'

I frown and fix my eyes on the horizon. 'Sometimes the truth does stare us in the face, but we just choose not to look.'

Dad sighs and wraps his arm around me. He holds me tight.

I pick a piece of dune grass and twist it in my fingers. 'I used to think maybe Mum was too important for us. Maybe she had been chosen for special missions. I thought one day I'd find her in the Amazon jungle saving river dolphins or other animals. I even thought maybe she was an alien from another world sent to save our planet.' My eyes blur with tears despite my smile. 'But I know that's not true now.'

I feel Dad's arm pull me closer still.

A deep ache knots inside my chest. 'We may never know

what really happened the night she disappeared,' I say. I press my fingers into the sand. 'But I know Mum died that night.'

I sink my head onto my knees. It feels as if everything I've kept inside is draining out of me, through my fingertips into the cool, cool sand below. 'If she had lived she would have found a way back. She'd be here with us now. She'd be here, because above everything else, she loved us, didn't she?'

I look up at Dad and see his face is wet with tears. I lean into him and stare out to sea. The ocean is flat and calm. Turquoise blue. Small waves crest and run along the shoreline.

'We'll build a new boat, Kara,' he says. He wipes the tears from his face. 'You and me, we'll build a new boat for us to sail in.'

I squeeze Dad's hand and close my eyes. I feel the warm sun on my face. A sea breeze lifts my hair and whispers past me through the dry dune grasses. I hear the curl of surf unfurl along the sand. Above, a seagull cries. I open my eyes and watch it sail across, powder white against a deep blue sky. This whole place feels alive somehow. I feel part of it, as if it's in me too. Maybe this is how Mum felt. Maybe this is how she always knew the dolphins would return. I feel it now. I feel in this moment of deep ocean stillness.

White Dolphin

I feel them rising through the water.

'Dolphins,' I yell.

I slide down the dune to the beach and cross the high tide line of shells and seaweed. My feet slap on the hard wet sand until I am running in the furling waves along the shoreline. I am running alongside the dolphins, their blue-grey bodies arching through the water, the sunlight shining from their smooth wet backs. Their dorsal fins rise and curve above the water, a whole pod of dolphins cruising through the sea.

Then I see her. I see Angel leap from the centre. A flash of white, she somersaults in the sunlight and slaps the water with her tail, scattering diamond drops of spray.

'Angel,' I yell.

I wade out beyond the breaking waves.

'Angel!'

She leaps again and I watch her twist and turn before she plunges back into the water. In this golden evening sunlight I feel chosen somehow, as if she's given me the chance to see through into her world.

I know deep down inside, the white dolphin will never be alone.

The vast blue ocean is waiting for her, and this is only the beginning of her story.

Dear Reader,

Have you ever wished you could swim with wild dolphins? Have you ever dreamed of diving into clear waters and swimming alongside them, watching them twist and turn around you? Well, I have too. When I was young, I used to dream I could a have a dolphin friend, a dolphin only I could talk to. That memory gave me the inspiration behind White Dolphin. In fact, White Dolphin started off as a story for much younger readers about a girl who could talk to dolphins. But the more I researched about dolphins, the more I realized how complex and fascinating they are and that there was no need to give them the power of human speech or any magical properties in my story.

Sadly, dolphins are endangered. But they are only the tip of the iceberg of endangered animals beneath our oceans. Whole habitats are threatened from overfishing, pollution, and acidification of the water. But for this story, I wanted to focus on Kara and her fight to protect the bay of her home town from the threat of commercial dredging. Dredging for scallops around our British coasts has intensified over the past forty years. It involves pulling massive metal rakes across the seabed, ripping up anything and everything, netting whatever lies on the seabed. Reefs that have developed over thousands of years can be reduced to rubble in minutes. Dredging leaves barren wastelands of our ocean floor. The Lyme Bay Project in Dorset has shown that the seabed can begin to recover, given sufficient time. But if dredging goes on unabated, then what is lost will be lost forever.

Knowing that our fragile oceans continue to be destroyed, out of sight and out of mind, scares me greatly. When will we notice? When there are no more dolphins leaping out of the sea? When there are no more fish on our plates? I wanted to write a story to show that our fishing communities are important and that sustainable fishing is possible, but only through protection of vulnerable habitats. I wanted to keep alive my dream of swimming with wild dolphins one day.

So the story I wrote became White Dolphin.

Gill Lewis

Top Twelve Fascinating Dolphin Facts

1. Dolphins are mammals.
As all mammals, dolphins give birth to live young and the mothers nurse them with milk.

2. Dolphins eat fish and squid.
Dolphins swallow their food whole, despite having teeth in their mouths.

3. Like other mammals, dolphins have lungs and need to breathe air to survive.
They breathe through a blowhole on the top of the head and must rise to the surface frequently to inhale fresh air before diving again.

4. Dolphins use a technique called echolocation to navigate and find food.
Dolphins send out clicks that are returned from other objects in the water (just like an echo). This way a dolphin can locate food, other dolphins, predators or rocks.

5. Dolphins are social beings.
Dolphins live in groups called 'pods' and work together as a team to raise their young and find food.

6. There are thirty-seven different species of dolphin.
There are thirty-two species of ocean dolphins and five species of river dolphins.

7. The largest dolphin is the Orca, also known as 'killer whale'.

Orcas are named as whales because of their size, but they really belong to the dolphin family.

8. The most popular dolphin is the 'bottlenose dolphin'.

Bottlenose dolphins are the ones most often seen in TV series, movies and sea life centres.

9. Dolphins are warm-blooded.

They are surrounded by a thick layer of fat called 'blubber' just below the skin which helps them to stay warm.

10. Dolphins don't sleep, they snooze!

Dolphins have to be conscious to breathe so only half their brain ever sleeps at one time.

11. Dolphins communicate efficiently.

Dolphins can make a unique signature whistle that may help individual dolphins recognize each other.

12. Dolphins are endangered.

Humans are the greatest threat to dolphins: environmental pollution, habitat destruction, and overfishing are the main reasons why so many dolphin species are endangered.

USEFUL WEBSITES

If you want to find out more about protecting our oceans, check out these websites:

World Wildlife Fund for Nature: www.wwf.org.uk

Blue Marine Foundation: www.bluemarinefoundation.com

Ocean Conservancy: www.oceanconservancy.org

Marine Conservation Society: www.mcsuk.org

Finding Sanctuary: www.finding-sanctuary.org

The Wildlife Trusts: www.wildlifetrusts.org

Marine Stewardship Council: www.msc.org and www.fishandkids.org

Born Free Foundation: www.bornfree.org.uk

Whale and Dolphin Conservation Society: www.wdcs.org

British Divers Marine Life Rescue: www.bdmlr.org.uk

Save Lyme Bay Reefs: www.savelymebayreefs.org

Want to help?

Why don't you . . .

1) Buy sustainable fish where you see the Marine Stewardship Council (MSC) logo.

2) Write to your MP about sustainable fishing and cleaning up our seas.

3) Be a volunteer at your local Wildlife Trust and help to clean up your beaches.

4) Adopt a dolphin with the Whale and Dolphin Conservation Society: www2.wdcs.org/hych/adopt/dolphin/dolphin.php

5) Raise money for an organization that helps to support dolphins.

Acknowledgements

This book couldn't have been possible without the help of many people.

I'd like to thank James Barnett of British Divers Marine Life Rescue for information on dolphin strandings (www.bdmlr.org.uk), Dave Murphy of the Finding Sanctuary Project for his wealth of experience as a fisherman and his invaluable insight into providing a sustainable future for all who use the sea (www.finding-sanctuary.org), members of the RYA sailability for their inspiration and technical advice (www.ryasailability.org.uk), Mikey Jones for showing me that anything is possible, and Mylor Sailing School for teaching an old dog new tricks.

I'm indebted to my agent Victoria Birkett and to Liz Cross and all the staff at Oxford University Press for pulling this story out of the hat.

Biggest thanks as always to Roger, Georgie, Bethany, and Jemma.

My research about the effects of commercial scallop-dredging came from the Lyme Bay Project funded by the Wildlife Trusts (www.savelymebayreefs.org). Their twenty-year study of the reefs off the Dorset coast has shown not only the full impact of damaging fishing practices but also the potential for marine habitats to recover if given protection and sufficient time. Protection has to be the key to marine conservation, because at our current rate of plundering the oceans' resources, time is running out.

Gill Lewis spent much of her childhood in the garden where she ran a small zoo and a veterinary hospital for creepy-crawlies, mice, and birds. When she grew up she became a real vet and travelled from the Arctic to Africa in search of interesting animals and places. She worked in Cornwall for several years and spent many hours of her spare time in the cold Atlantic, learning how to fall off a surfboard.

Gill now writes books for children. Her debut novel, *Sky Hawk,* was published to much critical acclaim and has been translated into twenty languages. The publishers of *Sky Hawk* generously sponsored a satellite-tagged osprey through the Highland Foundation for Wildlife, fulfilling Gill's dream that her writing could contribute directly to wildlife conservation.

She lives in the depths of Somerset with her husband and three children and writes from a tree house in the company of squirrels. She still loves to visit Cornwall, but prefers to take the bodyboard to tame the waves instead.

Also by Gill Lewis

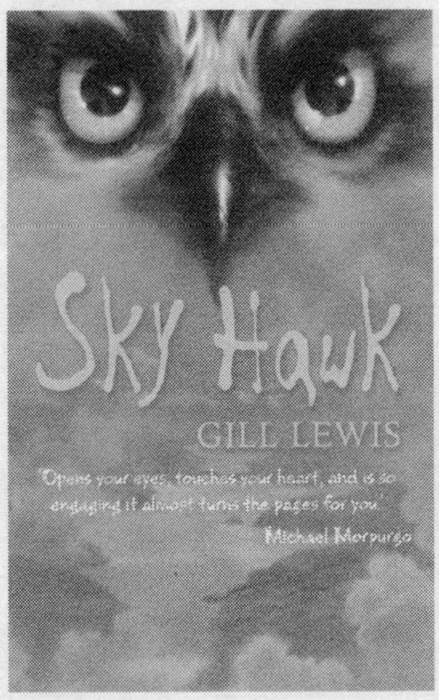

Something lives deep within the forest . . .
something that has not been seen on
Callum's farm for over a hundred years.

Callum and Iona make a promise
to keep their amazing discovery secret,
but can they keep it safe from harm?

The pact they make will change lives forever.

ISBN 978-0-19-275624-4

Penguin A

Africa in Prose
Edited by O. R. Dathorne and Willfried Feuser

Africa in Social Change *P. C. Lloyd*

African Outline *Paul Bohannan*

The African Past *Basil Davidson*

The Discarded People *Cosmas Desmond*

The Liberation of Guiné *Basil Davidson*

The Maghreb in the Modern World *Samir Amin*

Modern Poetry from Africa
Edited by Gerald Moore and Ulli Beier

Nasser's Egypt *Peter Mansfield*

Religion in Africa *Geoffrey Parrinder*

The Rise of the South African Reich *Brian Bunting*

South Africa: The Struggle for a Birthright
Mary Benson

The Struggle for Mozambique *Eduardo Mondlane*

Unity or Poverty? *Reginald H. Green and Ann Seidman*

Penguin African Library

Which Way Africa?

The Search for a New Society

Basil Davidson

A man would have to be very brave or very foolhardy to try to forecast precisely the pattern of Africa's future. Where events outrun the printing-presses, discretion is the better part of omniscience.

In *Which Way Africa*? Basil Davidson, the well-known writer on African affairs, has steered clear of political ju-ju. Instead – and infinitely more to the purpose – he has made what is the only up-to-date and comprehensive analysis in English – and probably in any language – of the social, economic, and political motives, myths, ideas, and beliefs which underlie modern African nationalism. Recent events have shown the world an Africa poised on the threshold of new ventures, an Africa in flux. Only such an analysis as the author has successfully achieved in this volume can help to delineate the kind of societies which will now tend to emerge there.

Other volumes in the Penguin African Library are listed overleaf.

Penguin African Library

Class and Colour in South Africa 1850-1950

H. J. and R. E. Simons

'How long will it last?' is the question most often asked about the prospects of white supremacy in southern Africa. Not whether, but when will revolutionary nemesis overtake the regime?

The authors of this book make no predictions. Their aim is to give the reader the historical and sociological data which he needs to form his own opinion. In a critical analysis of the Labour and National movements in South Africa they explore the questions of how and why over the last hundred years the white working class traded its socialist principles for a share of white power. And they also provide the first detailed study of interactions between the two wings of the resistance against white domination.

Specially written for the Penguin African Library by two political activists, *Class and Colour in South Africa 1850–1950* incorporates much material drawn from primary, hitherto untapped sources. It opens new horizons for students of race relations, colonial nationalism, the class theory and South African history.

Penguin African Library

A Short History of Africa

Roland Oliver and J. D. Fage

For some years now there has been an urgent need for a concise history of Africa. Although much has been written on different regions of Africa and different periods of her long development – colonial histories of the European powers, current affairs articles on the emergent countries, studies of Africa's prehistory – there has been nothing that offers the general reader an overall view of African history from the earliest times to the Pan-African meetings at Monrovia and Casablanca. Drawing on archaeology, oral tradition, language relationships, social institutions and material cultures, the editors of the *Journal of African History* now present *A Short History of Africa* which not only assembles the most authoritative views of their colleagues into an absorbing narrative, but also contains some original conclusions that take the study of Africa a stage further.

'Admirable in its quality, its balance, and its scholarship' – *Sunday Times*

Geography of the U.S.S.R.

J. P. Cole

In area the U.S.S.R. is the largest country in the world, stretching almost half-way round the northern hemisphere and divided into eleven time zones. It has the world's third greatest population, increasing at the rate of 3½ million a year. Three quarters of its total population is still to be found in the European part, whereas many of the best natura l resources lie in the eastern region of the country. This presents a major problem for Soviet geographers and economists. But if the vast size is a disadvantage in some respects, it at least ensures that natural resources are plentiful.

This book provides a regional geography of the U.S.S.R. with an economic approach. It covers physical background, historical growth, population, natural resources, regional planning, transportation, agriculture and industry. A concise and straightforward study, it is intended mainly for the non-specialist.

More about Penguins and Pelicans

Penguinews, which appears every month, contains details of all the new books issued by Penguins as they are published. From time to time it is supplemented by *Penguins in Print*, which is a complete list of all available books published by Penguins. (There are well over three thousand of these.)

A specimen copy of *Penguinews* will be sent to you free on request, and you can become a subscriber for the price of the postage. For a year's issues (including the complete lists) please send 30p if you live in the United Kingdom, or 60p if you live elsewhere. Just write to Dept EP, Penguin Books Ltd, Harmondsworth, Middlesex, enclosing a cheque or postal order, and your name will be added to the mailing list.

Note: *Penguinews* and *Penguins in Print* are not available in the U.S.A. or Canada

Pelican Books

The Geography of African Affairs

Paul Fordham was born in Norfolk in 1925 and went to the Friends School, Saffron Walden, for most of his schooldays. During and after the Second World War he spent some three and a half years as a 'Bevin-Boy' miner in Derbyshire. In 1950 he graduated in geography from Leeds University and, after brief spells as a tram conductor, jobbing gardener, and schoolmaster, spent the next ten years as a Resident Tutor in the Adult Education Department of Nottingham University, first in Lincolnshire and later in Derbyshire.

While still at school, Paul Fordham read Julian Huxley's *Africa View* which first made him want to teach *about* Africa and, later, to teach *in* Africa. In 1961 he went to Makerere University College to be Resident Tutor in Buganda for the Extra-Mural Department, moving after a year to become Principal of the College of Social Studies (a residential college for adult education) at Kikuyu, in Kenya. He was Director of the Institute of Adult Studies, University College, Nairobi, from 1966 to 1968. He then returned to England and worked for the Schools Council on secondment from the Department of Education and Science. He is now Director of Extra-Mural Studies in the University of Southampton. In 1950 he married a fellow student and they have two sons.

The Geography of African Affairs

Paul Fordham

Third Edition

Penguin Books

Penguin Books Ltd, Harmondsworth,
Middlesex, England
Penguin Books Inc., 7110 Ambassador Road,
Baltimore, Maryland 21207, U.S.A.
Penguin Books Australia Ltd, Ringwood,
Victoria, Australia.

Published in Pelican Books 1965
Second Edition 1968
Third Edition 1972

Made and printed in Great Britain by
C. Nicholls & Company Ltd
Set in Monotype Plantin

Contents

Part 2 – Regional Studies

List of Tables

List of Maps

Preface to the Second Edition

Anyone who has the effrontery to deal with so vast a subject in so small a compass must needs offer a convincing explanation for doing so.

Africa is large, its problems complex, and their solution increasingly pressing. We are often called on to express opinions about African affairs – and yet most people seem to lack that basic geographical knowledge about the continent which is an essential beginning for any sensible appraisal of political issues.

It was in my teaching of University Adult Education Classes in England that I found a need for such a book as this. I have not sought to write a complete Geography of Africa. What I have tried to do is to select from the whole mass of geographical facts about Africa south of the Sahara such information as seems important for an understanding of current political and economic problems. In doing this I have had in mind both the interested layman and those students of Geography who may wish to read a little farther than the normal confines of their subject.

This does not set out to be a work based on original research. The basic information and many of the ideas have been sifted from the writings of experts in a number of different fields. I hope that those who may be stimulated by this book will turn to them for further guidance.

Most of the sources used should be available on request from any good public library. They have been chosen with an eye both to availability and usefulness. The notes at the end of each chapter should therefore be regarded as a first guide to further reading. Statistics have been taken largely from the standard statistical reference books available in the larger reference libraries. The most useful sources of this kind are the *U.N.*

Statistical Yearbook, the *U.N. Yearbook of International Trade Statistics* and *The Statesman's Yearbook*.

My thanks to Mr and Mrs G. H. Moore, Mr A. H. Thornton, Mr H. C. Wiltshire, Mr P. Kinyanjui, Mr D. Macharia and my wife for many helpful suggestions and much needed encouragement. Also to Miss T. Kabacubya who typed most of the original manuscript.

University College, Nairobi, Kenya
December 1966 P.E.F.

Preface to the Third Edition

New material has been added where appropriate and all existing data have been revised. To the standard references mentioned above should be added *The Europa Yearbook* and *Africa Handbook* (Penguin Books). Students wishing to keep up to date with a rapidly changing continent should consult *Africa Digest* and *Africa Report*; for more lengthy papers, *African Affairs* and *Journal of Modern African Studies.*

My thanks to Miss Susan Burgess who typed the additions and alterations for this edition.

Schools Council, London
December 1970 P.E.F.

Part 1 A General Survey

1 A Land to Live In

SIZE

If you were asked what sort of mental picture you have of the land of Africa you would probably reply that it was hot; possibly you would add that it was wet, and you might even go on to talk of jungle, wild animals and unpleasant insects. On the other hand, if you have knowledge of people who have lived in one or another of the 'white settler' countries, you might have a quite different mental picture. You might talk then of summer all the year round, fertile soils, wonderful sunshine and spectacular scenery. In either case you would be describing a part as if it were the whole, forgetting Africa's truly continental scale. For Africa *is* a continent, and a very large one at that.

To say that Africa is 5,000 miles long from north to south and some 2,000 miles wide even at its narrowest point gives the true measure of the distances involved. These measurements really come to life when one compares this size with countries which may be more familiar (Map 1). Can India really be as small as that? A huge country of nearly 400 million people, itself the greater part of what is known as a 'sub-continent'? Of course it is not India which is small: it is simply dwarfed by its much bigger surroundings. Even 'little' states like Ghana compare favourably in size with England and Wales while some, like Sudan, approach the size of India itself. Countries of this size are likely to contain a great variety of environments within their own borders, quite apart from the greater variety to be found in the continent as a whole. This variety will be considered in subsequent chapters, but size has other consequences too.

In countries which are technically backward and where communications have not been well developed, the larger the size of the territory the greater the problems of government will be. All governments have to exercise a minimum of physical control and operate a workable administrative system or else they cease

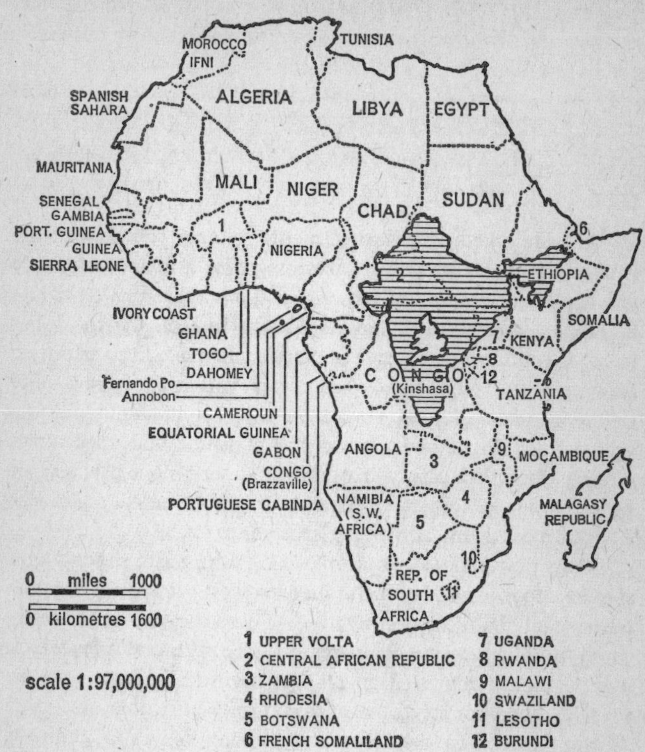

MAP I. The size of Africa, compared with England and Wales, and with India (without Kashmir)

to govern (as the government of the Congo Republic ceased to govern in the summer of 1960). If they are authoritarian and have sufficient force at their disposal they may solve the problem as the Belgians did in the Congo by establishing an efficient system of airfields, strategically placed paratroops – and a monopoly of aeroplanes. If they wish to remain in any sense democratic, however, their authority must derive from a working minimum of popular consent, and for this there must be a working minimum of political cohesion (or 'solidarity' or 'national sentiment') throughout the entire country. This is the

real difficulty. Apart from the educated minority this national sentiment hardly exists and has to be created. Even in a relatively small state like Ghana the government had to contend in the early days of independence with an official opposition which was a coalition of tribal interests rather than dissidents loyal to the new nation as a whole. In these circumstances the government found itself defending and promoting national solidarity with methods which may have seemed 'undemocratic', and which led to a major political upheaval in 1966.

The difficulty over political cohesion in new states as big and diverse as those of Africa is largely one of the present. When it has been overcome, size becomes an advantage rather than a hindrance. For, except in a few overcrowded areas like Rwanda, Burundi or parts of Kenya or Nigeria, there is room to expand and develop; room for the population to grow (as it is beginning to grow) and be absorbed; room to contain a growing and much needed labour force; room to experiment with new agricultural techniques to produce the food for the next generation as well as the food for today; above all, there will be room to live, as economic development in overcrowded lands frequently produces new troubles as well as solving old ones. 'A million peasants can dwell happily where a thousand car owners would chafe in frustration.'[1] Africa is fortunate to the degree that this is not her problem. One of the attractions for the Europeans who have settled there has been the space for work, travel and leisure. This space will remain one of Africa's greatest assets for a long time to come.

PHYSICAL ENVIRONMENT

There are few who would deny that before this century Africa was – in the Western, technical, sense – the most backward of all the continents. This does not imply that nothing worthwhile came out of Africa before the Europeans arrived. There was a great deal that was worth while, about much of which we are still largely ignorant.[2] But, in comparison with the great civilizations of Asia, Europe and the Americas, Africa does appear to have lagged behind in *material* achievements, and it is of more than academic interest to speculate on the possible

reasons for this. There are those who would attempt to justify racial discrimination on the grounds of some 'innate inferiority' belonging to native Africans, an inferiority deduced from the assumption that they have not 'achieved' anything. Almost all reasonable men in the twentieth century consider this explanation absurd. What we can say is that there are certain aspects of Africa's physical environment which *by themselves* would account for any backwardness which Europeans found there.

First and foremost is the aspect of isolation. Most of us are what we are because of what we learn from our family, our friends, our neighbours, our enemies and, above all, what we learn from the experience of the past. Most of us are content to learn, to imitate, to adapt, but not to invent. This process of learning and the accumulation of knowledge thrives on contact with other peoples and other ways of life, and stagnates in isolation. It is remarkable how all the really primitive peoples who survived into the nineteenth and twentieth centuries did so in extreme isolation and by adaptation to environments into which no other peoples were able or thought it profitable to penetrate. The Bushmen of the Kalahari Desert, the Australian and Tasmanian aborigines, and the 'Indians' along the southern tip of South America are examples which spring immediately to mind. Most Africans were not as isolated as this, but they were cut off to a large extent from contacts with the outside world. In the days before the European conquest of the seas, the Sahara Desert constituted a considerable barrier to communications,* and right down to the nineteenth century there were other barriers which militated against effective, constructive contact.

RELIEF

In relief, Africa is a vast plateau surface, with narrow coastal plains. The plateau is divided into a series of smaller plateau surfaces of different heights, often with abrupt edges both at the rim of the continent and at places in the interior. Land is higher in the south (where it averages 3,000 ft) than in the north (where it falls away to about 1,000 ft). Although generally flat and monotonous it is characterized by large shallow depres-

*But see pp. 101–103 below for medieval trans-Sahara contacts.

sions, some of which form what the geographer calls basins of inland drainage whose rivers end in inland lakes and swamps.

One further physical feature of note is the Great Rift Valley system of east Africa, of which the Red Sea forms part. The whole system is some 4,000 miles long and up to 100 miles wide, producing great local variations in relief, climate and vegetation. It contains most of the great lakes of east Africa, and the giant

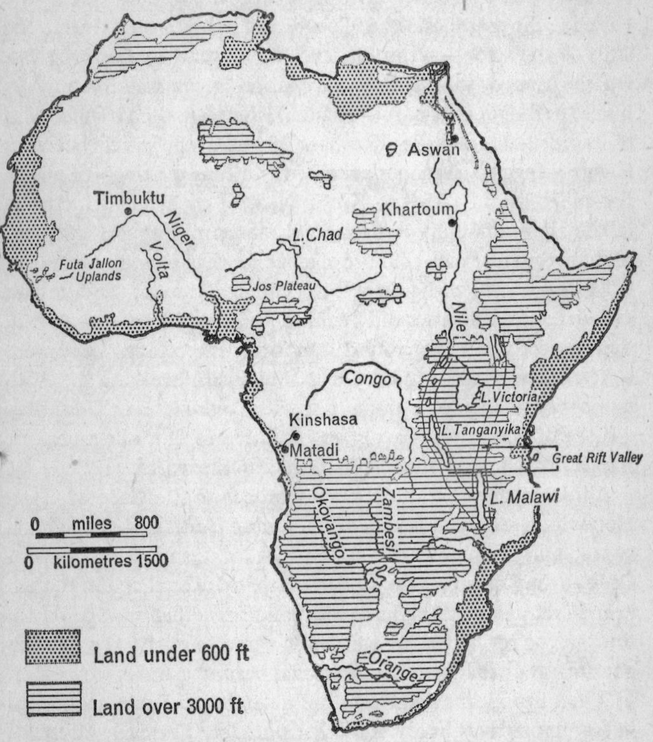

MAP 2. Relief and drainage (simplified)

volcanoes along its edges, with which are associated some of the continent's most fertile soils.

The edge of the plateau is always steep, sometimes spectacularly so, as with the Drakensberg in South Africa. It is these

steep edges to the plateau which have contributed so much to isolation. For early explorers the easiest way to penetrate a new land is to sail or paddle up the rivers – these are the natural lines of communication. But in Africa not one of them is navigable very far from the sea. They all 'fall off the edge' of the continent. The Nile, the most obvious entry into the continent, is famous for its cataracts, and farther south for its floating vegetation and swamps, which render it useless for navigation. With the Orange, the Zambesi, the Congo and other great rivers, the story is the same – waterfalls and rapids soon hinder progress. On the Congo, for example, navigation is possible for only 85 miles (to the present port of Matadi); there are then a succession of rapids and falls to Kinshasa,* where the river becomes navigable again. In modern terms this means a railway of nearly 200 miles from Matadi to Kinshasa, with consequent increases in the time, difficulty and cost of transport. For the early explorers, the river proved more of a barrier than a path.

Moreover, when the early European explorers of the fifteenth and sixteenth centuries did begin to find out more about Africa, their object was to get round it, not to penetrate it. They were concerned with finding a route to India, with breaking the Arab monopoly of the spice trade, not with colonization. What they did see of Africa was hardly an incentive to find out more, for Africa turns her most inhospitable face to the world.

All down the west coast from Morocco to the Cape of Good Hope there are a succession of uninviting landfalls – the Sahara, swamp and dense forest on the Guinea coast, the Namib Desert. Only at the Cape does the land seem to invite settlement, though even here the Dutch had no intention of establishing a colony at first, only a re-victualling station on the way to the East. It was not until 1685 that active colonization began.

When Europeans and Arabs did begin to penetrate, they went in search of slaves, ivory and other plunder. The early efforts of the Portuguese to 'civilize' and Christianize in the Congo area[3] gave way in the seventeenth century to the sort of destructive contact which became characteristic of all European penetration for over 200 years. This contact was not of the kind to provide a release from isolation and a stimulus to new effort and growth.

* Formerly Leopoldville.

Inwards from the extreme south and north, isolation remained an important aspect of African life until this century.

In addition to isolation there were other aspects of great difficulty which were presented to man by his physical environment. Difficulties are not always a disadvantage. They may be a desirable, even a necessary, stimulus to civilization. With Toynbee one may say that

> Ease is inimical to civilization . . . The greater the ease of the environment, the weaker the stimulus towards civilization.[4]

or agree with Burke, that

> . . . difficulty . . . has been the glory of all the great masters in all the arts to confront and to overcome; and when they had overcome the first difficulty, to turn it into an instrument for new conquests over new difficulties . . .[5]

Nevertheless there must come a point when the stimulus provided by difficulty becomes instead a crushing burden. This has certainly been true of the physical environment in Africa.

CLIMATE

The climate in its direct effects on human beings has often been stressed, perhaps over-stressed. There are few parts of Africa where the climate is debilitating for human beings all the year round, and even in these areas the pith helmet and the spine pad are things of the past. What is increasingly realized is that the *indirect* effects of climate, particularly on water supply, soils and disease, are of much greater significance in human terms. It is these which have been barriers to human progress in the past and which can only now be overcome with the technical aids of the twentieth century.

The climates of Africa possess three significant aspects. First, the continent's position about the equator determines the equatorial or tropical nature of most of its climates. Only the extreme north and the extreme south lie outside the tropics, and there are few places anywhere in the continent where plant growth is ever checked by cold. This occurs only in the highest mountain areas.

Secondly, because most of the continent is at least 1,000 ft and

often considerably more above sea level, there are very few places in Black Africa where temperature is excessively high. Only along the west coast, the Congo basin, and the coastal strip of east Africa are there mean annual temperatures of over 80 degrees – temperatures which, especially when combined with high humidities, are generally agreed to be rather enervating.

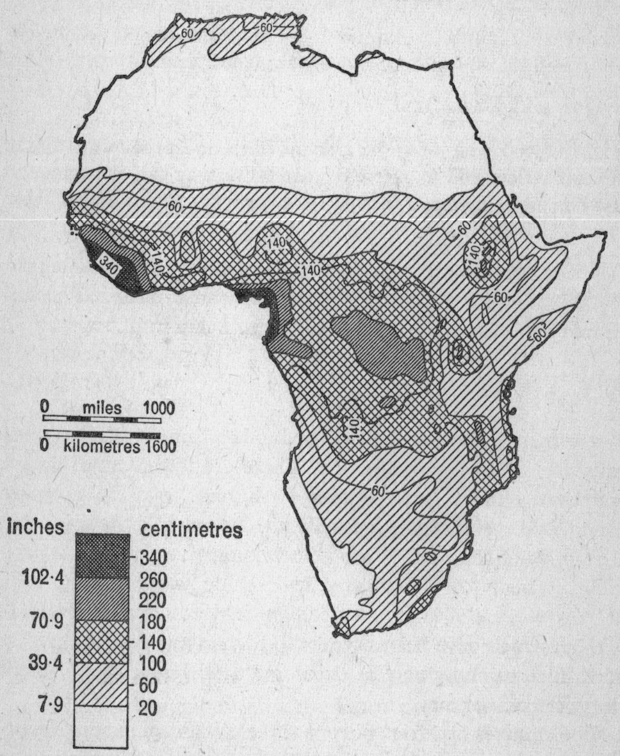

MAP 3. Mean annual rainfall

Thirdly, water rather than temperature is the critical factor. Water shortage is perhaps the most important limiting factor of the physical environment today, for 'water is scanty in at least three quarters of Africa south of the Sahara'.[6] Around the equator, where no month is really dry (except in parts of Kenya

and Somalia) and there are generally two rain maxima in spring and autumn, there is not generally a water problem. Very rapidly, however, as you move away from the equator, these two rain maxima merge into one rainy season (summer), the length of the dry season grows, and the amount and reliability of the rainfall steadily decrease.

Water is put to many and varied uses in modern society. As the standard of living rises, so does the standard of sanitation and plumbing and the consequent consumption of water. The creation of industry brings many problems in its train, not least of which is the consumption of water. Conservation of water for industrial use is already a serious problem on the Witwatersrand in South Africa.[7]

Fisheries, both natural and artificial, are likely to play an increasingly important part in an Africa still chronically short of enough protein foods. All these, as well as the demands of irrigation, transport and water power, will have to be met in the Africa of the future.

With the exception of South West Africa, Bechuanaland, Somalia, the Sahara and parts of Tanzania, Ethiopia and Kenya, there is enough total rainfall over the whole of inter-tropical Africa. It is the unreliability of the amount and the length of the dry season which constitute the problems. Methods of control must aim to reduce or eliminate the run-off of water, to allow its gradual use throughout the dry season.

SOILS

The poverty of soils in tropical Africa has been a hindrance to agriculture in most areas. Any advanced civilization must rest on the production of a food surplus, but if everyone is struggling to produce enough (or less than enough) to eat, there will be little time and opportunity for that division of labour so essential to the accumulation of material wealth.

It used to be thought, because so much of tropical Africa is covered with luxuriant vegetation, that the underlying soils must necessarily be rich. Only remove this dense plant cover, it was argued, and fertile agricultural land would be revealed. We now know that this is not so. In the wetter areas, soils under tropical

forest wear out very rapidly when the land is cleared. Such land must be left fallow again for long periods at a time unless some artificial methods of regeneration are applied.

Tropical soils are poorer and more fragile than those of temperate regions. Great care is needed in using them, if their further destruction and impoverishment are to be avoided. These conditions give tropical agriculture a precarious character which is absent from the temperate belt.[8]

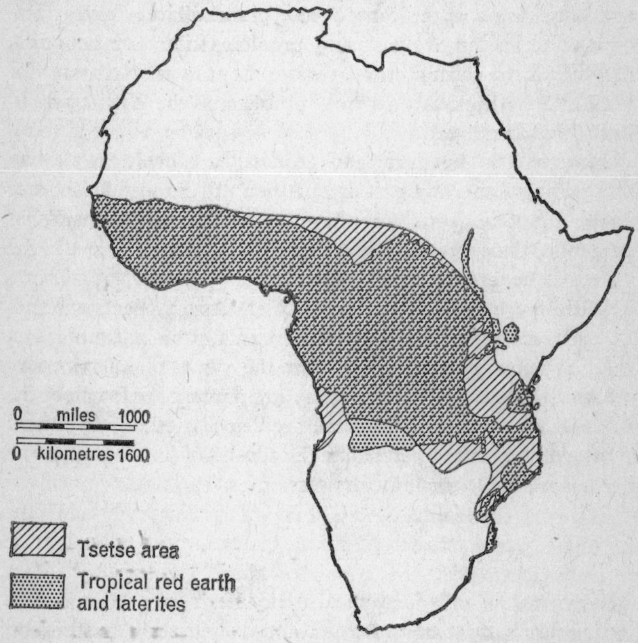

MAP 4. Tropical soils and the tsetse fly

The answer to the apparent paradox of luxuriant vegetation on poor soil is that the tropical forest lives in a state of equilibrium with itself and takes very little nourishment from the soil. For parts of the Congo it has been estimated that between 20 and 25 tons of leaves and branches fall on each acre every year. This enormous quantity of organic material quickly decomposes under the prevailing climatic conditions and forms the humus

and salts on which the trees directly feed. But it never becomes part of more than the top few inches of soil. Once you clear away the trees, you destroy the equilibrium, and the soil is revealed in all its actual poverty.

This general poverty of tropical soils is caused by the climate under which they are formed. Myriads of insects (especially termites) which flourish in the hot, wet areas, begin the decomposition of organic matter. These, together with the countless micro-organisms, soon convert the branches and leaves into humus and the humus into soluble salts. If they are not used within a few weeks of their formation, they are washed away (or 'leached') by the heavy rain. Tropical soils are thus poor in plant foods, and highly acid because any available lime is soon leached away, while the rapid conversion of humus into soluble salts prevents the storage of these salts for use by cultivated plants. Even the application of manure has an effect over months rather than the years enjoyed by temperate soils.

Experiments have shown that the activity of micro-organisms in decomposing humus is increased fairly rapidly by a rise in the average temperature. In Java, the 'humus content of the surface layer of the soil was shown to rise from 5 per cent at an altitude of 1,000 feet above sea level and a mean annual temperature of 76 degrees F (24·5° C) to 14 per cent at an altitude of 3,250 feet and a mean temperature of 68 degrees F (20° C).'[9] This range of temperature is about the same as the difference between much of Uganda and the tropical coast lands of east Africa. Away from the higher parts of the east African plateau, mean annual temperatures in tropical Africa are well above 70 degrees F. The only tropical soils which are naturally fertile are those which have not yet had time to become poor – those formed from fairly recent non-acid volcanic ash, as in parts of east Africa on the margins of the Rift Valleys, or those derived from recent river alluvium, as in a few small areas near the coasts. Only the Nile Valley in the north provided any natural fertility comparable with the great river valleys of south and east Asia.

Two further problems accentuate the poverty of African soils: soil erosion and lateritization.

Soil erosion, 'a malignant form of a natural phenomenon',[10] is essentially a man-made problem. Leave the soil with its natural

protective plant cover, either forest or grassland, and malignant erosion does not occur; but once this cover is removed, the opportunities for wind and rain to do damage are greatly increased. Bush clearance by burning, the unthinking transference of European methods and tools to an African environment and overgrazing have all contributed to the exposure of African soils and their removal by wind and rain.

Unless ploughing is always done by following the contours, the furrow becomes a gulley after a tropical deluge, and a gulley which becomes deeper and wider with each downpour. Lack of humus in the soil reduces its rate of water absorption, with a consequent increase in the rate of run-off and removal of top soil. In the dry season, soil reduced to a powder can quickly and dramatically be removed either by wind or by the next heavy rain. It is, in fact, in the drier areas that the problem is at its most acute, and these are just the areas which have some of the best soils in Africa. As you move out of the area of poor soils, you move into the areas where erosion and poor water supply are of increasing significance.

Most of the red soils of the tropics are lateritic to a greater or lesser extent. Pure laterite, described by Gourou as a 'pedological leprosy'[11] and 'utterly infertile,'[12] is a rock rather than a soil. Roads can be made of it as well as buildings, and it stands up to weathering rather better than some rocks. It is composed of the hydroxides of iron and aluminium in various proportions, is formed as the end product in the creation of soil from other rocks under tropical conditions and in its pure form contains absolutely nothing that plants can absorb.

In areas with a dry season, laterite forms as a hard crust on the surface of the land. During the dry season, water percolates upwards, bringing with it in solution the hydroxides of iron and aluminium which are deposited at the surface as a hard pan or crust. In those areas which have no significant dry season, as in the Congo Basin, the laterite forms at a depth varying from 18 inches to 9 feet, but even here it may quickly be exposed if the processes of man-induced soil erosion get to work.

Laterite is a dead soil, a rock which does not decompose and on which chemical erosion has no effect. Areas whose surface is formed by laterite are worthless. Soils in which laterite is incompletely formed

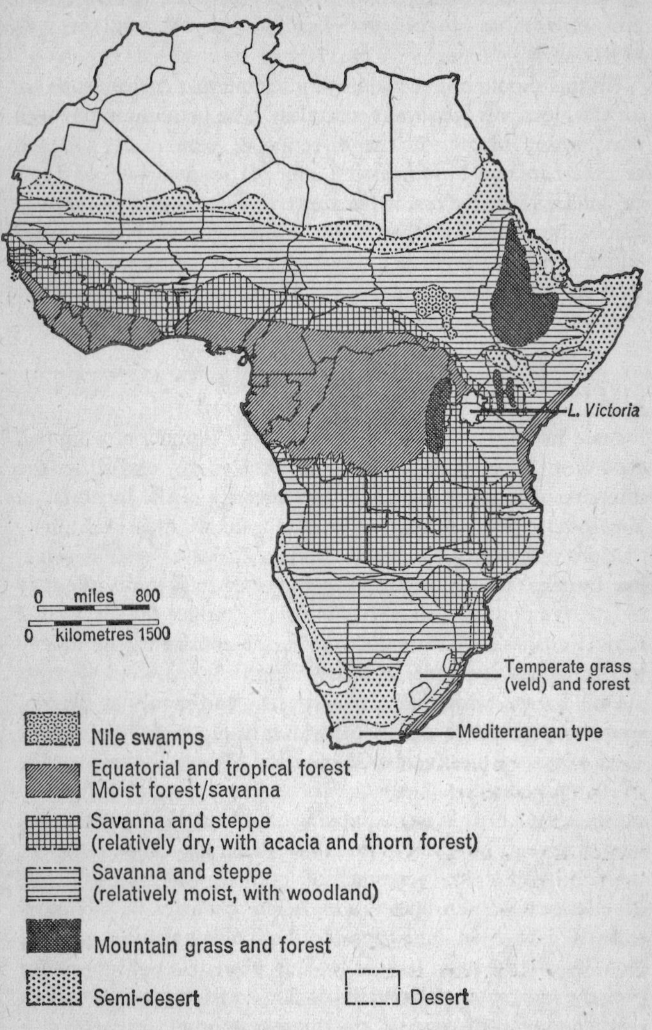

MAP 5. Natural vegetation south of the Sahara. This map also shows political boundaries. (For greater detail see R. W. J. Keay, *Vegetation Map of Africa*, 1959)

may be cultivated if they offer a good physical texture, as in certain gritty soils observed in the lower Congo valley; but they are very poor nevertheless.[13]

All this should not be taken as indicating that African soils are for the most part *potentially* worthless. The pendulum may well have swung too far in the direction of pessimism, and soil scientists are now busy stressing some of the advantages of tropical soils.[14] Nevertheless, it remains true that these soils do need to be improved, and that, without the knowledge of modern agricultural science, little more than the prevailing shifting cultivation was possible in the past. This did not provide the productive base for the development of an advanced civilization.

DISEASE

Disease has certainly constituted a serious limitation to human activity in Africa. Even today it saps the energy and stifles the initiative of millions – perhaps the majority of the inhabitants. To all those diseases familiar to Europeans we must add a host that are peculiar to the tropics and to Africa as well as some, like Bubonic Plague, now almost forgotten in Europe. We may today have the knowledge to eliminate or reduce the diseases of Africa, but, as with so much else in the continent, the money and the skilled personnel are still lacking.

One disease, which affects both cattle and man, has been of supreme importance and is still widespread. Carried by various species of tsetse flies (genus *Glossina*, see Map 4), the importance of Trypanosomiasis (sleeping sickness in man and nagana in cattle) lies not only in its debilitating effects on the human beings who survive it, but even more in its calamitous consequence for the rearing of stock over much of inter-tropical Africa. In the development of European and Asian civilizations domestic animals have been indispensable, both for transport and for food. One of the main reasons for European material superiority over the indigenous inhabitants of the Americas was the lack in that continent of any of the more important domesticable animals (the Plains Indians did not acquire the horse until it had been introduced by the Spaniards). In Africa the problem was not their absence, but lack of opportunity to rear and maintain

healthy stock. The effect on material achievements was the same.

Today it is possible to combat Trypanosomiasis by the use of insecticides, immunization, elimination of wild game and by the clearance of bush, the breeding ground particularly of the *mortisans* group of tsetse flies which are the chief carriers of nagana. These flies cannot maintain themselves in completely open country, such as that cleared for cultivation, or in dense forest. Both immunization and bush clearance are expensive,

TABLE I

Number of medical practitioners in selected countries

Country	*No. of doctors*	*No. of inhabitants per doctor*
Angola	387 (1964)	13,140
Botswana	21 (1966)	27,430
Cameroun	196 (1965)	26,680
Ivory Coast	218 (1966)	17,980
Liberia	96 (1965)	11,150
Nigeria	1,300 (1965)	44,620
Malawi	84 (1965)	46,900
Rwanda	53 (1966)	62,380
Senegal	214 (1966)	16,730
Sierra Leone	144 (1965)	16,440
Sudan	567 (1966)	24,590
U.K.	55,800 (1963)	840
India	77,780 (1962)	5,800

SOURCE: *United Nations Statistical Yearbook 1968*, Table 206.

however, while the indiscriminate use of insecticides and the killing of game are to be avoided. The final elimination of sleeping sickness will depend on how much money and skill is made available for the job, and it is encouraging to note that drugs for immunization are now becoming cheaper.[15]

There are several ways of classifying African diseases – according to the way they are spread, their causative organisms, or the

way of life pursued by their human sufferers.[16] This last seems the most sensible way for this study and is the one adopted here. Using it, we can establish four main categories.

The first contains all those diseases especially associated with the primitive rural life – still the lot of most of Africa's peoples. These are diseases spread mainly (though not entirely) by the insect carriers of disease, and they will only be eliminated or reduced in importance with improved housing, water supply and generally improved standards of hygiene. They include malaria, sleeping sickness, yellow fever and pneumonia.

The second group are those specifically associated with insanitary conditions and habits, some of which have become more prevalent as Europeans have encouraged the greater movement and mixing of peoples, crowding into urban slums, and also as clothing habits have changed. 'Dirty clothes are a poor substitute for clean nudity.'[17] They include plague, typhus, leprosy, various worm parasites and bilharziasis. Cholera, formerly absent from Africa, must now (1971) be added to this group.

The third group are those whose spread is mainly due to ignorance, like the venereal diseases and yaws, a disease whose symptoms are very similar to those of syphilis, but which is spread from infected cuts and to which young children are particularly prone.

The fourth group are the diseases due to malnutrition, of which kwashiorkor has received most attention in recent years. The name is used for a complex of symptoms associated with severe malnutrition, especially protein deficiency, a complex which affects large numbers of children just after weaning, when they are put on to a diet consisting almost entirely of starchy food. In 'certain parts of Africa it is probable that the majority of the children in the second and third year of life suffer from kwashiorkor.'[18] Among the symptoms are retarded growth, swollen bellies and permanent damage to the liver and possibly other organs. There is also a death rate of at least 30 per cent. In later life the high incidence of cirrhosis and cancer of the liver is thought to be due to childhood kwashiorkor. 'In England it is often said that a man is as old as his arteries. In tropical Africa it would seem to be more true to say that a man is as old as his liver.'[19]

In one sense we might place most of Africa's diseases in the

last category, because they are nearly all of them aggravated by the prevalent malnutrition. A pioneer study in this field was that of Orr and Gilks, in 1931, on the Masai and Kikuyu tribes of Kenya.[20] The Masai lived traditionally on a diet of milk, meat and raw blood, one which is unusually high in protein, fats and calcium. The agricultural Kikuyu live mainly on cereals, roots and fruit, one more nearly typical of most of Africa. It was found that the average male Masai was 5 inches taller, 23 lb heavier and had a muscular strength 50 per cent greater than his Kikuyu counterpart. Disease among the Kikuyu was much more prevalent, especially bone deformities, dental caries, anaemia, pulmonary conditions and tropical ulcer. Among the Masai only rheumatoid arthritis and intestinal stasis were more prevalent than among the Kikuyu. The improvement of health in Africa is to a large extent a question of improving diets.

Possibilities for the future development of Africa will be considered in Chapter 5, and the fact that past and present difficulties have been emphasized here does not mean that they cannot be overcome. Isolation has probably been the most important factor making for backwardness in the past, and the difficulties of the environment could not be effectively challenged until this isolation had been overcome. Much of the initial conquest by Europeans did not stimulate Africans to greater achievements, it merely added to their burdens. It is only now, in the middle of the twentieth century, that Africans have both the opportunity to develop on their own, and knowledge of the outside world to help them do so. Africa is still a land of difficulties, but they need not remain the crushing burdens that they have been in the past. They can now take their place with those of Burke as a stimulus to further effort. The test of the 'innate capacity' of Africans lies in the future and not in the past.

Even when talking of the past we should be wary of judging purely from a European standpoint. It is true that on the level of material culture much of Africa was in the early iron age and there were areas with less technology than that. There was, however, some elaborate social and political organization, especially in west Africa, while the influence of African art and music on that of Europe has been profound and far-reaching during the course of this century. Perhaps we may allow the

last word to one of Africa's most primitive stone-age men, a Bushman from the Kalahari Desert:

'What is considered the worst thing a man can do?' I once asked Tsonoma (the Medicine Man). He answered, without hesitation, that the gravest offence was to fight with someone else in the clan. It was considered unworthy and stupid. For that reason a boy who showed signs of aggressiveness was closely watched by all the adults and taken out on long, tough hunting trips to learn sense and discipline. In their legends, there are no heroes who attain distinction by force of arms...[21]

Notes on Chapter 1

1. R. A. Piddington, *The Limits of Mankind*, 1956, p. 2.
2. Basil Davidson, *Old Africa Rediscovered*, 1959, and *The Lost Cities of Africa*, 1959, for pioneer studies in the new African history.
3. See J. Duffy, *Portuguese Africa*, 1959, Chap. 1.
4. *Study of History*, Vol. 2, 1934.
5. *Reflections on the Revolution in France*, World Classics edn, pp. 184–5.
6. E. B. Worthington, *Science in the Development of Africa*, 1958, p. 114.
7. See Chapter 12 below.
8. P. Gourou, *The Tropical World*, 2nd edn, 1958, p. 13.
9. P. Gourou, op. cit., 4th edn, 1966, p. 21.
10. L. D. Stamp, *Africa*, 1953, p. 101.
11. P. Gourou, op. cit., 2nd edn, p. 21.
12. ibid., p. 20.
13. ibid., p. 22.
14. E. B. Worthington, op. cit., p. 140.
15. *Kenya Dairy Farmer*, June 1969. Article on 'The Treatment of Trypanosomiasis'.
16. The approach of E. B. Worthington.
17. E. B. Worthington, op. cit., p. 360.
18. J. C. Carothers, *The African Mind in Health and Disease*, W.H.O., 1953, p. 71.
19. ibid., p. 71.
20. J. Boyd Orr and J. D. Gilks, *The Physique and Health of Two African Tribes*.
21. J. Bjerre, *Kalahari*, 1960, p. 110.

SUGGESTIONS FOR FURTHER READING

As well as those books already mentioned more detailed information on the substance of this chapter may be found in:

E. Huntington, *Mainsprings of Civilization*, 1945.

G. V. Jacks and R. O. Whyte, *The Rape of the Earth*, 1949.

W. G. Kendrew, *The Climates of the Continents*, 1953 (Chapter 5).

D. H. K. Lee, *Climate and Economic Development in the Tropics*, 1957.

T. A. M. Nash, *Africa's Bane: the Tsetse Fly*, 1969.

B. W. Thompson, *The Climate of Africa*, 1965.

A number of general geographies of Africa have been published in recent years including:

H. de Blij, *A Geography of Subsaharan Africa*, 1964.

R. J. Harrison Church, J. I. Clarke, P. J. H. Clarke and H. R. J. Henderson, *Africa and the Islands*, 1964, is one of the best general geographies of Africa, especially regional geography.

A. T. Grove, *Africa South of the Sahara*, 1967.

W. A. Hance, *Geography of Modern Africa*, 1964.

Alan B. Mountjoy and Clifford Embleton, *Africa: a geographical study*, 1965, is very good on physical geography. Its human geography is more uneven.

R. M. Prothero (ed.), *A Geography of Africa*, 1968. A symposium of regional essays which focus on environmental, historical, economic and socio-political themes.

Appendix to Chapter 1

Some Notes on the Principal Diseases of Tropical Africa

DISEASES PARTICULARLY ASSOCIATED WITH PRIMITIVE RURAL LIFE

They are likely to disappear or be reduced in importance only with improved housing, sanitation and water supply – i.e. greater insulation from the wild environment. They include in particular those diseases carried by biting winged insects.

Malaria. Recently reduced in a systematic campaign conducted by W.H.O. (World Health Organization) against the malarial mosquito.

Yellow Fever. A disease of monkeys which occasionally assumes epidemic proportions in man. Transmitted by mosquitoes. In the 1951 epidemic in Nigeria there were 600 deaths out of 5,500 cases.

Trypanosomiasis (sleeping sickness in man, nagana in cattle). Spread to animals and man by tsetse flies of various species. Methods of control include the use of insecticides and bush clearance (to eliminate flies), destruction of wild game (to eliminate tolerant animal hosts) and the immunization of domestic animals and man. Immunization lasts only up to six months.

Onchocerciasis. Infestation by filarial worm and transmitted by a fly which lives near rivers and streams – hence the name *River Blindness* which is applied to the condition which often develops.

Pneumonia and Tuberculosis, common causes of death among Africans, may also be included in this category.

DISEASES PRIMARILY DUE TO INSANITARY CONDITIONS AND HABITS

Some of these are an increasing problem due to the movement of people into overcrowded towns and cities.

Trachoma. Very high infection rates often leading to partial or total blindness. Antibiotics are effective.

Typhus. Both louse-borne and flea-borne varieties.

Typhoid Fever and intestinal infections especially prevalent in urban slums.

Hookworms. Infestation is high. Live in the small intestine, taking blood from the host. Common cause of anaemia and general debility. Easy to treat but re-infestation is usual.

Plague. Spread by fleas and still occurs, though speedy control is possible.

Relapsing Fever, both tick-borne and louse-borne, is another herd disease which sometimes assumes epidemic proportions.

Leprosy might come either in this or the next category. Although still a serious problem, it is not in fact easy to catch and usually occurs only after long contact with an infected person. Segregation and treatment may eventually eliminate this disease.

Bilharzia (see below) could also come either in this or the next group.

DISEASES WHOSE DISSEMINATION IS MAINLY DUE TO IGNORANCE

The Venereal Diseases, of which gonorrhoea is native to Africa and syphilis has been imported. High infection rates especially for the former (80 per cent in some areas).

Yaws is closely related to syphilis although not a venereal disease. It should probably come in the category of diseases associated with primitive rural life.

Bilharzia. Caused by a worm, the life cycle of which passes through man and certain species of water snail. Occurs in water and streams throughout tropical Africa. Debilitating, especially for the undernourished.

DIETARY DEFICIENCY DISEASES

Many of the diseases in the first three categories are made worse by the prevalent inadequate diets. Of the specific deficiency diseases, *Kwashiorkor* is the most important (see text), while *Tropical Ulcer* is also a serious problem in some areas.

2 Peoples and the Old Economic Order

RACES AND TRIBES

Most of those belonging to the broad racial division of mankind that the anthropologist calls 'Negroid' live in Africa; and, of those that do not, most have descended from the slaves sold out of Africa in the last 400 years. There is great variety within the Negroid group, but Africa south of the Sahara is essentially Negro in a way which is true of no other major part of the world.

Just where and when the Negro evolved we cannot say with any certainty. The origin of man in general and of the Negro in particular provides fascinating fields of speculation for the scholar and a confusing maze of conflicting theories for the layman. Most theories of man's origins have pictured a single centre of evolution from which men have moved outwards over thousands of years, later becoming differentiated into various racial types as a result of subsequent evolution in isolation from one another. Many have thought of South West Asia as the original home of mankind, but the archaeological discoveries of Leakey and others in east and south Africa suggest that the origins of man may lie in Africa rather than elsewhere. Which centre of origin is finally accepted depends on what is discovered in the future, and is unlikely to affect the generally accepted view that the area of differentiation of the Negro lies somewhere in Africa, probably in the west. The period during which the different human types became differentiated stretches back into remote pre-history, when it is likely that movement both into and out of the central and southern parts of the continent was much easier than today.

During the Pleistocene ice ages in Europe, the Sahara Desert did not exist. Instead, northern Africa had a climate and vegetation not unlike that of Western Europe now, and there was no

question of isolation from the rest of the Old World. It was only with the retreat northwards of the European ice sheets that the gradual drying out of the Sahara began, a process which probably first impeded human movement somewhere between 10,000 and 5,000 B.C. This period of Saharan desiccation coincided with the discovery of how to produce food by cultivation and the domestication of animals. These discoveries, particularly associated with the civilizations of ancient Egypt, Mesopotamia and the Indus valley, probably spread south of the Sahara during the second or third millennium B.C.

Today the Sahara is the great human divide between Negro Africa to the south and Caucasoid* to the north: between the Africa which has been isolated and the Africa which has been in sustained contact with Europe and Asia. There has been some mixing along the fringes in the west and some more extensive inter-mixture in the east, especially in the southern Sudan, Ethiopia, Somalia, Kenya and Uganda. Nevertheless, the Himalaya mountains[1] are the only other land barrier in the world across which there is such a contrast in 'racial' type.

'Racial' is placed in inverted commas because even in Africa the isolation of human groups has never been complete enough for long enough to permit of any racial 'purity' in the biological sense. As is the case elsewhere in the world, each group merges almost imperceptibly into its neighbours. Moreover, the exact knowledge required to make a proper classification of the races of Africa is not available, and we still have to rely on a classification which is based primarily on language and only to a lesser extent on physical features. Language is a poor criterion on which to rely, because languages spread farther and faster than the physical types which may have originated them. What follows should be regarded as the sort of generalization which may well have to be revised when the knowledge at our disposal has improved.

In the most remote, impenetrable and difficult areas live two groups of people whose physical distinctiveness and ways of life mark them out as peoples apart – the Pygmies of the Congo

* The anthropologists' term for the huge group of mankind which stretches from Western Europe south-eastwards to India. It is perhaps best described as the 'white/brown' race.

Basin and the Bushmen of the Kalahari Desert. Both have been pushed into their present homelands by the entry of materially more advanced peoples into the more favourable environments. Both are hunters and gatherers with a stone-age culture, and both are probably doomed to extinction or absorption like other

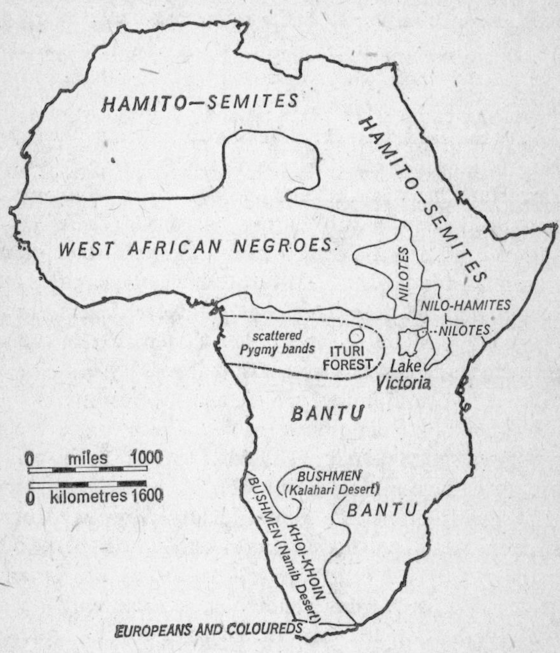

MAP 6. Major 'racial' groups in the eighteenth century. (Principal sources: J. H. Greenberg, *Studies in African Linguistic Classification*, 1955; I. Schapera, *The Khoisan Peoples of Southern Africa*, 1930).

primitive hunters before them. They are small in number (about 100,000 Pygmies and 50,000 Bushmen) but were undoubtedly more numerous and widespread in the past. Their present ways of life and small physique probably represent comparatively recent adaptations to the unfavourable environments into which they have retreated.[2]

Pygmies

The Pygmies are normally less than five feet tall, with arms very long in relation to their legs. Their skin is yellowish to dark brown and their bodies are covered with light downy hair. They have large prominent eyes, flat noses and are generally prognathous.* They live in small bands of about fifty individuals, hunt with bows and poisoned arrows and gather berries and roots.

They have come to rely on the surrounding agricultural tribes with whom they exchange game and other forest products for cultivated foods. 'Almost nowhere today do Pygmies occupy independent tracts of land. Rather they are attached in small bands to particular Negro chiefs or headmen in a relationship which, though reciprocal, is clearly dependent ...'.[3] Many of the Pygmies have been absorbed into these surrounding tribes and, where not absorbed, they have often adopted the agricultural life of their Negro neighbours. As far as is known, there is no distinct Pygmy language.

Bushmen

The Bushmen are a fascinating remnant group now confined to the Kalahari Desert and its margins but who were at one time or another found over the whole of Africa. We know this largely because of their skill as cave painters, for examples of their art have been found in the Sahara and in east Africa as well as in the south. That it is Bushmen art we are tolerably sure, not only on the grounds of style, but because of the depiction of people with one of the unique physical features of the Bushmen – an exaggerated inward curvature of the base of the spine and a fatty deposit on buttocks and thighs known as steatopygia.[4] Bushmen also use (together with the Khoi-Khoin or Hottentot) a distinctive type of language containing 'click' sounds, and traces of these, too, are still found among some east and south African tribes.[5]

The Bushmen are physically short (just over 5 feet), slender

* A term referring to the normal Negroid characteristic, whereby the face below the forehead, and especially the jaw, is projected forward.

in build, with yellow to brown skin and 'peppercorn' hair, the hair so tightly spiralled as to leave bare patches of skin showing between the 'peppercorns'. They have high cheek bones, flat noses, high and broad foreheads and pointed chins. Their eyes are narrow and almond-shaped but not Mongoloid, and they are not prognathous except where they have intermixed with Negroes. Materially, they are like the Pygmies in leading a simple hunting life with bows and poisoned arrows, although unlike the Pygmies they are completely dependent on their own resourcefulness in a particularly harsh environment. Their social organization is extremely simple, and it is as artists that they have made their unique cultural contribution.

Apart from these remnant groups, Africa south of the Sahara is the homeland of various Negro peoples. In the west, cut off by the Sahara to the north, the sea to the south and a broad belt of forest to the south-east, there seems to have been least human movement. Here are found people who show in clearest form the physical features characteristic of the Negro. In the east, on the other hand, there has clearly been much more movement. The more open country to the east of the Nile swamps and west of the Ethiopian Highlands provides a narrow, if difficult, route between north and south, and as a result, the peoples of east, central and southern Africa are much more variable in physical type.

West African Negroes

West African Negroes number more than 90 million people. They are usually over five and a half feet tall,[6] with dark brown to black skin, spiralled but not 'peppercorn' hair and broad flat noses. Their lips are usually fully everted and there is pronounced prognathism.

The West African Negroes are usually cultivators, with few cattle, and their true homeland is the savanna country away from the coast, although they have moved into the forest zone since about the beginning of the Christian era. Among the tribal groupings some of the better known are the Ashanti, centred on Kumasi in Ghana, and the Hausa, Yoruba and Ibo of Nigeria.

In social and political organization and in the practice of the

plastic arts West Africans were far advanced before the coming of Europeans to the coast. There were a number of highly organized states like Ashanti, Dahomey and the Yoruba kingdoms, with elaborate military organization and complex legal systems. The artistic achievements of Benin and the Yoruba areas are well known, but all through the area woodworking, textiles and craftsmanship in gold and silver were very highly developed.

Away from the west, most of central and southern Africa was probably occupied by Pygmy and Bushman hunters until after the beginning of the Christian era. Today it is occupied by various Negro groups, many of whom are significantly different in physical type from the Negroes of the west. There is great physical variety in both east and south Africa and signs in many areas of relatively recent and incomplete 'racial' mixture.

Hamites

The Hamites were at one time thought to be recent intruders into eastern and southern Africa and to have altered both the culture and physical type of the various Negro tribes that they found there. Recent archaeological research has now shown, however, that Caucasoid physical types have lived in east Africa for at least six or seven thousand years. The southward movement of these 'proto-Hamites'* into east Africa pre-dates by several thousand years the entry from the west of Bantu-speaking Negro cultivators.

These 'proto-Hamites' possibly account for the markedly Caucasoid physical features found in many of the tribes of east and southern Africa. Those groups amongst whom such features appear most common are pastoralists, until recently often forming a distinct caste ruling over their more numerous neighbours who live by cultivation. Examples of this dual cultural and social system are the Hima and Iru of Ankole in Uganda and the Tutsi and Hutu of Rwanda and Burundi. In the case of both the Hima and the Tutsi, narrow noses and faces make them physically as well as culturally distinct from their more Negroid neighbours. Many of the Hima and Tutsi feel a sense of superiority associated with this physical distinctiveness. Similar narrow

* So called by Leakey.

noses and faces can be observed in the ruling families of some other tribes, notably the Ganda in Uganda.

Nilo-Hamites and Nilotes

The Nilo-Hamites (about 2 million) and the Nilotes (about 10 million) are distinguished mainly on linguistic but partly also on cultural grounds. They live in parts of the southern Sudan, Kenya and northern Tanzania, and most of them are pastoralists, either nomadic or semi-nomadic. Some groups have adopted the more sedentary life of their Bantu neighbours, like the Nilo-Hamitic Nandi and Nilotic Luo of western Kenya. Many of the Nilotes, notably in the southern Sudan, are distinguished by their tall stature and extreme long-headedness.

Bantu

The Bantu, numbering more than 90 million people, are much the most important group of Negroes outside the West, covering almost the whole of Africa south of about 5 degrees north latitude. Like the other two groups they are separated on linguistic rather than racial grounds, although most are physically distinct from West Africans. In the east, and especially in the south, they are neither so dark nor so prognathous, but in the north and west the differences are less marked.

The Bantu have spread out into most of the lands they now occupy only within the last 2,000 years, and much of their occupancy is clearly more recent than that. There is some difference of opinion as to where they originated, but the linguistic evidence points to the area of the Cameroon highlands.[7] Bantu languages are so closely related that their present wide dispersal is likely to have been a relatively recent one. 'As little as 2,000 years ago Bantu may have been a single language spoken in an area much smaller than that occupied today by its descendants. . . .'[8] In any event they would have been unable to colonize the forest zone in such large numbers until they had acquired imported food plants (see pp. 50–53 below), and one writer[9] has placed their entry into the Congo rain forest as late as the seventeenth century.

Most of the eastern and southern Bantu combine cultivation (a woman's job) with cattle keeping (the prerogative of the men). Only where the existence of the tsetse fly prevents effective stock-rearing are cattle absent. In the west, a forest environment confines them to cultivation.

Khoi-Khoin (Hottentots)

Khoi-Khoin (Hottentots), numbering about 24,000 today, are physically and linguistically more akin to the Bushmen than other groups, but, being pastoralists, are culturally quite distinct. They are taller and more prognathous than Bushmen and are usually regarded as a cross between Bushmen and proto-Hamites, perhaps originating in the Great Lakes region and migrating southwards with their cattle to their present habitat. They helped to form the present Cape Coloured population, and the lighter skins of the southern Bantu may be accounted for by mixture with them and with the Bushmen.

SUBSISTENCE ECONOMIES

Types of Economy

With the exception of the pastoral Nilotes, Nilo-Hamites and Khoi-Khoin, and a few hunting and fishing peoples, the great majority of Africans – outside the industrial areas of southern Africa – are engaged in agriculture or in agriculture combined with pastoralism. Even where the reverence for cattle is strong pure pastoralism is possible only in the tsetse-free areas.

This agriculture is mainly *subsistence* or *semi-subsistence* farming, where the main emphasis is placed on production for use rather than sale of the staple food crops. It has been estimated that in all African countries outside the Republic of South Africa the majority of working Africans are still engaged in this traditional type of agriculture,[10] and that over the whole of tropical Africa between two thirds and three quarters of the total cultivated area is still used for subsistence production.[11] In traditional agriculture, cash crops may be entirely absent or they may be grown on a regular basis. Much of Uganda's

cotton crop, for example, is grown on small semi-subsistence holdings.

Traditional agriculture is practised in most areas by the system known as *shifting cultivation* or *bush following*. Both these terms

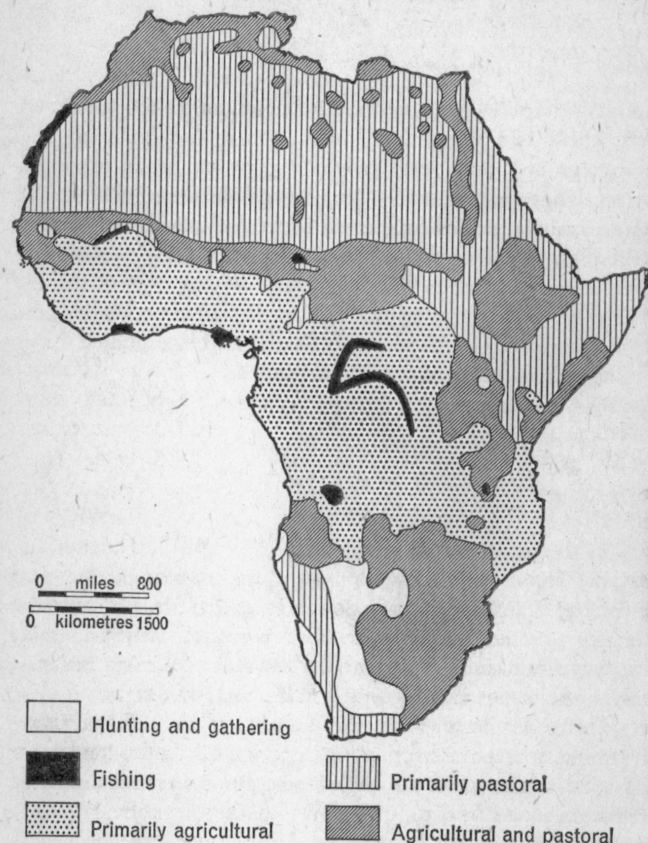

MAP 7. Distribution of types of subsistence economy. (Adapted from G. P. Murdock, *Africa: its Peoples and their Culture History*, 1959, p. 18)

have been criticized for their imprecision, as they cover a wide range of agricultural and land use systems, depending on the

nature of the soil. In almost all areas the land cannot sustain permanent cultivation without a fallow period to restore its fertility. The farmer (or the whole population) must therefore 'shift' to new land after a period of cultivation. The degree to which cultivation is 'shifting' will depend on the length of the fallowing period which is necessary.

At one extreme there are weak, leached soils which may require as much as twenty-five years for their regeneration after only two or three years of cultivation. At the other, there are soils which

will sustain permanent crops or repeated cultivation of annuals almost indefinitely, or which will regain their fertility after a rest period not longer than the period of cultivation if this is not unduly prolonged. On such soils, where climatic conditions are favourable, one finds systems of permanent cultivation and stable habitations – or, at least, an agriculture that is 'shifting' in a degree not much greater than the 'shift' from arable to ley on a well-managed English farm.[12]

Shifting cultivation has been described as 'the greatest obstacle not only to the immediate increase of agricultura production, but also to the conservation of the production potential of the future, in the form of soils and forests . . .'[13] An intensification of agriculture and the transition to a money economy is probably impossible under this system. However, Worthington argues that it 'is admirably suited to the soils and climate of Africa, provided the area of land is sufficiently large'.[14] Adequate fallowing does produce the necessary regeneration of the soil's fertility, and clearance in small patches reduces the chances of excessive soil erosion. A recent careful study of African agriculture[15] points out that it is not traditional agriculture that is responsible for declines in fertility but the unplanned introduction of cash crops coupled with increasing population pressure. Trouble begins when the pressure of population on the land reduces the periods of fallow and, as a consequence, fertility and soil structure begin to deteriorate.

This pressure on the land is a serious problem in many areas and is likely to increase as death rates drop with the improvement in health standards. Dudley Stamp has calculated for Nigeria how much land is required under traditional agriculture. For Southern Nigeria he says

> I worked on the basis that the average family was 3·6 persons and that each family required the produce from two acres of cultivation annually. If the land is allowed to rest seven years after one year of cultivation, each family would actually require sixteen acres of village land. This gives a population density of 144 per square mile as the maximum which can be supported. . . . In Northern Nigeria, with a lower and more precarious rainfall, I calculated . . . a density of eighty-eight per square mile, above which the land would be over-populated.[16]

These critical densities are already exceeded in these and many other areas.

Staple Food Crops

The staple crops grown in subsistence agriculture are those which give the maximum return of starchy food in a particular natural environment. Although the details vary,[17] tropical Africa can be divided into five main areas on the basis of the staple food types that are grown:

1. The forest areas west of the Bandama river in the Ivory Coast, where rice is the staple food crop. The area covers much of Guinea, Sierra Leone and Liberia.
2. The other forest areas of west and central Africa, where various tropical roots – cassava (manioc), yams, taro (cocoyams) and sweet potatoes are dominant.
3. The drier, more northerly areas of the west, where cereals are of major importance, especially millets and sorghums, with some subsidiary maize, rice, groundnuts and cow peas. Towards the southern edge of this region, in the relatively moist savanna areas, sweet potatoes are also grown.
4. The savanna country of the south and east, where maize is usually more important than millets and sorghums.
5. The Great Lakes area, where the plantain (green banana) forms the basis of the food supply.

Each crop tends to be dominant in the environment to which it is most suited and large areas of tropical Africa might remain uncultivated if any major group was missing. Millets and sorghums or maize are vital outside the forest areas; the tropical roots, plantains or rice are vital within them – and yet only the millets and sorghums are native to Africa. The others have all

been introduced into Africa since the beginning of the Christian era, and some are of much more recent date than that. Guinea yams east of the Ivory Coast and African rice to the west probably enabled man's conquest of the forest to begin, but these are not today's major staples in the forest areas.[18]

Thus, with the food plants native to Africa, the cultivating peoples could make effective penetration of none but the savanna country. Penetration of the equatorial and tropical rain forest, for which few suitable native plants were available, was only made easy with the introduction of the present food staples from outside the continent. It is not therefore surprising that the

TABLE 2
Major tropical African food plants by type and origin

	Africa (South of Sahara)	*S.E. Asia*	*America*
Cereals	*Millets & Sorghums*	*Rice*	*Maize*
	African rice		
Legumes	Cow pea		Haricot bean
			Lima bean
Tubers & roots	Earth pea	*Taro*	*Cassava*
	Guinea yam	*Yam*	Ground nut
			Sweet potato
Fruits & tree crops	Oil palm	*Plantain*	Pineapple
	Gourd	Banana	Pumpkin
	Watermelon	Coconut	Squash
	Tamarind	Mango	Tomato
			Avocado
			Papaya
Condiments	Kola		
	Coffee (Ethiopia)	Ginger	Cocoa
		Indian hemp	Red pepper
Indulgents		Sugar cane	Tobacco
		Pepper	
		Clove	

Crops which are dominant in the subsistence economy of particular areas are italicized.

SOURCE: Murdock, *Africa: its Peoples and their Culture History*, 1959.

earliest well organized African states were in the western Sudan* savanna country with millets and sorghums as the staple foods. The expansion of the Bantu into much of the southern and eastern parts of the continent did not take place until the arrival of exotic food plants from Asia.

These Asian food plants – yams, cocoyams and plantain in particular – were probably introduced to the east coast some time during and after the first century A.D., as this coast has had trading posts at least since then, posts established either by people of Indonesian origin, or Persians, or, since the seventh century, by Arabs.[19] The coastal traders were interested in the products of the interior, particularly slaves and ivory, and their expeditions into the hinterland were no doubt responsible for the initial westward diffusion of the Asian food plants. Once the Bantu had adopted them, they were able to displace the Pygmies and Bushmen from their former habitats and to reveal 'a capacity for explosive expansion paralleled, among all the other peoples of the world since the dawn of recorded history, only by the Arabs after Mohammed, the Chinese, and the European nations since the Discoveries . . .'[20]

Plants of American origin – notably maize and cassava – have clearly been introduced more recently, and were brought into West Africa by the Portuguese in the sixteenth century, to feed their slaves before and after shipment. Asian food plants may already by this time have reached the west coast from the east, enabling more effective colonization of the coastal forest zone from the inland empires.

The discovery of new foods does not necessarily presuppose the actual movement of large numbers of people at the same time. The knowledge may be passed on from village to village over the centuries until it has spread thousands of miles from its original source. Some such process has been outlined for the spread of cassava (manioc) in the Congo basin.

Late in the fifteenth century the Portuguese established relations with the King of the Congo at his capital some 200 miles inland from the mouth of the Congo, and for over a hundred years they maintained close relations with the Congolese. The rulers of the Kingdom

* The term normally used for the northern part of west Africa, and not to be confused with the state of the same name which covers most of the eastern Sudan.

of Congo apparently looked on the Europeans as representatives of a superior culture and were highly receptive to the innovations which they brought – so much so that by '1506 the King of Congo was the Christian ruler of a more or less Christian realm and recognized as such by the King of Portugal and by the Pope'. It would appear that at an early stage the Portuguese introduced manioc . . .[21]

Manioc, important in northern Angola as far back as the 1660s, had by 1885 been adopted by the Baluba Empire, a state covering most of what was formerly Katanga. It had taken just over 200 years for the knowledge of cassava cultivation to spread about 1,000 miles inland. If the Asian food plants from the east travelled at anything like this speed, they would have reached the Guinea coast before the arrival there of the Portuguese.

The races of Africa and their ways of life before the modern colonial period are thus fairly clearly discernible in broad outline. Before the Christian era there were established Negro civilizations in the west, Bushman and Pygmy hunters, together with Caucasoid 'proto-Hamites' in the east, south and centre of the continent. Then, during the following centuries, came the importation of alien food plants, bringing in their wake the explosive expansion of the Bantu. They mixed with the earlier stocks, so creating greater racial complexity than in the more negroid west. The east African plateau from Kenya southwards to the Republic of South Africa is relatively open country, so that once the edge of the continent has been breached, movement is comparatively easy. It is here that there is the linguistic and racial meeting point of most of the major groups, quite apart from the more recent introductions of Indian and European races and cultures. The term 'Bantu' alone covers great racial and cultural complexities.[22]

In spite of the emphasis which many Africans themselves place on cattle, their economies are – with a few exceptions – based on agriculture, an agriculture which is mainly of the traditional subsistence or semi-subsistence type and which is only now beginning to change. Yet side by side with this subsistence economy there exists today a completely different type of agricultural economy, one which is commercial in motivation and usually modern in technique. Often this commercial agri-

culture is run by Europeans and has certainly been introduced by them. The most extreme contrasts are to be found in the Republic of South Africa, with its highly successful European farming and the still primitive agricultural methods of the poor and overcrowded African reserves. The marriage of these two contrasting types of agricultural activity is one of Africa's important tasks for the immediate future. That it is a possible and potentially rewarding task can be seen in the remarkable agricultural progress of Kenya since independence.

Notes on Chapter 2

1. Which divide the Mongoloid peoples of north and east Asia from the Caucasoids to the south.
2. See R. Oliver and J. D. Fage, *A Short History of Africa*, Chap. 1, Penguin African Library, 1962.
3. G. P. Murdock, *Africa: its Peoples and their Culture History*, 1959, p. 49. But see C. Turnbull, *The Forest People*, 1961, for an idealized view of Pygmy life by an anthropologist who has lived amongst them.
4. These paintings also have remarkable similarities to the much earlier efforts of stone age man in Europe. See L. Adam, *Primitive Art*, 1954.
5. Notably the Sandawe of N. Tanganyika and the Xhosa and Zulu of South Africa.
6. Height is a poor yardstick, except in extreme cases, as it is very much affected by diet.
7. J. H. Greenberg, *Studies in African Linguistic Classification*, 1955. Revised as *The Languages of Africa*, 1963, Mouton & Co., The Hague.
8. Oliver and Fage, op. cit., p. 29.
9. W. O. Jones, *Manioc in Africa* – quoted in B. F. Johnston, *The Staple Food Economies of Western Tropical Africa*, 1958, p. 177.
10. J. C. de Wilde *et al.*, *Agricultural Development in Tropical Agriculture*, (2 vols.), 1967.
11. ibid., p. 21.
12. W. Allan, *The African Husbandman*, 1965, pp. 5–6. This is a detailed and readable account of African agriculture by an agricultural scientist of great experience and imagination. His work on carrying capacities and critical population densities is of major importance.
13. F.A.O. Staff, 'Shifting Cultivation', in *Tropical Agriculture*, July 1957, quoted in Johnston, op. cit., p. 266.

14. op. cit., p. 11.
15. W. Allan, op. cit.
16. L. D. Stamp, 'Land Utilization and Soil Erosion in Nigeria', in *Geographical Review*, 1938, pp. 32–45 and quoted in Stamp, *Africa*, p. 151.

17. SOME CHARACTERISTICS OF THE MAJOR CROPS

Millets and *Sorghums* need less water than any other cereals, and are unique in being able to stand periods of drought, after which they recover to recommence growth normally. They are also resistant to hot dry air, a fact of special importance in the west, with its periodic 'Harmattan' winds blowing off the Sahara. They are tolerant in their soil requirements and have a fairly short growing season. Low yields are the rule in the difficult conditions under which they are usually grown, but they have proved particularly suitable to savanna country.

Rice in the west is usually upland rice, which does not need flooded paddy fields for its cultivation. Swamp rice with its much higher yields but also more complicated techniques of cultivation has only been grown on a large scale in recent years, and in commercial as distinct from subsistence farming.

Maize needs more water than millets and sorghums, although it is partially drought-resistant, except at the 'tasselling' stage. It does not like dry heat, which probably explains why it is less important in the west than in the east and south. Its great advantage is that cultivation is much easier than for millets and sorghums, while the yields are higher in suitable conditions. On the other hand, owing to the wider spacing between the plants, it does encourage soil erosion.

Plantains need fairly rich soils, good drainage and an ample, well-distributed rainfall. In such favourable areas very high yields are possible. These areas occur on the volcanic soils of the Great Lakes region and in Cameroon.

Cassava (*Manioc*) is the most versatile of the tropical roots. Even on poor soils it will give high yields, a fact which probably explains its increased use on some of the exhausted soils

of Nigeria. It gives a certain yield even in soils unsuitable for all other crops and is very easy to cultivate.

Yams occur in several varieties, some of which can survive under drier conditions than cassava.

Taro (*Cocoyams*) have similar requirements to cassava, but can survive on less well-drained soils and in shade. With their large leaves they are often planted as a crop to protect young cocoa trees from the sun.

Sweet Potatoes need less moisture than the other tropical roots and will mature in 3–4 months.

For more details on crops see F. R. Irvine, *A Textbook of West African Agriculture, Soils and Crops*, 1953.

18. See J. D. Fage, 'Anthropology, Botany and the History of Africa', *Journal of African History*, 1961, II, 2, p. 299.
19. The Portuguese were also active along the east coast from the sixteenth century.
20. Murdock, op. cit., p. 271.
21. Johnston, op. cit., p. 177, quoting W. O. Jones.
22. But see Noni Jabavu, *Drawn in Colour*, 1960, for a vivid and highly individual account of two different Bantu societies.

3 Europe Goes into Africa

EARLY CONTACTS

The period of colonial rule in Africa has been relatively short. For over 400 years the coastline had been known and increasingly dominated by the European powers, but the interior remained unknown and unwanted until the end of the nineteenth century. This was not only because of the inhospitable coasts and the difficulty of penetrating beyond them, but also because what was considered useful to Europeans could be had without bothering to penetrate far inland. Small coastal forts were all that were required to provide bases for ships on their way to the known riches of the East and to act as depots for the plunder of the interior. Gold, ivory and, above all, slaves could be brought to the European forts by native middlemen.

The Portuguese were the earliest coastal explorers and the first of Africa's European colonists. Creeping southwards along the west coast, the ships of Prince Henry the Navigator had already reached south of the Gambia by the time of his death in 1460, and they had brought back with them their first cargoes of gold and slaves. By 1484, Diego Cão had reached the mouth of the Congo, and before the century was out Vasco da Gama's discovery of the Cape route to India made possible the rapid expansion of a Portuguese empire in the Indian Ocean.

North of Cape Delgado, on the east coast, the Portuguese found the Arabs already entrenched. From their coastal bases the Arabs were able to obtain precisely the same African commodities that interested the Portuguese; like them, they failed to penetrate into the interior until well into the nineteenth century.

The Portuguese monopoly of west Africa and of the slave trade lasted until the end of the sixteenth century, when it was broken by a number of west European countries. French, English, Danes and Prussians all established rival forts and

entered the trade, but it was the Dutch who really ousted the Portuguese from their dominating position, both in west Africa and in the Indian Ocean. In the west the Portuguese were driven from all their strongholds except on the coast of what is now Portuguese Guinea and Angola. In the east they were similarly driven southwards by the Arabs to what is now Moçambique.

The slave trade reached its height in the eighteenth century, and the Dutch and English were the chief carriers. Various estimates of the number taken out of Africa have been made, but it was certainly not less than ten million and may well have been more. One careful calculation gives twelve million for the Atlantic trade alone, while the Arab trade in the east probably involved even greater numbers,[1] covering as it did a much longer period of time.* What has horrified subsequent generations produced no moral qualm among those involved, and it took thirty-one years from the date of the first unsuccessful motion against the slave trade in the British House of Commons to the final abolition of slavery for Britain itself in 1807. The long period for which the trade flourished has been called

> an appalling illustration of the strength which vested interests can acquire, and of the extent to which familiarity with crime can deaden the conscience and blur discrimination between plain right and wrong. The first British African Company was formed for honest trade, and ships sent to the Gambia refused to buy negro women offered for sale by a negro on the ground that Englishmen did not buy and sell 'any that had our own shapes' . . . but slave trading became the mainstay of West African commerce. Thenceforward there was no question as to the morality of the traffic; the great issue was whether it should be monopolized by a company or thrown open to competition. . . . Slave labour had become a matter of course . . .[2]

The slave trade was, however, more than a crime against humanity and a challenge to the conscience of Europe. Many of its effects were to endure much longer than the trade itself, influencing the life of Africa today as an inevitable legacy from the past. Of these effects, there are three of outstanding importance.

Firstly, there are the effects arising from the forcible mass movement of millions of Negroes to the Americas, where they

*It started before the Christian era.

have increased in numbers and extended their range of distribution since the days of slavery. They have become integrated in varying degrees with the societies in which they now live, but, because of the consciousness of colour that those with lighter skins have forced upon them, they have never completely lost their sense of identity with their African origins. For some, like those who supported Marcus Garvey in the 1920s, this sense has implied an eventual return to Africa; for others it has meant participating in African emancipation from the outside by encouraging the 'Pan-Africanist' movement; while for the majority it has at least entailed an emotional affinity with all other Negroes. In the U.S.A. the term 'Afro-American' is preferred to Negro, and in all instances, their sense of identity has given them a heightened interest in the welfare of Africa – an interest which the political leaders of the U.S.A. and the countries of the West Indies (and increasingly of South America) can afford to ignore only at their peril.

Secondly, the slave trade perpetuated the isolation of the interior long after normal trade and empire building would have opened it up. The interior of Africa became the preserve of the slave traders and their agents, a locked-up land in which there was neither room nor opportunity for the teacher, scientist or missionary. The slavers could obtain all they wanted from their bases on the coast. It was in their interests, as Livingstone saw so clearly, to keep Africa an 'unknown' continent, just as the only way to kill the slave trade was to open up the interior and provide both facilities and security for honest trade.[3]

Thirdly, slave trading helped to destroy the native civilizations of the interior. It did so in two ways: by maintaining a state of perpetual inter-tribal warfare, as tribe raided tribe to secure captives to sell to the slavers, and by the depopulation of whole areas over a long period of time. It thus helped to reinforce the European belief that nothing good could come out of Africa except what was put into it by Europeans. It helped to perpetuate the myth that the Negro was inherently inferior, so that as late as 1928 a distinguished Englishman could write:

> The Negroes of Tropical Africa specialized in their isolation and stagnated in utter savagery. They may even have been drifting away from the human standard back towards the brute when migratory

impulses drew the Caucasian, the world's redeemer, to enter Tropical Africa ... mingle his blood with that of the pristine negroes and raise the mental status of these dark-skinned, woolly-haired, prognathous retrograded men ...[4]

Echoes of this attitude were still to be heard in the British House of Lords in 1961:

> As I went to it [the United Nations] I really got the impression that there was a convention of nigger minstrels going on ... the Commonwealth is a piebald set-up, and a piebald set-up is a poor form of organization that will never last.[5]

The one exception to the general European lack of interest in the interior was that of the Dutch in South Africa. The first settlement was established in 1652, when Jan Van Riebeeck was commissioned to build a fort and re-victualling station at the Cape of Good Hope for ships of the Dutch East India Company. Although the Company did not intend to establish a colony, it soon realized that the most economical way of obtaining fresh food was to import Europeans to farm the land. In 1687 a policy of active colonization was initiated, and by 1706 the colony consisted of 1,641 people, who by this time had spread far out into the hinterland in search of more land and freedom from the restrictions of authority. By 1779 the settlers had their first clash with westward-moving Bantu tribes in the region of the present Ciskei reserve.*

To the Afrikaner, ever since, the black African has remained the enemy on the other side of the frontier, however absurd this has become geographically.

Apart from the movement inland of the Cape Dutch, Africa remained an unknown land to Europeans until the great explorations of the nineteenth century: explorations which were to draw the main outlines of the interior and to provide that foundation of geographical knowledge on which the political partition of the continent was to be based.

EUROPE TAKES OVER

The earliest explorations and the earliest political divisions took place in the west. Under the auspices of the African Association

* See Chapter 12 below.

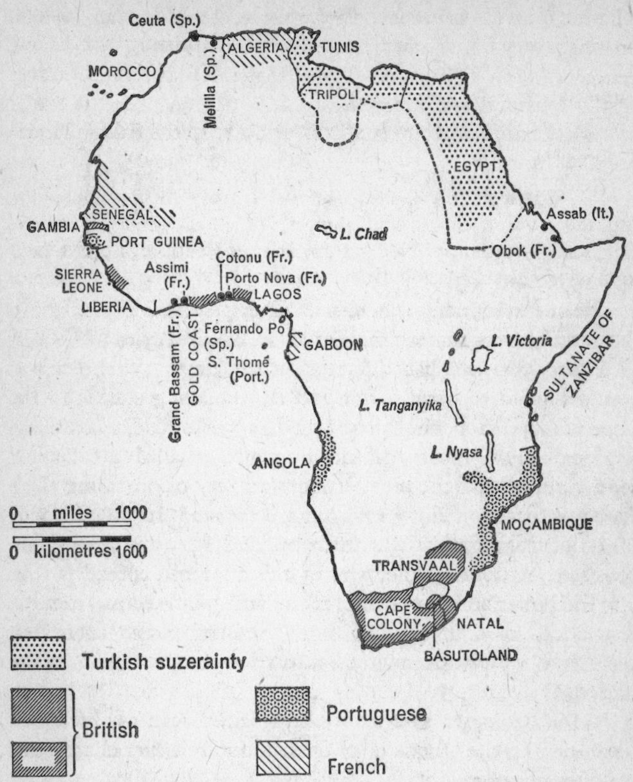

MAP 8. The pattern of alien rule, 1880. (From J. D. Fage, *An Atlas of African History*, 1958, p. 46)

of London, Mungo Park visited the Gambia river in 1795 and made his way overland to the river Niger. Prior to this journey it was believed that the Gambia and Senegal rivers were the outlets for a westward-flowing Niger. He returned to the Niger ten years later with the intention of following its course to the sea, but he was unsuccessful and died believing that the Niger and the Congo shared the same estuary. It was not until the 1830 journey of the Lander brothers that the outlet of the Niger was finally discovered.

Political involvement in west Africa by the European powers remained very small until the last two decades of the nineteenth century. Intervention in the hinterland at this time was usually reluctant and designed for the protection of the trading, missionary and humanitarian interests already established there.

The British navy had been the chief instrument in the suppression of the slave trade, and to this end bases had been acquired* in order to drive out the slavers, encourage legitimate commerce and facilitate the advance of 'civilization'. There was, however, little desire to acquire an empire.

One of the unforeseen consequences of this peaceful European intrusion into the affairs of west Africa was a further breakdown of tribal authority, especially on the coast, and a consequent increase in unrest and warfare. In the Gold Coast, for example, Britain was drawn into wars with the Ashanti in 1863 and 1864 – wars which brought trade to a standstill. Such seemed the hopelessness of the situation that a Select Committee of the House of Commons was led to recommend a withdrawal from all existing bases in west Africa apart from Sierra Leone.[6]

A withdrawal of this nature was easier to recommend than to achieve. However reluctant the original involvement may have been, Britain's commitments tended rather to increase. Far from withdrawing from the Gold Coast, a further Ashanti attack in 1873, threatening as it did the existing British bases, led to an extension of British influence over the coastal Fanti and, in 1874, to the establishment of the Gold Coast as a Crown Colony. Even if it had wanted to, Britain dared not give up its west African responsibilities for fear of offending humanitarian opinion.[7]

The French, too, were reluctant to engage in colonial expansion at this time. Except for the colonial government in Senegal, they were content to have the same sort of indirect influence through missionaries and traders that Britain sought to exercise. In Senegal, which appears to have developed 'a local expansive power of its own',[8] the urge to empire took hold early, and the advance inland to the upper Niger began in 1876. When the French government finally did take an interest in a west African empire (after 1882), the systematic eastward penetration from

*Sierra Leone in 1808, Gambia in 1816 and the Gold Coast in 1821.

Senegal over the previous few years gave them an important advantage over their rivals.

The west had been explored, but the whole of the central and eastern parts of the continent remained unknown when David Livingstone started on his first journey in 1841. Moving northwards from the Cape of Good Hope he discovered Lake Ngami in Bechuanaland eight years later, mapped out the upper Zambezi in the following year, and arrived at Luanda on the coast of Angola in 1854. In another two years he had made the first coast-to-coast crossing of the continent, discovered the Victoria Falls, and mapped out the whole of the Zambezi river. Previously an agent of the London Missionary Society, he embarked on his second journey in 1858 as a government servant with consular authority, exploring during six more years the Shire river and the Shire highlands of Nyasaland (now Malawi).

Meanwhile, farther north, Burton and Speke moving west from Zanzibar had discovered Lake Tanganyika in 1858. Their journey, together with the later ventures of Speke and Grant and those of Sir Samuel Baker, had at last found the source of the Nile by the time Livingstone returned in 1864. It still remained to determine the source of the Congo and whether or not Lake Tanganyika was linked with the Nile.

Livingstone started on his final journey in 1866, exploring in what is now Zambia. He died on the shores of Lake Tanganyika in 1871, and it was left to Stanley to solve the final river problem of Africa. In 1877 he succeeded in passing down the Lualaba and Congo rivers to the sea. The main physical features of the continent were now known to Europe and the stage was set for the 'scramble' by the European powers for pieces of African territory, a scramble which in less than twenty years was to transform the political map and trace today's international boundaries.

'The scramble for Africa' rates an important place in most history books of the period, but much less is known about it than is popularly supposed. Up to the 1880s none of the European powers had shown much interest in taking on more responsibilities in tropical Africa. They had been content to protect the interests of private citizens already established there while holding back from more formal commitments to empire-building.

Now the political map of Africa was to be re-drawn and almost the whole of the continent placed under European rule. What was it that set off this partition?

The motives of statesmen were certainly mixed, and the Leninist 'search for markets'[9] is rather too simple an explanation to be more than part of the truth. In fact there was never enough investment in tropical Africa to provide for the creation there of the vast consumer markets which may be expected to arise in the future. This does not imply that a search for markets was not one of the motives behind the scramble, but there was much more to it than that. Raw material needs in Europe were also important, and so were philanthropy, missionary endeavour, strategic pressures – like the protection of Britain's sea-route to India – and the search for political prestige *in Europe itself*.

Europe was ruled by a 'balance of power', in which one of the major tests of prestige and influence was the loss or gain of territory. What had happened in the past to Poland and more recently to Alsace was now to occur in Africa. European diplomats began to use stretches of African soil, known to them only as coloured areas on inaccurate maps, as bargaining counters in the struggle for power in Europe.[10]

A careful analysis of cabinet and other government papers[11] has shown that – for Britain at least – the overriding motive in acquiring a new empire in Africa was a concern for the security of the routes to the old empire in India. This meant a keen interest in the east coast, where there were thought to be few opportunities for trade, and much less interest in the west, where the chief commercial opportunities were known to be. It meant, above all, that stability in Egypt was the first priority in Africa for Britain's late Victorian statesmen.

The British occupation of Egypt in 1882 was undertaken to protect the Suez Canal and to prevent its control by a hostile government. It was not meant to be the start of a scramble for territory elsewhere in the continent, but this it turned out to be. The occupation of Egypt alienated France from Britain and gave Germany an opportunity to exploit their differences to her own advantage.

By altering the European balance the occupation of Egypt inflated the importance of trivial disputes in tropical Africa and set off a

scramble. Quickened by the hope of prising the British out of Cairo, the French drove deep into West Africa, while the Germans took their opportunity to irrupt into East and West Africa, in an attempt to extort British support in Europe. Hence the taking of Egypt ended the age when private merchants and consuls, acting through African authorities, could dominate the east and west coasts by influence alone. Once the French and German governments for diplomatic purposes began to back their own traders against British firms, trade turned into a business of territorial claims.[12]

There were plenty of traders and adventurers already active in Africa to whom the European governments could now turn to help them in their own power struggles. One of these was Stanley who, in 1878, returned to the Congo under the auspices of the newly formed International Association of the Congo, a body international only in name and in reality under the control of its President, Leopold, King of the Belgians, acting in his personal capacity.

Both France and Portugal were also active at the mouth of the Congo, and the Association soon found itself in dispute with these countries over territorial claims. To settle the disputes between these rivals, Bismarck of Germany called the Berlin Africa Conference of 1884–5.

The Conference produced the Berlin Act, an instrument signed by all the major European powers. It aimed 'to foster the development of trade and civilization, to further the moral and material well-being of the native populations', and to abolish slavery in the area. It provided for the establishment of a free trade area and for the neutralization of the whole of central Africa in the event of a European war. It also attempted to regulate the process of further territorial acquisitions by the powers.

Immediately following the Berlin Conference the area allotted to the International Association was organized as the 'Congo Free State' with Leopold as King – again in his personal capacity. It became a classic example of misrule and exploitation. Leopold seems to have run a kind of rake's progress through the Congo. Concessions were given to companies which went into partnership with the government. The native population was deprived of its land, driven to forced labour and treated with horrible cruelty.[13] The atrocity charges were fully authenticated and led

the British Foreign Secretary to declare that the state had 'morally forfeited every right to international recognition'.[14] The worst features of misrule ceased after Leopold's death, and the State was taken over as a Belgian colony in 1908.

The rest of the partition tale is best told on the accompanying maps and was virtually completed in the ten years following on the Berlin Conference. In the east, British and Italian Somaliland, Uganda, Kenya and German East Africa all appeared. In the west, the essentials of present-day boundaries were established while, in the south, Rhodes's advance northwards with his British South Africa Company had frustrated the claims of Portugal to all the lands between Angola and Moçambique. German–British affairs in Africa were settled by the Anglo-German Treaty in 1890, which, among other provisions, exchanged Heligoland for British control over Zanzibar.

THE DRAWING OF FRONTIERS

The newly independent African states are no more free of the frontiers of the 'scramble' than they were in their colonial past. Some, like Ghana, Guinea and Mali, have made abortive attempts to escape from the old boundaries. Only British and Italian Somaliland, the Republic of Cameroun and the Southern Cameroons and Tanganyika and Zanzibar (Tanzania) have so far united in practice across colonial frontiers. The first (and only) mutually agreed alteration of an existing frontier between two independent African states took place between Mali and Mauritania in February 1963.[15] This conservatism over frontiers is not surprising, for the administrations and other vested interests which have developed within the artificially created boundaries are no less strong than tribal and economic interests which pull across them.

Not only was the partition undertaken solely in the interests of Europe, but the advance into the hinterland was inevitably made from existing bases on the coast. Thus in west Africa most of the colonies came to have a north–south orientation quite at variance with the human and physical divisions, which run east–west. Again, in the Rhodesias the advance had to take place from the existing Cape Colony, avoiding the Portuguese-held

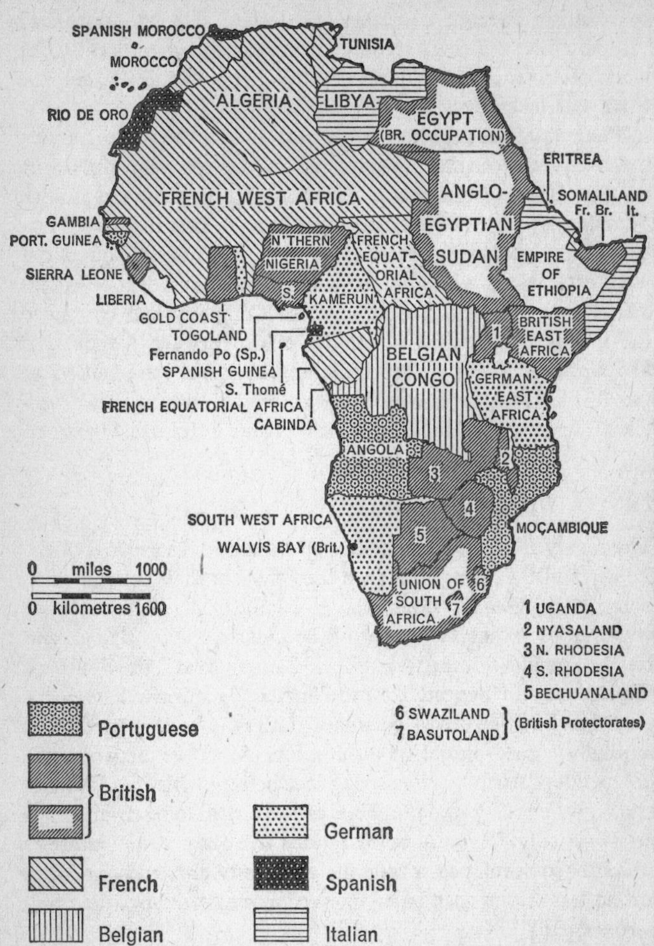

MAP 9. The pattern of alien rule, 1914. (From J. D. Fage, *An Atlas of African History*, 1958, p. 48)

coasts and the Boer Republics, and moving across the most open type of terrain.

British colonization was conducted either by chartered companies, as in Southern Rhodesia, or by officials who took the

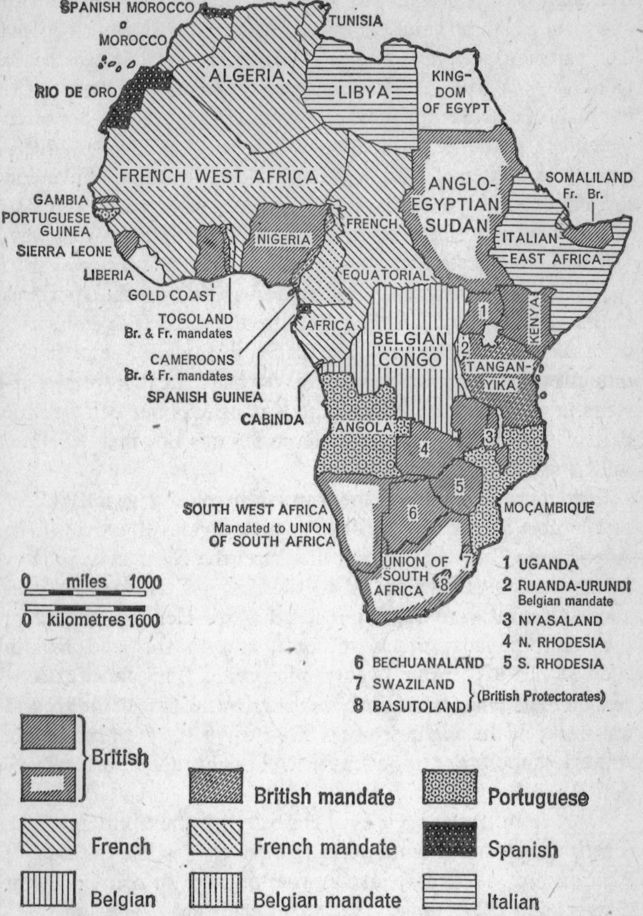

MAP 10. The pattern of alien rule, 1939. (From J.D. Fage, *An Atlas of African History*, 1958, p. 49)

existing native authorities under their protection, as in Northern Rhodesia and Uganda. The two methods of taking control have had profoundly different effects on subsequent development. In the Rhodesias, for example, the south was conquered by a

chartered company and was given internal self-government in 1923: the north was not conquered by the British South Africa Company and was governed as a Protectorate until it became, in October 1964, the independent state of Zambia. Whatever the methods of colonization, control by one country or another often depended on the local initiative of individual officials or adventurers – a matter of who arrived first or who could prove and maintain effective occupation. The curious southward extension of Katanga into Northern Rhodesia was promoted in this way.

The Congo State had already given a minerals concession to the Katanga Company, whose representative on the spot was Captain Carstairs, a Canadian. Both he and the British emissaries from the south wished to stake claims in the area, since it was thought to be very rich in mineral deposits. In the event, Carstairs arrived first (1891) and the Katanga copper belt became part of the Congo; though the frontier was not finally settled until 1930.

Even more curious in shape than southern Katanga is the sliver of Namibia (South West Africa) which divides Botswana from Angola – the Caprivi Strip, so called after the German negotiator at the discussions which led to the Anglo-German Treaty of 1890. General von Caprivi insisted upon German access to the Zambezi from the west coast, and to this end Britain allowed her a corridor twenty miles wide. This fanciful concession to mapmakers in Europe who knew nothing of the ground was never of the slightest use to Germany[16] but is of increasing strategic importance to South Africa in fighting guerilla infiltration.

Apart from this geographical curiosity are the frontiers which constitute economic and political obstacles to the welfare of Africans today. We may take as examples the British Colony of Gambia and the boundary between Ghana and Togoland.

Gambia is a 'Caprivi Strip' all on its own. In shape a worm-like intrusion into the state of Senegal, it is 300 miles long and in places only 13 miles wide, with a population of just over a quarter of a million. It lies astride the navigable section of the Gambia river, which is itself one of the finest stretches of navigable water in the whole of Africa. Ocean-going ships can reach 150 miles up river from Bathurst, and but for the existence of

political boundaries the Gambia would undoubtedly be the main outlet for the trade of both Senegal and Mali.

British control of the Gambia meant that the French had to make alternative transport arrangements, and the Gambia has been used only for local traffic. As the Senegal river is much less navigable, the main line of communication has been the railway from Kayes to Dakar, built in 1923, an expensive undertaking which also required the costly construction of a large artificial harbour at Dakar. This would all have been unnecessary if the more convenient Bathurst could have been utilized.

Not only has the separation of Gambia from its hinterland led to the wasteful construction of railway and port facilities in Senegal and the neglect of the Gambia itself, but the development of part of Senegal has also been retarded. Gambia separated the southern province of Casamance from the rest of the country, and because of the difficulties of communication economic development there has been slow. Only in 1947 did Britain agree to give the French direct transport facilities between the two parts of Senegal.

The Ghana–Togo boundary divides the Ewe people into two more or less equal parts. Numbering rather more than one million in all, about half now live in south-east Ghana and the rest in southern Togo. Prior to independence repeated representations about their division were made by Ewe leaders, both at the League of Nations and at the U.N.* The Ewe tended until recently to prefer British to French rule, and there was at one time some movement of population from the French to the English side of the frontier. Their agitation for unity received support from nationalist leaders in the Gold Coast, but since the independence of Togo the Ewe there have shown no significant interest in joining independent Ghana.

Whatever the difficulties that the existing frontiers create, it is clear that they will be slow to change now independence has been achieved. The establishment of an independent government creates a vested interest in the perpetuation of the existing political unit – or at any rate in the prevention of its absorption by its neighbour.[16]

* Most of the territory involved was under League mandate or, later, U.N. Trusteeship.

As has been seen, Europe surrounded and exploited Africa long before the interior was seized or even explored. When the interior was finally opened up, it was from a mixture of motives – some benevolent and some selfish – but all of them assumed the supremacy of Europe and the benefits which would result from European rule.

This is not the place to draw up a balance sheet on colonialism, but it has been shown that the hurried and largely haphazard nature of the scramble for Africa did little good from the outset to some of the areas involved. Lasting frontiers were established which cut across both ethnic and economic interests, and which to many of those drawing them were simply lines on inadequate and little understood maps.

Subsequent developments have brought remarkable changes during the last sixty years. The Eurocentric view of Africa has gradually given way to a recognition that the continent matters for itself and that the interests of the inhabitants should ultimately determine policy. It remains true, however, that even the most revolutionary changes have up to now taken place within the geographical framework, the main political outlines of which were established during the scramble at the end of the nineteenth century.

Notes on Chapter 3

1. R. Coupland, *East Africa and its Invaders*, 1938, p. 35.
2. C. P. Lucas, *The Partition of Africa*, 1922, pp. 50–51 and Coupland, op. cit., Chap. 1.
3. Lucas, op. cit., p. 53.
4. Sir H. H. Johnston, *The Opening Up of Africa*, 1928, p. 25.
5. Lord Brabazon of Tara, 23 March 1961, *Hansard*, Vol. 229, No. 57, Cols. 1277–9.
6. R. Robinson, J. Gallagher and A. Denny, *Africa and the Victorians*, 1961, p. 30.
7. ibid., p. 33.
8. ibid., p. 163.
9. See J. A. Hobson, *Imperialism*, 1902, and V. I. Lenin, *Imperialism, the Highest Stage of Capitalism*, 1916.
10. C. E. Carrington, 'Frontiers in Africa', in *International Affairs*, Vol. 36, No. 4, October 1960, p. 431.
11. Robinson, Gallagher and Denny, op. cit.
12. ibid., p. 162.
13. Lucas, op. cit., p. 85.
14. Sir Ed. Grey, quoted ibid., p. 85.
15. I. Wm. Zartman, 'A Disputed Frontier Settled', in *Africa Report*, August 1963. There have also been some other settlements of frontier disputes but no other transfers of territory have taken place.
16. For a more detailed treatment of these and other frontier problems see R. J. Harrison Church, *Modern Colonization*, 1951, Chap. 7, and I. Wm. Zartman, 'The Politics of Boundaries in North and West Africa', in *Journal of Modern African Studies*, August 1965. This is an excellent study of one part of Africa. It also contains a full bibliography on African frontier problems.

    See also J. D. Hargreaves, *Prelude to the Partition of West*

Africa, 1963, and C. G. Widstrand (ed.), *African Boundary Problems*, 1969.

On slavery, see also Nordholt, *The People that Walk in Darkness*, 1960, and Basil Davidson, *Black Mother*, 1960.

4 Natural Resources and Economic Development

The improvement of living standards and the elimination of poverty are aims which are shared by all the countries of Africa whatever their political complexion. The belief in the possibility of achieving these aims is, however, something new, and the will to do something about it is even newer. It is easy to forget that most African governments only began comprehensive economic development with the end of the Second World War. As a result there is a tremendous amount of knowledge still to be gained about the continent's natural wealth and even more about the best ways of developing it.

Outside South Africa, the economic potential of the continent remains largely underdeveloped, with only isolated pockets here and there of intensive economic activity, both in commercial agriculture and in industry. There is little manufacturing, although major growing points exist in cities like Lagos, Nairobi or Salisbury. Most of the economic development has been concentrated on those crops (like cocoa in Ghana) or minerals (like copper in Zambia) unobtainable in Europe or obtainable more cheaply in Africa. In each instance the markets lie outside Africa, and development has been undertaken in response to an overseas demand. Another type of development has taken place where favourable climates have attracted European settlers (as in Kenya and Rhodesia). Because of their European contacts these settlers have succeeded in attracting a disproportionate amount of investment capital, a fact which has helped to maintain the uneven character of development in the continent as a whole.

African poverty is real enough. Even allowing for considerable margins of error, the figures in Table 3 show an average so low that it is difficult for the West European or North American to imagine it.

TABLE 3

National income per head in selected countries (1964 estimates in pounds)

United Kingdom	838·2
Republic of South Africa	178·7
Ghana	89·5
Kenya	30·4
Uganda	27·5
Tanzania*	22·8

SOURCE: *U.N. Statistical Yearbook 1965*, pp. 80–84 and 544–5.

*Former Tanganyika only.

POPULATION

The people of any country are important economically both as consumers and as producers. Fears of over-population, which have in recent years led to a greater emphasis on their role as consumers, should not make us forget that as producers people are the first essential economic resource which any country must have. There are about 255 million people in tropical and southern Africa, and although in a few areas population density is high, the continent as a whole is still very sparsely inhabited; over large areas the density falls below twenty persons to the square kilometre (Map 11). This low density is certainly a reflection of the real present poverty, whatever may be the potential wealth in terms of population and production.

Most of the patches of denser than average population seem to be connected with development beyond a purely subsistence economy. Those based on industry are not included on the map and are all in South Africa, notably on the Witwatersrand and near Cape Town, Port Elizabeth and Durban.[1] The other higher densities (shown on the map) are almost entirely agricultural.

In the east there are five main areas: the coast from Mombasa to Dar-es-Salaam, the Lake Victoria region, the highland areas of Kenya and of Tanzania and south Malawi. Although these areas differ greatly in their climates, soils, crops, racial complexity and social systems, most have moved beyond a system of subsistence agriculture, and a considerable proportion of effort is

devoted to producing crops for sale.* Similarly in the west the two discontinuous belts of higher density are based partly on cash crops – groundnuts and market gardening in the northern areas, and palm oil and cocoa in the southern.[2]

*The chief exceptions to this generalization are the highlands of Rwanda and Burundi where unusual soil fertility and a favourable climate for agriculture support very high densities.

TABLE 4

Population (1967 estimates)

	Population (in 1000s)	Area (in sq. kms.)	Density (per sq. km.)
West Africa (English-speaking)			
Nigeria	61,450	923,768	67
Ghana	8,139	238,537	34
Sierra Leone	2,439	71,740	34
Gambia	343	11,295	30
Liberia	1,110	111,369	10
West Africa (French-speaking)			
Guinea	3,702	245,857	15
Mali	4,657	1,240,000	4
Niger	3,546	1,267,000	3
Dahomey	2,505	112,622	22
Upper Volta	5,054	274,200	18
Ivory Coast	4,010	322,463	12
Senegal	3,670	196,192	19
Mauritania	1,100	1,030,700	1
Togo	1,724	56,000	31
*U.D.E.A.C.**			
Cameroun	5,470	475,422	12
Chad	3,410	1,284,000	3
Central African Republic	1,459	622,984	2
Gabon	473	267,667	2
Congo (Brazzaville)	860	342,000	3
Eastern Africa			
Kenya	9,928	582,644	17
Uganda	7,934	236,036	34

*Union Douanière et Économique de l'Afrique Centrale. (Founded in 1966 on the basis of former French Equatorial Africa plus Cameroun. Chad withdrew in 1968.)

TABLE 4 – *contd*

	Population (in 1000s)	Area (in sq. kms.)	Density (per sq. km.)
Tanzania	12,173	939,701	13*
Rwanda	3,306	26,338	126
Burundi	3,340	27,834	120
Ethiopia	23,667	1,221,900	19
Somalia	2,660	637,657	4
Sudan	14,355	2,505,813	6
Former Spanish and Portuguese Territories and Congo (Kinshasa)			
Congo (Kinshasa)	16,354	2,345,409	7
Angola	5,293	1,246,700	4
Moçambique	7,124	783,030	9
Sâo Tomé and Príncipe	58	964	62
Portuguese Guinea	528	36,125	15
Equatorial Guinea			
Fernando Po, Annobon	76	2,034	37
Rio Muni	201	26,017	8
Central Africa (English-speaking)			
Zambia	3,945	752,614	5
Rhodesia	4,530	389,361	11
Malawi	4,130	117,800	35
Southern Africa			
Republic of South Africa	18,733	1,221,037	15
Namibia	594	824,292	1
Lesotho	885	30,355	29
Botswana	593	600,372	1
Swaziland	385	17,363	22
Total population	254,913		

*Zanzibar and Pemba, 134 to the sq. km.

The economic development of Africa has been even more patchy and haphazard than the population distribution indicates; there are great contrasts in the rate of economic growth from territory to territory and even within individual countries. Existing economic activity is carried on in a series of economic 'islands', often separated by great spaces devoted almost entirely to subsistence agriculture. These islands can usually be classified under three headings: the coastal areas, where access to overseas

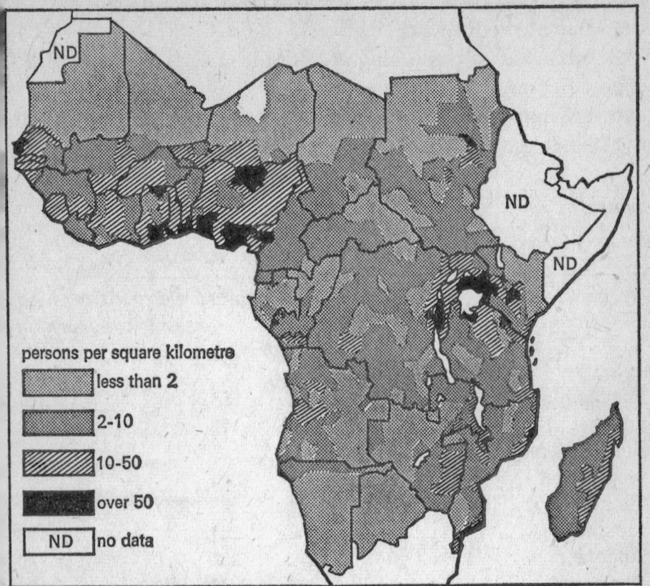

MAP 11. Population density

Figures for some non-African countries for comparison

	Population (in 1000s)	*Area (in sq. kms.)*	*Density (per sq. km)*
U.S.	199,118	9,363,387	21
India	511,125	3,263,373	156
France	49,866	547,026	91
Belgium	9,581	30,507	314
U.K.	55,068	244,030	226

SOURCE: *U.N. Statistical Yearbook 1968*, pp. 78–80.

markets is easy and of long standing; the highland areas, where superior climates and soils have attracted European farmers; and the mining centres. 'These distinct and separate economic islands combined make up perhaps 4 per cent of the area of

tropical Africa, but probably account for at least 85 per cent of the value of produce entering world trade.'[3]

Another way of comparing present incomes is to examine the export figures, for African countries live by the export of food and raw materials in so far as their inhabitants are engaged in the money economy at all.

TABLE 5

*Value of exports and imports 1967**

	Imports	*Exports*	*Exports per head of population*
	(Millions of U.S. dollars)		*(U.S. dollars)*
Zambia	429	658	167
Liberia	125	153	138
São Tomé and Príncipe	5	8	138
Ivory Coast	263	325	81
Mauritania	23	69(1966)	63
Rhodesia	262	264	58
Angola	275	238	45
Ghana	307	278	34
Sierra Leone	90	70	29
U.D.E.A.C.†	404	346	29
Congo (Kinshasa)	265	443	27
East African Community‡	596	572	19
Togo	45	32	19
Moçambique	199	122	17
Guinea	53	58 (1966)	16
Malawi	80	56	14
Nigeria	626	677	11
Niger	46	26	7
Dahomey	48	15	6
Portuguese Guinea	16	3	5
Mali	52	17	4
Upper Volta	36	18	4

*Only countries for which comparable figures are available are included.

†Union Douanière et Économique de l'Afrique Centrale (Congo (Brazzaville), Central African Republic, Chad, Gabon and Cameroun. Formed 1966: Chad left the Union in 1968).

‡Kenya, Uganda and former Tanganyika only.

SOURCE: *U.N. Statistical Yearbook 1968*, pp. 394–5.

Partly for reasons of prestige and partly from sound economic motives African countries would like to reduce their dependence on the export of primary products. Industry has been seen as necessary both to satisfy national pride and for economic well-being. If a country relies solely on the export of primary products it is inevitably at the mercy of economic conditions in the advanced industrial countries. A slight fall in industrial production in Europe, for example, can lead to a catastrophic fall in the export income of an underdeveloped country. Nevertheless, the development of manufacturing industry is likely to be a slow process and there has been a welcome change of emphasis in some countries towards rural development rather than the unattainable dramatic industrial growth which was envisaged in earlier years.

Private capital is always more readily available for the expansion of mining, and public investment will have to continue to concern itself above all with improving basic services like transport and power supplies ('infrastructure' in economic jargon), and with improving productivity and the quality of life in rural areas. Certainly the export of primary products either from the land or from the mines will provide the main source of revenue for some time to come. In some countries – especially those of east Africa – tourism is an increasingly important industry.

AGRICULTURE – THE PRESENT POSITION

The land devoted to producing crops for sale – both in the internal and external markets – varies from one quarter to one third of the total cultivated area of tropical Africa, but even where the proportion of cash-crop production is high, it is all too often concentrated on one or two crops of high profitability. Not enough has been done to develop other lines as an insurance against a fall in prices. Dependence on groundnuts in Senegal and Gambia and cocoa in Ghana means prosperity while prices are high but may lead to disaster with a fall in overseas demand. This dependence on one or two crops is probably inevitable as long as development is left uncoordinated and uncontrolled, because such crops are immediately profitable, while those increases in production which have occurred in recent years have

followed the classic African pattern in being largely haphazard and in response to overseas demand.

Coffee production in 1964 was over twice the level of that in 1950, with expansion particularly rapid in former French West Africa, Cameroun, Congo (Kinshasa) and east Africa. Tea production has nearly trebled since 1950, with Kenya the leading African producer, and there have been similar spectacular increases in rubber production, especially in Nigeria. Sisal shows an increased output – 40 per cent for Africa as a whole in the decade 1953–63 – but there have been price falls over the last few years. Synthetic alternatives to sisal are now becoming competitive and this may have a serious effect on large producers like Tanzania and Kenya.[4]

These increases are impressive and economically important to the countries concerned, but all of them are for crops which are either luxuries or industrial raw materials, and there has been much less effort and investment put into the production of food, which is still largely the function of subsistence agriculture. However, Africa is beginning to participate in the 'Green Revolution';[5] the use of improved seeds and farming methods have turned Kenya into a maize exporter, while in the Ivory Coast rice production more than doubled in the nineteen sixties.[6] These successes, together with the earlier achievements in the export crops, lend support to the view that the islands of commercial farming could be extended and that 'there is sound reason for the belief that trans-Saharan Africa could become much more productive agriculturally than hitherto'.[7]

MINING AND POWER SUPPLIES

It is clear that Africa is rich in both minerals and power supplies, although there is much exploratory work still to be done. The deficiency in coal[8] is offset by a large hydro-electric potential – about 28 per cent of the world total – and for a large number of minerals Africa is already a leading producer. With few exceptions, production has increased rapidly since pre-war days, in some cases spectacularly so. Oil has only recently become important, with the beginnings of production in Gabon in 1957, Nigeria (former Eastern Region) in 1958 and Angola in 1959.

However, production is already almost ten times as great in the N. African countries (Algeria, Libya and the United Arab Republic).

As with any generalizations made on a continental scale, the figures in Table 6 conceal not only differing growth rates for different countries, but also the fact that mineral production is unevenly spread throughout the continent. Out of a total of thirty-six countries in tropical and southern Africa, twelve are major producers with another six as significant minor producers.[9] (See Map 12.)

By value about half of the total mineral output is in South Africa, with approximately another third in Zambia and the Congo (Kinshasa). There are, however, a few important minerals

TABLE 6

Production of some important minerals (excluding N. Africa)

	Level of production 1938	*Level of production 1967*
	(Thousands of metric tons except where otherwise stated)	
Bauxite	0·4	2,316
Chrome	171	808
Coal		53,052
Copper	399	1,159
Gold (kilograms)	454,696	993,273
Iron	681	26,657
Lead	32	124
Manganese	415	1,904
Petroleum (crude)	5·3	19,619
Tin (metric tons)	20,961	21,739
Zinc	20	210

SOURCE: *U.N. Statistical Yearbook 1957* and *1968*.

not found in any quantity in these three leading mining countries, notably bauxite, tin and oil. Like much of commercial farming, mining has been developed for the overseas market, and – because of the greater capital required for development –

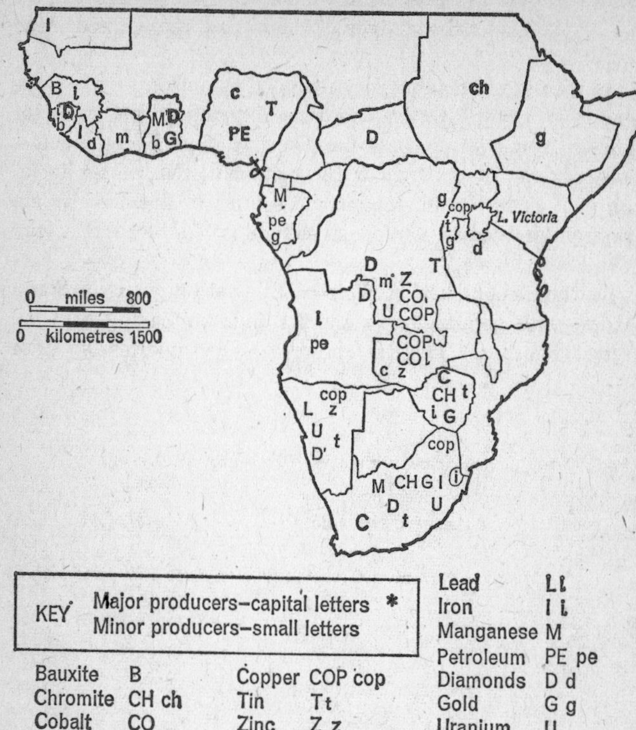

MAP 12. Main mineral producing areas

has remained in the hands of a few large enterprises, most of them controlled by foreign financial interests. The great exception is the Oppenheimer empire in the Republic of South Africa controlling De Beers (diamonds) and Anglo-American (gold-mining), as well as much else.*

TRANSPORT

In a continent where vast distances still separate the highly productive economic 'islands', and where, as a result, transport is both costly and inefficient, it is of the greatest importance both

*See note 9, p. 97 for definitions.

to reduce costs and to increase efficiency. In the various national development plans so far initiated, between one third and two thirds of all expenditure up to 1959 had gone into the building of roads, railways, and harbour installations,[10] and there is no doubt that much more similar expenditure is still required. This is, however, one of the easiest purposes for which prestige investment is likely to be forthcoming on political grounds, as in the case of the Tanzam railway (to be financed by China) and road building in east Africa by West Germany.

The haphazard and uncoordinated development of transport in the past has contributed to the haphazard development of the continent as a whole. Once established, a transport route may attract other forms of investment through the access to markets which it provides. In Senegal the major part of groundnut production is strung out along the railway, as in Gambia it lines the river. Increase the transport facilities, and more farmers would be able to turn from subsistence to commercial farming. In Tanganyika, on the other hand, one of the factors which led to the choice of sites for the ill-fated Groundnut Scheme was the existence of a railway, and it was not until later that the same sites were found to be physically and climatically unsuitable for groundnut production. This particular railway is a good example of those built for political and strategic rather than for economic reasons.

The period of greatest activity in railway building – 1890 to 1914 – coincided with the consolidation of European power in the areas 'allotted' to the various metropolitan countries. Outside of South Africa, the railway map is still dominated by unconnected tracks extending into the existing political units and built largely for strategic reasons. The line from Mombasa to Kisumu was built between 1896 and 1901 at the expense of the British Government in order to consolidate British power in Uganda. Later, white settlement was encouraged in the Kenya highlands partly to bring more business to a costly railway. Of course, railways were never as important strategically as they seemed at the time, and the most grandiose strategic dream of all – the Cape to Cairo railway – never materialized. This was conceived as the lifeline of the British Empire in Africa and was to link together all the British territories *en route*. The first link was

built in 1897 to Bulawayo by Rhodes's British South Africa Company, skirting the independent Transvaal and passing through recently protected Bechuanaland. By 1905 it had reached Northern Rhodesia and, in 1910, the Copper Belt. By then the Imperial Route seemed less urgent. Already in the 1890s

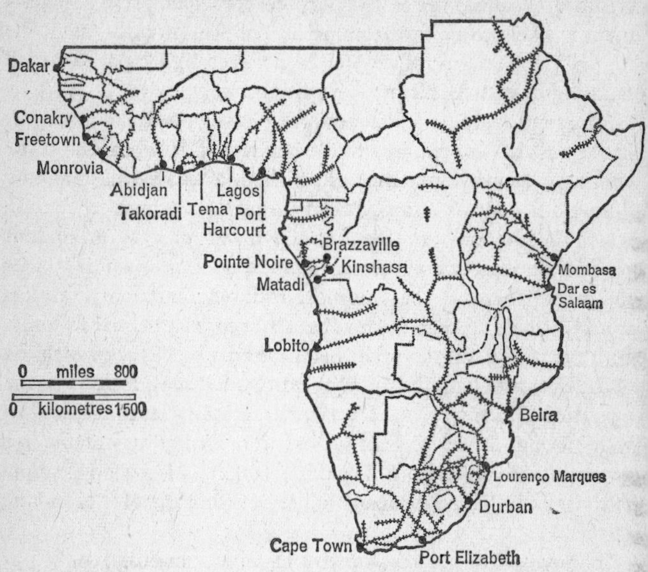

MAP 13. Railways and major ports

Rhodesia had been linked with Beira, as a way to the sea for a vigorous and growing settler community. When a further advance was made in the inter-war years, it was to the Congo as an outlet for the newly developed copper mines. Strategic considerations were beginning to give way to economic ones, although – as with political boundaries – their legacy is still with us.

Two other important facts emerge from the railway map: the existence of a network of lines only in South Africa and the very few international links which yet exist. The South African network is a result of earlier and more intensive economic development; the international links provide outlets for Zambia, Rhodesia and the Congo. Each of these areas is dependent on

the Portuguese territories for its access to the sea. Even with encouragement from official Belgian sources to use the all-Congo route, it was still cheaper to use the Portuguese railways and ports for more than two thirds of the Katanga trade. Now, with Zambia increasingly anxious to reduce dependence on unfriendly neighbours a politico-strategic railway is once more under construction – the Tanzam link to the Tanzanian coast.

Since the end of the Second World War, roads rather than railways have been built to link the existing lines and to open new areas. Most of the railway construction has been undertaken for the export of minerals – iron in Liberia, copper in Uganda and the new line from Rhodesia to Lourenço Marques built to relieve the congested route to Beira. Apart from these new lines, and some significant extensions in Sudan, the main effort has been put into roads, and most authorities are agreed that this is the most economical method of transport development at present.[11]

No map of roads is included, because the road 'system' of tropical Africa exists more in the minds of cartographers than as a dependable network on the ground. Bold red lines representing main roads are likely to turn out narrow rutted tracks – adequate for light traffic when it is dry but frequently impassable after heavy rain. The time and material employed in coping with inadequate roads represents an increasingly heavy loss to countries embarking on ambitious development programmes.

DEVELOPMENT FOR THE FUTURE

Economic development up to the standard of European countries lies in the far distant future. Even the growth rates predicted in the various national development plans seem optimistic when one remembers the conditions necessary before they can be met. Nothing less than a social revolution will be required in many areas before modern production methods can be achieved, as well as a large amount of capital investment, much of it from the developed countries. Private capital from the advanced industrial countries is unlikely to be attracted to a low-interest area while there remain more lucrative fields of investment at home. It therefore falls to governments and international lending agencies

to make up the deficit, though the inadequate 1 per cent target is far from being achieved.*

Only countries with easily exploitable minerals have been able to attract large quantities of private investment, and the uneven distribution of these minerals has been a major cause of the patchy and uneven development to which we have referred.

Before the Second World War, investment – both public and private – was heavily concentrated on South Africa, which up to 1936 received nearly half the total of Africa's capital inflow. Table 7 shows the distribution of investment in the rest of Africa south of the Sahara.

TABLE 7
Tropical Africa

Estimated investment of capital per head of population up to 1936

	£
Rhodesias	38·4
Belgian Congo	13·0
Angola and Moçambique	*9·8
British East Africa	8·1
British West Africa	4·8
French Colonies	3·3

SOURCE: Lord Hailey, *African Survey*, 1956, p. 1321.

*Much of this was for port and railway development to serve the Rhodesias and the Belgian Congo.

The situation was revolutionized after the war by the decisions of the metropolitan governments to initiate long-term development plans. The British Colonial Development and Welfare Act of 1945 made money available for the individual British territories. The French F.I.D.E.S.† of 1947 aimed at comprehensive planning for France and her dependencies as a single unit, and Belgium initiated a ten-year plan for the Congo in 1950. The

*Set in the Pearson Report, *Partners in Development*, 1969.

†Fonds d'Investissement et de Développement Économique et Social des Territoires d'Outre-Mer. Since 1958, F.A.C. – Fonds d'Aide et de Co-operation.

Portuguese have launched a series of small-scale development plans since 1938.

French investment, in particular, has increased dramatically since the Second World War. Between 1954 and 1958, public investment in the French Community territories amounted to £14·3 per head of population. For the British territories (excluding the Rhodesias) the comparable figure was £4·1 per head.

Investing Scarce Capital

In investing scarce capital, a choice has often to be made between the large, potentially highly productive but also costly schemes, and smaller less spectacular projects. These smaller projects may be relatively less productive in potential, but frequently cost less and bring quicker returns to the participants. One such scheme was the agrarian reform in central Kenya, much of which was promoted as a by-product of security needs during and after the Mau Mau Emergency.

The former 'Kikuyu Reserve' is a fertile, well-watered area in the Kenya Highlands. During this century over-population, over-stocking and primitive farming methods had all helped to bring about a deterioration of soil and an increase in discontent. The causes of discontent were as much political as economic but the economic problems were real enough.[12] In the Fort Hall and Kiambu districts there are population densities of about 1,000 to the square mile, an extremely high figure for a rural area. As well as soil erosion, low productivity resulted from the excessive fragmentation of holdings.

Prior to the Emergency, the Kikuyu lived in scattered settlements. Part of the security measures during the Mau Mau rebellion was the forcible 'villagization' of the Kikuyu and the consolidation of fragmented holdings.* In addition, under the Swynnerton Plan of 1954, £10m. was invested in the improvement of farming methods and the introduction of cash crops. As a result the face of the land has been transformed. Now there are not only villages where none existed before, but rows of crops and trees planted along the contour, cultivated terraces, and

*There was much justified opposition to the *enforcement* of the improvements outlined below.

farmers who are enjoying a cash income for the first time in their lives. The density of population is at last being matched by the intensive cultivation of available land.

Elspeth Huxley has described the working of the scheme:

> A typical planned small-holding of from ten to twenty acres will have cash crops like coffee, pyrethrum, and pineapples,* together with some grazing for livestock, fodder, and food crops. Most of the small-holders have adopted the officially approved farm plan or lay-out.
>
> Farm lay-outs are not compulsory, but in the Central Province, where everyone was moved into a village during the Emergency and needed permission to move out while it lasted (October 1952 to January 1960), farmers were not normally able to settle until they had accepted the principle of these simple plans. . . .
>
> A farm lay-out will suggest to you where to put your homestead and sheds, to site your paddocks on the contour, the best place for a firewood plantation . . . where to grow your food. The basic principle is that all arable land should spend about half its life under grass, generally on a seven- or eight-year cycle.[13]

There is much to criticize in Kenya land reform – compulsion, an early lack of attention to marketing, and too few jobs for the landless. When individual ownership of land has replaced tribal ownership, the owner-occupier may become richer in the process, but his poor relations find it increasingly difficult to live off his production and end up by helping to swell the army of unemployed in the towns. The improvements are, however, small enough to be well-understood, and their results have not been too remote in time. Other examples of successful small-scale land improvements are the *paysannat* schemes of French Equatorial Africa, which aim at settling peasant farmers on land newly cleared for them by government agency. One such scheme that has worked well is the Mandingou *paysannat* in the Niari valley of ex-French Congo.

> A score or so of villages, comprising several hundred families, have been established on good soils, and in close proximity to both the road and railroad linking Brazzaville and Pointe Noire. Each village is surrounded by, or adjacent to, a number of fields that the administering authority has had mechanically cleared and ploughed. These

* After much experimentation, tea is now the dominant crop in the higher areas.

fields may be anything up to 100 or 150 acres in size. Each family with two working adults has been given approximately seven acres of arable land. ... This land they sow and cultivate by hand as directed by their supervisors. The crops grown are the peanut ... sweet potato, urena (a fibre that has all the uses of hemp and some others besides), manioc, maize, and a variety of green crops for ploughing under; they are grown according to a strict four-year rotation. In addition to the arable land each family has been given a pig and about half an acre of land for coffee.[14]

Large-scale Development

The first of the spectacular improvement plans to reach the news headlines in the post-war world was the *Groundnut Scheme* in Tanganyika. In conception, it was an attempt to have the best of all possible worlds; to combine the pre-war notion of Africa as a supplier of Europe's food and raw materials with the post-war notion of development for the sake of African advancement. Twenty-five million pounds was allotted to the original scheme in 1948, and it was aimed to produce over 500,000 tons of groundnuts annually within five to six years.

Speed on a large scale was deemed to be essential, although it proved to be the chief cause of failure. It was thought necessary to increase the supply of fat to food-rationed Britain, and the heavy political opposition to the scheme demanded a spectacular political success. Three sites were selected after only a hurried examination of soils, climate, terrain and communications, and it was not really surprising that the scheme turned out a costly failure, a gamble that did not come off. Drought, bush clearance, difficulties of soil cultivation, and the blunting of mechanical tools were some of the many natural difficulties encountered, and by 1951 the scheme had to be reduced to the pilot project that it ought to have been in the first place. This has done invaluable research work on the problems of commercial farming in the three areas.[15] A glance at Map 23 illustrates one of the difficulties which could have been avoided if the information had been obtained before the scheme started. Not one of the three chosen areas lies within the region where there is even a fair prospect of receiving thirty inches of rainfall each year. The *East African Royal Commission Report* (1955), from which the

map is adapted, notes that the areas where there is little prospect of obtaining thirty inches (areas in which Kongwa and Nachingwea are situated), 'are those where the reliability of a thirty-inch rainfall is too poor to allow arable farming to be normally possible'. The areas where there is a poor or a fair prospect of obtaining thirty inches (in which Urambo is situated) 'are those where the indifferent reliability of a thirty-inch rainfall produces marginal conditions of a kind which do not necessarily preclude arable farming, but which place distinct limitations upon the likelihood of its success . . .'[16]

The Volta River Project in Ghana

A number of factors have combined to make the large-scale development of river valleys appear the key to rapid economic growth in a number of African countries. The plateau edge which led to isolation in the past can provide the key to future development of cheap hydro-electric power, as has already been achieved at Owen Falls in Uganda and at Kariba in Rhodesia. Concurrently with the provision of power can go essential water control and conservation. There is, too, the experience and enthusiasm of American and other foreign engineers who have helped in similar large-scale development at home and whose ideas have been influential in the drawing up of preliminary plans. Finally, the spectacular nature of many of the schemes finds favour with governments for political reasons, either because they may provide quick popularity at home or because they may attract more investment capital from abroad.

The Volta River project was first mooted in 1924, and various plans had been drawn up from time to time – the last in 1959 – to provide for the construction of a large dam across the Volta River at Akosombo. The resulting lake was enormous, stretching for some 300 miles across half the length of Ghana and influencing the whole of the surrounding area.

Initially the plan had four main purposes – the provision of an aluminium smelter near the dam site for which power was not then available, the further development of bauxite mining, the improvement of transport facilities, and the irrigation of part of the Accra plains. A new port has been made at Tema, and work

was completed on the dam and hydro-electric station in September 1965. The aluminium smelter* was completed in 1967. The project is both expensive and spectacular, economically and politically. It will enable Ghana not only to maintain but to increase her lead in living standards, as well as helping her to support her claim to political leadership among African states. However, the capital cost has been high. Over £70m. for Volta River Authority responsibilities (mainly the dam and power facilities), more than £12m. for resettlement of 78,000 people displaced by the new lake – and over half of this £82m. has been raised within Ghana itself. Such expenditure has contributed in no small measure to Ghana's short-term economic problems.

The Kariba Dam

The highly publicized Kariba Dam was begun in 1954 and finished in June 1959. Lake Kariba – 175 miles long – has been full since early 1962. Development of the ancillary power stations and transmission lines is due for completion in 1972. It is, of course, a great achievement, both for the engineers and workmen who built it and for the government which was able to finance it. It will undoubtedly bring great benefits to Zambia and Rhodesia in the future – cheap power for the further development of mining and manufacturing, water conservation for irrigation and other purposes and fishing to provide much-needed protein foods. But these are still future benefits, and the dam at present is still only a wonderful piece of window-dressing to catch the attention of the outside world, both politicians and investors. It has not yet improved the lives of many individuals, and like other large schemes it has been immensely costly in scarce capital. It may help to attract further investment, but will certainly postpone some of the immediate benefits which might have accrued from smaller and less expensive schemes. For the former Federal Government† precariously placed at home, an improvement in the lives of the people it was supposed to serve might have been thought more important than impressing the outside world.

*V.A.L.C.O. (Volta Aluminium Co. Ltd), a consortium of two American companies, is responsible for the aluminium smelter.

†Of Rhodesia and Nyasaland.

Before Kariba was begun 'a decision had to be taken between the two great schemes for hydro-electric power, Kariba and Kafue. Kariba was the bigger, the more expensive and the slower . . . (but) . . . by the time Kafue was finished more power would be needed'. Kafue was also a wholly Northern Rhodesian scheme, and Kariba is on the border between Zambia and Rhodesia. 'So sharp was the controversy between these two bodies of opinion that little was heard in Rhodesia of a third view, that a much higher priority, perhaps at the expense of these schemes, should have been given to plans for putting money directly into the pockets of African farmers by irrigation and cooperative marketing.'[17] Investment will not be attracted to a government unless it is seen to be economically progressive; nor will it be attracted to one with serious political unrest on its hands. Kariba may yet be a costly casualty in the conflict between Rhodesia and Zambia.

This brief consideration of the three schemes outlined here points a number of lessons for the future. Of these the first and most important is the need for adequate information and for the preliminary research necessary to acquire it. If the development really cannot wait on careful preliminary planning, then the small scheme which is also a pilot project runs less danger of being a spectacular failure – either economic or political – than the large venture. In any event, experiment will be required as well as planning, and we may need to challenge some fundamental assumptions in the process. For example, it was thought until quite recently that the use of large tsetse-infested areas to produce animal protein necessarily required the elimination of fly and the improvement of animal husbandry. Now it has been shown that

> over much of Africa's wild land a given area will produce a larger weight of animal protein – meat – and might be made to yield a larger financial profit, if cropped for game – that is to say by killing surplus wild animals for meat or hides – than through the medium of cattle or any domestic stock.[18]

Even a wholly African government has to carry the people with it; proper attention to adult education in general and agricultural extension in particular is one way of doing this.

Another lesson for the future is the need for the right political conditions. In Ghana, careful publicity and an African government produced a climate of opinion favourable to the success of the Volta project. It is, in addition, a scheme which has received much careful preparatory planning. Kariba on the other hand, while a technical success, has been a political success only abroad and among the Rhodesian Europeans, not among the Africans. Future benefits seem to them less important than present needs.[19]

Finally, we must not forget that the large schemes may themselves help to accentuate the uneven economic development of the continent which we have already noted. Large schemes need a great deal of money to implement, and much of this will have to come from commercial sources. Countries which have readily exploitable minerals or confident European minorities may well find it easier to attract scarce capital than those whose obvious natural resources are less. In east Africa, for example, the contrast between development on Mt Kilimanjaro or in Buganda and such areas as the West Nile district of Uganda is greater than the contrast between farming areas of Western Europe and the former regions. Again, within individual territories unbalanced economies need to be balanced. Ghana needs the industrial development which the Volta project will bring, but Ghana's neighbours need to be brought up to her standards. Rhodesia and Zambia desperately need investment in agriculture as well as in an industry which has already outpaced the subsistence economy. 'Attention needs to be given to the underdeveloped areas within the underdeveloped whole.'[20]

Given that we find the right questions to ask and that the right answers are not too long in coming, then there is still time for Africa to develop both profitably and peacefully. As we noted in Chapter 1, there is still space in Africa, space to grow, to develop and to increase the richness of human choice. The population explosion is only just beginning there. By the time it really gets under way the answers should have been found.

Notes on Chapter 4

1. See Chapter 12 below.
2. For a full discussion of population distribution see Wm. Brass *et al.*, *The Demography of Tropical Africa*, 1968.
3. W. A. Hance, *African Economic Development*, p. 5.
4. *U.N. Economic Bulletin for Africa*, Vol. V, January 1965, pp. 9–10 and 20–23. Sisal accounts for one third of Tanzania's foreign exchange earnings.
5. L. R. Brown, *Seeds of Change: The Green Revolution and Development in the 70s*, 1970.
6. ibid., p. 5.
7. J. Phillips, *Agriculture and Ecology in Africa: a Study of Actual and Potential Development South of the Sahara*, 1959, p. 376.
8. Known coal reserves are mainly confined to the Republic of South Africa and Southern Rhodesia. The whole continent contains less than 1 per cent of probable world coal reserves. The production of coal per annum:

South Africa	49,300,000 tons
Southern Rhodesia	2,739,000 tons
Zambia	399,000 tons
Moçambique	282,000 tons
Nigeria	203,000 tons
Congo (Kinshasa)	127,000 tons

SOURCE: *U.N. Statistical Yearbook, 1968*, pp. 185–6.

9. Definitions of 'major' and 'significant minor' as follows:

	Major (1000s of metric tons except where stated otherwise)	*Significant minor*
Bauxite	1,500+	300+
Chrome	200+	10+
Coal	2,000+	200+
Copper	300+	15+
Diamonds (metric carats)	1m.+	0·5m.+
Gold (kgs.)	10,000+	700+
Iron	4,000+	400+
Lead	100+	20+
Manganese	200+	50+
Petroleum	10,000+	500+
Tin (tons)	5,000+	500+
Zinc	100+	20+

10. United Africa Company *Statistical & Economic Review.* Special issue on transport in Africa, March 1961, p. 4.
11. United Africa Co., op. cit., and W. A. Hance, op. cit., pp. 116–17.
12. See C. Rosberg and J. Nottingham, *The Myth of Mau Mau,* 1967.
13. E. Huxley, *A New Earth,* 1960, pp. 212–13.
14. G. H. T. Kimble, *Tropical Africa,* 1960, Vol. 1, p. 178.
15. The scheme is more fully considered in Phillips, op. cit., Chap. 32.
16. *East Africa Royal Commission 1953–5 Report,* 1955 (Cmd. 9477), p. 254.
17. Philip Mason, *Year of Decision,* 1960, p. 57.
18. Sir Julian Huxley, 'Cropping the Wild Protein', *Observer,* 20 November 1960, p. 23.
19. *Monckton Commission Report,* p. 135.
20. Hance, op. cit., p. 286.

At the time of independence many African countries had reports on their economic development prepared by the International Bank for Reconstruction and Development. Examples are *The Economic Development of Uganda* (1961) and *The Economic Development of Kenya* (1962). Compre-

hensive government development plans were prepared and published after consideration of these reports and have since been regularly revised.

There is a large and growing literature on African economic development. W. A. Hance, *The Geography of Modern Africa*, 1964, provides a useful survey of the economic geography of the continent. Nicolas de Kun, *The Mineral Resources of Africa*, 1965, is a mammoth compendium of information by a mining engineer. J. Sheffield (ed.), *Education, Employment and Rural Development*, 1967 (East African Publishing House for University College, Nairobi) examines the interrelationships of a number of development problems in Kenya, which have wider implications for Africa as a whole. G. Hunter, *Modernizing Peasant Societies*, 1969, makes a brave attempt to synthesize experience and development problems in both Asia and Africa.

See also John C. de Wilde *et al.*, *Agricultural Development in Tropical Africa*, 1968, for detailed consideration of a number of agricultural development schemes, and B. W. Hodder, *Economic Development in the Tropics*, 1968, for a geographer's clear summary and reference source to the literature in this field. W. M. Warren and N. Rubin (eds.), *Dams in Africa*, 1968, is also useful.

Part 2 Regional Studies

West Africa

West Africa is the home of some of the finest achievements of the early Negro civilizations. It was also able to advance most rapidly towards political independence in the mid twentieth century. Partly this is because the climate has not encouraged much white settlement, so that educational and economic advance for Africans has not been impeded by the presence of an alien and privileged settler community. Here, too, there has been specialization on a number of tropical crops like cocoa and the oil palm. This, unlike the exploitation of minerals, has brought wealth to thousands of small cultivators rather than to huge industrial companies.

West Africa has, however, shared with the rest of Africa the political fragmentation imposed by Europeans, and boundaries were settled without regard for the physical and human divisions of the area.

It comprises the states of former French West Africa,* the former mandated territory of Togoland, Portuguese Guinea, Liberia, Gambia, Sierra Leone, Ghana and Nigeria. With about 104 million people, it contains nearly half the population of tropical Africa. Also included in this study are Equatorial Guinea (formerly Spanish) and the transitional thinly peopled zone of former French Equatorial Africa (Chad, Central African Republic, Congo (Brazzaville) and Gabon), and Cameroun, containing another 12 million people speaking mainly Bantu languages.

The great contrast in west Africa is between the southern forest zone and the northern savanna lands. The forest has here been the area of difficulty – difficult to penetrate and difficult to settle without the importation of alien food crops. In the

*Mauritania, Mali, Niger, Senegal, Guinea, Ivory Coast, Dahomey and Upper Volta.

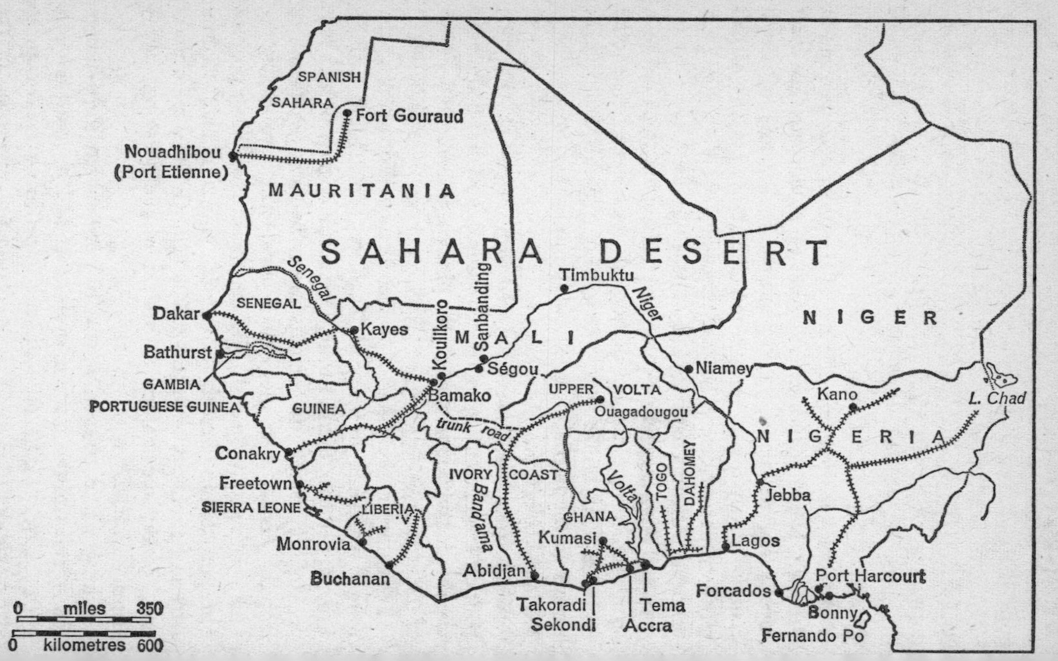

MAP 14. West Africa

savanna lands, on the other hand, movement was easy and native food plants were available to sustain a relatively large population. Eastwards from Senegal, through Mali and Upper Volta to Northern Nigeria, lies a belt of relatively high population density in which a number of important states developed during the medieval period, of which Ghana from the ninth to the eleventh centuries and Mali in the fourteenth century were the most important.

Not only did these savanna states have the advantages of easy movement and adequate native food plants, but, from the first century A.D., they were in regular and sustained contact with Mediterranean civilization. Trade in goods and ideas was carried across the Sahara by camel caravan, and the stimulus of this contact was an important source of progress.

This early supremacy of the savanna country began to be reversed in the sixteenth century, when West Europeans finally broke the Arab monopoly of trade with the Guinea coast. The trans-Saharan caravan routes decayed and the coastal forest zone was henceforth the area in greatest contact with the outside world; contact which was often destructive but which eventually led to the emergence on the coast of an educated African *élite* and the beginnings of modern economic development. Both these events have been of considerable significance in the emergence of independent west African states.

5 Nigeria: Cross-Section of the West

In size, variety of peoples and environments, as well as in the challenges which these present for future development, Nigeria in many ways exemplifies the problems of tropical Africa as a whole. Size and human variety set problems of political cohesion. There are the usual problems of water supply, poor soils and disease, while the general level of poverty is as low as anywhere in Africa. Stretching from the dense forests of the south to the margins of the Sahara, Nigeria provides therefore a revealing cross-section of west African life, in many ways typical of the whole region.

Size and the variety of its environments do, however, give it advantages denied to many of its neighbours. The economy of the whole is varied, and the unity imposed by British rule has survived a disastrous civil war which at one time threatened to destroy it.

The third largest territory in area and the largest in population, Nigeria is bound to exert tremendous influence on its neighbours if it retains its unity. It is a land some four times the size of the United Kingdom and has between fifty and sixty million people.

MAJOR TRIBAL GROUPINGS

Nigeria at the time of independence was a federation with three strong regional governments and a federal government to cover all three regions. Each of the original regions is the core area of one or other of the major tribal groups – Hausa in the North, Yoruba in the West and Ibo in the East – though no region was linguistically or culturally homogeneous.

Prior to independence there was considerable local pressure for many more regions, and no less than fifteen were demanded at

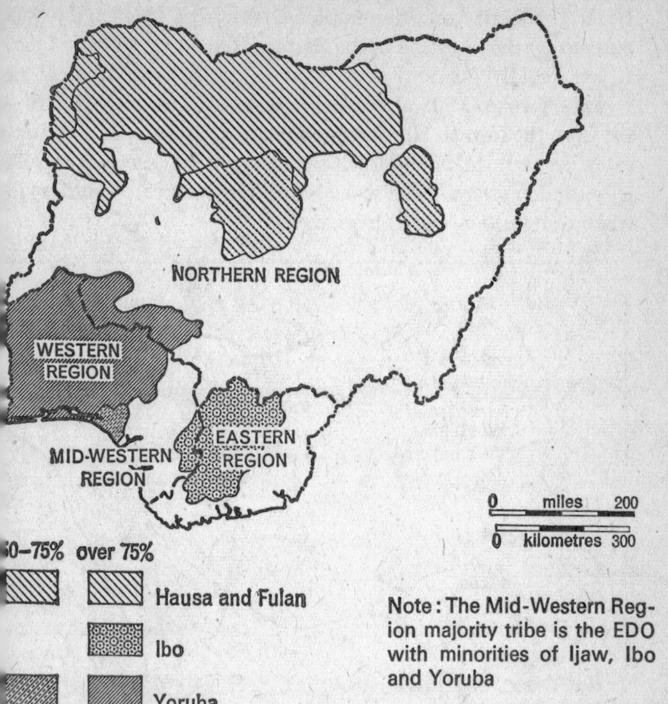

MAP 15. Nigeria: tribal nuclei and regional boundaries, 1963

the 1957 London Conference. These demands were successfully resisted, however, and the constitutional difficulties of creating new regions were made fairly formidable.* These difficulties were overcome in 1963 in the case of the new Mid-West Region, consisting of the Delta and Benin provinces formerly belonging to the West, and with its capital the ancient city of Benin. It was a product both of local opposition to Yoruba domination and of the 1962–3 political crisis in the Western Region[1]. On 30 November 1966 the Federal Government announced that not less than eight and not more than fourteen states would comprise the new

*(a) Two thirds majority in favour in both federal houses.
(b) Approval by a majority of Houses of Assembly of the existing regions.
(c) A referendum with 60 per cent of the new state's registered voters approving.

Federal Nigeria, but the implementation of this policy was delayed by the secession of the Eastern Region on 30 May 1967. It was rapidly put into effect after the collapse of 'Biafra' on 7 January 1970. Federal Nigeria now consists of twelve states – six from the former Northern Region and three from the East, together with the Mid-West, Lagos and the West (which lost only the Lagos area). No more states may be created until 1976 when the position will be reviewed.

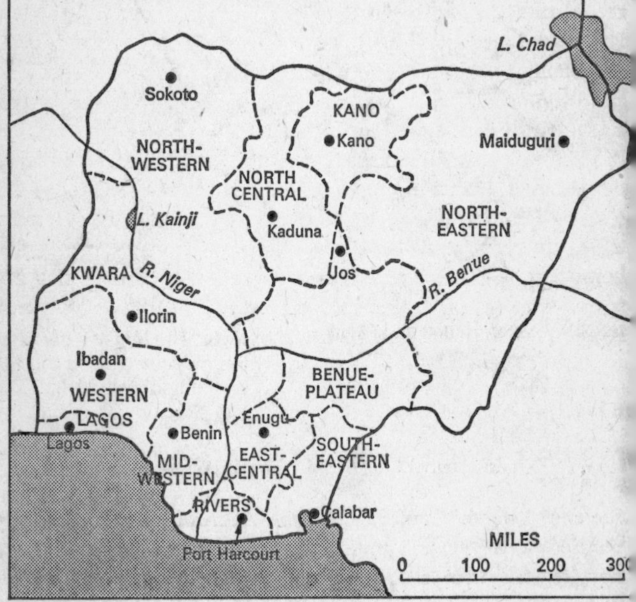

MAP 16. Nigeria: state boundaries, 1970

More than three quarters of the population in the West is Yoruba-speaking, two thirds of the population in the East was Ibo-speaking, and about one third of the population in the North had Hausa as its first language, the use of which is constantly spreading. There were considerable minorities of Yoruba in the North (as well as in neighbouring Dahomey).

The North – according to the last census figures – contained rather more than half the total population, and in consequence

the Federal Government was largely dominated by northerners until the upheavals of 1966. The creation of the new states is designed to end the political instability caused partly by the previous imbalances.

Population census figures in Nigeria had important political implications. Seats in the Federal House of Representatives were allocated on a population basis and, with political parties still largely based on the regions, the census figures could alter radically the political balance of power between them. As a result, there have been two census counts in Nigeria in the last few years (1962 and 1963), the results of which have both been in dispute.* The 1963 figures were, however, accepted as official and meant that the North kept its preponderance in the former Federal House of Representatives.[2]

Finally, it should be noted that the Hausa did not dominate numerically in the North to anything like the same extent as did Yoruba and Ibo in West and East respectively. This greater tribal diversity was, however, offset by the greater cultural homogeneity which comes from the practice of Islam. Only the so-called Middle Belt, the southern part of the former Northern Region, does not have a Moslem majority.

HISTORICAL OUTLINE

Both the north and the west of the country have a long tradition of political and military organization.

In the north, the Hausa states arose from the twelfth century onwards, becoming converted to Islam in the fourteenth century as a result of contacts with traders and missionaries from Mali to the west.[3] They were then brought under the rule of one political system with the Fulani revolution of the early nineteenth century.

The Fulani, a cattle-keeping nomadic people (in contradistinction to the crop-growing Hausa), had been moving into the Hausa states since the fifteenth century, frequently constituting an intellectual and religious *élite* whose reforming zeal

*1963 Census figures: North 29,777,986, East 12,388,646, West 10,278,500, Mid-West 2,533,337, Lagos, 675,352. Total 55,653,821. Source: *The Times*, 26 February 1964.

seems to have been the main cause of the Fulani seizure of political power. In consequence a large region formerly the preserve of a number of independent states was brought under a single government. And it was not only the Hausa states which were brought under Fulani rule. The new empire was able to extend its frontiers as far south as the Benue river in the east, and south of the Niger well into the Yoruba areas of the west, bringing with it for the first time an extension of Islamic religious influence. Hodgkin takes the view that

> European commentators have tended to underestimate the extent to which the Fulani Empire survived through the nineteenth century as an effective political unit. It was, of course, a state of a broadly 'feudal' type, in which the various provincial governors ... enjoyed a large autonomy, and revolted from time to time against the central power; but it remained discernibly a state.[4]

When a British protectorate was established over Northern Nigeria in 1900, much of the existing political structure was retained under a system of 'indirect rule'. The northern Emirs, together with their councillors and officials, became officials of the new native administration.

One important consequence of the treaties made by the British Government with the Moslem Emirs was that Christian missions were in general not allowed into the exclusively Moslem areas. As a great deal of the educational system has been in the hands of the missions, there is now a considerable contrast in standards of literacy between the north and the south of the country. In the north, literacy in Roman script is under 5 per cent outside the Yoruba minority areas and the non-Moslem tribes of the Jos plateau, while literacy in Hausa (Arabic script) is nowhere greater than 15 per cent. Literacy rates in the south are up to 25 per cent in many areas, but only in parts of the former Eastern Region is this figure exceeded. One result of this contrast in literacy standards has been the importation into the north of clerks and others from among the southern tribes, especially the Ibo. This importation was resented by many in the north, particularly since it was accompanied by radical pressures. This resentment resulted in the tribal conflicts of 1966 and the subsequent mass exodus of Ibos to their own home area.

The Yoruba states – of which the chief were Oyo and Benin –

arose between the eleventh and fourteenth centuries. From the seventeenth century onwards secular power was predominantly in the hands of the Alafin of Oyo, while both Oyo and Benin accepted the spiritual authority of the Oni of Ife. By the nineteenth century the Yoruba states were in decline. Fulani expan-

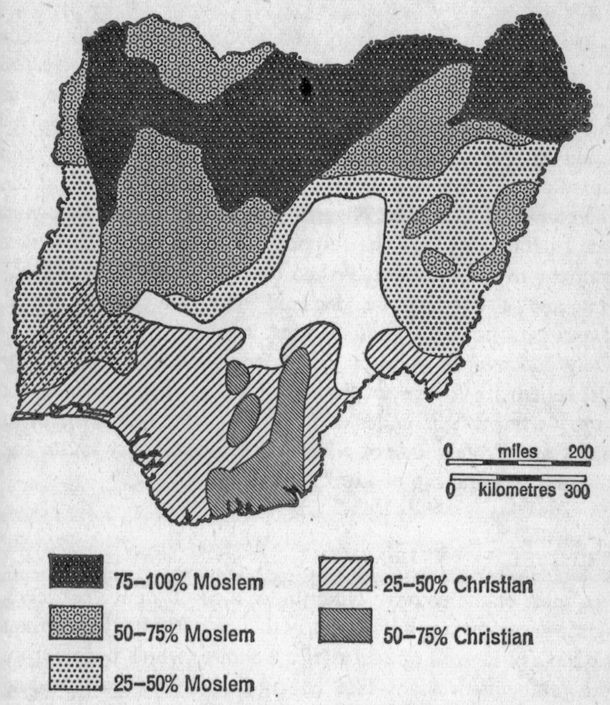

MAP 17. Nigeria: the frontiers of Islam and Christianity. (Modified from J. Spencer Trimingham, *Islam in West Africa*, 1959)

sion had detached some of the more northerly areas, while pressure from Dahomey in the west and the depredations of the slave trade had reduced political stability and cohesion in the region.

The Ibo have no such tradition of political and military organization, and before the establishment of British rule were

organized in small family and kinship groups. Perhaps this is one reason why Christian missions have had more success in the Eastern Region than elsewhere in Nigeria. Only here are there areas with over half the population Christian.[5] Attempts to rule the Ibo areas through native authorities were not successful, because there were no suitable native authorities through which to rule.

British occupation was achieved piecemeal from the 1860s onwards. Lagos was occupied in 1861 and a colony created there in the following year. The Oil Rivers Protectorate was established in 1885 in the region of the Niger delta, being renamed the Niger Coast Protectorate in 1893. Then in 1899 control passed from the Foreign to the Colonial Office, and the Protectorate of Southern Nigeria was formed in the following year. In the same year the responsibilities of the Royal Niger Company to the north were taken over by the British Government and a Protectorate declared over Northern Nigeria. Government in both protectorates, however, was not completely effective for another nine or ten years. The last partly independent areas were not absorbed until 1914, when the whole country was brought under one administration and the unified Colony and Protectorate of Nigeria began its history under the Governor Generalship of Lord Lugard.

THE PHYSICAL ENVIRONMENT

With most of the country lying under 2,000 ft above sea level, Nigeria is everywhere a hot country to live in, having in common with most of the rest of west Africa a climate which people from more temperate regions find enervating. There is a gradual increase in height of the plateau surfaces from south to north, but this has little effect on temperature except on the central Jos plateau, parts of which rise to over 4,000 ft.

The south has the smallest range of temperature, both between day and night and between the hottest and coolest months. Moving north the daily range increases, as do the differences between the hottest and coolest months, so that the north experiences both the hottest days and the coolest nights.

TABLE 8
Temperature contrasts in Nigeria

	Mean monthly maxima	Mean monthly minima
Calabar (in the south-east)	81·6 to 89·4	72·3 to 74·5
Nguru (in the north-east)	87·3 to 103·6	53·8 to 74·3

SOURCE: K. M. Buchanan and J. C. Pugh, *Land and People in Nigeria*, 1955, p. 30.

Nigeria is typical of Africa as a whole in that rainfall and water supply are far more significant than temperature in limiting or stimulating human activities. Rainfall exceeds 120 inches along parts of the south-east coast, but the amount falls away rapidly to north and west, where large areas have only between 20 and 40 inches. More important than the crude annual totals is the northward increase in the length of the dry season, so that areas which may seem to have quite comfortable annual totals have, for at least part of the year, insufficient water in the soil for the growth of crops. Even Calabar in the south-east has a period of two months when moisture loss from the soil is greater than rainfall, although it receives over 100 inches annually and there is no month which is completely dry. It must be concluded from this that there are few parts of the country and indeed of the whole of west Africa where full use can be made of favourable growth temperatures without irrigation. Over more than half of Nigeria the annual need for water is greater than the rainfall. This assessment pays no regard to the requirement of animal stocks, human consumption, and industry. Long-term development will clearly have to include major irrigation schemes on the Niger and Benue and the completion in 1967 of the Kainji Dam is a first essential step in the rational use of water resources[6] (and see below).

THE SUBSISTENCE ECONOMY

The fundamental contrast in subsistence agriculture is that between the grain economy of the north and the root economy of the south. These represent adaptations to a grassland and a

forest environment respectively. There is some overlapping in the Middle Belt, but this is away from the main areas of dense population. In the southern root economy, yams and cassava are the main crops, with subsidiary rice and beans, while, especially in the south-east, the oil palm is important in both subsistence and commercial agriculture. Over most of the country cultivation is by the normal African bush fallowing system, and one part of Yoruba country has been described as follows:

> The area is cleared in February and ... burned soon after ... The main crops of yams and corn are planted with the first rains together with pumpkins, melons and calabashes. When the first corn* is harvested in June, beans, cassava, okra and cocoyams may be planted. A second crop of corn is planted in August and harvested in October or November; yams are harvested in September or October.[7]

The fallow period in this area may be from eight to fourteen years, but in parts of Ibo country has been dangerously reduced as a result of population pressure.

The northern grain economy is devoted mainly to millets and sorghums, with guinea corn as a subsidiary crop and groundnuts on the lighter soils. Around the larger towns more permanent cultivation has been developed, associated with the availability of animal manure, light, easily worked soils, and wells and streams for irrigation. The most extensive area of this type is around the city of Kano.

POPULATION DISTRIBUTION

The three main areas of high density roughly correspond with the three main tribal nuclei, and also with those areas which are the major contributors to commercial agriculture. In between the high density areas of north and south lies the thinly populated Middle Belt, comprising two fifths of the country's area, which has only one fifth of the population. Poor soils, low rainfall and scanty ground water have contributed to poverty in population and wealth. Even more important, probably, have been centuries of slave-raiding and warfare, both from north and south. With a population constantly reduced in this way, tsetse-infested bush country had been able to encroach on once

*i.e. maize.

cultivated land, making it all the more difficult to settle again once warfare and slaving ceased for a while. The existence today of this wide, thinly peopled area between north and south helps to emphasize the differences between the Moslem north and the other two regions.

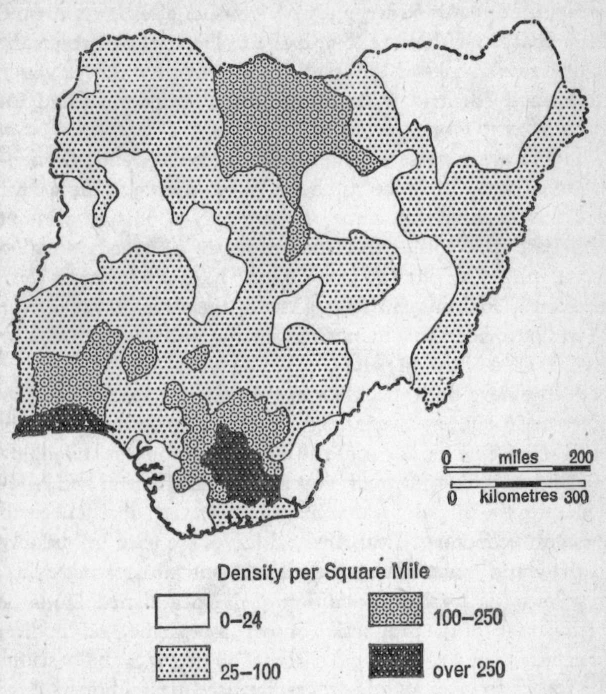

MAP 18. Nigeria: population density.

High densities in parts of the north have been facilitated by the light, easily worked soils, good ground water supplies for irrigation and the absence of tsetse fly. Strategic position on the trans-Saharan caravan routes has also been important, as has the political stability provided by powerful empires. In recent years the coming of the railway has provided the necessary outlet to the sea for the development of commercial agriculture and a consequent increase in wealth and population.

A more powerful political organization than their neighbours have enjoyed also helped the Yoruba to maintain their numbers in spite of slave-raiding – numbers increased in recent years with the opportunities provided by the growing of cash crops like cocoa. The Yoruba areas are characterized by a high concentration of people in large towns, unusual elsewhere in rural Africa. Ibadan, with more than half a million people (about the size of Leeds), ranks as the largest city in tropical Africa which is not wholly dependent on an imported commercial and industrial activity for its growth.*

The Ibo areas possess some of the highest population densities in Africa, with some patches of 1,500 people to the square mile, thus ranking with some of the highly populated areas of South-East Asia and approaching a degree of over-population unusual in Africa. The Ibo seem to have been protected by their dense forest environment from some of the slave raiding of the past and have been able to increase their wealth and numbers by the cultivation of the oil palm.

The Ibo have been fortunate in this, since – apart from sensitivity to drought and waterlogging – the oil palm is tolerant in its soil requirements. Most of the cultivation consists in looking after wild or semi-wild trees, and in the East-Central and Mid-West states the oil palm is dominant in both the subsistence and the export economies. Leaf ribs and leaves are used in building and thatching; palm wine makes a pleasant intoxicating drink, and palm oil is a valuable addition to the local diet. Palm oil is used overseas for the production of soap, margarine, and candles, among other things; while palm kernel oil provides the basis for soap, toilet preparations and other pharmaceutical products.

COMMERCIAL AGRICULTURE

The wealth of Nigeria lies mainly in agriculture, which occupies at least 80 per cent of the working population and accounted for about 55 per cent of the Gross Domestic Product in 1965–6. Commercial farming occupies about one quarter of the land under cultivation and is concentrated in three main areas of

*Greater Lagos, for example, is larger than Ibadan but is mainly a commercial and industrial centre of twentieth-century origins.

dense population. Each area, with its distinctive natural environment, is characterized by different export crops: cotton and groundnuts in the north, cocoa in the Yoruba areas, and palm oil and kernels in the south-east.

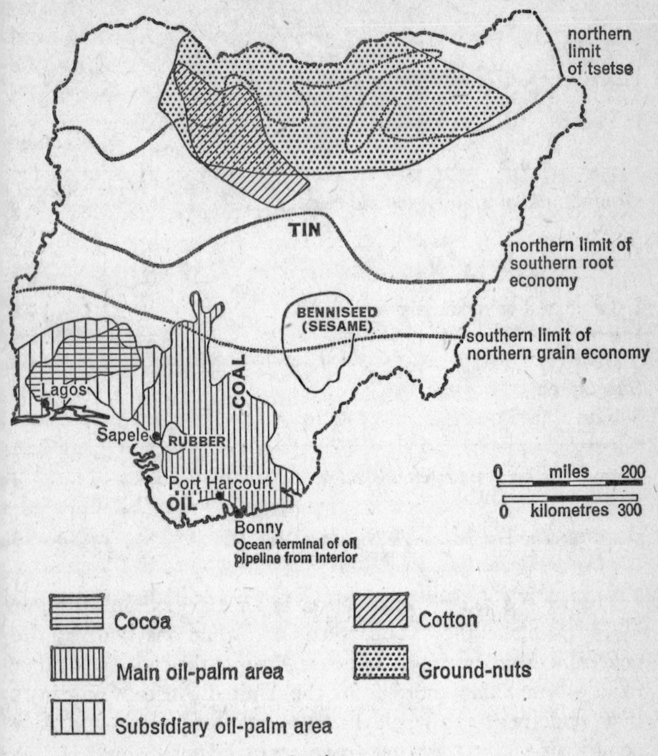

MAP 19. Nigeria: export production

The dependence of each concentration of population on one or two export crops is typical of the smaller independent countries of west Africa. United in one political unit, they become complementary to each other and a source of national strength. With the exception of cocoa, there is considerable local consumption of these crops and, as a result, considerable local trade between the three regions. The Middle Belt at present provides

a small food surplus for export to the other areas, a surplus which should be increased in any future agricultural expansion. There is little plantation agriculture, and most of the export production is in the hands of smallholders.

TABLE 9

Nigeria. Exports in 1968 (by value)

	percentage
Groundnuts, groundnut oil and cake	24·8
Cocoa	24·5
Petroleum	17·5
Tin	6·4
Palm oil and palm kernels	4·8
Rubber	2·9
Timber	1·6
Raw cotton	1·5
Other	16·0
Total value N£211·1 million (£246·9m. sterling)	

SOURCE: *The Europa Yearbook*, 1970, Vol. II.

Rubber has ranked with cotton as an export crop in recent years, owing to the establishment of plantations both by the government and by private interests. Prior to the civil war, timber exports, including those from the United Africa Company's huge undertaking at Sapele, had also increased. Hides and skins come mainly from the tsetse-free areas of the north.

MINERALS AND POWER SUPPLY

The only major mineral export, other than oil, is tin from the Jos plateau, where it has been worked for over fifty years by Europeans and before that by local smelters.

Nigeria is fortunate in having both workable coal deposits and proved oil reserves. The coal is of low quality and is used mainly on the railways and for electricity production, but both uses are

important in a country which has not yet developed hydro-electricity to any extent, except on the Jos Plateau for the use of the tin industry. Total production amounts to rather less than one million tons annually.

High-cost coal production is not likely to increase in the future, since lower-cost oil output is now growing. Though it was first produced in exportable quantities no earlier than 1958, heavy investments have now been made in the oilfield of the Niger delta. Production reached over two million tons in 1961 and over five million tons by 1966. Before the outbreak of the civil war the new refinery at Port Harcourt was able to meet Nigeria's domestic needs as well as having an exportable surplus for Chad and Niger.

Although the war seriously interrupted the industry there has been a spectacular recovery, and in 1970 Nigeria became one of the world's top ten oil producers. Production is now running at more than 60 million tons per annum and is expected to be double that by 1975. New pipelines are being built and the Bonny and Forcados terminals improved.[8]

TRANSPORT

At least 30 per cent of development plan money in the 1960s was spent on the improvement of railways, roads, harbours and water transport. The railway system is still only single-track and, like most other African railways, is now heavily overloaded. Road traffic, especially of commercial vehicles, has increased enormously in recent years, but only a few trunk roads have tarred surfaces and many are impassable in the wet season.

With the improvement of inland transport arrangements, port installations already working at peak capacity will have to be improved. Lagos handles over twice as much cargo as the other major port, Port Harcourt, and in both there are already costly delays in the turn-round of ships because of congestion. The improvement of Port Harcourt is complicated by the shifting and constantly silting channels of the Niger delta, and by the damage of war. Improvements are now once again in hand.

Most important for the future of Nigeria will be the development of the Niger and Benue rivers. These rivers, so impressive

on the map, are not as yet the aid to trade and movement which they will become in the future. Up till now they have served rather to divide than to unite the country, and they need to be improved for navigation, for irrigation, and for power supplies, the more so because such a large part of their course lies in the under-populated and relatively neglected Middle Belt.

Research work on river improvement was started by a Dutch firm in 1953, and as a result the Escravos* scheme for improving navigational outlets in the Niger delta was initiated. This has been particularly important in facilitating the development of the oil industry in the area. The same Dutch firm also investigated possibilities along both the Niger and the Benue and published its most comprehensive report in 1959.[9]

Both rivers are seasonal and irregular in flow, and any scheme must consist of a series of dams to impound flood water and provide a controlled discharge for both navigation and irrigation, as well as the necessary head of water for the generation of power. The first of the series of dams was started in 1964 at Kainji, north of Jebba on the Niger. When the power complex is completed it will provide a major source of electric power as well as the beginnings of irrigation works and flood control in an undeveloped part of the Middle Belt. The careful preparatory research work has been one of the most thorough investigations ever carried out on one of the world's great rivers.

Large size and population, regional variety and divisions and the usual problems of developing a backward economy in a difficult tropical environment: these are the most important facts to remember in considering Nigeria's future role.

*Named after the major outlet.

Notes on Chapter 5

1. D. B. Abernethy, 'Nigeria Creates a New Region', in *Africa Report*, March 1964.
2. J. P. Mackintosh, 'How Many Nigerians?', in *New Statesman*, 13 March 1964, pp. 390–92.
3. T. Hodgkin, *Nigerian Perspectives*, 1960, p. 23.
4. ibid., p. 41.
5. See the map of religious distribution in J. Spencer Trimingham, *Islam in West Africa*, 1959.
6. B. J. Garnier, *The Moisture Resources of Nigeria and their Utilization* in *Natural Resources in Tropical Africa*. Report of a symposium held at Makerere College, 1955.
7. P. A. Allinson, 'From Farm to Forest', in *Farm and Forest*, Vol. II, No. 2 (1941), pp. 95–6. Quoted in K. M. Buchanan and J. C. Pugh, *Land and People in Nigeria*, 1955, p. 105. This is the best single book on Nigerian geography.
8. 'Nigeria Starts Again: a Survey', in *Economist*, 24 October 1970.
9. *River Studies and Recommendations on the Improvements of the Niger and the Benue*, by N.E.D.E.C.O., 1959.

In addition the following are recommended:

R. J. Harrison Church, *West Africa*, 1968, Chap. 26.
G. B. Stapleton, *The Wealth of Nigeria*, 1958.
J. Coleman, *Nigeria: Background to Nationalism*, 1960.
Robin Hallet, *People and Progress in West Africa*, 1966. An excellent short study of the whole of West Africa, focusing on the problems of development.

6 English-Speaking West Africa

Ghana, Sierra Leone, Gambia and Liberia share with Nigeria the use of English as their official language. Gambia was acquired by Britain (from 1817 onwards) in order to prevent French possession of an important navigable river, while both Liberia and Sierra Leone were founded as homes for freed slaves from the Americas. Ghana, the former Gold Coast, became a British colony in 1874, although there had been British settlements there since the seventeenth century.

GAMBIA

Gambia as a geographical absurdity has already been discussed.[1] Its very existence is one of the best examples of European folly in the political fragmentation of the continent. Varying between 13 and 30 miles wide and extending for nearly 300 miles along both banks of the navigable Gambia river, it is almost entirely surrounded by the territory of Senegal.

The river is not only the reason for Gambia's existence but remains its life-line of communications. All of the population (just over 340,000 in 1967) live within striking distance of the river and are dependent on it for their links with the outside world.

Ninety per cent of the population are peasant farmers whose production for sale is almost entirely limited to groundnuts. In 1968–9 the value of groundnut and groundnut oil exports amounted to over £4,065,000.[2]

Groundnuts, first exported in 1830, are grown on the lighter sandy soils away from the riverside swamps, especially in the middle river areas, while the riverside and coastal swamps, useless for groundnuts, are now being developed for rice cultivation. Rice has not yet replaced millets as the staple food, but it is already the preferred food of most Gambians and may well

replace millets in the not too distant future. Rice acreages have increased rapidly in recent years, largely due to a government-sponsored attempt to make the colony self-sufficient in food.

One interesting feature of the economy is the annual migration into Gambia of between five and ten thousand 'strange farmers', who come from Portuguese Guinea, Senegal, and Mali to grow groundnuts. They are given land and houses by their hosts in return for labour service, and return to their homes after the harvest in November.

Gambia was the last British colony in west Africa to achieve its independence (1965), largely because its future as a viable entity seemed uncertain. To the outside observer the only rational solution seems to lie in some sort of union with Senegal, but development in the colonial period was entirely at variance with progress towards such a union. The lack of any well-developed communications between the two territories, the development of an artificial port at Dakar instead of the more suitable Bathurst, and different systems of colonial administration all combined to make union difficult. Moreover, Senegal's earlier independence made Gambians resist any suggestion that they should simply be incorporated into an existing state and so lose their identity.

The first step in bringing about closer cooperation between the two countries was completed in 1958 with the trans-Gambia road linking northern Senegal with Casamance.

A U.N. Report of 1964[3] considered three alternative solutions to relations between Senegal and Gambia: (a) full union, (b) a Senegambian federation,[4] and (c) an 'entente' between the two countries. In fact the 'entente' solution finally adopted has meant little more than agreement on defence matters.

Legitimate trade with Senegal is still small, but smuggling is important to the Gambian economy. Import duties are generally lower at Bathurst than Dakar, and it has been estimated that some 10 per cent of Gambian imports and about 15 per cent of the revenue from import duty is accounted for by goods destined for illegal import into Senegal.[5]

SIERRA LEONE

Sierra Leone is a small, mountainous country, a little smaller than Scotland, which occupies a unique place in formerly British West Africa. It represents in practical terms the early stirrings of Europe's conscience over the evils of the slave trade, and was established at the end of the eighteenth century as a home for ex-slaves, most of whom had fought with Britain in the American Revolution and who were settled at Freetown in 1792.

During the nineteenth century the British used Freetown as their main naval base for the suppression of the slave trade, and the capture of slaving ships led to the settlement of more slaves in the colony, so that by 1833 over 34,000 freed slaves had been settled there.[6]

This colony was by no means the country we know today. The ex-slaves were settled in a small area of the peninsula – in and to the south of Freetown – which constituted the Colony proper, and was ruled directly by the British Government until independence. Most of the country, which was not settled by ex-slaves, was only taken over in 1898 as 'Protectorate' and ruled indirectly through the native chiefs.

The descendants of the ex-slaves, numbering only about one tenth of the population today, are known as Creoles and have until recently had little contact with the peoples of the interior. The vast majority of the population live outside the Creole area in the Protectorate.[7]

Rivalry between Colony and Protectorate, between Christian and non-Christian, between Creole and non-Creole continues down to the present day, largely as a result of Creole exclusiveness and sense of superiority.

This sense of superiority stems from a variety of causes. The system of indirect rule through the chiefs in the Protectorate, distinct from direct rule by the British government in the Colony, helped to maintain a barrier between the Creoles and the rest of the population, while the Creoles enjoyed superior educational facilities and even developed their own language.

Fourah Bay College – the oldest institution of higher education in west Africa – was founded in 1827 at Freetown, and students there have been awarded Durham University Degrees since

1876. Since the mid nineteenth century the Creoles of Freetown have had access to an education denied to most other west Africans for nearly 100 years. Already by 1859 the first Creole Doctor of Medicine had graduated from a British university, and ever since the Creoles have supplied a steady stream of educated and qualified men not only for their own country but also for other parts of English-speaking Africa.

Their sense of superiority thus stems in part from the advantages they enjoyed in training and education. Not till 1927 did the first non-Creole qualify as a medical doctor – the country's first Prime Minister, Sir Milton Margai.

Creole exclusiveness has also been aided by the development of Krio – a form of English with some Spanish, French and Portuguese words. It has no written tradition because it is the language of a group educated in English, but it is preserved in folk-tales and proverbs and used as the language of social intercourse in the Creole community.

For the rest, the peoples of the Protectorates are composed of thirteen different tribes speaking as many different languages or dialects. There are, however, two major tribes – the Mende of the north and the Temne of the south – both with about 30 per cent of the total population.

Like other similar stations along the west coast, Sierra Leone proved a proverbial 'White Man's Grave'. Between 1814 and 1885 no less than five Governors and seven acting Governors died at their posts or on the way home, usually of malaria or yellow fever. As a result of advances in preventive medicine the country is no longer very unhealthy, but for much of the year the climate is uncomfortable, especially on the coast. Monthly mean temperatures at Freetown range from 78 to 82 degrees F. and in the rainy season, from June to September and beyond, there may be long periods of steady rain. Freetown has an annual rainfall of 118·7 inches.

The very high rainfall and the intensity of the rains lead to rapid run-off, severe leaching, and a high degree of lateritization. Coupled with this there is a density of population – unusual in this part of west Africa – which has in turn led to the removal of some 95 per cent of the original forest cover.[8]

In the subsistence economy rice, especially upland rice, is the

main food crop. Only in parts of the north-east is the country dry enough for millets, while in the north-west and centre cassava replaces rice. These inland areas suffer in extreme form all the hazards, both natural and man-made, to which agriculture is subjected in tropical Africa; leaching, lateritization, soil erosion and bad farming practices have seriously reduced their potential. It is in the coastal swamps, therefore, some 20 miles in width, that the future of Sierra Leone's agriculture would seem most profitably to lie.

Mangroves are being cut and swamps being cleared to make way for the growth of swamp rice. Over the last seventy years some 80,000 acres have been developed. Swamp clearance is hard and expensive, but once it is completed the work of cultivation is comparatively easy.

TABLE 10

Sierra Leone. Food crop acreages

Upland rice	570,000
Swamp rice	80,000
Millets and sorghums	30,000
Maize	25,000
Cassava	46,000

SOURCE: Colonial Office, *Annual Report 1959*.

There is no doubt that further increases in swamp rice acreages would help to halt soil degradation in the interior by reducing the cultivation of upland rice and would eventually enable the country to become a rice exporter. In recent years, however, rice has had to be imported owing to a diversion of labour from farming to the more profitable digging for diamonds.

The major agricultural export at the moment is oil-palm kernels, mostly from semi-wild trees in the vicinity of Freetown. Other agricultural exports are piassava (for raffia), kola nuts, coffee, cocoa and ginger, but these make only a small contribution to the national income.

In the last fifteen years the economic future of Sierra Leone has changed dramatically with the rapid increase in the production and export of iron ore and of diamonds.

TABLE II
Sierra Leone. Exports in 1968 (by value)

	percentage
Diamonds (from 35 per cent in 1959)	60·3
Iron ore	13·4
Palm kernels	11·4
Cocoa	2·4
Bauxite	1·9
Other	10·6
Total value 75·6 million leones (£37·8m.)	

SOURCE: *The Europa Yearbook*, 1970, Vol. II.

This upsurge in mineral production has placed the economy of the country on a much firmer base than before. As a purely agricultural land it would hardly have had the resources to attempt tackling the challenge of independence with any hope of success. Now it can look forward to the development of an economy which already possesses some degree of diversification.

There has been considerable controversy over the mining of diamonds. In the early 1950s it was discovered that diamonds could be picked up quite easily in the river beds – and therefore marketed illegally in defiance of a monopoly granted to a private corporation. Police were unable to control the thousands of illegal miners who entered the diamondiferous areas in search of this new source of wealth, so that the corporation's monopoly had to be terminated and the private diggers allowed to mine under government licence. The government was initially alarmed at the illegal mining, as it suffered considerable losses of revenue. The outcome has, however, proved satisfactory in several different ways. Wealth has been spread more widely in a country which is still very poor; people have been encouraged to move away from their villages and prosper elsewhere; and it has reduced the grip of foreign capital on the country's economic life.[9]

Iron ore production has nearly doubled over the last ten years in response to private foreign investment. Further development in this and other fields is likely to be hampered, however, by poor and difficult communications. The 2 ft 6 ins. gauge railway has served a useful purpose, especially for the oil-palm districts, but road development only really started after the Second World War. It took till 1950 before the road into neighbouring Guinea was completed.

In sum it can be said that a comparatively diverse economy and access to overseas investment in the mines gives Sierra Leone a certain stability.

LIBERIA

Liberia was like Sierra Leone in being founded by philanthropists as a home for ex-slaves, though the organization concerned there was the American Colonization Society. The first party of freed slaves was landed in 1822, and from then onwards the colony received a steady stream of immigrants, especially slaves freed by the American Navy. Liberia differed from Sierra Leone, however, in gaining its independence as early as 1847.

Lacking either techniques or capital, and landed on an inhospitable coast, the freed slaves never had a chance to do more than merely survive in stagnation and chronic indebtedness. Their state became a symbol to which those seeking to prove Negro inferiority could point. Up to 1939 Monrovia had no telephone system, piped water or sewage disposal; there were no railways, roads or ports; and the government was notorious for its corruption and despotism.

There is the same division as in Sierra Leone between the descendants of returned slaves (the Americo-Liberians*) and the vast majority of the inhabitants, except that the Americo-Liberians have not enjoyed the educational opportunities of the Creoles of Sierra Leone. Even as late as 1948 there was not one indigenous medical practitioner in Liberia. Until after the Second World War, the rule of the Americo-Liberians over the rest of the population was absolute. The first independent re-

*About 2 per cent of the people in the country are Americo-Liberians.

public in tropical Africa had a native policy no different from that of a colonial power, with district commissioners operating under a system of indirect rule.

The Americo-Liberians came to spend more and more time playing a closed game of politics and pursuing an elaborate social life which was modelled on that of the white plantation aristocracy in the American South. For over a century a wide gulf continued to exist between them and the vast majority of the population in the hinterland, a population which remained one of the most primitive and isolated in the whole of Africa. The master–slave pattern which they had known in the American South was transported by the Americo-Liberians to Africa. They were the masters; the native population, the slaves.

For years a small group of men 'played musical chairs with the available government offices'.[10] There were no skilled workers, and the only cash income received by any Liberians went to the politicians.

By the 1930s the country had sunk so low that an international commission judged it guilty of procuring forced labour from among its own native population. Labourers were being shipped with the connivance of government officials from Liberia to French Gabon and Fernando Po, under conditions scarcely distinguishable from slave trading.

The modern development of Liberia stems from the beginnings of the Firestone Rubber Company's operations in 1926. Since then Liberia has been developed (and largely controlled) by a few large American firms, though since the end of the Second World War U.S. government investment has also played an important part in development.

Firestone has two estates, a large one near Monrovia and a small one near Harper. By 1945 over 95 per cent of exports were of rubber and this still forms 15 per cent of Liberia's total export trade, despite subsequent diversification of the economy.

In spite of its dominant position in the economy, Firestone employs less than 30,000 people. Its operations, indeed, provide a perfect example of Africa's highly developed economic islands in the midst of a stagnant subsistence economy. The plantations themselves are very efficient, giving the highest yields per acre of any rubber estates in the world.

TABLE 12
Liberia. Exports in 1968 (by value)

	percentage
Iron ore	70·0
Rubber	15·0
Diamonds	5·3
Other	9·7
Total value $169 million (£70·4m.)	

SOURCE: *The Europa Yearbook*, 1970, Vol. II.

In addition to profitably growing rubber, Firestone has established all the modern civic amenities in the vicinity of its estates, and has branched out into other fields of manufacturing activity. Medical, health and educational services, roads, a hydro-electric plant, a radio station and factories producing rubber products are examples of the company's activities and interests. In 1955 nearly 40 per cent of government revenue came from Firestone.

Since 1945 the American government itself has taken a direct interest in Liberia's development, starting with the construction between 1945 and 1948 of a huge new deep-water harbour at Monrovia, which cost $20 million. Between 1950 and 1958, U.S. government loans and grants to Liberia amounted to over $10 million, and have been used for economic surveys, the development of agriculture, and the beginning of a network of communications and other essential public services.[11]

Other large companies besides Firestone have also taken a hand. The Liberia Company has interested itself in plantation agriculture and communications, while the Liberia Mining Company has added a new and important commodity to Liberia's list of exports. High-grade iron ore some 45 miles north-west of Monrovia in the Bomi Hills is being successfully worked, following the completion of the mineral railway in 1951. This development was followed by even greater growth at other centres, notably at Mt Nimba and in the Bong Hills. Exports are now running at over 20 million tons a year, and it is estimated that

there are deposits of 400 million tons of high-grade and 250 million tons of lesser-grade ore still to be worked.

Another of Liberia's booming activities in recent years has been the growth of her merchant fleet. With Panama, she provides for the world's shipping one of the best-used flags of convenience, which gives owners the advantages of low registration fees and taxation with little external control over their ships. Between 1954 and 1959 the total tonnage of Liberian-registered ships rose from 1·22 million tons to over 11 million tons.

From sad and dismal beginnings Liberia has made substantial strides during the last thirty years, both in economic development and in the reform of her government and administration. There is still very heavy reliance on a few large American companies, of course, and the U.S. still takes most of Liberia's exports. Yet Liberia has begun to take a respectable place in the community of independent African states, and the sneers of less than forty years ago are now unjustified.

GHANA

Ghana is the richest country in tropical Africa. The income per head of its 8·1 million population is around £90 a year, and though this is not very high by European standards, it is three times as high as the average income per head in some other African states. This is one reason why Ghana was able to achieve independence before her neighbours. Linked with this greater prosperity was an older and more developed educational system which had by the 1950s produced a potential administrative *élite*. One measure of this greater wealth, educational advance and political progress is given by figures of newspaper circulation. (See Table 13.)

Ghana consists of the former Gold Coast Colony (the 50–150 mile wide coastal strip), Ashanti (inland from the former colony and centred on Kumasi), the Northern Territories, and that part of the former German colony of Togoland which elected to join newly independent Ghana in a U.N.-sponsored plebiscite.

The Northern Territories are relatively poor and undeveloped, resembling the thinly populated Middle Belt of Nigeria, since

Ghana does not extend far enough northwards to embrace areas similar to the more thickly populated and Moslem-dominated north of Nigeria. Only in the extreme north-eastern tip of the country are population densities as high as those in the south. The politically and economically important areas of Ghana are Ashanti and the former Colony.

As elsewhere in west Africa, foreign settlements remained coastal until the late nineteenth century. From 1874 onwards these settlements were administered by Britain as the Gold Coast Colony, but inland the Ashanti Confederation of native states continued to exert considerable military and political

TABLE 13

Daily newspapers. Copies in circulation per 1,000 of population in selected countries

Daily newspapers		*Copies in circulation per 1,000 of population*
South Africa	(1961)	57
Ghana	(1966)	37
Rhodesia	(1965)	15
Sierra Leone	(1966)	10
Kenya	(1966)	9
Angola	(1964)	9
Liberia	(1966)	9
Zambia	(1966)	8
Uganda	(1965)	8
Gambia	(1959)	5
Cameroun	(1964)	4
Tanganyika	(1962)	3
Ivory Coast	(1966)	3
Chad	(1965)	0·4

SOURCE: *U.N. Statistical Yearbook 1968*, pp. 774–5.

power. In a series of seven Ashanti wars (the last in 1900) this obstacle to British expansion was eliminated and the Asantehene exiled to the Seychelles, from which he did not return until 1924. But there was no destruction of the native administration,

and Ashanti regional feeling and pride were able to flourish under the British system of delegating as much local administration as possible to the existing native authorities.

When constitutional discussions took place immediately prior to independence, most Ashanti leaders would have preferred a federal system such as was to be developed in Nigeria, but here there was no approximate balance between Ashanti and the Colony, as between south and north in Nigeria. The Colony contained the greater part of the population, possessed the higher educational standards, and had produced the dominant political leadership, a leadership moreover which had turned away from tribalism and regional loyalties towards the establishment not only of a strong Ghana, but an ultimately united Africa.

The main component of political opposition in Ghana at the time of independence was Ashanti separatism. For the first ten years of independence 'liberal' opposition increased under the strong rule of Nkrumah's Convention People's Party, but the strength of Ashanti separatism declined. Increasing discontent in all areas led to the overthrow of Nkrumah in 1966.

The wealth of Ghana is heavily dependent on cocoa, of which it is the world's leading producer, and which accounts for over half of its exports. Most of this comes from southern Ashanti, where over one fifth of the working male population is growing cocoa.[12]

The tree, native to South America, was introduced to Ghana, where conditions proved to be ideal for its cultivation. It needs fairly good soils, dislikes too much rain as well as a pronounced dry season (60 inches of well-distributed rain is ideal) and must be provided with shade. It needs little labour in cultivation and was, therefore, capable of rapid adoption by African smallholders. In spite of the ravages of swollen shoot virus disease (12 million trees were cut out between 1946 and 1961) cocoa continues to be the chief cash crop, often at the expense of food crops which have to be supplemented by imports.

Cocoa provides most of Ghana's wealth, but minerals are also important, and their significance is likely to increase in the future. Like cocoa, production of all the major minerals is confined to southern Ashanti and the coastal regions, with the

richest concentration in an area close to the Kumasi–Takoradi railway.

Gold, diamonds, timber and manganese are the present principal contributors to national income after cocoa, but the immense bauxite deposits west of Kumasi are likely to overtake these once the Volta River project is under way

The completion of the Volta River project will not only help to raise Ghana's already relatively high living standards and diversify her economy, but will provide opportunities for population growth and economic development in a thinly peopled area formerly devoted largely to subsistence agriculture.

TABLE 14
Ghana. Exports in 1967 (by value)

	percentage
Cocoa	54·7
Timber	8·4
Gold	7·6
Diamonds	5·1
Manganese	3·1
Other	21·1

Total value 338·8 million cedis (£138·2m.)

SOURCE: *The Europa Yearbook*, 1970. Vol. II.

Notes on Chapter 6

1. See Chapter 3 above.
2. *The Europa Yearbook*, 1970, Vol. II.
3. U.N. Department of Social and Economic Affairs, *Report on the Alternatives of Association between the Gambia and Senegal*, March 1964.
4. 'Senegambia' existed as a British Crown Colony from 1765–83.
5. P. Robson, in A. Hazlewood (ed.), *African Integration and Disintegration*, 1968, p. 119.
6. R. J. Harrison Church, *West Africa*, 6th ed., 1968, p. 301. For a detailed account see R. R. Kuczynski, *Demographic Survey of the British Colonial Empire*, Vol. 1, *West Africa*, 1948, Chapter 2.
7. 1948 population figures: Colony 124,657; Protectorate 1,858,275.
8. F. J. Martin, *A Preliminary Survey of the Vegetation of Sierra Leone*, 1938, quoted in Harrison Church, op. cit., p. 304.
9. C. Fyfe, 'A Peaceful Achievement in Africa', in the *Listener*, 27 April 1961, p. 726.
10. W. A. Hance, *African Economic Development*, pp. 235–6.
11. ibid., p. 226.
12. R. J. Harrison Church, *West Africa*, 6th ed., 1968.

See also:

E. A. Boateng, *Geography of Ghana*, 1965.
J. I. Clarke, *Sierra Leone in Maps*, 1966.
C.O.I., *Sierra Leone: the Making of a Nation*, 1950.
C.O.I., *Sierra Leone*, 1961.
C. Fyfe, *A History of Sierra Leone*, 1962.
H. A. Gailey, *A History of the Gambia*, 1964.

H. R. Jarret, *A Geography of Sierra Leone and Gambia*, 1954.
R. Lewis, *Sierra Leone*, 1954 (Corona Library).
L. A. Marinelli, *The New Liberia*, 1964.
A. T. Porter, *Creoledom*, 1963.

7 French-Speaking Africa, Portuguese Guinea and Equatorial Guinea

The rapidity with which political independence came to the former French colonies was spectacular even by African standards. It represented a dramatic reversal of traditional French policy towards her dependencies, out of which have emerged fourteen different independent states. Twelve of these fourteen were incorporated in the former French West Africa and French Equatorial Africa, while the former German colonies of Togo and Cameroun were held under U.N. Trusteeship.

As early as 1848 France had granted full citizenship rights to the people of the Senegalese coastal towns, but throughout the rest of Black Africa the policy pursued was one of permanent close association with France rather than complete assimilation. Ultimately full assimilation might come, but only after the completion of France's civilizing mission – a mission which would be completed only when all of francophone Black Africa was fully French in language and culture.

In pursuance of this policy, administration was increasingly conducted through a French-educated African *élite*, and the traditional authorities were either replaced or their powers allowed to lapse. The French-speaking educated African had more political power and therefore less political grievances than his English-speaking counterpart. African politicians sat in France's Parliament, became cabinet ministers, and generally participated in the political life of the metropolitan country in a way which would have been unthinkable in Britain. These French Africans were frequently said to be more French than the French; and there were many who thought it unlikely that such men would wish to take their peoples to full independence from France.

The group which led the breakaway movement was the Guinean Democratic Party of Sekou Touré. Under the terms of

the French referendum in 1958 General de Gaulle offered the overseas territories of France a choice between full internal autonomy, within a new French community, or immediate independence. In the event, Guinea opted for immediate independence and the rest for internal autonomy.

Guinea represented in 1958 the extreme nationalist wing in French African politics. 'It will fall to us,' said Sekou Touré, 'to preserve, for Guinea and for Africa, the honour of African Man.... We shall vote "No" to a community which is merely the French Union re-christened.... We shall vote "No" to inequality.'[1]

Guinea stood alone in 1958. French aid was stopped, experts withdrawn, and trade agreements terminated. But it proved impossible to isolate the rest of French Africa from the rush to independence which Ghana and Guinea had started. There were those like Mali and Senegal which wanted collective independence for the whole of French West Africa. There were those like the Ivory Coast which wanted neither complete independence nor federation. One and all, however, with varying degrees of enthusiasm, found it expedient to follow the lead of Guinea and Ghana. After Guinea, there was no complete break between France and its other former colonies, and all the other states continued to receive French economic aid and technical assistance.

It has already been shown that the level of French investment in her overseas territories since 1948 was considerably higher than Britain's in English-speaking Africa.[2] It should be said, of course, that this was more than ever necessary because the level of pre-war investment had been so abysmally low – much lower than in the British colonies which were, as a result, economically more advanced. This new high rate of investment has been maintained and indeed even increased since the attainment of independence, but it has been coupled with the encouragement of inter-territorial economic planning for the whole area and much closer economic ties with France than the ex-British colonies have with Britain. With the exception of Guinea, the ex-French territories do about 70 per cent of their trade with France.[3]

As in the rest of the continent, development has been very

uneven; countries with a favourable coastal situation have been able to advance much farther and much faster than the inland states. In 1956, Senegal accounted for 35 per cent and the Ivory Coast for 44 per cent of the total exports of French West Africa. And this imbalance has been maintained in the era of overall economic planning. In the west, Senegal and the Ivory Coast received much the largest share of the total funds available, partly no doubt because so much investment was for port and communications development to serve the whole area. Similarly the Congo (Brazzaville) was developed as the main hub of communications for the whole equatorial region, with all external trade passing through Pointe Noire.

TABLE 15

French Government investment in tropical africa 1947–57

	£ million
Senegal	46·8
Ivory Coast	36·3
Congo	30·3
Mali	26·4
Guinea	26·2
Chad	18·6
Central African Republic	16·8
Dahomey	16·6
Gabon	16·5
Upper Volta	14·5
Niger	8·4
Mauritania	5·0

SOURCE: *French Economic Assistance in West and Equatorial Africa: A Decade of Progress 1948–58* (French Government Publication).

STATES OF THE SAVANNA ZONE

MALI

Mali has at least one town which everyone can recognize – Timbuktu. Like Kano in Nigeria, this ancient city owed its importance to its situation astride the trans-Saharan caravan routes and the existence of available water for irrigated

agriculture. This combination of circumstances also helps to explain the rise in the same area of medieval Mali, from which the modern state is named, and which reached the peak of its power in the thirteenth and fourteenth centuries. Trans-Saharan contacts are now once again suggested, by means of a trunk road from Algeria (to Gao in Mali), to be built with French and Czech assistance.

French penetration from Senegal began in the 1860s and 1870s. The railway from Kayes was begun in 1881 and opened to Koulikoro in 1904, thus linking the upper limit of navigation on the Senegal to the navigable middle Niger. From then until 1960 this railway remained the main link with the sea and carried the major part of Mali's external trade. After the political break with Senegal in August of that year, the 'life-line' was closed for the first time in over fifty years and Mali sought to develop an alternative route through Guinea; as a result a railway from Bamako to Kankan is being built with Chinese assistance. At present, the only practicable alternative lies by trunk road and railway through Upper Volta and the Ivory Coast to Abidjan. The railway through Senegal was re-opened on 22 June 1963 with better relations between Senegal and Mali.

Mali is larger in area than Nigeria but has far fewer people (4·7 million in 1967). The southern part of the country is in the same latitude as northern Nigeria, while the north extends far into the Sahara. It is, therefore, a dry land, and agriculture without irrigation is only possible in parts of the south. Even in the extreme south of the country the rainy season is short. Because of this, together with high temperatures and rapid evaporation, Bamako's annual rainfall average of 44 inches is not very effective for agriculture, although it would be more than enough in temperate latitudes.[4]

Both for communications and for production, the life of Mali centres on the Niger valley, and it is here that most of the people live.

The chain of lakes and water channels stretching southwards from Timbuktu is all that now remains of the former inland delta of the Niger and the lake into which it drained. Even today, however, the river gradient is slight, and the consequent annual floods have been used for centuries, both for crop grow-

ing (millets) and for seasonal pasture. The area of lakes and channels from Diafarabé to Timbuktu is known as the live delta; the stretch from Sansanding to Diafarabé, the dead delta.

Irrigation in both parts of the delta was extended by the French. In the live delta, work has been undertaken on a generally small scale under the Department of Agriculture. The dead delta has been the area of operations for one of Africa's most ambitious irrigation schemes, the Niger Office project.

The Niger Office, a state organization, was set up in 1932, and its main engineering work has been the construction of a dam at Sansanding, begun in 1934 and finished in 1941. Its effect has been to raise the river level some fourteen feet, with the aim of making 'live' again the dried-up water channels from former years.

Into this hitherto unproductive region African colonists have been brought from other parts of Mali and from Upper Volta, to be organized into cooperatives called Native Agricultural Associations. These are financed partly by the Office, partly by the members, and act both as providers of credit and as marketing agencies. Every colonist must observe certain cultivation requirements, but after paying annual dues and contributing towards the food and seed reserves of the Association, each member may sell either through the cooperative or elsewhere. In this way individualism and modern techniques are combined with traditional attitudes towards communal life.[5]

Preceding and accompanying the development of this project went years of research into soil, crops, and marketing organization. During the 1930s the whole region became 'a vast agronomic laboratory',[6] including fruit orchards, a rice station, a cotton research station, and an animal husbandry laboratory; but nearly four decades of expensive experimentation have achieved only limited success.

Grandiose in conception, the original project envisaged over 1 million irrigated hectares employing about 800,000 colonists, and aimed to grow enough cotton to free France from American supplies. It has been in full operation since 1947, but by 1954 had been extended to include only 50,000 hectares and less than 40,000 colonists.[7]

The emphasis is now on rice rather than cotton, as this has been found more suitable for the poor soils and inexperienced farmers. Critics of the scheme argue that the expenditure of $175 million to irrigate 50,000 hectares of rice fields was stupid, and there is certainly some similarity between this partial success of the Niger Office and the failure of the Tanganyika Groundnuts Scheme. Deficient technical planning and administration were contributory factors, but in this case disappointing results appear to have stemmed chiefly from a shortage of labour. Mali is not a country with a problem of over-population and the Niger Office is still far from earning a return on the capital invested.[8]

Live delta irrigation has been improved and extended by the Department of Agriculture, using simple and inexpensive methods to modify the annual floods, to conserve available water supplies and to extend the cultivable area. Although cultivation methods are inferior to the Niger Office project, the cost is negligible and the Department has irrigated more than three times the acreage of the more expensive scheme.[9]

These two methods of land improvement in Mali provide a further example of the dilemma facing agricultural improvers all over Africa today. The large scheme, expensive in capital and skilled manpower, is probably the best in the long term. On the other hand, the short-term simple improvements are likely to bring more immediate benefits to more people, at a time when the large scheme has hardly begun to show results.

With the help of both types of improvement, Mali had in the 1950s become a food-exporting country. It produced each year some 14,000 tons of rice surplus to its needs, about 6,000 tons coming from areas developed by the Department of Agriculture and about 8,000 tons from the Niger Office areas.[10] However, surpluses have been declining steadily in recent years and negligible quantities were exported from 1961–4. The same areas also produce large quantities of fish, some of which is exported. Groundnuts are an increasingly important export crop though production fluctuates. Most of the rice crop is now consumed locally.

Outside these main agricultural areas the wealth of the country is in cattle, sheep and goats, thousands of which are exported annually to the Ivory Coast, Ghana and Nigeria.

TABLE 16
Mali. Exports in 1968 (by value)

	percentage
Cotton	39·4
Live animals	30·8
Fish	13·6
Groundnuts	10·6
Other	5·6
Total value 2,650 million Mali francs C.F.A. (£2m.)	

SOURCE: *The Europa Yearbook*, 1970, Vol. II.

SENEGAL

Senegal, with its coastal situation and consequent control over inland lines of communication, rivals the Ivory Coast for the leadership of French-speaking Africa, but the reasons for its supremacy over many of its neighbours lie in its strategic situation and political experience rather than in any inherent economic strength.

The port of Dakar was developed from 1898 as a naval base and subsequently became a great centre of air communications and an important port of call on both South American and African shipping routes. Indeed, it was developed by the French to be the administrative centre for the whole of French West Africa. As a result there have come to this city of over 350,000 inhabitants many of the abler and more ambitious people from the surrounding areas. Its favourable climate has attracted over 30,000 European residents[11] and it already has an established industry in soap, textiles, canning, oil refining and other products. Dakar without the rest of French West Africa is, however, rather like Vienna without the Austro–Hungarian Empire – a capital without a country – for the rest of Senegal is, like Gambia, heavily dependent on groundnut production.

About 40 per cent of the cultivated area is devoted to groundnuts, and most of the rest to the staple food – millets. Groundnut exports date back to the 1840s, encouraged by the needs of

French soap manufacturers, and were given an opportunity to grow by subsequent railway development. Unlike the production of neighbouring Gambia, many of the nuts are processed in local refineries.*

Efforts to diversify the economy include the Senegal Delta irrigation scheme, under which over 13,000 acres have, since 1948, been irrigated for swamp rice cultivation. This has not, however, been a financial success so far. Pumping is expensive and the infertile soils mean that annual applications of fertilizers are necessary. Natural phosphates form a recent welcome addition to local production.

Senegal has been heavily dependent on the usefulness of Dakar. Its future would seem equally dependent on the goodwill of neighbouring states, including Mali, with whom relations were broken in 1960 and not repaired until three years later.

MAURITANIA

Mauritania is, in population, the smallest of the states in ex-French West Africa, with less than a million people, most of them nomadic. The country is largely desert and its very existence has been challenged by Morocco, which claims the whole of the territory as its own. This challenge to Mauritania's existence has embittered relations between Morocco and the French-speaking states of Black Africa, for these last are very jealous of their territorial integrity, however colonial the genesis of their frontiers.

Interest has quickened in this barren desert country with the plans laid in 1952 to exploit the iron-ore deposits in the Kedia d'Idjil Hills in the far north-west, inland from Spanish Sahara.

As so often in Africa, the overriding problem was transport. The nearest port, in Spanish territory, is not particularly good. Nouadhibou (Port Étienne) is better and belongs to Mauritania. A line has been built entirely in Mauritania, including a 1¼ mile tunnel costing £3m. designed to avoid some eight miles of Spanish territory.

*Of total exports in 1968, 35·5 per cent of 37,385 million francs (£63·8m) were groundnut oil, 21·9 per cent groundnuts, 11·1 per cent were oil-seed cake and meal and 6·8 per cent natural phosphates (*Europa Yearbook*, 1970, Vol. II).

The largely Anglo–French consortium (M.I.F.E.R.M.A.),* formed to exploit the ore, has built an air-conditioned town for 5,000 people at each end of the railway. Water is supplied from local wells and from distilled sea water at Nouadhibou.[12]

Total exports of all products in 1961 were only valued at 535 million francs, of which over half was fish. Now, with the expansion of mining, the economic prospects have been transformed. Mauritania's exports are running at over 18,000 million francs annually (£30·7m.), about 90 per cent of which is iron ore. Nearly five million tons were sent overseas in 1967, with the United Kingdom, Germany, France, Belgium, Luxemburg and Italy the best customers.[13]

Surprisingly enough, another large source of future income may be tourism. Nouadhibou has pleasant beaches and a temperature from November to May which ranges between 54 and 84 degrees F. In the ever-widening search for a quiet and sure escape from the European winter, Mauritania may come to rank with currently more fashionable refuges.

UPPER VOLTA

Upper Volta lies in one of the most densely populated parts of the west African savanna zone. Its population of 5 million is greater than that of the Ivory Coast in a rather smaller area, but its density bears little relation to the richness of its natural resources or the development of its economy. It is a poor and infertile land, almost entirely devoted to agriculture, with a degree of over-population unusual in this part of Africa. The reasons seem to lie in a long period of political stability and successful Mossi† resistance to the Fulani invasions of the nineteenth century.

Over-population and underdevelopment have led to a considerable migration of workers into neighbouring countries. Some have gone to Mali as colonists in the Niger Office scheme, some to work in the mines and on the cocoa farms of Ghana.

Economic ties with Ghana are close, but Upper Volta is associated with the Ivory Coast, Niger and Dahomey in the loose partnership of the Conseil de l'Entente. In an effort to

*Mines de Fer de la Mauritanie. †The chief tribe of the country.

encourage closer economic association within the Conseil and promote development, the railway from the Ivory Coast was extended to the capital, Ouagadougou, but much of Upper Volta's trade still goes through Ghana.*

NIGER

Niger is slightly smaller in area than Mali but larger than Nigeria, with only some 3·5 million people. Of these the Hausa constitute the biggest group (about a million), and Niger thus has close cultural as well as geographical links with northern Nigeria, links made stronger by the fact that Niger's line of communications with the outside world lies through Kano.

The population is concentrated in the south-west along the Niger river, and the main export crop is groundnuts.† Niger is drier than Mali, and there are accordingly fewer cattle for export. The cattle trade is, like the export of groundnuts, directed through Kano. Niger is one of the most remote of the African states and its biggest immediate economic problem is the development of adequate communications with the outside world.

STATES OF THE WEST AFRICAN COAST

GUINEA

Guinea is agriculturally the poorest of the three states, and has the smallest population (3·7 million in 1967). Until a few years ago its main exports consisted of bananas and citrus fruits from plantations on the Fouta Djallon, many of which were owned by non-Africans. Increasingly, however, it has been realized that Guinea's economic future is as an industrial rather than an agricultural country.

This is surprising at first sight, because varied relief has produced an unusual climatic variety, which in turn has provided possibilities for a varied agriculture. Rice and palm oil from the coastal swamps, fruit from the Fouta Djallon and tea and coffee

*Total exports in 1968 were valued at 5,290 million francs (£9m.), of which more than 60 per cent were live animals, with some cotton and groundnuts (*Europa Yearbook*, 1970, Vol. II).

†Over 60 per cent of a total value of 7,125 million francs (£12·1m.) (*Europa Year book*, 1970, Vol. II).

from other highland areas have all developed to some degree. All are hampered, however, by the quality of Guinean soils.* Guinea contains some of the world's most extensive deposits of laterite which, together with high and heavy rainfall and consequent washing away of top soil, make large areas almost useless for agriculture. If a land with similar soils existed in Europe two thirds would be regarded as unsuitable for either arable or pastoral farming. It has been estimated that

about 60 per cent of the country ought not to be cultivated ... About 30 per cent could be used if proper cultivation and anti-erosion methods were employed. Only about 10 per cent, mostly situated on the east coast and in river valleys, is capable of being cultivated without particular precautions.[14]

Although Guinea could conceivably be made more than self-sufficient in food, it is in its resources of bauxite, iron and hydro-electric power that the real wealth – and so the main hope for the future – of the country lies.

As long ago as 1912 bauxite was discovered on the Los islands, offshore from Conakry, the capital. This was in easily worked surface deposits, but no attempt was made to exploit them until 1949, when a French subsidiary of the Aluminium Laboratories of Canada began operations. The first shipment of ore left Guinea in 1952, and by 1955 annual production had risen to nearly half a million tons. Because the ore was not needed in France and was of a type not treated by any European plant, it was shipped to Canada for processing.

The Los island deposits are expected to be exhausted soon, and in anticipation of this event development, including the building of an alumina plant and a railway to the coast, was undertaken by the same company and by Halco (U.S.) in far richer deposits at Boké, about 100 miles north-west of Conakry.

More important still has been the discovery and working of yet richer deposits in the Fouta Djallon by an international consortium of companies known as F.R.I.A., whose alumina plant began production in 1960. The firm is financed largely by French, Swiss and American capital, and development has included the building of a dam on the Konkouré river at

*This is also true of much of Liberia and Sierra Leone.

Sonapité to provide cheap hydro-electric power. A further dam and alumina plant at Kerovane on the Konkouré is to be financed by the Russians. Agreement in principle on this project was reached in July 1965.

Iron ore is also worked near Conakry with capital provided from private Western sources. One third of the finance comes from the British Iron and Steel Corporation, and the major part of the output is used by the United Kingdom.

TABLE 17
Guinea. Exports in 1964 (by value)

	percentage
Alumina	59·8
Bananas	10·1
Palm nuts and palm kernels	6·6
Coffee	6·3
Iron ore	5·5
Diamonds	4·5
Other	7·2

Total value 11,086 million francs (£18·9m.)

SOURCE: *U.N. Yearbook of International Trade Statistics 1964*, p. 288.

Guinea is poor and even less developed than some of her neighbours, but she possesses the same advantages in the situation of her exploitable minerals as Britain enjoyed in the early days of the industrial revolution. Like most British coalfields, the iron and bauxite reserves are near the coast, and transport is accordingly cheap. Moreover, they are reserves which are attracting private investment capital in a way which countries without such mineral deposits cannot hope to do.

Guinea's chief problem now is to finance the less profitable side of her development plan – the dams, further transport facilities, agricultural improvements, and social services – the growth of which was stopped short by the sudden withdrawal of French capital in 1958.

Since independence there has been a considerable growth of

trade with East Germany, Czechoslovakia and the Soviet Union, but few reliable statistics are available for recent years.

Communist Chinese and Russian methods of rapid economic growth do seem to have an attraction for the leadership. In an interview in 1959, Sekou Touré, President of Guinea, expressed himself determined to go ahead with the first Konkouré Dam. 'We shall build it with our own hands if necessary,' he said, and cited developments in China as an example.[15] His own aim is to develop Guinea as an industrial country based on cheap electric power, producing aluminium houses, boats for river navigation, aircraft, trains and cars.

The truth seems to be that Guinea is determined on an industrial future and that for scarce capital she will go wherever she can get it. If it is not forthcoming in sufficient quantities, she may have to resort to popular mobilization on the communist Chinese or Russian model.

IVORY COAST

Ivory Coast ranks with Senegal as one of the two richest components of former French West Africa. In addition, under the formidable leadership of M. Houphoüet-Boigny, it has played a leading role in seeking to maintain close economic and political ties with France.

TABLE 18
Ivory Coast. Exports in 1967 (by value)

	percentage
Coffee	31·6
Wood	27·1
Cocoa	17·2
Bananas	3·7
Pineapples	3·0
Manganese	0·5
Other	16·9

Total value 80,263 million francs C.F.A. (£137m.)

SOURCE: *The Europa Yearbook*, 1970, Vol. II.

Economic development has until recently been hampered by lack of a suitable port, as Abidjan was cut off from the sea by a persistent sand bar. Only in 1950 were the engineering problems overcome, the Vridi canal opened, and Abidjan able to be developed as a major trade outlet.

The economy is based almost entirely on agriculture and the processing of agricultural products, although there is a small diamond and manganese mining industry.

Unusually for west Africa, about a quarter of the coffee crop is produced on European-owned plantations; but cocoa, introduced from the Gold Coast, is nearly all produced by African smallholders. Ivory Coast ranks as the third largest coffee producer in the world.

TOGO

Togo is one of the smallest independent states in Africa, consisting of that part of former German Togoland which became a French mandated territory in 1919. The part allotted to Britain elected to join independent Ghana. Togo is almost entirely an agricultural country and over half of all exports consist of cocoa and coffee, with subsidiary palm kernels and copra. More recently the mining of phosphates has made a welcome addition to the national income.*

Remarkably, among the former subjects of France, many people in Togo are literate in an African language and not in French. This is particularly true of the Ewe, for whom the Germans soon worked out an orthography and started to teach it. Like Swahili in Tanganyika, this has been an important factor in the development of nationalism, and may be measured particularly in the concern of the Ewe to be united with their fellow Ewe across the border in Ghana.

Togo is also remarkable in that it also has an English press which comes in from Ghana. There has been much population movement and commerce across the border, and many Ewe can speak and read English as well as (or instead of) French.[16]

It was thought at one time that the Ewe leaders of Togo

*1968: total exports were valued at 9,549 million francs (£16·3m.) (phosphates 33·8 per cent).

would wish to join with Ghana, but an independent existence has proved more attractive to them.

DAHOMEY

Dahomey has close affinities with neighbouring Nigeria. Just as the Ewe are divided between Togo and Ghana, so the Yoruba-speaking people spill over from Nigeria into Dahomey.

Like the Mossi of Upper Volta, Dahomey had a powerful indigenous political organization prior to French occupation. One consequence of this is that there has been considerable development of African-owned plantation agriculture, a system established in the mid nineteenth century by the labour of prisoners.

At present Dahomey is an entirely agricultural country, but deposits exist of high-grade iron ore and chromite.

TABLE 19
Dahomey. Exports in 1965 (by value)

	percentage
Palm oil and products	69·4
Cotton	4·6
Groundnuts	2·9
Other	23·1
Total value 3,304 million francs C.F.A. (£5·6m.)	

SOURCE: *The Europa Yearbook*, 1970, Vol. II.

THE EQUATORIAL STATES

CAMEROUN

The population is concentrated in two main areas. The first, in the far north, south of Lake Chad, corresponds in population and economic activities with Northern Nigeria; the second, in the south-west, is where the main wealth of the country lies.

Cameroun, like Togo, was divided in 1919 between French

and British administered mandates. By a plebiscite held in 1961, most of the former British area (i.e. the Southern Cameroons) elected to rejoin with independent Cameroun rather than with Nigeria. The Northern British Cameroons elected to join Nigeria.

There have been considerable economic and political problems in the way of integrating East and West Cameroun, not least the geographical isolation of the latter. This isolation has been overcome by the construction of new road and rail links, notably a new road across the Mungo and Wouri estuarine system between Victoria, Tiko (in the west) and Douala. This has reduced a difficult 240 km. road journey to only 56 km. This means that it has been possible to start developing the roadstead of Victoria into a deep water port; the expansion of Douala is limited by its position and by dredging problems.

New railways have also featured in recent developments. An extension of the Douala–Nkongsamba line strengthens ties with the West, while plans have been made to extend the Trans-Camerounais line beyond Ngaoundéré through to the cotton-growing areas of Chad.

German development of plantation agriculture in the fertile highland areas of the south-west was continued under subsequent administrations. The plantations are mainly African-owned, and the chief export crops are cocoa, coffee, palm kernels, bananas, cotton, rubber and timber.

There is a smelter at Edea for processing bauxite and, although deposits exist south of Ngaoundéré, the raw material is currently imported from Guinea.

In 1963 Cameroun produced almost half the Gross Domestic Product of those countries which in 1966 formed the Union Douanière et Économique de l'Afrique Centrale,* and has an encouraging diversity of growth points for the future.[17]

CHAD

Chad is the most remote of all the former French colonies. Not only are its communications with the outside world poor, but so are its internal communications. Few roads exist and these are of

*Cameroun, Central African Republic, Chad, Congo (Brazzaville) and Gabon.

TABLE 20
Cameroun. Exports in 1967 (by value)

	percentage
Coffee	28·8
Cocoa	25·2
Alumina	13·4
Timber	6·9
Cotton	4·7
Rubber	2·9
Palm products	2·6
Bananas	1·9
Other	13·6
Total value 37,540 million francs C.F.A. (£64m.)	

SOURCE: *The Europa Yearbook*, 1970, Vol. II.

poor quality. The northern half of the territory is semi-desert and populated by dissident tribesmen in revolt against the central government. In the central areas the land is too dry for anything except extensive cattle farming. Only in the south-west is there enough rainfall for crops, and here cotton has been developed as a cash crop.* Increased production of cotton and meat, with reduced transport costs for their export, are the main lines of development likely to be followed in the future.

The whole area has been hampered by lack of good communications. The coastal rain-forest prevented the early development of transport links with the more populous interior, while the generally low density of population (less than five per square mile) makes modern roads and railways extremely costly undertakings. Extension of the Trans-Camerounais railway into the southern areas would improve economic prospects.

CENTRAL AFRICAN REPUBLIC

This is potentially a rich country where cotton, coffee and cattle provide a firm agricultural base. Since 1962 diamond mining has

*Of total exports worth 6,635 million francs (£10·2m.) in 1967 over 80 per cent were cotton (*Europa Year Book*, 1970, Vol. II).

developed rapidly, providing much-needed income for investment in other sectors of the economy.

TABLE 21
Central African Republic. Exports in 1968 (by value)

	percentage
Diamonds	53·0
Cotton	23·4
Coffee	12·1
Wood	3·3
Other	8·2
Total value 8,816 million francs C.F.A. (£15m.)	

SOURCE: *The Europa Yearbook*, 1970, Vol. II.

GABON

It is Gabon, however, which has the best immediate prospect of income for future development. Gabon, the land of Schweitzer's 'Primeval Forest', now exports oil, uranium, thorium and manganese with the aid of Franco-American investment.* Manganese from Moanda is exported by rail through Pointe Noire, while another new railway link is being built from Libreville to the iron deposits at Mékambo. Refined oil will be produced at a new plant being built at Port Gentil.

CONGO REPUBLIC (BRAZZAVILLE)

Much of French investment in former Equatorial Africa concentrated on the improvement of communications, especially the expansion of port facilities at Brazzaville and Pointe Noire and the construction of the rail link between them. This accounts for the very high rate of post-war investment in Congo (Brazzaville) as compared with its neighbours. Brazzaville, like Dakar in the west, was designed to be both the administrative capital and

*Mineral output in 1968 was: crude oil, 4·6 million tons, manganese, 1·3 million tons, uranium, 1,370 tons, and gold, 512 kgs. (*Europa Yearbook*, 1970, Vol. II).

the economic hub of the whole of Equatorial Africa. Independent Congo, like Senegal, is heavily dependent on the cooperation and goodwill of its neighbours.

TABLE 22

Congo (Brazzaville). Exports in 1967 (by value)

	percentage
Wood	40·6
Diamonds*	32·3
Others (including less than 0·1 per cent of petroleum)	27·1
Total value 12,190 million francs C.F.A. (£20·8m.)	

SOURCE: *The Europa Yearbook*, 1970, Vol. II.

*Either from Central African Republic or smuggled from Kasai in Congo (Kinshasa).

MALAGASY REPUBLIC

The Malagasy Republic (Madagascar), an island of almost continental proportions, is both geographically and culturally a transitional zone between Africa and Asia. Its people seem to have come originally from both these continents, though the former ruling group (Merina or Hova) is probably of Asian origin. The population of 6·7 million is about one fifth Hova. Farming techniques suggest an African origin for most of the people but the national language – spoken by all groups – has affinities with the languages of Indonesia.

Rice is the staple food, covering about half the cultivated area, but plantation crops loom larger in the export figures.* Madagascar is a leading world producer of graphite but the total amount involved is small. There are extensive deposits of mica, nickel, copper and chromite.

The continuing close relationship between France and most of her former colonies has had two important results, one

*Total exports in 1967 were 25,711 million francs in value (£43·9m.). Coffee 31·5 per cent; spices 9·9 per cent; sugar 8·2 per cent; rice 7·1 per cent; raphia 3·5 per cent; other 39·8 per cent (*The Europa Yearbook*, 1970).

political and the other economic. Politically, although France has lost an empire, she has gained ten or eleven independent allies. In an age where votes in the U.N. General Assembly are important in international affairs, the support of the French African states has, on occasions, been of immense importance to France. For example, they succeeded in modifying U.N. General Assembly resolutions over Algeria and enabled France to continue until 1962 to postpone a settlement.

The economic result of continuing close association is possibly longer-lasting. When France joined the European Common Market she took her African territories with her. This means that the exports of French Africa have duty-free entry into the whole Common Market area, but that other African exports do not unless the countries concerned negotiate special agreements. Cocoa from the Ivory Coast, for example, has a tariff advantage over cocoa from Ghana. If Britain entered the Common Market without negotiating similar privileges for Commonwealth countries, it would have to admit French African products duty free, while imposing tariffs on goods from Commonwealth countries outside the Common Market. As they stand at present, the Common Market arrangements in Africa serve to perpetuate economic and political divisions between the French- and English-speaking areas.[18]

EQUATORIAL GUINEA

This gained its independence from Spain in October 1968 and consists of *Río Muni*, sandwiched between Cameroun and Gabon together with the volcanic islands of *Fernando Po* and *Annobon* which, like their Portuguese counterparts, have had their fertile soils developed for plantation agriculture, developed from the turn of the century with cocoa as the main crop, together with some coffee and palm kernels. Like São Tomé, Fernando Po imports migrant labour on a contract basis, much of it from the Ibo areas of Nigeria. Ninety per cent of the cocoa exports of Equatorial Guinea come from Fernando Po.

PORTUGUESE GUINEA

Portuguese Guinea is Portugal's remaining foothold in west Africa. Set between the Senegalese province of Casamance and independent Guinea, it is the third smallest political unit in west Africa, with only about half a million people. African guerilla groups claim control of more than half the country.

Unlike the other Portuguese territories, it is not a country of extensive white settlement[19] or of plantation agriculture. As with its southern neighbour, many of the coastal mangrove swamps have been cleared for rice cultivation: like that of its northern neighbour, its main export crop is groundnuts. Together with palm products, these make up about 80 per cent by value of the colony's exports.

Notes on Chapter 7

1. Speech to Territorial Conference of P.G.D., 14 September 1958, in Conakry. Quoted by T. Hodgkin and R. Schachter in 'French-speaking West Africa in Transition', special issue of *International Conciliation*, May 1960, p. 420.
2. See Chapter 4 above.
3. Much of Guinea's trade has been switched to Eastern Europe, which in 1959 took 16 per cent of exports and sent 9 per cent of imports. (Hodgkin and Schachter, op. cit., p. 423.)
4. G. Harrison Church, *West Africa*, 1968, p. 254.
5. V. Thompson and R. Adloff, *French West Africa*, 1960, p. 369.
6. ibid., p. 368.
7. John C. de Wilde *et al.*, *Agricultural Development in Tropical Africa*, Vol. II, 1968, p. 288.
8. ibid.
9. ibid., p. 247.
10. G. Harrison Church, op. cit., p. 245.
11. ibid., p. 251.
12. Climatically it is far superior to Bathurst in Gambia.
13. G. Harrison Church, 'Problems and Development of the Dry Zone of West Africa', in *Geographical Journal*, June 1961.
14. Tim Brierley, 'Mauritania', in *Geographical Magazine*, February 1965. *The Europa Yearbook*, 1970, Vol. II.
15. G. Harrison Church, *West Africa*, p. 389.
16. Article by Edwin S. Morrisby in the *Guardian*, 7 January 1959.
17. Committee on Inter-African Relations, *Report on the Press in West Africa*, 1961, p. 24. (Mimeographed. Distributed by

Dept of Extra-Mural Studies, University College, Ibadan, Nigeria.)

18. P. Robson, in A. Hazlewood, (ed.), *African Integration and Disintegration*, 1968, p. 31.
19. See also Aaron Segal, 'Africa Newly Divided', in *Journal of Modern African Studies*, March 1964, p. 73.
20. 1950 population 508,970 of which

Balante	160,296 (the coastal people)
Fulani	108,402
Manjalus	71,712
Mandingo	53,750
Whites	2,263

SOURCE: Texeiria da Mota, *Guiné Portuguesa*, 1954.

See also:

Philip Neres, *French-speaking West Africa*, 1962.

Wm. J. Faltz, *From French West Africa to the Mali Federation*, 1965.

R. J. Harrison Church, *West Africa*, 6th ed., 1968, has useful chapters (27 and 28) on both the former Spanish and the Portuguese islands. These chapters also contain bibliographies of the Spanish and Portuguese literature on the islands.

Central Africa

8 Angola, Moçambique, São Tomé, Principe, and Congo (Kinshasa)

Portugal was the first European country to colonize in Africa; Belgium, one of the last. Both have ruled over enormous territories and both ruled with a paternalistic attitude to their subjects. They allowed no political opposition to develop and no political leaders to mature. Both have attracted world attention only in the last few years. There were, however, significant differences in the policies and programmes of the two countries.

The Belgians in the Congo, while intending to stay as rulers for a long time to come, started on a long-term programme leading to eventual self-government and undertook an ambitious ten-year development plan, financed largely by the mining industries of Katanga and Kasai. The Portuguese, on the other hand, have only been actively developing the interior of either Angola or Moçambique for the last twenty-five years, and they still regard all their overseas possessions as integral parts of the mother country. Portuguese policy is in theory fully assimilationist; that is, all the inhabitants of their territories are entitled to the full rights of citizenship once they have achieved the required standard of 'civilization'. Very few Africans have, however, acquired this status of *assimilado*.

In the early 1930s the Salazar régime began to revive the consciousness of Portugal's imperial destiny as intrinsic to its programme of national regeneration, a revival stirred by such phrases as 'the magnificent certainty that we are the third colonial power in the world'.[1]

The sense of destiny has been strengthened in recent years by unparalleled economic progress, rising white immigration, rapid urban and industrial growth and increasing support for Portugal's own stagnant economy. 'Angola and Moçambique between them contribute directly or indirectly, up to 25 per cent of Portugal's national budget.'[2] In this new consciousness of empire,

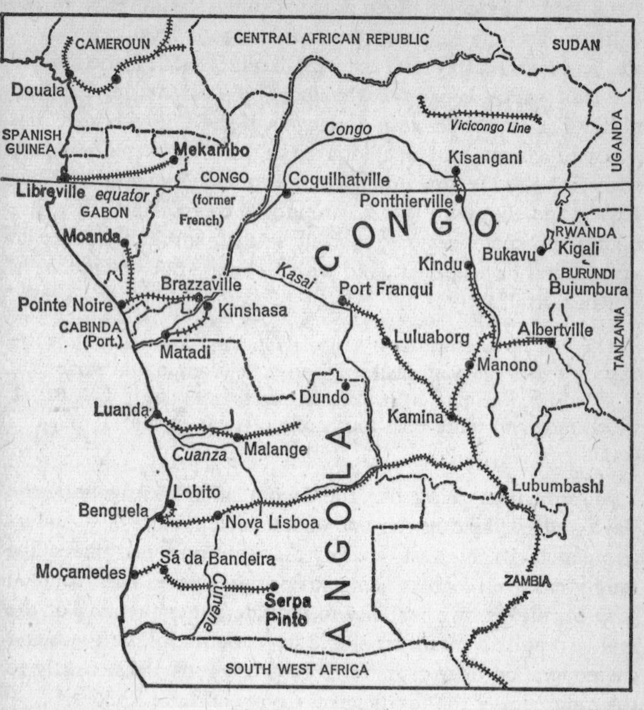

MAP 20. The Congo and Angola

the territory which has loomed largest in the minds of both politicians and economic planners is the relatively unknown land of Angola. Some four times the size of the United Kingdom, Angola is the promised land of the Portuguese Empire.

ANGOLA

The coastal strip (up to 100 miles wide) is kept both arid and cool for the latitude by the cold Benguela ocean current, which

flows along the coast. Even Luanda, only 600 miles from the equator, has only eleven inches of rain a year. Inland, however, the land rises sharply, and the rainfall increases. It is the interior plateaux which constitute the focus of current development plans. The north, between Malange and the Congo border, has a tropical climate and plantation agriculture has been developed, with coffee as the main crop. In the centre (Bié) around Nova Lisboa and the south (Huila) around Sá da Bandeira, there are higher and cooler regions, sparsely settled, admirably suited to agricultural development, and with a climate not unlike that of Portugal itself.[3]

The first three centuries of Angola's history, from about 1550 to 1850, is a chronology of small wars and expeditions in the interior and of a dedicated commerce in black humanity, most of it with Brazil, which made up more than four fifths of total exports during this period.[4]

More than anything else, the depopulation of Angola by the slave trade is the cause of one of its chief handicaps – under-population. In this vast territory there are only just under five million people, of whom some 300,000 are white. This, coupled with Portugal's own inability to provide either the men or the money required, meant economic stagnation until the 1950s and the emigration of workers to more prosperous areas, chiefly to the industries of the (ex-Belgian) Congo and the Rhodesias.

The boom of the last twenty years is associated both with agricultural settlements for whites and, more recently, with the development of mining. Mining has developed along the Luanda railway for manganese, iron ore, asphalt, phosphates and petroleum.

The economy is also boosted by the 'invisible' exports of the transit trade from Congo and Rhodesia, and a large part of railway and port development had been paid for by British and Belgian private capital.* Angola's other principal sources of revenue are coffee, diamonds, iron ore, fish and a variety of agricultural products. Diamonds were, until recently, the

*The biggest shareholder in the Benguela railway is the British Company, Tanganyika Concessions. With political disorders in the Congo, much more copper traffic came to this railway. Traffic again increased with the diversion of Zambian copper exports from Rhodesia after U.D.I.

colony's chief export and are won from workings near the Congo border across which lies the much bigger diamond field of Kasai. Mining is controlled by the Diamond Company of Angola (Diamang). Tucked away in this remote corner of the country with its headquarters in a garden city of its own creation (Dundo), Diamang is a colony within a colony and very much its own master.

The fishing industry and the processing of fish meal, much of which, like the country's coffee, goes to the United States, are both centred on Benguela and Moçamedes, towns far more reminiscent of Portugal than of Africa.

TABLE 23

Angola. Exports in 1968 (by value)

	percentage
Coffee	45·2
Diamonds	17·4
Iron ore	8·2
Maize	3·1
Sisal	2·5
Cotton	2·4
Wood	2·4
Fish meal	1·7
Dried fish	1·5
Fuel oil	1·3
Other	14·3

Total value 7,796·4 million escudos (£108·3m.)

SOURCE: *The Europa Yearbook*, 1970, Vol. II.

White Settlement in Angola

The central and southern highlands are the scene of an experiment unparalleled in Africa today – the settlement of Portuguese families as smallholders working their own land and tending their own cattle without the help of native labour.

Deliberate encouragement of white settlement did not start until the 1940s, when it was decided officially for the first time that 'the rich extensive colonial lands, undeveloped and sparsely populated, are the natural complement for metropolitan agriculture.... In addition they will take care of that part of the metropolis's excessive population which Brazil does not wish to accept'.[5] A further reason is the drive to demonstrate to Africans, by example, the Portuguese way of life.

Early efforts at planned colonization on the Huila plateau were not very successful, but in 1952 began the first of a series of planned colonization projects known as *colonatos*. The site of the first pilot scheme was at Cela on the Amboin plateau, about 240 miles north-west of Nova Lisboa. Here by 1954 over 200 Portuguese families had been installed, each receiving a house, seeds, livestock, and over 100 acres of land. A conscious effort was made to re-create the atmosphere of rural Portugal, and wherever possible immigrants were chosen from the same home district.

The white population of Angola grew from 44,000 in 1940 to 110,000 in 1955 and has now topped 300,000. The centre for current immigration and rural development plans is on the southern Huila plateau. The railway has been extended inland from Sá da Bandeira to Serpa Pinto, hydro-electric and irrigation schemes are being undertaken on the Cunene river, and further *colonatos* being prepared. Out of a total of £36 million earmarked for Angola in the 1953 six-year Development Plan, over £27 million went to Huila.[6] Oil is the latest resource to be exploited, starting in 1969 and with excellent prospects forecast.

White settlement on the land has also been undertaken in Moçambique, although the climate is less suitable there and the numbers involved are not yet quite so high. Portugal clearly intends to extend the *colonato* system, particularly in the south of Angola and in Moçambique following on the building of the Cabora Bassa dam (see below). Since Portugal is committed to establishing the Portuguese way of life in Africa, since the colonists are forbidden to use African labour, and since in southern Angola there is a relative abundance of land, it was hoped that friction between Africans and Europeans would be kept to a minimum. Nevertheless, increased immigration is already creating discontent. The available funds are being spent on pro-

jects which benefit primarily the European colonists.[7] Job opportunities for Africans are decreasing as the number of poor white immigrants increase, some of whom drift to the cities rather than stay on the land. Many manual jobs are now taken by Portuguese immigrants and colour consciousness has already led to violent clashes in territories which at one time boasted a culture bar rather than a colour bar. Increasingly, Portugal's social as well as political policies come to resemble those of South Africa and Rhodesia.

Angola is really five very different worlds – the old-established and hitherto easy-going coastal towns, the Diamang Concession in the far north-east, the sparsely settled and almost untouched eastern half of the country, the central and southern highlands with their unique experiment in mid-twentieth-century white settlement, and the plantation agriculture of the north.

In this last area, there is a tribal overlap with both Congo Republics. The area around the mouth of the Congo river is occupied by the Bakongo people whose memories go back to a united kingdom in the fifteenth and sixteenth centuries.

MOÇAMBIQUE

White colonization in Moçambique has been less effective although there were in 1950 some 50,000 Europeans living in the colony, mostly in Beira or Lourenço Marques, fine modern cities, which live off the transit trade from Rhodesia and the Republic of South Africa. Some agricultural *colonatos* have been started, but on a smaller scale than in Angola. The most notable is at Guijà on the Limpopo. Much of the country is low-lying and malarial, and there has been considerable emigration of workers into the Rhodesias, Malawi and the Republic.

The *Cabora Bassa* dam, on which work started in 1968, and the Zambezi Valley Development Project, should together transform the territory's economy. The dam will be one of the world's largest and will create a lake over 160 miles long. It will allow irrigation of 3·5 million acres and will enable Zambezi valley deposits of iron, coal, manganese and chrome to be developed. It is intended that much of this work will be done by Portuguese immigrants – who would come in in such numbers that the

whole ethnic balance and political future would also be transformed. This is one reason why the project has aroused so much opposition in independent Africa, where it is seen as a symbol of white supremacy. Another is that it will tie the economy even more closely to that of South Africa. The electricity produced is to be linked to the South African grid and, indeed, purchase of electricity by South Africa is necessary to ensure the dam's economic viability.

Another mining development proposed is of iron ore in Namapa, to be exported through Nacala – said to be the finest natural harbour in eastern Africa. This harbour is also likely to become a major outlet for Malawi once the Nacala–Vila Cabral railway is extended (late 1970) to that country.

TABLE 24
Moçambique. Exports in 1968 (by value)

	percentage
Cashew nuts	23·1
Cotton	14·3
Sugar	9·3
Tea	6·6
Copper	6·2
Vegetable oils	4·2
Wood	4·1
Sisal	2·0
Other	30·2

Total value 4,420·2 million escudos (£64·3m.)

SOURCE: *The Europa Yearbook*, 1970, Vol. II.

However, until these developments begin to mature, Moçambique remains an essentially agricultural country with a list of export crops notable more for their variety than their volume. But it is clear that with a comprehensive investment programme and a settlement of political problems the country could one day play a much more significant role than has hitherto been the case.

SÃO TOMÉ AND PRÍNCIPE

Recent charges of forced labour in Angola[8] confirmed by a U.N. investigation have re-awakened interest in similar charges against Portugal early in this century;[9] charges which led to a boycott by Cadbury Brothers of cocoa from São Tomé.

São Tomé and Príncipe are small islands lying some 200 miles off-shore from Gabon and Spanish Guinea.

Occupied by Portugal since the fifteenth century, they have a population of about 60,000 and are organized for the production of cocoa and coffee on large plantations. Much of the labour is provided by Africans brought over from the mainland on four- or five-year contracts, many of them from the Ibo areas of Nigeria. They are paid a minimum wage equivalent to £1·50 a month, with free food, barrack lodging, and medical attention. Another source is the labour of prisoners and unconvicted detainees, of whom there are large numbers.

Although there is no colour bar, cultural and economic differences mean that there are in fact self-contained 'racial classes' with rigid occupational and social immobility. Efforts are being made to reform the contract labour system into a permanent one by means of grants of land.[10]

It is clear from the high value of exports per head of population* that São Tomé is one of the most likely places where charges of 'colonial exploitation' can be made to stick. The standard of living is no higher than in the rest of Portugal's colonies and the conclusion must be drawn that, whatever the liabilities of colonial ownership, São Tomé is for Portugal a very profitable piece of real estate.

CONGO (KINSHASA)**

Belgium's only colony† started out in 1908 with a legacy of misrule and maladministration from the Congo Free State of King Leopold. It moved through a period when it became the

*See Table 5.

**Changed its name to Republic of Zaire in October 1971.

†Rwanda and Burundi, formerly Belgian-administered U.N. Trust Territories, are considered in Chapter 10.

envy of some of its neighbours as a model of benevolent paternalism and, more recently, back again not so much to misrule as to chaos and international dispute.

Prior to the riots of January 1959 in Leopoldville, the Congo had indeed seemed miraculously peaceful and wonderfully prosperous. There were more and more children going to school, more and more hospitals – and no politics. Said the Belgian information service: 'It is true that no one votes in the Congo; they work. The Belgians prefer administration to politics.'[11] When politics did come, they came with devastating suddenness to a colony which was in many ways educated for 'work' but completely undeveloped for 'votes'. Belgium boasted of the fact that 40 per cent of school-age children were in school (compared with 19 per cent in the Rhodesias), but neglected to mention that less than 3,000 (1960) had completed more than seven years' schooling and that most of that schooling was in the many local vernacular languages.[12]

The absence of higher education and the use of the different tribal languages as the media for school instruction meant that such political consciousness as had developed was local and tribal rather than national, a factor furthered by the enormous size of the country – as big as Western Europe – and its relatively tiny population (16·3 million in 1967). Of this number, only about a million are urban. At the time of independence there were about 110,000 whites.

The Congo is dominated physically by the immense shallow depression known as the Congo Basin, and the extensive river system which drains it. Here, in the central and western areas, lie those thousands of square miles of sparsely inhabited equatorial forests which are often thought to characterize the whole. But the Congo is a land of great variety in the challenges and opportunities which are offered by a whole series of different environments.

Roughly south-east of a line drawn through Kinshasa (Leopoldville), Luluabourg and Kisangani (Stanleyville), the dense forest ceases. Moving southwards, distances from the equator are great enough to bring about an increase in the length of the dry season, until ultimately the land rises to the high plateau of Katanga, where temperatures are considerably modified by alti-

tude and the seasonal aridity of the land is intensified by poor and rocky soils.

To the east of the forest areas the land rises slowly and then spectacularly to the high, moist, but cool lands round the east African lakes of Kivu, Tanganyika, Edward, and Albert. Here were fertile plantations and tourist centres, which may one day rival more well-known places in popularity. Bukavu on Lake Kivu was described as 'a combination of Lake Lucerne and the Bay of St Tropez'.[13] Sadly, however, it is just these areas which have been most neglected and most devastated since 1960 as a result of civil strife.

The diverse parts of this great country are tied together geographically by the Congo river system, both for transport and the actual or potential production of power.

The Congo river is fed by streams which arise some distance away on both sides of the equator. As a result some of the tributary streams are experiencing the Northern Hemisphere dry season at the same time as others are experiencing the Southern Hemisphere wet season – and *vice versa*. This means that the Congo–Lualaba main stream has one of the most even flows of any great river in the world.

As well as an even flow, the Congo is also noted for the falls and rapids which impede navigation at a number of points. Passing up-stream from the Atlantic, the first and major obstacle is a series of falls and rapids from the port of Matadi to Kinshasa at Stanley Pool. There is then a clear stretch of over 1,000 miles to Kisangani, where navigation is again impeded – by Stanley Falls. From Ponthierville the river (now the Lualaba) is again navigable a further 200 miles to Kindu.

This combination of even flow and major navigation obstacles means that the Congo is an excellent source of hydro-electric power but that its usefulness as a major highway is severely limited. Nevertheless the Belgians succeeded in making the Congo and its tributaries into a major transport system by a series of linking railways to overcome the rapids and falls. Loading and unloading at the rail-river trans-shipment points is, of course, costly, but not as expensive as a more extensive railway network and the neglect of cheap water transport. The first linking railway to be built, finished in 1898, was the link from Matadi

to Leopoldville (Kinshasa), an essential prerequisite if the Congo Basin was to be opened to trade at all. The cost in money and lives (over 2,000) was great, but without it the Congo would have remained in isolation. Other links run from Kisangani to Ponthierville, Port Franqui on the Kasai head of navigation to Lubumbashi and Zambia, Kindu to Kabalo and, the most recent, from Kabalo to the Lubumbashi line.

This coordination of river and rail transport links has been accompanied by the development of the Congo's different environments into a complementary economic whole. Rivers and railways link each productive area and provide lines of both urban and rural settlement between them.[14]

Some regions and provinces* are heavily dependent on one or two export products, but taken as a whole the economy has been well diversified. If the Congo retains its unity, indeed, this diversified development will be a great asset for the future. If not each region will be the poorer, or else far too dependent on one or two major commodities.

By 1964 the value of exports had risen almost to pre-1960 levels (24,000 million francs in 1959) from the disastrous fall of the early 1960s (4,000 million francs in 1960). Mining has been able to improve on the levels of 1960 and copper production reached a record 360,000 tons in 1969.[15]

The economic life of the Leopoldville area is centred on the ports of Kinshasa and Matadi, through which passes most of the Congo's trade. In addition there are some plantations for palm oil, cocoa, rubber and coffee. Many of those for palm oil are controlled by Lever Brothers' subsidiary, the Compagnies des Huileries du Congo Belge.

The falls below Kinshasa have a tremendous hydro-electric potential as yet undeveloped; the Belgians preferred to build small barrages to serve the various industrial and urban centres. Although some coal is mined, most of the Congo's power is provided by these small barrages. In 1968 work began on the first stage of a large power scheme in the Inga region.

The central areas are the least developed, and most heavily forested, areas, though with the 1968 discovery of oil, more

*The six provinces of pre-independence days have now been divided into twenty-one, mostly on a tribal basis.

development is planned. South Kasai towards the Angola border is the centre of the diamond industry, controlled by the Forminière (Société Internationale Forestière et Minière du Congo), and satisfies most of the world demand for industrial diamonds.[16]

TABLE 25
Congo (Kinshasa). Exports in 1967 (by value) excluding uranium

	percentage
Copper	59·5
Palm oil and kernels	6·9
Coffee	5·8
Diamonds	5·4
Cobalt	4·8
Tin	3·8
Zinc	3·4
Rubber	2·7
Other	7·7
Total value 65·232 million zaire (£54·4 m.)	

SOURCE: *The Europa Yearbook*, 1970, Vol. II.

North of Kisangani is the largest area of European-established plantations in the country, and is served by the 2 ft gauge Vicicongo railway (Société de Chemins de Fer Vicinaux du Congo). Cotton, coffee, palm oil, palm kernels, rice and lumber all start their long journey from here, whence they are shipped down the Congo.

This area, and also around Kivu, has a balance of economic activities and contains some of the most attractive and comfortable areas in which to live. Tin is mined in Kivu and at Manono and there are plantations for cinchona, tea, coffee and pyrethrum. Even grapes are grown near Lake Kivu, giving two vintages a year from rich volcanic soils.

Before independence Katanga provided up to 60 per cent of the Congo's revenue,[17] with only some 17 per cent of the population, which fact alone helps to explain separatist tendencies. The area is heavily dependent on its copper, cobalt and uranium production, as not only are the soils poor but the Union Minière,

unlike its counterparts in Zambia, has done little to encourage any agricultural activity.

Katanga was very much the creation of the Union Minière. It was a barren, thinly-peopled land before the company began to exploit the rich and easily-worked copper deposits. Many workers were imported from other parts of the Congo, and a deliberate policy of both settled labour and rapid African advancement in industrial skills was pursued. Alone among the developed areas, Katanga did not need to rely on river transport. The railway routes to Lobito and Beira are cheaper than the all-Congo route.

The Congo was developed by Belgium as an economic whole. Much of it was well prepared for economic advance, but at the same time was kept politically mute. Inevitably, this lack of political education and experience meant that local and tribal influences remained strong, while political movements dedicated to disrupting Congolese unity could combat those seeking to preserve it. Even the first and most important agitation for independence was not conducted by the unity-minded M.N.C. (Mouvement National Congolais) of Patrice Lumumba but by the tribal Abako party, representing the Bakongo tribe. In the elections of 1960 there were 110 competing political parties, most of them local and tribal groups. Only the M.N.C. – the largest single party – stood for national unity.

The other tribal party of some significance was the Conakat of M. Tshombe in Katanga. Supported by the Lunda and Bemba, as well as by most of the Europeans and industrialists in the province, it gained a narrow majority in the 1960 elections,[18] with the Balubas providing the main opposition (Balubakat) in the north. Both Lunda and Bemba extend into Zambia, but in the quite different political atmosphere in this former British territory tribal nationalists are not very popular with local African politicians.

Belgium's mistakes were so obvious and disastrous that it is easy to belittle the achievements. For much progress in the economic and social fields was made, particularly over the final decade of Belgian rule. It is still fair comment to say that the Belgians in the Congo were 'enlightened industrialists but short-sighted politicians'.[19]

Notes on Chapter 8

1. Quoted by J. Duffy in *Portuguese Africa*, 1959, p. 270.
2. J. Duffy in Colin Legum (ed.), *Africa: a Handbook*, 1965, p. 291.
3. Sá da Bandeira has 64·6 degrees F. mean annual temperature and 43 inches rain.
4. Duffy, op. cit., p. 49.
5. Salazar, 1943, quoted in Duffy, op. cit., p. 337.
6. P. B. Stone, 'New Development in South Angola', in *South African Geographical Journal*, December 1957.
7. ibid.
8. See Basil Davidson, *The African Awakening*, 1955.
9. H. W. Nevinson, *A Modern Slavery*, 1906.
10. R. J. Harrison Church, *West Africa*, 6th ed., 1968, Chapter 28.
11. Quoted by Colin Legum in 'What Went Wrong with the Congo', *Observer*, 14 August 1960.
12. Quoted by Clyde Sanger in the *Guardian*, 23 February 1961.
13. T. Marvel, *The New Congo*, 1949, p. 208.
14. The revolution in the life of Kasai brought about by the railway is discussed in H. Nicolai and J. Jacques, *La Transformation des passages congolais par le chemin de fer, l'exemple du BCK*, 1954.
15. 'Mobutu's Magic', in *Economist*, 5 September 1970.
16. Hailey, op. cit., p. 1516.
17. It is impossible to be more precise because of lack of information about uranium production.
18. *Congo Tribes and Parties*, Royal Anthropological Institute, 1961. In the elections, Balubakat gained five seats in the Senate as against seven for Conakat. In the Chamber of Representatives Balubakat gained seven seats as against eight for Conakat. See also Colin Legum, *Congo Disaster*, Penguin Special, 1961.

19. Basil Davidson in *New Statesman and Nation*, 24 April 1954.

See also C. Hoskyns, *The Congo Since Independence*, 1964. R. H. Chilcote, *Portuguese Africa*, 1967, for historical data and comment on current politics.

9 Rhodesia, Malawi and Zambia

These three countries were joined together in the Federation of Rhodesia and Nyasaland in 1953 amidst a storm of controversy both in Africa and in Britain. Advocates of Federation won the day largely on the economic arguments advanced: that the economies of the three territories were complementary and that they would be more prosperous together than apart. Opposition to Federation came from those with political objections, especially the Africans of Northern Rhodesia and Nyasaland. They feared that the effective control of Southern Rhodesia by the European minority and the system of segregation practised there would be extended northwards under a federal system. They argued that economic cooperation was possible without political union and that any economic advantages would be outweighed by political disadvantages.

Africans in Southern Rhodesia were somewhat less hostile to Federation, probably because they hoped their own position would be strengthened by association with the more liberal north. Some Europeans in Southern Rhodesia also opposed Federation on similar grounds, fearing that they would be swamped by the black majority in the northern territories.

Ten years later the Federation was dismantled. Nyasaland became the independent state of Malawi and Northern Rhodesia the independent state of Zambia (1964). Rhodesia declared her independence illegally in 1965, an act which has had important economic as well as political consequences (see below, pp. 183 and 188).

Political opposition to Federation had increased since 1953, especially among Africans in the north. The Monckton Commission[1] reported that they 'were left in no doubt that genuine opposition to Federation on the part of Africans in the Northern Territories has grown more intense.'[2] The Africans pointed out that attachment to Federation had held up political progress and that this was more important than any possible

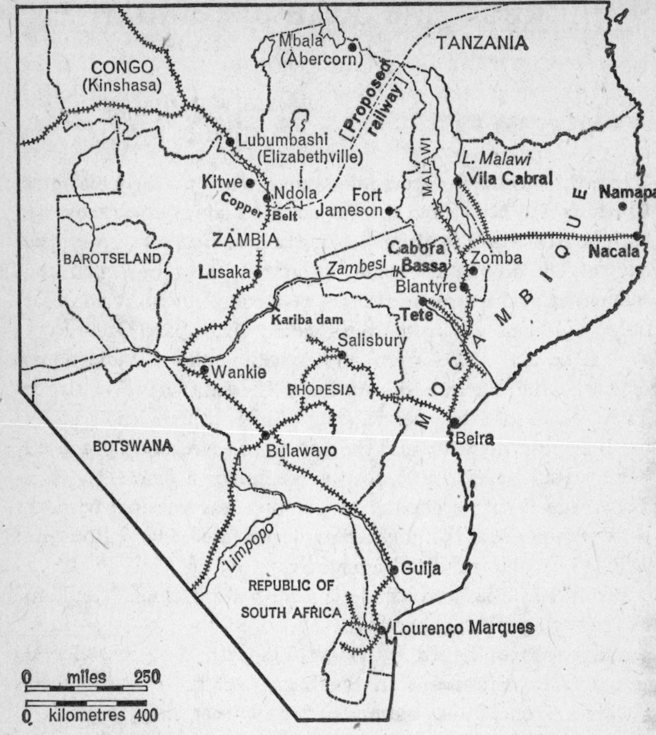

MAP 21. Central Africa and Moçambique

economic advantages, which they tended to discount anyhow.

The breakdown of the conference of 1960, assembled to review the Federal Constitution, made it clear that further inter-territorial development was impossible until the future constitutions and direction of development of the individual territories had been worked out. The three territories certainly made strange political bedfellows.

Northern Rhodesia and Nyasaland were Protectorates, controlled ultimately by Governors appointed by the British Government. Even before U.D.I. Rhodesia's European minority ruled itself. It is the largest of all the European communities in southern Africa outside the Republic and has had full internal

self-government since 1923. Whereas in the two Northern territories the interests of the Africans were clearly paramount, and government was largely indirect through the native chiefs, in the south it seemed right and proper – in 1923 – to concede to the British pioneers in Rhodesia what had already been granted to those in Canada, Australia, New Zealand and South Africa. Even in 1923, however, the granting of internal self-government to the Southern Rhodesian whites was clearly a marginal case and could only have been done on the expectation of a further increase in the numbers involved. Today they number only about 7 per cent of the total population in that territory.

TABLE 26

Rhodesia, Zambia and Malawi. Population Estimates

	(in 1,000s to the nearest thousand)		
	Rhodesia (1969)	*Zambia (1969)*	*Malawi (1966)*
Europeans	230	70	7
Africans	4,840	3,973	4,042
Others	24	13	10
	5,094	4,056*	4,059

SOURCES: *The Europa Yearbook*, 1970, Vol. II.
U.N. Demographic Yearbook, 1969.
H.M.S.O. *A Yearbook of the Commonwealth*, 1970.

RHODESIA

Rhodesia is a land some two or three times as large as England and Wales but the productive wealth of the country is concentrated into less than half the total area. About one third is the unhealthy Low Veld, lying below 2,000 ft, much of it tsetse-infested and malarial and having an uncertain rainfall. The Low Veld covers large tracts of the country on both its northern and southern boundaries – along the Zambezi in the north and the Limpopo in the south.

The most important area is the High Veld (generally from four to five thousand feet), where a combination of altitude,

* Census figure (corrected for under-enumeration).

good soils, adequate rainfall and some exploitable minerals have concentrated the European population and as many of the Africans as can find employment there.[3] The High Veld stretches from the south-west to the north-east, from the neighbourhood of Bulawayo to that of Salisbury. It is a fairly narrow strip about 50 miles wide covering about 20 per cent of the area of the country. North and east of Salisbury are two narrower extensions of the High Veld, both over 5,000 ft in altitude. The eastern extension is the larger and continues over the border into Moçambique.

The High Veld contains the line of rail* and the major towns. In the north-eastern area around Salisbury, rainfall is adequate (over 30 ins.) for crop cultivation, but in the south-west, in areas of 25 ins. of rainfall or less, ranching becomes more important. Here in the south-west are most of the country's important minerals, among them asbestos, chrome and gold. Away from the High Veld the altitude of the plateau surface falls away on both sides to the Middle Veld (3,000–4,000 ft) and beyond that to the Low Veld.

The Middle Veld covers between 40 and 50 per cent of the total land area and although much of it is good land it has been less developed than the High Veld and it has poorer communications. Much of it is African-owned and it is here that there are the greatest concentrations of the rural African population.[4] Coal is found in the Middle Veld at Wankie in the north-west.

The European Population

The European population came to Southern Rhodesia as conquerors and the facts of that conquest have coloured their attitudes ever since.

Prior to the European occupation, much of the south and west of the country was under the rule of Lobengula, King of the Matabele. This warlike tribe was centred on the site of modern Bulawayo from where they forced their attentions and exercised their authority (by cattle raiding) over the less well-organized Mashona to the north and east.

*Except that from Bulawayo through Wankie to Livingstone. This is the Middle Veld.

European penetration was initiated by Rhodes's British South Africa Company, which in 1888 succeeded in obtaining from Lobengula the right to mine minerals throughout his domains. The Company obtained a Royal Charter from the British Government in the following year. Although the mineral concession contained no rights of settlement, Company rule was soon extended to the Mashona areas. By 1893 Lobengula himself was driven from his Kraal and the whole territory brought under Company rule.

This conquest is still seen today by white Rhodesians as part of a glorious Imperial past and is taught as such in Rhodesian schools. The national holidays of Rhodes Day, Founder's Day, Pioneer Day and others, all help to drive the point home. Moreover, the conquest is not seen as aggression but as a valiant pioneer struggle against natural obstacles – including the natives. In this respect it resembles the American view of their own 'manifest destiny' in occupying the whole of the United States. The pale echoes of the U.S. Declaration of Independence in Rhodesia's U.D.I. indicate that white Rhodesians continue to view themselves in this heroic image. In the case of Rhodesia, however, there were an inconveniently large number of natives still left when the occupation was completed. Nevertheless, development assumed that Southern Rhodesia would remain solely a white man's country.

As E. Clegg puts it:

> Economic development was thought of as being entirely in the hands of Europeans. They were creating a new world, their world. The African was needed as an instrument to help in that creation: he was not wanted as a permanent feature of it. His home was the tribal village. This attitude was not surprising. The African was a naked savage; his life bounded by the spear and primitive agriculture. To think of the differences between the races being bridged was to stretch human credulity unreasonably.[5]

Unfortunately for this point of view, the material differences between the races have narrowed, while the political gulf remains as wide as ever.

The structure of the European population has been analysed by Colin Leys.[6] Among other things, he points out that this population is still largely made up of immigrants as distinct from

those who are Rhodesian born, and that urban manual workers form an important element in the community.

Over two thirds are immigrants, a majority of whom have moved into Rhodesia from Britain, having stayed some time in South Africa. In addition, schooling and university education as well as holidays are often taken there, so that the influence of South African racial ideas on the European community has been strong. Further, most of the immigrants move into manual jobs where they have little social and economic security and where they are rapidly made aware of the potential economic competition of Africans.

TABLE 27

European employment (men only). Southern Rhodesia and England & Wales, 1951

	Southern Rhodesia percentage	*England & Wales* percentage
Agricultural		
1. Farmers	15·1	2·1
2. Farm workers	0·6	5·2
Non-Agricultural		
3. Professional and administrative workers, employers and shopkeepers	25·8	16·7
4. Clerical workers	10·8	5·1
5. Shop assistants	6·2	3·4
6. Skilled manual workers and foremen	38·5	40·5
7. Semi-skilled and unskilled manual workers	1·7	24·7

SOURCE: 1951 Population Censuses, Southern Rhodesia and U.K. Quoted in C. Leys, *European Politics in Southern Rhodesia*, 1959.

It will be seen from Table 27 that the three really striking differences between the Southern Rhodesian employment pattern and that of England and Wales are the larger number of farmers, the smaller number of farm workers, and the smaller

number of unskilled and semi-skilled workers outside agriculture. These are, perhaps, what we should expect without access to statistics. A country which depends on agricultural exports may be expected to have a larger percentage of farmers than Britain, while the unskilled and semi-skilled work is mostly done by non-Europeans. What may be surprising to the outsider is that so many Europeans are engaged in manual work at all. This certainly has great political significance.

No less than 40·2 per cent of employed male Europeans are engaged in non-agricultural manual work. If some of the clerical workers and shop assistants are included, we can assume that nearly half the European population is dependent on jobs in which Africans are beginning to acquire skills and into which they demand entry. Many of these jobs have been 'traditionally' European, at rates of pay which a poor country like Rhodesia cannot afford on a mass scale. The standard of living of large numbers of Europeans would thus be directly threatened if entry to employment was made to depend entirely on ability. In present political circumstances there is no threat to the white skilled labour force, because the number of skilled Africans is still too few, but it could place a high proportion of Europeans' jobs in jeopardy if the Europeans give up their political control.

The racial division between unskilled and skilled work has been aided by the educational system. The education of whites is universal and free. The education of Africans, especially in secondary education, still lags far behind. State expenditure on education per head of population is ten times as high for Europeans as for Africans.[7] Both in job reservation and in education the Europeans still form a privileged caste. Their privileges can only be maintained by the continuance of white political control.

The European population is essentially urban, the African still essentially rural, although the African drift to the towns is gathering momentum as industrialization proceeds. These urban areas are the centre of European life and the chief growing points of the economy, but land and land policy are still crucial.

The *Land Apportionment Act* of 1931 was the cornerstone of land policy and the basis of segregation in Southern Rhodesia. The Whitehead Government had been preparing to abolish it but it was kept in force by its successors until replaced by

the *Land Tenure Act* of 1969. Under the terms of the Land Apportionment Act the whole country was divided into African (44·4 million acres) and European (35·6 million acres) areas, plus some areas of Crown and unreserved land (16·5 million acres) not then allocated (mostly in the Low Veld). The Land Tenure Act makes this division more rigid by abolishing the Crown lands and adding to the European, so that both Europeans and Africans now have 44·95 million acres with 6·6 million acres of 'National' land. The European area is a continuous belt of country including the lines of rail and contains all the main

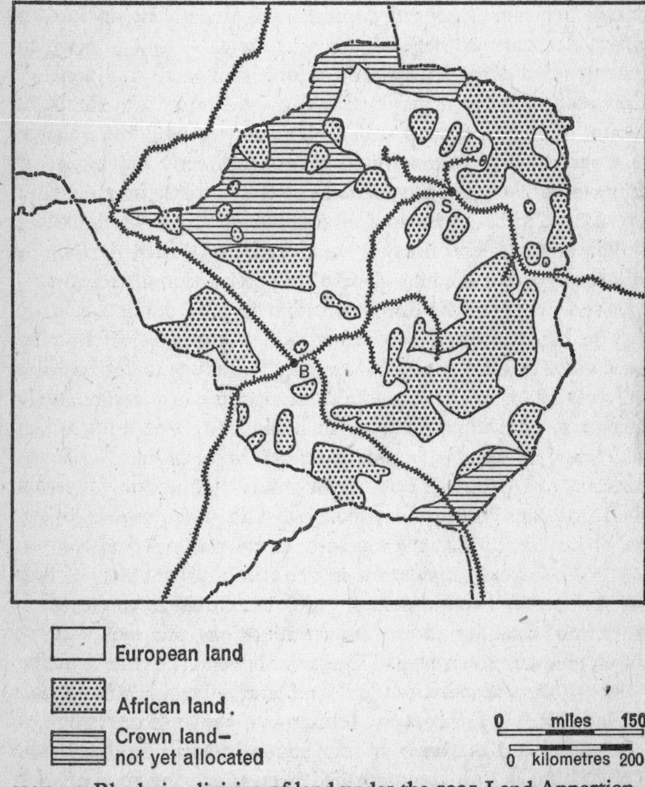

MAP 22. Rhodesia: division of land under the 1931 Land Apportionment Act

towns and most of the High Veld. The African areas are discontinuous tracts of land, mostly in the Middle Veld.

The allocation of land under the Land Apportionment Act was based on false assumptions about future African needs for land which left no room for future expansion. It was assumed that European enterprise would grow: African farming would remain static. Moreover, those Africans living in the European area were gradually to be removed to the areas reserved for native purchase.[8] Already by 1939, however, the number of African farmers in the areas reserved to them exceeded the 1931 estimates and the African areas were becoming seriously overcrowded. This has not prevented the continuing resettlement of Africans from empty lands into the overcrowded reserves and the removal of any possibility of further expansion by the passing of the new Act.[9]

The Land Apportionment Act also slowed down the integration of non-Europeans into urban life. It kept the towns as whites-only areas and the African comes to work there on sufferance. He is not allowed to own land, live in other than approved 'locations' and, until the late 1950s, suffered all the indignities of a rigid social colour bar. These restrictions were beginning to break down[10] but the process was a slow one and has been reversed since U.D.I.

Overcrowding in the reserves, and the inability of an increasing number of Africans to live off the land allocated to them, has increased the drift of Africans to the urban areas. This drift has been accelerated by the Native Land Husbandry Act of 1951. This Act, which was designed to improve African agriculture, and the Land Apportionment and Land Tenure Acts, which were designed to achieve segregation, have worked together to sharpen the political conflicts within Rhodesia. They have had the effect of limiting the land available for individual Africans and of swelling the African population of the towns. It is here that the social and political conflicts between white and black have increased and African pressure on the European community to share its privileges has been greatest.

Such reforms as have been implemented in Rhodesia were too few and too late to convince the Africans of the two northern territories that they wish to be associated with a Rhodesia ruled

by Europeans. With the break-up of the Federation, Rhodesia's Africans have been placed in a much weaker and more exposed position politically.

Economic Development

The early hopes of a South African-type prosperity based on gold soon gave way to more sober efforts – and achievements – based on agriculture. In spite of subsequent industrial growth, tobacco remained the mainstay of the economy until U.D.I. The 3,000 tobacco farmers accounted for nearly one third of all export revenue in 1964 and were an important political force in the country. Economic sanctions seem to have been most effective in preventing the export of tobacco and the crop has been reduced to 40 per cent of its original level, most of which is bought and stockpiled by the government. Less than 2,000 farmers now grow tobacco and diversification into maize, wheat, cotton or beef is being encouraged.[11]

TABLE 28

Rhodesia. Exports (by value) in 1964 (Published statistics for later years are unreliable)

	percentage
Tobacco	34·1
Asbestos	7·9
Gold	5·6
Iron and steel	5·1
Other manufactures	11·5
Chrome*	2·0
Coal products	1·7
Other †	32·1
Total value £126·5 million	

SOURCES: *U.N. Yearbook of International Trade Statistics, 1964*, p. 662. *East Africa and Rhodesia*, Vol. 42, p. 813.

*Of which Rhodesia is one of the major world suppliers.

†Mainly agricultural products other than tobacco.

During and after the Second World War, Rhodesia became the most important manufacturing country in southern and tropical Africa outside the Republic.

Under careful government protection, Rhodesia has been able to build up a remarkable range of industries. Among them are the first iron and steel works in southern Africa outside the Republic, an oil refinery (1964), textiles, cement, agricultural implements, food and drink, soap, paints and tyres. These are concentrated in and around Salisbury and Bulawayo and have been able to grow because of the high cost of imports and the necessity to absorb European immigrants. This industrial growth was boosted by the formation of the Federation in 1953, with its accompanying inflow of capital and business confidence and access to the protected markets of the north. In the decade 1950–60 some £500 million was invested in Rhodesia, mostly in the urban areas. Iron and steel manufacturing and a wide range of secondary industries have reduced Rhodesia's dependence on primary production and diversified the economy.[12]

Before U.D.I. nearly one third of Rhodesia's exports went to the U.K. and about one third to Zambia; the U.K. importing mainly primary products, Zambia coal and manufactured goods.

This is not the place to attempt the difficult task of passing judgement on the effect of economic sanctions to date. Many more of Rhodesia's exports have been moving south since U.D.I. and sanctions appear to have had a crippling effect only on the tobacco industry. There has also been some diversification of agriculture and an attempt to encourage import substitution industries. To the outside world the Rhodesian government appears to have conducted a successful holding operation – slow growth certainly, but equally certainly no collapse.

MALAWI

This is overwhelmingly the poorest of the three countries and is dependent for its livelihood both on the production of its own agriculture and the annual export of labour to work in the mines, industries, and farms of Zambia, Rhodesia and the Republic. Up to one third of the adult male labour force is away from

home at any one time.[13] The Monkton Report noted in 1959 that

> The Gross Domestic Product of Nyasaland was £19 a head, of Northern Rhodesia £81 and of Southern Rhodesia £89. Without any exploitable mineral resources, with long and expensive communications, a peasant population swollen by continuing immigration from Portuguese Territories and with restricted scope for European enterprise . . . and for the employment which such enterprise offers, the economic opportunities open to Africans are few.[14]

The post-colonial government is, above all, concerned with extending those opportunities. To this end, Dr Banda's régime has found it expedient to open diplomatic relations with South Africa and to accept that country's economic aid. Good relations with Portuguese Moçambique are also encouraged and a railway from Lilongwe through to Nacala is being built.

Malawi is like Uganda in having been penetrated by missionaries before a Protectorate was established. Scottish missions were active from the 1870s and, before the coming of official British rule in 1891, sometimes acted as the government. Slave raiding and inter-tribal strife had so broken down the old tribal structure that the missions found themselves in the position not of replacing an existing government but of providing government where none existed.

Malawi is a land of very varied relief and consequently of climate. Three main types of terrain may be distinguished. The hot and unhealthy lowlands of the Shire river and the shores of Lake Nyasa, the cooler plateaux, between three and four thousand feet, and the still higher plateaux between five and eight thousand feet. Maize is the staple diet on the plateaux and cassava on the lake shore.

Population, both African and European, is concentrated in the southern highlands. Communications are good here, soils are fertile and the climate pleasant for human comfort. Land alienated to white farmers (about 5 per cent of the whole country) is mainly concentrated in the south.

The chief cash crops of tobacco, tea, groundnuts, coffee and cotton are produced both on the European-owned farms and by African farmers. The latter are mostly smallholders in a transitional stage between subsistence and commercial agriculture. Supplementation of a predominantly subsistence holding by

some cash crop is common. Malawi is the leading Commonwealth producer of tung oil (used in paint manufacture).

TABLE 29

Malawi. Exports in 1967 (by value)

	percentage
Tea	27·1
Tobacco	25·5
Groundnuts	20·7
Cotton	4·1
Tung oil	1·7
Cassava	1·6
Other	19·3
Total value £16·5m.	

SOURCE: *The Europa Yearbook*, 1970, Vol. II.

ZAMBIA

The former Protectorate of Northern Rhodesia lies between Nyasaland and Rhodesia, both geographically and economically. Much of the country is too remote from good communications to have seen much development,[15] and is still largely devoted to subsistence agriculture. There is, however, a zone of more intensive development – both in agriculture and in mining – along the line of rail.

Most of Zambia is high plateau country on the watershed between the Congo and the Zambezi, having a tropical climate modified by altitude. It is hotter than the High Veld of Rhodesia, but only the valleys of the Zambezi and Luangwa are excessively hot. It has not, however, the climatic attractions for Europeans offered by the more favoured areas of its southern neighbour.

Except along the line of rail, European settlement and commercial farming were confined to two small areas; one near Abercorn in the north, which looked to Tanganyika for its

contacts with external markets, and the other near Fort Jameson, whose communications were mainly through Malawi. However, these two areas have now been largely given over to small-scale African farming, while there is a growing European farming area around Mkushi, east of Broken Hill.

The *Copperbelt* lies between Broken Hill and the Congo border, and is a continuation of a similar area in what was formerly Katanga. Its development has created the wealth and many of the political problems of Zambia. The first mine, at Bwana Mkubwa, produced low-grade copper in the 1920s, but it was with the discovery of far richer deposits and the beginnings of their exploitation in 1931 that the story of the Copperbelt really begins.

In the 1920s European miners were brought in by the mining companies at relatively high wages because at that time no suitable local labour existed, except for the unskilled work. These miners, through the Northern Rhodesia Mineworkers' Union (an entirely European body, formed in 1926), were able to consolidate their position and, until just before Independence, to monopolize all the skilled work at rates of pay about ten times as high as those for unskilled work. They thus had the same direct economic interest in the continuance of white political control as have the manual workers of Rhodesia,[16] and continued to resist, with decreasing effectiveness, the growing strength of African nationalism.

TABLE 30

Zambia. Exports in 1968 (by value)

	percentage
Copper	94·8
Zinc	1·6
Cobalt	0·6
Other	3·0

Total value 544·4 million kwacha (£318·4m.)

SOURCE: *The Europa Yearbook*, 1970, Vol. II.

There are seven main mines on the Copperbelt, producing copper and much smaller quantities of zinc, cobalt, gold, silver, lead, and manganese. So one-sided has been the economic development of the country that well over half the Africans in employment are working in or near the Copperbelt.[17] Most of the commercial agriculture is concentrated along the railway which serves the Copperbelt, and is largely a supplier of the domestic market, although tobacco and smaller quantities of other crops like groundnuts and tobacco are produced for export.

The Copperbelt has attracted not only immigrant Europeans, but also somewhat larger numbers of Africans from outside Zambia, many of them from Malawi, and the Portuguese Territories.

ECONOMIC RELATIONS

The complementary nature of the economies of the three former Federal Territories was often stressed at the time. A common market of eight and a half million people seemed an attractive alternative to political and economic fragmentation. As the Monckton Report put it:

> The more advanced agriculture and light industries of Southern Rhodesia are balanced by the heavy extractive industry in Northern Rhodesia and vice versa; coal from Wankie is used to smelt copper in Northern Rhodesia and the railway system transports both; tea from Nyasaland is drunk in Salisbury; meat raised in Matabeleland is eaten on the Copperbelt...

Moreover, the Federal Government was able to attract a considerable amount of foreign investment. Most of this investment went into the building of Kariba dam and into the industries of Rhodesia, however, and simply served to increase the Federation's already uneven development.

Of the former Federation's exports, over two thirds by value were of two commodities – Northern Rhodesian copper (47·3 per cent) and Rhodesian tobacco (19·5 per cent).[18] But both the production of export commodities and the new industrial growth bore little relation to the production and income of the vast majority of the inhabitants – those still engaged in subsistence or semi-subsistence agriculture. Most of them were quite

unimpressed, therefore, when told of the Federation's economic achievements. As two African members of the Monckton Commission put it:

> It is true to say that the economic advantages which have accrued from the Federation resulted in high standards of living for Europeans ... and created some employment for Africans in Southern Rhodesia and Nyasaland...
>
> It is wrong in our view for the Commission, when dealing with Kariba, to say that Africans were going to benefit as a result of this hydro-electric scheme. The Commission visited most of the African municipal townships ... and saw that in the majority of cases hardly any of these townships were supplied with electricity at all...[19]

Even the economic achievements have been challenged since its dissolution. As Arthur Hazlewood has pointed out,[20] the Monckton Commission had no evidence for its assertion that the rate of economic growth was greater after 1953; only for Southern Rhodesia do the data suggest any acceleration in the rate of growth after federation.

The uncertain political future of the area makes it difficult to comment on the economic future of these three former 'partners'. Malawi is still poor and will need to export her labour for some time to come. Moreover, her government has shown a willingness to cooperate with both Portugal and South Africa which has not been welcomed by her northern neighbours.

Zambia is poor, too, but has the enormous long-term advantage of plenty of income for investment from the mines. In the short term, her dependence on Rhodesian coal, electricity, transport facilities and consumer goods severely limits her political freedom of action. The policy of sanctions against Rhodesia has damaged the Zambian economy in spite of British support. The continuation of the Rhodesian crisis can only mean a continuing crisis for Zambia. The air-lift and lorry-lift of oil from Tanzania is both costly and inefficient while the Tanzam railway outlet, although now begun, must take some years to build.

Rhodesia is busy forging new links with her prosperous southern neighbour. Generous quotas on Rhodesian manufactures entering the Republic, adequate supplies of oil from the south and enthusiastic moral support have helped the

Rhodesian economy show surprising buoyancy in the face of world hostility.

The outcome of events in Rhodesia is bound to be decisive in determining the degree of future economic relations between the three states.

Notes on Chapter 9

1. *Report of the Advisory Commission on the Review of the Constitution of Rhodesia and Nyasaland*, 1960. Cmnd. 1148.
2. ibid., pp. 17–18.
3. See George Kay, *The Distribution of the African Population in Southern Rhodesia: Some Preliminary Notes*, 1964, Rhodes-Livingstone Institute, Lusaka.
4. ibid.
5. E. Clegg, *Race and Politics*, 1960, p. 33.
6. In *European Politics in Southern Rhodesia*, 1959.
7. David Wigg, 'African Education in Rhodesia and Zambia' in *Teacher*, 18 October 1968.
8. African land was divided into the 'reserves' and 'native purchase areas'. In the latter, freehold tenure was introduced and attempts were made to improve farming methods.
9. The effects of the Land Apportionment Act are fully considered in R. Gray, *The Two Nations*, 1960, and Philip Mason, *Year of Decision*, 1960. Demographic effects are considered in G. Kay, op. cit.
10. As, for example, the abolition of separate counters in P.O.s and the building of permanent urban housing for Africans on ninety-nine year leases.
11. Africa Bureau, *Fact Sheet No.* 2, 1970.
12. C. Legum (ed.), op. cit., pp. 177–8.
13. *Report of the Nyasaland Commission of Enquiry (Devlin Report)*, 1959, pp. 7–8.
14. *Monckton Commission Report*, p. 57.
15. But see G. Kay, 'Agricultural Progress in Zambia's Eastern Province', in *Journal of Administration Overseas*, Vol. V No. 2, April 1966.
16. For a short history of the industrial colour bar see *World Today*, May 1955, and E. Clegg, op. cit.

17. Colonial Office, *N. Rhodesia Annual Report*, 1960, p. 13.
18. *U.N. Economical Survey of Africa since 1950*, p. 168.
19. *Monckton Commission Report*, p. 135.
20. Arthur Hazlewood, *African Integration and Disintegration*, p. 206.

Eastern Africa

10 Kenya, Uganda, Tanzania, Rwanda and Burundi

East Africa is a land of great variety; in physical features, climate, human types, economic development, and political evolution alike. There are few places on the earth's surface where, in the space of a few hundred miles, you can experience such a range of contrasts. You can pass from high mountain snows to the deepest lake-filled troughs lined with tropical vegetation; from the invigorating climate of the highland areas to the dusty heat of the rift valley floors, or from bustling modern cities to a countryside still largely devoted to subsistence agriculture. It would, moreover, be false to make a firm distinction between developed towns and an underdeveloped countryside. There are great differences between one area and another. Particularly in Kenya, you can move from a fully commercial agriculture to the poorest subsistence farming or from fertile volcanic soils, like those round Kilimanjaro in Tanzania, to the poor and eroded pastures of the Masai on the floor and margins of the rift valley. Finally, there are in East Africa all the clashes of tribal and racial interests present in other parts of the continent and great contrasts in the types of state which have emerged from the race to independence.

These diverse environments and their many difficult problems have been given a certain unity by two facts, one physical and the other political.

Away from the coast, the encircling arms of the eastern and western rift valley systems are a unique feature of the African physical scene and are responsible for many of the region's physical and human contrasts. The western rift mountains and lakes cut east Africa off from the Congo Basin and from Zambia while the eastern and western rift highlands alike contain fertile volcanic soils and some of Africa's highest population densities. In between the two arms the plateau surface centres on th

fertile, well-watered and thickly-populated Lake Victoria depression.

Politically, with the exception of Rwanda and Burundi, all the territories have been under British rule and use English as an official language.* Most of Kenya was a Crown Colony, except the coastal strip which was a Protectorate; Uganda and Zanzibar were Protectorates, while Tanganyika was administered by Britain under U.N. Trusteeship. Both Tanganyika and Ruanda-Urundi were German colonies in the years before the First World War but Belgium became the administering power for the latter country and tended, until the late 1950s, to make little distinction between Ruanda-Urundi and the colony of Congo. The former British territories have enjoyed common tariff arrangements and certain common services, like railways, posts and telecommunications.† The future maintenance of these common services and arrangements remains a key issue in the international relations of the three countries.

LAND AND CLIMATE

East Africa may conveniently be divided into five natural regions which, as so often throughout the continent, cut right across the political boundaries.

The coastal fringe, varying in width from ten to forty miles, has an equatorial climate with abundant though not excessive rain and accompanying tropical vegetation. This part of east Africa has had centuries of contact with the outside world, contact which is reflected in the cosmopolitan racial, cultural and architectural character of the cities of the Swahili-speaking coast.

Prior to the coming of British and German rule the coast was controlled by the Sultan of Zanzibar. Germany bought the Tanganyika coast for £200,000 in 1890, but the Kenya coast became a Protectorate over which the Sultan of Zanzibar still had some claim until 1963.

*Kenya and Tanzania also use Swahili.

†These are administered by the East African Community, formerly the East African Common Services Organization, and, before that, the East African High Commission. See below.

The coastal hinterland, for the most part dry and uninviting, cuts off the coast from the great population centres of the interior. Whereas the coast has long been known to the outside world the inland areas were only well known towards the end of the nineteenth century. In Kenya the zone is one of semi-desert and in most of the long rail haul from Mombasa to Nairobi (about 300 miles) there are few people and little economic activity. This dry zone becomes more marked as you move northwards in Kenya and the whole northern half of the country is semi-desert or desert. In Tanzania the coastal hinterland is better watered and inland from Tanga contains the extensive sisal estates which are the country's principal source of export revenue.

The highlands of the eastern rift, mainly over 5,000 ft, are a discontinuous zone with many natural advantages of soil and climate. Temperatures are comfortably modified by the altitude, the soils are deep and, like most volcanic soils, have a valuable reserve of natural fertility when not abused. The climate and the crops grown tend to vary with altitude rather than with season or latitude and there may be great variety within a small area. In the Kenya Highlands, for example, you can see wheat, oats, barley, pyrethrum,* tea, coffee and pineapples all flourishing within a few miles of each other.

The western rift highlands of Rwanda, Burundi and western Uganda are less well known and, because of their distance from the sea, less developed. They are, however, naturally fertile and support a dense African population. Rwanda and Burundi together have over six and a half million people (1967), more than the whole of Angola.

The interior plateau, lying between the two rift systems and about 4,000 ft above sea level, is largely arid or semi-arid bush country, much of it infested with tsetse fly. The chief exception to the general aridity is the land on the margins of Lake Victoria. The lake has considerable local influence in producing a climate with a well-distributed rainfall. As a result, the Nyanza and Western provinces of Kenya, the southern half of Uganda and, to a smaller extent, the lake shores of Tanzania are able to support a dense and relatively prosperous population.

It will already be evident from this description that there are

*A daisy-like flower used in the making of insecticides.

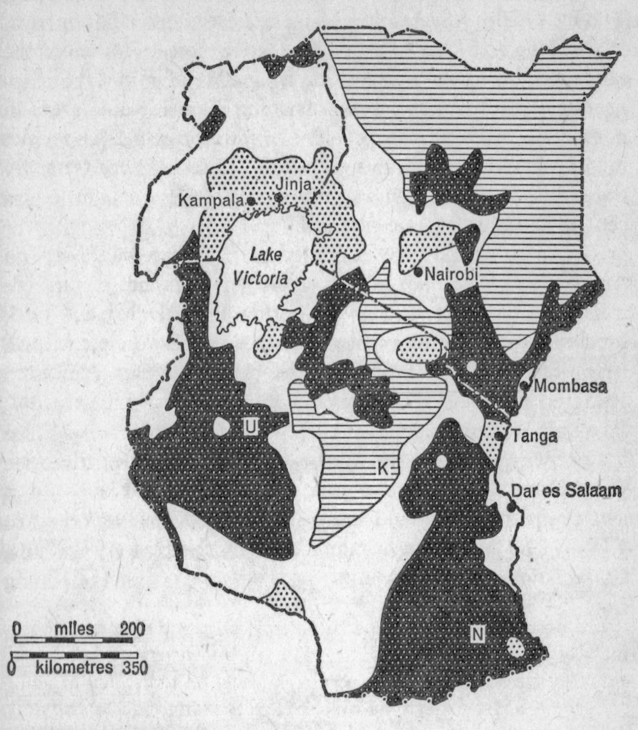

MAP 23. Kenya, Uganda and Tanzania: population, rainfall and tsetse fly. (Sources: *E. Africa Royal Commission Report*, 1955; 'Exporting to East Africa', *Board of Trade Journal*, 25 August 1961, p. 5)

considerable areas of east Africa too dry for successful farming. The East Africa Royal Commission estimated that a fair prospect of receiving 20 inches of rain a year was necessary for successful ranching and a fair prospect of 30 inches of rain a year was necessary for successful arable farming. Considerable areas do not measure up to these standards. In addition, much land which might otherwise be suitable for cattle is infested with tsetse fly. Some 10 per cent of Kenya, 32 per cent of Uganda, and 60 per cent of Tanzania is tsetse-infested.[1]

The areas of extreme difficulty are illustrated in Map 23. Areas which have both a poor chance of 30 inches of rain and tsetse infestation are useless for both arable farming and cattle ranching. Areas with less than 20 inches are also useless without irrigation.[2] Small wonder that the people of east Africa are scattered in islands of high density in those areas which are more favourable to human activity.

Contrasts between the fertile and the infertile, the well-watered and the arid, are so great in east Africa that land hunger and competition for land are pressing problems, especially in Kenya. The position was summed up by the East Africa Royal Commission in 1955 as follows:

> If a panorama picture could be taken slowly, and over a period, of the way people are living in East Africa, the most striking feature of it would be a restless anxiety to obtain and hold on to the land. Land is still, for the vast majority, a basic necessity from which each family derives its own food by its own physical effort. Where this can be done with the least effort for the greatest result, people have tended to collect and tend to want to stay. This tendency has been accentuated by the difficulty of penetrating the unknown where tsetse and lack of water have proved insurmountable obstacles, and by the hazards of uncertain rainfall over such a large part of the region. Thus the places where good rainfall, good soil, water and grazing are most easily obtained, the risks of human and animal disease most easily avoided, are in the greatest demand. As population has increased – and this has generally been greatest in these most favourable localities – so has pressure increased in two directions, outwards, so as to get more land if possible and to obtain as fertile land as possible, and inwards, towards a more devastating use of the land itself. The inward pressure, under contemporary systems of land usage, is affecting production from the soil adversely. This is the most serious aspect of the land

problem. The outward pressure results in conflict wherever fertile land is short . . .[3]

PEOPLES AND POLITICS IN KENYA, UGANDA AND TANZANIA

TABLE 31
Population of Kenya, Uganda and Tanzania, late 1967 estimates (in thousands)

	Africans	*Europeans*	*Arabs and Asians*
Kenya	9,671	42·0	231·0
Uganda	7,829	9·7	91·4
Tanzania	10,452	15·0 (1966)	111·5 (1966)
Zanzibar (1963)*	298*	0·65	20·06†

SOURCE: *East African Economic and Statistical Review*, December 1967.

*Indigenous inhabitants (Arabs, Africans and Cormorians).
†Excluding Arabs but including Somalis.

Contrasts in the land and the distribution of population are paralleled by contrasts in the people themselves. Not only are there several immigrant groups to contend with – notably the Europeans, Asians, and Arabs – but the differences between the African tribes in language and political outlook are just as important in some areas.

East Africa is the meeting point for all the continent's major linguistic groups. Even the 'click' languages are represented in central Tanzania. The three groups of greatest importance are the Nilotic, the Nilo-Hamitic, and the Bantu, and of these the latter are by far the most important. Of the tribes whose numbers are around the million mark only the Luo are a non-Bantu people.

In Tanzania there are between 80 and 120 tribal groups, none of whom is numerically anywhere near the million mark except the Sukuma of the southern shores of Lake Victoria. Unlike some of the important tribes of Kenya and Uganda, the geographical situation of the Sukuma makes them remote from the capital city and centre of political activity. Partly for this

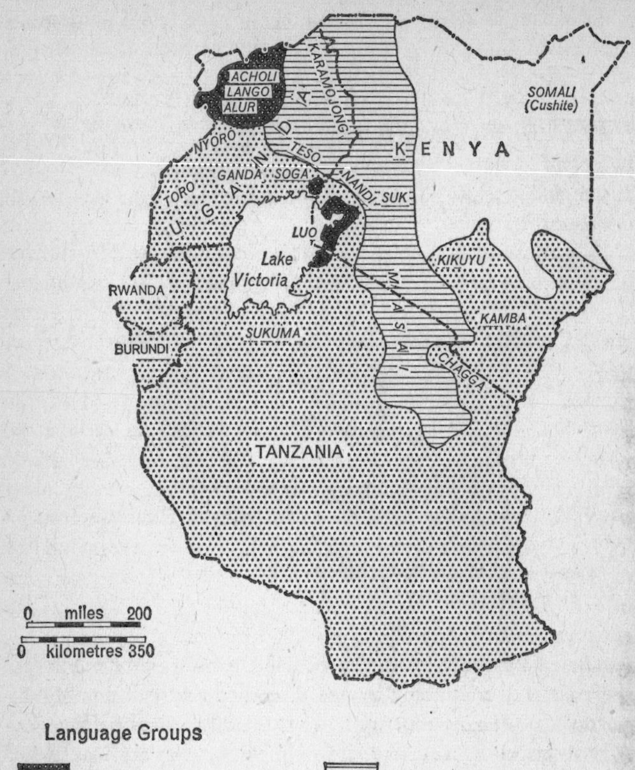

MAP 24. East Africa: major language groups. (Source: J. E. Goldthorpe and F. B. Wilson, *Tribal Maps of East Africa and Zanzibar*, 1960)

reason, there has never been any question or fear of Sukuma political domination as there has been of Baganda domination in Uganda, for example. While the ten largest tribes of Kenya make up between 80 and 90 per cent of the population, in Tanzania the fourteen biggest tribes make up only just over half the population.[4]

Tribalism in Tanzania has also been made less important by the use of Swahili as the language of instruction in schools, whereas in Kenya and Uganda the various vernacular tongues have been given greater encouragement.

Whatever the reasons, former Tanganyika on the verge of independence presented a remarkable picture of political unity. In the elections of 1960 no fewer than fifty-eight seats went to unopposed candidates of T.A.N.U.,* an achievement paralleled only in those countries where no effective opposition is allowed to exist. Tanganyika was joined in April 1964 by the former Sultanate of Zanzibar to form the United Republic of Tanzania. The islands of Zanzibar and Pemba were once the centre of trade and civilization on the east African coast. In the mid nineteenth century in particular, under the reign of Sultan Seyyid Said and his successors, Zanzibar became the commercial centre of the area with a flourishing trade in slaves and ivory. It is estimated that Zanzibar had an annual import of some 15,000 slaves during the first half of the nineteenth century.[5] Today the islands rely almost exclusively on the production and export of cloves and clove oil. In 1963 they formed 74 per cent of exports by value, the remainder consisting of coconuts and coconut products.[6]

The total population is over 300,000 of whom about 77 per cent are classified as Africans and about 16 per cent Arabs.[7] Traditionally the islands have been ruled by the Arabs, and the Zanzibar Nationalist Party, controlled by the Arab minority, still had a bare majority of seats in the legislature until the 1964 revolution swept the opposition Afro-Shirazi Party to power. This party is now the only legal political party on the islands while T.A.N.U. has become the only legal party on the mainland.

The fact that Tanzania's populous and productive areas are scattered around its periphery might well lead in the future to the emergence of regional discontent; this is made the more likely by the country's great size and poor communications. At present, however, we have the prospect of the continuance of a strong and popular central government.

In Uganda, the upheavals of 1966 and 1970 have upset the delicate balance of the politics of compromise which accompanied

*Tanganyika African National Union.

the federal constitution of 1962. Such a constitution seemed essential at the time in order to accommodate the wishes of the leaders of Buganda.*

The Ganda number about a million people and are numerically the largest tribe in Uganda. Moreover, their geographically central position places them at the centre of economic and political power. The capital city and seat of government are in Buganda, the country's road system radiates out from Buganda and the comparative wealth of the Ganda people has brought them greater educational and job opportunities than other tribes. At the time of independence in 1961, the average money income per head of Africans in central Buganda was nearly ten times as great as in parts of the Western Province and over twice as much as that in most other parts of the country.[8]

Buganda's former position of influence, which was due in part to this favourable geographical situation, was also strengthened by British colonial policy.

When a British Protectorate was established in 1900 it was convenient for Britain to control the country through the existing native administration. The agreement between Britain and the Kabaka's government not only confirmed the authority of that government but gave it a status far above that of the surrounding tribes. More than this, the Ganda were rewarded for their loyalty by British recognition of the annexation of territory from the less cooperative Nyoro. This annexation gave rise to the 'lost counties' dispute.

The claims of Bunyoro extended to five of the northern counties of Buganda and parts of two others, all of them claimed on historical grounds as once forming part of the lands of the Nyoro people. The dispute really centred on the three north-western counties in two of which (Buyaga and Bugangazzi) the Nyoro form an overwhelming majority of the population. For some decades prior to British rule Buganda had been expanding at the expense of Bunyoro so that two or three of the counties would probably have passed to Buganda without British intervention.

*Buganda, or the country of the Ganda, has given a modified form of its name to the whole of Uganda almost by accident. Buganda was the first part of Uganda to fall under British rule and was called 'Uganda' by the early administrators. As other bits and pieces of country were added, the name Uganda came to apply to the whole Protectorate and the country of the Ganda was given its proper name, Buganda.

It is doubtful, however, whether Buganda would have been able to acquire Buyaga and Bugangazzi when it did without British help. These two counties were returned to Bunyoro in May 1964.

One result of the earlier economic development in Buganda has been a considerable inward immigration from other parts of East Africa. The 1959 census showed no less than 47 per cent of the population of the province to be natives of other areas. Since the 1920s African immigrants have poured into Buganda in response to the greater economic opportunities existing there. They came from Rwanda, Burundi, Kenya and Tanzania, as well as other parts of Uganda, and worked as unskilled labourers on various construction works, non-African industrial enterprises and, for the Ganda themselves, on the land. Many returned home but, as with immigrant groups the world over, an increasing proportion have stayed. As far as non-citizens are concerned, this inflow of labour has now (1970) been stopped by the government and thousands without work permits have been expelled.

The 1966 constitution and the deposition of the Kabaka of Buganda weakened Buganda's political position *vis-à-vis* the rest of the country. It would, however, be a mistake to view the political events of the last few years as simply a question of Buganda versus the rest. The situation is far more complicated than that.

In Kenya, the main concentrations of population are in three widely separated centres, the Mombasa district, the highlands near Nairobi (the home of the Kikuyu) and Nyanza and Western Provinces (the home of the Luo, Luyia, Gusii and others). Each area has different languages, tribes, and economic problems. It would in any case be difficult to weld them into a cohesive political whole. Without a strong government at the centre the task appeared impossible. Such a government has emerged since independence and has succeeded in reducing regional opposition to the minimum necessary for effective cohesion. The independence constitution of 1963 divided the country into seven Regions and the Nairobi area. These have since been re-named 'provinces'. One province (the North East) is claimed by Somalia as part of 'Greater Somalia'. The majority of the people of this province are Somalis (as is the case with the Ogaden of

Ethiopia). 'Shifta' bandits from Somalia were an increasing terrorist menace to North East Kenya in the mid-1960s (see Chapter 11 below).

Kenya today is a firmly African country. But there is no doubt that in the past the politics of Kenya have been dominated by its most influential but by no means most numerous 'tribe', the Europeans.

The Europeans in Kenya number some 42,000 people. Although they nearly doubled their numbers between 1950 and 1960, they no longer control Kenya's political life and their future is uncertain. As elsewhere in east Africa, most of them live in the towns, especially Nairobi, and it is a myth to think of them as mainly settlers on the land.

The myth had some substance in the early days of white settlement. Europeans were brought in to farm on the Kenya highlands as a direct result of the building of the Uganda railway, which reached the site of modern Nairobi in 1899 and Kisumu in 1901. The railway had been built to reach the strategic headwaters of the Nile, to open up Uganda to legitimate trade, and to provide support for the Christian missions there. It was, however, a costly undertaking in both lives and money and, partly in order to make it pay, attention was soon directed to developing the highland areas of Kenya through which the railway passed. Under the stimulus provided by the enthusiasm of Lord Delamere and others, European farmers were encouraged to take up land on favourable terms from 1902 onwards and again, under special schemes for ex-servicemen, after the two world wars.

It has always been a small community – growing from just over 5,000 in 1914 to nearly 17,000 in 1931. In 1931 the largest occupational group was still in agriculture but was already being overtaken by government service and commerce. In 1948, out of the total 'gainfully employed' population, only 23 per cent were in agriculture and fishing. Government service, commerce, the professions and clerical occupations together accounted for over 62 per cent of the European population.

Nevertheless, in spite of the small numbers of people involved in farming, the land question continued to be of immense importance in Kenya politics. Alienation of the former 'white

highlands' formed the basis of race segregation in Kenya, just as the Land Apportionment Act did in Rhodesia. It made Nairobi primarily a non-African town and squeezed the Kikuyu between two sectors of European land, into their increasingly over-crowded reserve. It helped to sustain the Mau Mau rebellion and has resulted in exceedingly uneven economic development. Much money and skill has been put into the land in the former European areas while only recently has much money and effort been devoted to improving the African areas.

In Tanzania about 15 per cent of Europeans were in agriculture[9] but their diverse ethnic origins (Greeks, Germans and English among others), their peripheral location and their remoteness from the political and commercial capital of the country combined to reduce their political influence. In Uganda only a handful of Europeans are planters, most of the rest of them being employed in government and other service occupations.

The Asian community has been established in east Africa for longer than many of the African tribes themselves. The myth of the Kenya Europeans as largely 'settlers' is paralleled by the myth of Asians as largely descended from labourers brought in to build the Uganda railway.[10] Arab traders have been on the coast for close on two thousand years and Indians have probably been there for nearly as long. It would indeed be surprising if they had not.

The geographical unity of the Indian Ocean, and the ancient navigation routes across it based on regularly changing monsoon winds, means that the east African coast has always provided bases for the brisk trading activities of the area. As elsewhere in Africa, the settlements remained coastal until the nineteenth century, but the enterprise and civilization established there, though cosmopolitan, was essentially Asian and has left its mark on all the cities of east Africa which have developed since the opening up of the interior. 'Asian' in East Africa usually means either Indian or Pakistani, Moslem or Hindu, as well as the smaller Goan Catholic group.* Arabs are, for many purposes, also included.

The Asians have come to east Africa because of opportunities

*From Goa, a former Portuguese enclave in India.

for trade and the advantages of a better life for themselves and their children. Their contribution to the economic development of the area has been out of all proportion to their numbers.

Whereas the European has gone into east Africa to govern, to farm, or to engage in some relatively large-scale business enterprise, the small Asian shopkeeper has penetrated right out into the villages, creating a demand for goods where none existed before, providing most of the people's needs in consumer goods and, later, sometimes branching out into larger manufacturing or farming enterprises, as in cotton ginning or the sugar plantations of Uganda.

Whereas most Europeans were more or less temporary residents, the Asians came to stay. They may have thought of Britain, India or Pakistan as 'home', but this was more a sentimental than a real attachment. With the coming of independence, some of the Asians took out local citizenship; others decided they would be more secure as Indians, Pakistanis or British – especially the latter. Events since 1968 have shown that it was quite unrealistic to think it possible still to share east Africa's wealth *and* keep a foreign passport.

Two factors combine to make the Asians an object of prejudice from Africans and from Europeans. One is social and the other economic.

Many Asians are closely involved with one or other of the Asian religious sects, most of which are exclusive to themselves.[11] They thus tend to have their own independent social and cultural life and to be cut off from many of the people among whom they live.

They are also concentrated in occupations which arouse popular envy. Characteristically they are shopkeepers and businessmen. In the early 1960s in Tanganyika about 50 per cent of Asians were dependent on trade, in Kenya over 33 per cent and in Uganda over 50 per cent.[12] In both these respects they are like the Jews of Europe and are in the same danger of being subjected to discrimination.*

*For some evidence of prejudice see Paul Fordham and H. C. Wiltshire, 'Some Tests of Prejudice in an East African Adult College', *Race*, October 1963 and the symposium on *Racial and Communal Tensions in E. Africa*, 1965, published by the East African Publishing House, Nairobi.

The Asian came to east Africa to better himself and he usually succeeded. In doing so he also helped to improve east Africa. As the East Africa Royal Commission said:

> ... the remarkable tenacity and courage of the Indian trader has been mainly responsible for stimulating the wants of the indigenous peoples, even in the remotest areas, by opening to them a shop-window on the modern world and for collecting for sale elsewhere whatever small surpluses are available for disposal. The non-African trading system as it exists in East Africa is one of the most important assets which the economy possesses ...[13]

ECONOMIC DEVELOPMENT IN KENYA, UGANDA AND TANZANIA

All three countries are still primarily agricultural. They rely for their main source of wealth on the export of a few important crops, although both Uganda and Tanzania have the beginnings of both mining and manufacturing industry and Kenya has a fast-growing variety of manufactures, mainly of consumer goods for the local east African market.

In Kenya much of the export production in agriculture comes from large-scale farms in the former 'white highlands', the ownership of which has been diversified since independence. Production of small-scale farms is also increasing as a direct result of the land reforms of the last ten years and of the improved techniques with which they have been associated.

African farmers began earlier in Kenya a process which has now started in Tanzania and Uganda – the raising of output per man and per acre on the available agricultural land. If purchasing power is to be increased sufficiently to sustain a developing manufacturing industry it will be essential to raise farm incomes in all three territories, and this is now being recognized in current development plans. In Kenya, for example, agriculture in 1967 accounted for 30 per cent of Gross National Product, 50 per cent of employment and 60 per cent of export revenue. The accent in the 1970–74 Plan is on rural development, including processing and other industries in the rural areas. Only by an all round improvement in the quality of rural life will growth and stability be sustained.[14]

In Tanzania, as in Kenya, a high proportion of the export

production is in the hands of the large firms: sisal on large plantations in the Tanga area, coffee and tea in the highland regions. There is, however, a much greater proportion of small-scale farm production than in Kenya, notably of coffee around

TABLE 32

Kenya, Uganda and Tanzania. Exports in 1967 (by value)

	Kenya percentage	*Uganda percentage*	*Tanzania percentage*
Coffee	29·2	53·5	13·9
Sisal	3·8	nil	11·8
Cotton	1·1	23·4	14·8
Tea	13·8	5·3	2·5
Diamonds	nil	nil	13·1
Copper and alloys	*	8·4	nil
Meat and meat preparations	5·3	*	2·8
Hides and skins	3·2	2·5	1·6
Oil seeds, fodder etc.	*	4·3	2·7
Cloves†	nil	nil	5·3
Cashew nuts	*	nil	5·4
Pyrethrum and extract	5·4	nil	*
Petroleum products	13·3	nil	nil
Soda ash	2·0	nil	nil
Other	22·9‡	2·6	26·1
Total values in East African pounds (£ sterling)	53·5m. (£63m.)	64·6m. (£76·2m.)	84·4m. (£99·3m.)

SOURCE: *The Europa Yearbook*, 1970, Vol. II.

*Negligible.

†Zanzibar is the chief source of cloves, revenue from which is retained in that part of Tanzania.

‡Mainly manufactured goods including cement (2·6 per cent).

Mt Kilimanjaro and cotton and coffee from the southern end of Lake Victoria.

Both Kenya and Tanzania have a greater variety of export crops than some African countries, which makes a lowering of

price in any one commodity easier to bear. Uganda, however, is much too dependent on two crops, coffee and cotton, which together account for over 80 per cent of total exports by value.

Coffee is the most profitable for the farmer but is mostly of the low-grade *robusta* type (in contrast to Kenya *arabica*) and hard to sell in a coffee-glutted world market. Cotton pays the farmer less but has a more ready sale in the world market. In the case of both crops, output per man is too low and the increased production of recent years has largely come from taking more land into cultivation.

Uganda is more fortunate than her neighbours in having more land available which is suitable for arable farming. Indeed this may be one reason for the low farming standards in most of the country. The land and the climate are sufficiently good to support a relatively dense population at the subsistence level. There has been less of a challenge for survival than in Kenya and the tentative entry of most farmers into the money economy still has an air of incompleteness about it.

Mining has been developed in all three territories in so far as resources are known and transport available to tap them. Copper mining in Uganda had to wait on the completion of the western railway extension. Diamonds from Mwadui provide an increasing proportion of Tanzania's export revenue while Kenya, the poorest of the three in minerals, has developed the mining of soda ash at L. Magadi.

Tanzania has extensive reserves of coal and iron in the southwest which will become exploitable when the railway to Zambia is built. Zambia's politico-economic problems may yet be a blessing in disguise for Tanzania.

Industrial development is in its infancy in all three territories although Kenya now makes a wide range of consumer goods including shoes, petroleum products from the Mombasa refinery, processed foods, window frames, and glassware.

The difficulty of attracting industry to Uganda illustrates the major economic problem of east Africa as a whole: the raising of farm output and thus of purchasing power to stimulate local demand. When the government built the Owen Falls dam at Jinja to provide hydro-electricity, it was expected that spontaneous industrial growth would follow. In fact this did not

happen. Electricity made possible a textile mill, a cement factory, a copper smelter and a steel works using scrap as raw material, but there was no rush from other industrial users. Indeed it was said that 'hydro-electricity appears to have done more to brighten up the town at night, and to make life pleasanter for the better-off sections of the population than to promote industrial growth'.[15] Without an increasing local market there is little likelihood of further industrial expansion. The raising of farm output and farm incomes remains the first priority.

THE EAST AFRICAN COMMUNITY

This organization had its origins in 1947 as the E.A. High Commission (later called the East African Common Services Organization), to administer certain common services throughout British East Africa. There were the so-called 'self-contained' (i.e. self-financing) services like railways, ports, posts and telecommunications, and the 'non self-contained' services like research, meteorology and higher education, to which all the territories contributed. With independence the continued existence of these common services has presented a serious political problem.

Kenya, Uganda and Tanzania each participate in the Community. So far, most of the common services have continued and the common tariff against the outside world has been maintained. The question as yet undecided is the long-term future of the organization – will it be strengthened or will it succumb to increasing economic nationalism on the part of the three territories or to political rivalries between them?

It is clear that each country has benefited from the common economic links. Kenya has gained a market of over twenty million people for her manufactured goods and dairy products, Uganda has an assured outlet to the sea over which it has its share of control, while Tanzania, like the others, can draw on the services of the organization's skilled personnel.

These are assets which none of the countries can afford to lose. They will be unique in Africa if they survive intact without political integration.

All the east African countries were committed to a political

federation, but it has proved difficult to implement this intention in practice. The only definite political union so far is that of Tanganyika and Zanzibar (Tanzania).

When the High Commission was set up it was proposed that certain items should be included in the Commission's powers which were in fact excluded in the final agreement. These included things like industrial licensing and commercial legislation. They would not only have meant considerably more control over economic planning but also the giving up of more sovereignty than the territorial governments were willing to consider.

It is unlikely that the Common Services Organization can be strengthened immediately on the lines originally proposed in 1947. But attempts are being made to keep the main structure intact until closer political relations are achieved. The East African Community Treaty came into effect on 1 December 1967, and gave new hope for future cooperation. The history of rapid political federation in Africa has not been a happy one. Both Mali (Soudan-Senegal) and the United Arab Republic (Egypt-Syria) have ceased to exist, as has the Central African Federation. East Africa has the framework of a different and slower road to unity. It may, however, be more lasting if the goal is clear and the will to cooperate maintained. There is, at any rate, a unique opportunity to try.

RWANDA AND BURUNDI

These two countries were formerly parts of German East Africa which were, from 1919 to 1962, administered by Belgium under League of Nations Mandate and U.N. Trusteeship.* Both are densely populated agricultural countries with a rapidly increasing population and an acute shortage of agricultural land.

These are two of the poorest countries in Africa and most of the population is occupied with subsistence agriculture, but there has been increasing attention paid in recent years to the growing of cash crops, especially coffee, cotton and rice. Some tin is mined but the immediate prospects of other mineral development are not considered good.† Situated over 1,000 miles from

*As Ruanda-Urundi.

†Over 90 per cent of Rwanda's exports are of coffee and tin.

the sea, with poorly developed communications with the outside world, Rwanda and Burundi have been less developed economically than neighbouring countries and there has been a considerable outflow of labour to Uganda and to the mines of Katanga. In view of the lack of economic development, the recent (1970) expulsion of non-citizens from Uganda will exacerbate economic problems in Rwanda and Burundi more than in neighbouring Kenya.

One interesting new venture in the Canguzo and Mosso areas (bordering on Tanzania) has arisen out of refugee resettlement. Beginning in early 1967 and affecting some 100,000 people in the Canguzo area, work has proceeded on a rural development scheme involving drainage, tsetse-fly elimination, improved roads and social facilities and the establishment of small-scale rural industries; the annual value of crops being produced amounts to more than £0·6m. A larger plan under U.N. auspices started in mid-1968 in both areas and massive development is planned.[16]

In both Rwanda and Burundi about 15 per cent of the population are Tutsi and about 85 per cent are Hutu. There are also a few Twa pygmoid hunters. The Tutsi are pastoralists who entered the country between the fifteenth and the eighteenth century and who were able to subdue the more numerous agricultural Hutu.

Until recently this Tutsi rule was maintained in both countries, but in Rwanda the Hutu, through their party, Parmehutu, and the support of the Belgian administration, were able to depose the Tutsi king and to remove most of the Tutsi from positions of power. This revolution was accompanied in 1963 and 1964 by much violence and the outflow of refugees in their thousands to neighbouring Uganda, Tanzania and Congo (Kinshasa).

In Burundi, although the monarchy has been forcibly abolished, recent events have been somewhat more peaceful and there has been less friction between Tutsi and Hutu. The reasons for this are complex[17] and are certainly associated with a much greater variety of status groups in Burundi society than the clear Tutsi–Hutu division in Rwanda. Moreover the geographical distribution of the two groups is different in each country. In

Rwanda the Tutsi were spread evenly throughout the land, while in Burundi they are concentrated in the Bututsi region, here forming 80–85 per cent of the population. Most other areas have few Tutsi with one third of the country having virtually no Tutsi at all.[18] The Bututsi region is in the south of Burundi and thus geographically separated from Hutu–Tutsi strife in Rwanda.

Whatever the future of these poor and struggling states, it is unlikely that they will associate more closely with each other. The term 'Ruanda-Urundi' was always misleading when viewed in historical perspective.

A series of Hamitic kingdoms, including Ruanda and Urundi, were established in Central Africa, probably in the eighteenth century. These kingdoms, despite their common origins, were constantly at war with one another. The kings of Ruanda and Urundi were almost always enemies. . . . When the Europeans occupied the country they found two absolute monarchies, separate and distinct, each headed by a king, each with its own organization and its own language. . . . There is still very little contact between the indigenous authorities of Ruanda and Urundi, and their respective populations are still kept apart by their traditional particularism. Thus the administration had to abandon in 1951–2, because of the opposition of the people, a scheme to standardize the spelling of Kirundi and Kinyaruanda, languages which are so closely related as to call for assimilation if not complete fusion.[19]

Notes on Chapter 10

1. East Africa Royal Commission 1953–5, *Report*, pp. 256–7. Tsetse fly is on the increase in parts of Uganda and Kenya.
2. Even this possibility is limited. In the *Economic Development of Tanganyika* it is said that 'A rough calculation suggests that around 4 million acres could be opened up for crop production by irrigation or flood control. This is less than 2 per cent of the total area of the territory . . .' (Report of a Mission organized by the International Bank for Reconstruction and Development, 1961, p. 18).
3. *E.A. Royal Commission Report*, p. 279.
4. J. E. Goldthorpe, *Outlines of East African Society*, 1959, p. 40 (photolithographed and published by Dept of Sociology, Makerere University College). This book is an excellent summary and analysis of information available at the time on East African society.
5. L. W. Hollingsworth, *The Asians of East Africa*, 1960, p. 28.
6. U.N., *Yearbook of International Trade Statistics*, 1964, p. 722.
7. Central Office of Information, Zanzibar, 1961 (Fact Sheets on U.K. Dependencies).
8. *Board of Trade Journal*, 25 August 1961. Special article on 'Exporting to East Africa', p. 19.
9. Colonial Office *Annual Report*, Part II, p. 9.
10. See especially E. Huxley, *White Man's Country*, 1935, for one important source of the myth.
11. The chief exception is the Goan Roman Catholic Group.
12. Colonial Office, *Tanganyika: Annual Report*, 1960. *Kenya Statistical Abstract*, 1960. 'Non-African population', *Uganda Census*, 1959.
13. E. Huxley, op. cit., p. 65. See also L. W. Hollingsworth, op. cit., and D. Ghai, *Asians in East Africa: Portrait of a Minority*, 1965.

14. Z. Onyonka, 'Focus on Rural Development', in *Inside Kenya Today*, September 1970, p. 7.
15. W. Elkan, *The Economic Development of Uganda*, Oxford University Press, 1961, p. 60.
16. T. F. Betts in *Journal of Modern African Studies*, Vol. 7, No. 1, pp. 149–53, 'Zonal Rural Development in Africa'.
17. See R. Lemarchand, *Rwanda and Burundi*, 1970, for a lucid analysis. This book is both scholarly and eminently readable.
18. ibid., p. 25.
19. United Nations, *Report on Ruanda-Urundi*, 1957, p. 14.

See also:

S. J. Baker, 'The Distribution of the Native Population over East Africa', *Africa*, Vol. 10, 1937.

J. Huxley, *Africa View*, Chatto, 1931 – inevitably dated but still worth reading.

N. Leys, *Kenya*, 1924, for an early attack on land alienation. Well documented.

W. T. W. Morgan and N. Manfred Shaffer, *Population of Kenya*, Oxford University Press, 1966.

11 Sudan, Ethiopia and Somalia

These three countries are all marginal to black Africa and were, for this reason, left out of the first edition of this book. Only the three southern provinces of Sudan (Upper Nile, Equatoria and Bahr-el-Ghazal), with their predominantly Negro population, have close affinities with countries to the south. In the past few years, however, there has been increasing contact with their southern neighbours. Ethiopia has become the headquarters of the Organization for African Unity and has sought to play a leading role in African affairs; Sudan's domestic problems in the south have repercussions in Uganda, while the militant nationalism of the Somalis has from time to time upset relations with both Ethiopia and Kenya.

SUDAN

Sudan is the largest country in all Africa, with a population of only 14 million people – rather larger in area and slightly more thinly-populated than Congo (Kinshasa). As with most of Africa, the nation-state gained independence (1955) before the full development of national consciousness. A people with many different religions, languages and ways of life has not yet been welded into a united nation in spite of over 140 years of political unity. First unified through conquest from Egypt by Mohamed Ali in 1821, Turco–Egyptian rule was maintained until the success of the Mahdist revolt of 1885. From then until Kitchener's conquest in 1899, Sudan remained independent under the followers of the Mahdi.

The foundations of the modern state were laid during the long 'condominium' (1899–1955). This was a unique form of colonial rule whereby the country was – in theory – jointly administered by Britain and Egypt. However, Egyptian control was never

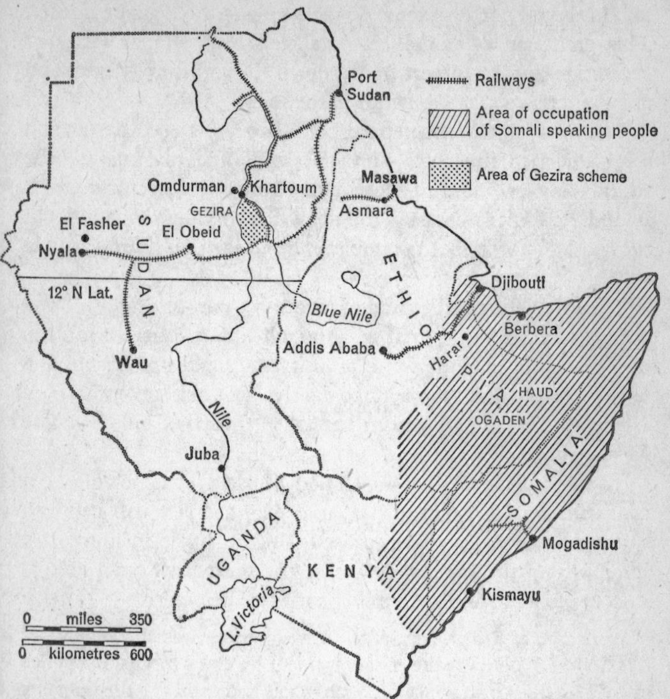

MAP 25. Sudan, Ethiopia and Somalia

more than nominal, even though Egypt retained throughout the condominium the right to share in Sudan's administration. Egypt developed 'a deep and well-founded suspicion that Sudan was being separated from Egypt, and an emotionally deep but legally and practically slight belief in her rights of sovereignty over Sudan and the Sudanese'.[1] Relations between Egypt and Sudan have been good since independence.

Land and People

Everywhere a very hot (and usually flat) country, the most significant feature of the physical environment is the gradual increase in total rainfall from north to south – from almost no

rain in the far north to some 60 inches along the Uganda border. This gradation of rainfall is paralleled by a similar series of vegetation zones – desert in the north through semi-desert and grassland to woodland savanna in the south.

The most significant natural boundary – between desert and semi-desert to the north and grasslands and savannas to the south – is very close to the country's most important cultural boundary. This is between the non-Moslem, negroid south and the Moslem north. Both boundaries lie close to the line of latitude 12°N.

The Moslem north contains about 75 per cent of the total population. Its various tribes, although widely different in ways of life, are given some sense of unity by the use of Arabic as a *lingua franca* and, most importantly, by their acceptance of Islam. Sudanese nationalism has taken firm root only in these Moslem areas.

To the south the tribes are all non-Moslem, some having been converted by Christian missionaries over the last half century. Sudanese nationalists have accused the British administration of emphasizing the distinctiveness of the southern Sudan and of encouraging the Christian missionaries in their work.

> The creation of a firm barrier to 'Arabicization' was the keynote of this Southern policy – the encouragement by every means of English as a *lingua franca*; an attack on Arab patois and names; – the unhappy memories of slave-trade were deliberately revived and kept alive . . .[2]

This view ignores the historical isolation of the south and the continuous contacts with Islam and the Arab world of the north. It has, however, resulted in the expulsion of European missionaries from the southern provinces. Whatever the policy of the British administration the difficulties of welding north and south into a united whole would in any case have been formidable.

The Economy

Sudan is almost entirely an agricultural country. Although nearly half of the export revenues come from one major irrigation scheme (the Gezira), the rural population is widely scattered, with methods of production related to the various rainfall régimes.

North of about 16°N latitude is the land of pastoral nomadism, except where cultivation is possible along the Nile Valley. In the far south a mixed subsistence economy of cattle-keeping and cultivation has made little contribution to the economy.

TABLE 33
Sudan. Exports in 1968 (by value)

	percentage
Cotton	59·8
Oil seeds, nuts, cake, meal and oil	20·9
Gum arabic	9·6
Hides and skins	1·8
Other	7·9
Total value 81·2 million Sudanese pounds (£67·8m.)	

SOURCE: *The Europa Yearbook*, 1970, Vol. II.

The chief zone of non-irrigated agriculture is known as the Central Rainlands, lying between 10½° and 15°N latitude. Here are grown both food crops (millet) and short staple cotton for export, as well as the production of gum arabic from wild acacia trees. Most of the world's supply of gum arabic comes from this area of Sudan. The chief towns of the Central Rainlands are El Fasher and El Obeid while just to the north lies the great Gezira irrigation scheme and the conurbation of Khartoum, Khartoum North and Omdurman. The Central Rainlands, the Khartoum area and the Gezira together form the economic and political heart of Sudan.

The Gezira (and its more recent extension, the Managil) is the most famous irrigation scheme in Africa. Started in 1925, it is operated on a partnership basis between the Government, the Sudan Gezira Board and the tenants. Each of these receives 32 per cent of the cotton crop. The rest is allocated to various social welfare funds.

It is often stated that the Gezira can be a model for other developing countries to follow and this view has been brilliantly set out by Arthur Gaitskell.[3] However, it should be remembered

that the Gezira has had the benefit of over forty years of development. Other African countries may be in too much of a hurry to follow this model of careful planning and the development of a cooperative spirit among all concerned.

ETHIOPIA

The heartland of Ethiopia remains the high tableland of the Ethiopian plateau, though the boundaries of the present state extend over the surrounding lowlands. Here in the isolated mountain valleys the remnants of the Christian civilization of Aksum* remained in being after the neighbouring coastal areas had been occupied by Moslem peoples. Rumours of its existence reaching Europe during the Middle Ages gave rise to various legends of the kingdom of 'Prester John', though no certain knowledge of this Christian kingdom reached Europe until effective Portuguese contact in the sixteenth century.[4]

The boundaries of the modern state in the south and west are substantially the same as those achieved by conquest in the early twentieth century by the Emperor Menelik. In the north, Eritrea was under Italian domination for most of this century but became part of Ethiopia after the Second World War.[5] Apart from the Italian occupation (1936–41) Ethiopia has been an independent country throughout recorded history.

Land and People

The dominant influence on the physical environment is altitude. Ethiopians themselves distinguish three distinct climatic zones based on altitude.

(a) *Kolla* is found up to 6,000 ft and is hot, dry thorn scrub.
(b) *Woina Dega* is found between 6,000 ft and 8,000 ft. Here the climate is sub-tropical and well-watered. It covers most of the plateau country and contains most of the populous and cultivated areas.
(c) *Dega*, above 8,000 ft, is temperate grassland where cereals like wheat and temperate fruits can be grown.

*Christianized in the fourth century A.D., Aksum relapsed into obscurity during the seventh-century rise of Islam.

The dominant ethnic group among Ethiopia's 23 million people are the Amharas. They number only about two million but form a closely-knit ruling class. Their language (Amharic) is the official language of the state and their religion (Coptic Christian) is the state religion. The power and wealth of the church is enormous. In the Christian areas it is estimated that about a fifth of the male population are priests and the churches dominate the villages both physically and socially.

More important numerically are the Galla, who live largely to the south of the highland areas. They form over half the population of Ethiopia and are also found in parts of northern Kenya. They are a relatively backward people only some of whom have been converted to Islam. They are linguistically and in physical type closer to the Somalis than to the Amharas.

The other group of major importance are the Somalis. Although they number less than half a million people they cover about one fifth of Ethiopia's land area (see Map 25) and are a serious political problem. (See pp. 220–222 below.)

TABLE 34
Ethiopia. Exports in 1966 (by value)

	percentage
Coffee	60·1
Hides and skins	13·8
Oil seeds, nuts and kernels	10·3
Other	15·8
Total value 2,586 million Ethiopian dollars (£43·1m.)	

SOURCE: *The Europa Yearbook*, 1970, Vol. II.

The Economy

The economy is largely undeveloped although the agricultural and hydro-electric potential is enormous. The chief physical barrier to development is poor communications. However, many would argue that a social revolution is at least as important a

prerequisite for economic growth as investment in roads and railways.

The chief export is coffee, most of which goes to the U.S.A.

SOMALIA

Somalia is unique among newly independent African states in that the nation-state has followed, not preceded, the development of Somali nationalism. The sizeable Somali minorities in neighbouring countries have given rise to territorial claims which threaten to disturb the peace of the whole of the Horn of Africa. Eighty-three per cent of the Somalis live in Somalia, 13 per cent in Ethiopia (Haud and Ogaden regions), 3 per cent in Kenya and 1 per cent in the French Territory of the Afar and Issa Peoples (formerly French Somaliland).

Land, People and Economy

Somalia is, for the most part, a desert or semi-desert country and three quarters of the population is nomadic. Only in the extreme south and in a small highland area in the north-west is rainfall adequate for cultivation. Elsewhere, agriculture is confined to small areas with sufficient ground water.

The camel is the mainstay of the subsistence economy and also contributes to export revenues (see Table 35 below). Migration of camel herders occurs not only within the Somali Republic but also (by agreement) across the border into the Haud area of Ethiopia. Apart from animal husbandry the only other economic activities of importance are the Italian-established banana plantations of the Juba and Webbe Shibeli rivers and the production of incense in the coastal areas.* Trade in animals and their products is mainly with Arabia.

BOUNDARY PROBLEMS

Most of the new African states are composed of a number of different ethnic groups and, as we have seen, political independence has come *before* a fully developed sense of national consciousness. It is quite otherwise with the Somali.

*From frankincense and myrrh trees.

Somali nationalism stems from a feeling of national consciousness in the sense of 'we' as opposed to 'they' which has existed among the Somali for many centuries. It was nurtured by tribal genealogies and traditions, by the Islamic religious ties, and by conflicts with foreign peoples. It ripened and became a political movement as a result of external influences – the establishment of alien governments, the impact of the Second World War, and the example of the struggle for independence in other countries.[6]

TABLE 35
Somalia. Exports in 1968 (by value)

	percentage
Live cattle, sheep, goats and camels	58·6
Bananas and plantains	28·1
Hides and skins	5·5
Wood and charcoal	2·3
Meat and meat products	1·4
Other	4·1

Total value 212 million Somali shillings (£12·4m.)

SOURCE: *The Europa Yearbook*, 1970, Vol. II.

Under twentieth-century colonial rule the Somalis were divided between five different political units.* The amalgamation of former British and Italian Somalilands into the Somali Republic in 1960 was seen by Somali nationalists as the first step in the creation of a 'Greater Somalia'.

Border conflicts have continued since that time. In Kenya, in the 1960s, infiltrating groups of Somali bandits (*shifta*) tied down large numbers of the security forces and the Kenya Government attempted both to close the frontier and to 'villageize' the nomadic Somali in an effort to overcome the problem. The common threat of Somali nationalist expansion has thrown Kenya and Ethiopia together in a working alliance.

It is important to realize that the threat is not simply physical. Both Kenya and Ethiopia exist as multi-tribal, multi-ethnic

*British Somaliland, Italian Somaliland, French Somaliland, Ethiopia and Kenya.

states. To admit that there is any substance in Somali claims is to admit a challenge to the very basis of their national development – that loyalty to the state must override loyalty to any particular ethnic or tribal group. The only peaceful reconciliation that seems possible is through a pan-African solution – the accommodation of Somali nationalism within a wider federal structure.

The possibility of such an eventuality has been brought much closer by the Arusha Agreement of 1967. Concluded under O.A.U. auspices, the agreement marks the end of four years of hostilities between Kenya and Somalia and the re-opening of diplomatic relations. It should be remembered, however, that this is the beginning of negotiations rather than the end of the dispute.

FRENCH TERRITORY OF THE AFAR AND ISSA PEOPLES

Formerly known as French Somaliland, this consists of the port of Djibouti and a small area of surrounding territory.

The Issas are a Somali-speaking group and form rather less than 50 per cent of the total population.

Notes on Chapter 11

1. Peter Kilner, in C. Legum (ed.), *Africa: a Handbook*, 1965, p. 95.
2. Beshir Mohammed Said, *The Sudan: Crossroads of Africa*, 1965.
3. A. Gaitskell, *Gezira: a Story of Development in the Sudan*, 1959.
4. See K. Pankhurst, *Ethiopia: a Cultural History*, 1955, and A. H. M. Jones and E. Monroe, *A History of Ethiopia*, 1960.
5. Federated with Ethiopia until 1962; now an integral part of the State.
6. Saadia Touval, *Somali Nationalism*, 1963, p. 84.

See also:

K. M. Barbour, *The Republic of the Sudan*, 1961.
A. A. Castagno, 'The Somali-Kenyan Controversy', in *Journal of Modern African Studies*, July 1964.
J. Drysdale, *The Somali Dispute*, 1964.
R. Greenfield, *Ethiopia*, 1966.
K. D. D. Henderson, *The Making of the Modern Sudan*, 1953.
C. Jesman, *The Ethiopian Paradox*, 1963.
I. M. Lewis, *The Modern History of Somaliland*, 1965.
I. M. Lewis, *A Pastoral Democracy*, 1961.
E. M. Luther, *Ethiopia Today*, 1958.
Mesfin Wolde Mariam, 'The Ethio-Somalian Boundary Dispute', in *Journal of Modern African Studies*, July 1964.
E. Ullendorf, *The Ethiopians: an Introduction to Country and People*, 1965.

Southern Africa

12 The Republic of South Africa

With the most developed economy, abundant resources, and the highest income per head in all Africa, the Republic is from one point of view the most favoured country in the continent. But because it also has the most acute racial problems, it is, from another point of view, the continent's unhappiest country instead. It is certainly the most modern – both in terms of economic development and of settlement.

THE PEOPLE

Prior to European settlement in the Cape during the seventeenth century, the western half of the Cape Province was sparsely inhabited by Bushmen hunters and Khoi-Khoin (Hottentot) pastoralists, most of whom were either exterminated or have since been absorbed into the Cape Coloured population.[1] The eastern half of Cape Province and the whole of the coastlands of Natal had been settled for many centuries by Bantu-speaking people. At the time of the European advance eastwards in the eighteenth century, the south-westward frontier of the Bantu lay approximately along the line of the Great Fish river. This line was the first point of violent conflict between Boer and Bantu and it is important to remember its location for two reasons. First, in any discussion of 'historic rights' between the two groups, the Boers can claim they were first only in the western half of the Cape Province, not in the rest of the country. Second, all the Bantu areas (or 'Native Reserves' as they used to be called) are in the north and east.

The bare numbers and percentages in Table 36 do not give a clear picture of the distribution of the various groups, and the figures should be read in conjunction with the distribution on Map 28. The most significant facts which emerge from this are

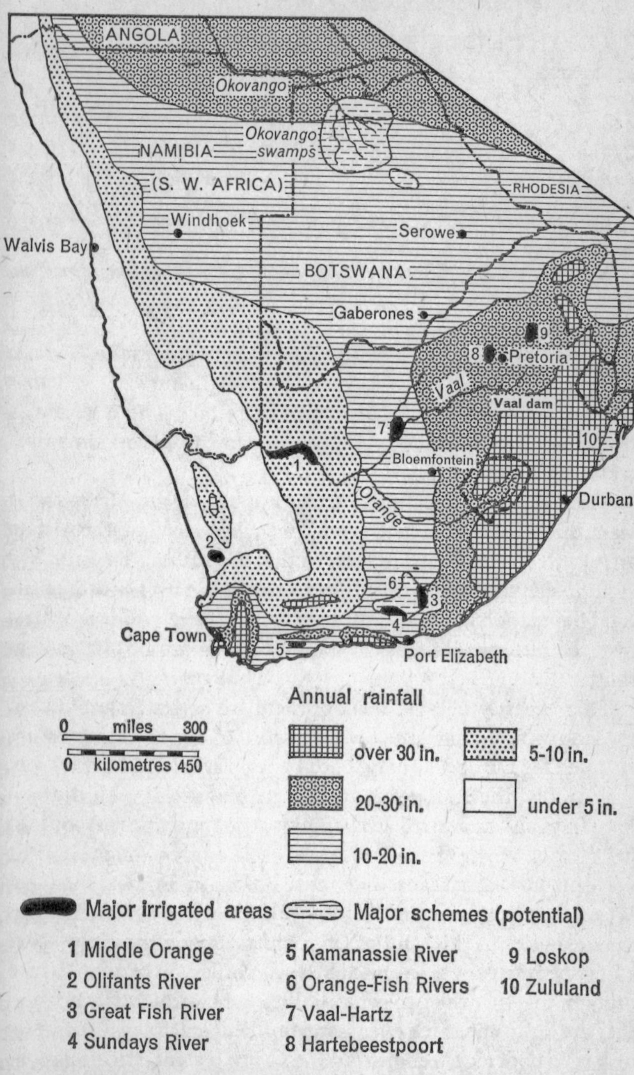

MAP 26. Water in southern Africa

TABLE 36
Population of the Republic by race (1969 estimate)

		percentage
Whites	3,639,000	18·9
Africans	13,042,000	68·3
Coloureds (including Cape Malays)	1,912,000	9·9
Asiatics	574,000	2·9
Total	19,167,000	100·0

SOURCE: Republic of South Africa, *State of South Africa, Yearbook*, 1970.

that there are comparatively few Africans (Bantu) in the Western Cape (where their place is taken by the Coloureds), and that most of the Indians (Asiatics) live in Natal.[2] There is, too, a difference in racial composition between town and country which we will deal with later.

The Europeans of South Africa are unique in Africa for at least three reasons. First, there are many more of them than anywhere else on the continent, so that they cannot be dismissed as an insignificant minority. They amount to 18·9 per cent of the total population and not only exercise complete political control over the rest, but do most of the jobs which can be classified as skilled.

This is partly because most of them are better educated than the non-whites, but also because most of the skilled jobs are reserved for Europeans only, both by legislation and by tradition.

Secondly, the Europeans are unique because of their division into English- and Afrikaans-speaking communities. About 40 per cent of Whites have English as their mother tongue and 60 per cent have Afrikaans. For most people in Britain, the Boer War is a remote piece of history, but for white South Africans the memories of this, and other conflicts among themselves, are still very much alive. In spite of the Act of Union of 1909, which brought together the two communities in political independence, they are far from united over many fundamental issues – attitudes to law, democracy, religion and, to some extent, race relations among the most important.

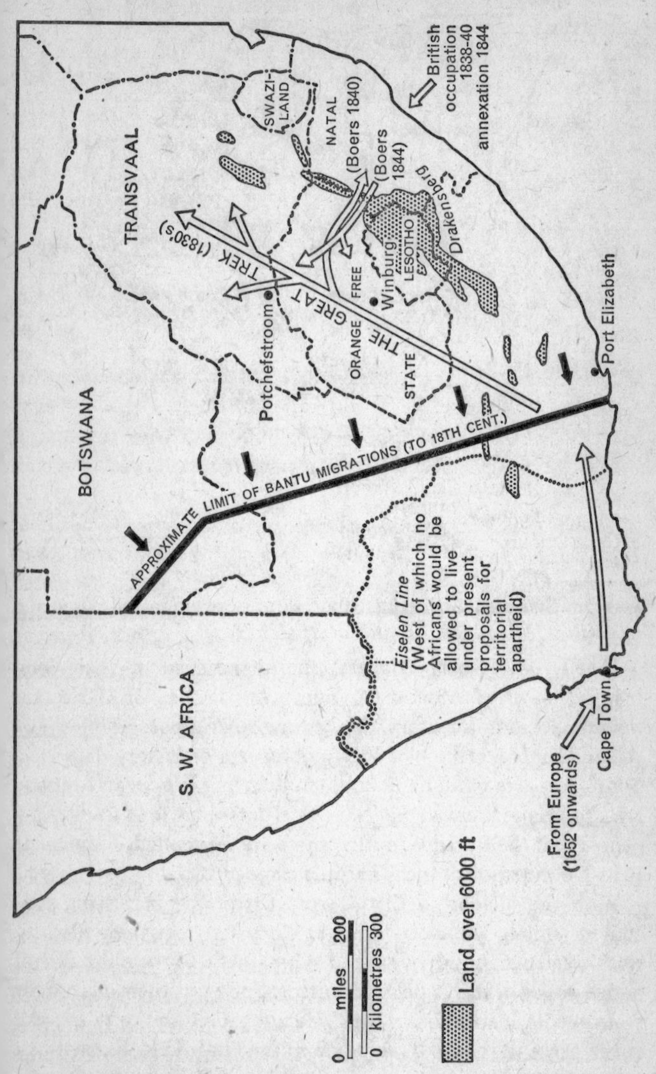

MAP 27. Main lines of European colonization in South Africa up to the middle of the 19th century

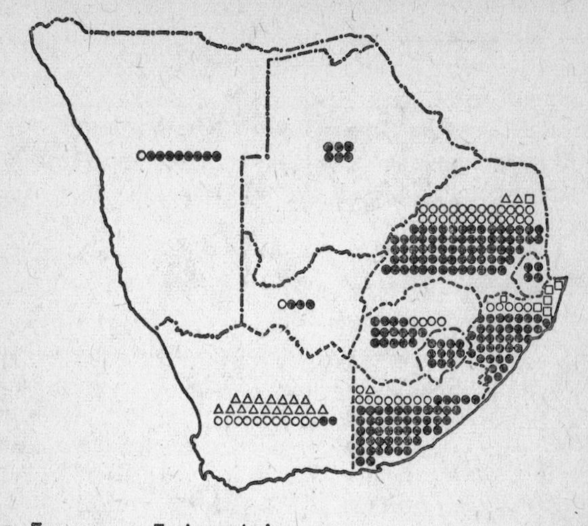

European ○ Bantu ● Cape Coloured △ Asiatic □ Each symbol represents 50,000 people (1951 census)

0 miles 350
0 kilometres 600

MAP 28. Southern Africa: distribution of population by region and race. (From J. D. Fage, *An Atlas of African History*, 1958, p. 51)

Finally, the Europeans are unique because of their long history in Africa. Most other European 'settlers' in Africa are newcomers in this century. White South Africans, and especially the Afrikaners, can look back to 300 years of history *in Africa*. South Africa is more home to them than any European country. By 1795 there were about 16,000 settlers[3] and it is from these people that the Republic's Afrikaners are descended. Permanent British occupation of the Cape only came in 1806.

With the advent of British rule there was increasing discontent among the Boer farmers. They felt that their identity was threatened and they were unsympathetic to the more liberal native policy of the Cape government. Such was their discontent that they decided to leave the Cape altogether and to undertake in the 1830s the Great Trek north to the High Veld, to establish what later became the independent Boer republics of the Orange Free State and the Transvaal.

The Great Trek involved at least 10,000 people, moving across 500 miles of mountain and plateau in convoys of ox wagons. To the east the way was barred by the human barrier of Bantu tribesmen and the physical barrier of the mountains of Basutoland and the Drakensberg. To the north-west the land was dry and uninviting. Only to the north-east was the way open, the native population greatly reduced in numbers by warfare, and the land suitable for both arable and pastoral farming. Some of the pioneers descended into Natal and founded Pietermaritzburg, but numbers migrated again on the annexation of Natal by Britain in 1844.

The Boer farmers settled down on the veld to enjoy their hard-won independence, preserving their Calvinist theology, evolving their own special language, and treating the natives according to their lights. 'There shall be no equality between Black and White either in Church or State,' said the original constitution of the Transvaal. Their present belief in apartheid

> is based not simply on fear of the African, but on the will to preserve the culture handed down through the centuries by the founders of White South Africa.
>
> It seems a bare inheritance, an inward-turned, unsmiling, dourly pious way of life, which has never flowered notably in literature, music, or the visual arts; but it has a kind of bleak dignity, and the story of the Afrikaner people is the story of a long fight to protect it against the British as well as against the Bantu.[4]

English-speaking white South Africans are of more recent origins, since many of them came after 1860 with the development of first diamond and then gold mining. Before this, settlers had been brought into the Cape in the 1820s and again in the 1840s and 50s – probably about 22,000 in all. In the same period (up to 1856) about 8,000 Europeans had settled in Natal.

Immigration on a large scale – mainly British – followed on the discovery of diamonds in the Cape and gold in the Transvaal. It was a development the Afrikaners did not welcome but could not stop. No accurate figures exist of immigration at this time, but some indication is given in the growth of the white population (from all sources) in Transvaal between 1890 and 1911 – from 119,000 to 421,000. This influx of '*Uitlanders*' has had its effect on the linguistic balance between town and country even

today. Until very recently English has been predominant in the towns (especially in the newer industrial centres) and Afrikaans in the countryside, and although Afrikaners have joined the townward movement in recent years, they remain rooted in 'pre-industrial Europe. The English section arrived after the industrial revolution which had transformed the country of their birth. They brought with them the modern ideas of commerce and finance....'[5] This urban dominance of the English-speaking Whites has meant that although the Afrikaners have for long been dominant in politics, they have until recently been under-represented in the professions (including the judiciary) and even more under-represented in business enterprises.[6]

The *Coloureds* are of exceedingly mixed racial origin and, like the Afrikaners, their roots go back to the early days of settlement at the Cape. About 90 per cent of them still live in the Cape Province, and about 90 per cent have Afrikaans as their mother tongue.

Their ancestors include Bushmen, Hottentots, Europeans, slaves (of Malayan, West African, Malagasy or Indian origin among others) and passing sailors of all races. Offspring of European–Hottentot unions have sometimes preserved a special identity and are known as Bastards; one of the best-known groups are the Rehoboth Bastards of South-West Africa. Only the Cape Malays have preserved their racial and cultural distinctiveness, due to the social cohesion which the practice of Islam has given them. They number today less than 100,000 people.

The formation of the Coloured community has been a continuing process right up until the present time. Between 1937 and 1946 there were, on average, about 700 'mixed' marriages annually,[7] apart from other less permanent unions; although, with the application of apartheid legislation, this process will no doubt decrease. There has, moreover, been a continuing traffic *from* the Coloured people of those whose physical make-up enabled them to 'play white'. Nobody knows how many have been absorbed into the White population or how many 'Whites' carry Coloured genes. Certainly many Whites must be partly Coloured, and one writer has estimated their number as at least half a million.[8]

The *Asians* are descended from indentured labourers brought over from India to work in the sugar plantations of Natal, and most of them still live in that province – over half in the city of Durban alone. Many have risen to wealth and influence there, although the majority are still poor. It has long been the dream of the Whites that the Indians would one day be repatriated to India. A state-assisted scheme has been in force since 1927, but the numbers taking advantage of it have never been great. Since the Second World War less than a thousand Indians have accepted this Government assistance.

The Bantu tribes had moved into the eastern half of South Africa from the north some centuries before White settlement at the Cape. Like the Whites, they displaced, absorbed or destroyed what indigenous inhabitants were already living there.

Although 'Bantu' is really a linguistic not a racial term, the South African Bantu do have a different appearance from the Negroes of West Africa. For example, many are of lighter skin colour, probably due to admixture with the yellow-skinned Hottentot and Bushmen. This relatively light skin colour is particularly noticeable among the Xhosa, some of whom have been known to 'play Coloured' in the same way that Coloureds have played white.

The two main groups of Bantu languages in South Africa are the Nguni and the Sotho. These are further subdivided according to the following table, which also gives the approximate percentage of Bantu which speak them.

It will be seen that the main groups of importance (roughly one third each) are the Xhosa, Zulu and Sotho, but it should be remembered that some of the urban Bantu know no tribal language. The Drakensberg mountains form the boundary between the Sotho and the Nguni groups in the same way that they formed the boundary between Briton and Boer in the nineteenth century. They also form a climatic divide at all times and are still a barrier to communications.

The Africans are the least urbanized of the South African peoples but they have been moving into the urban areas in ever increasing numbers during this century. In 1904 only 10·4 per cent of Bantu were town dwellers while, by 1960, 32 per cent lived in the urban areas – two thirds of these in the four main

TABLE 37

Bantu languages in the Republic, Botswana, Lesotho and Swaziland

		percentage
Nguni group	Xhosa	32
	Zulu including Ndebele	30
	Swazi	3
	Tsonga	3
	Venda	2
Sotho group	S. Sotho	10
	N. Sotho	10
	Tswana	8
	Other	2

SOURCE: *Tomlinson Commission Report.*

industrial centres,[9] where they congregate in shanty towns and 'locations' surrounding the White cities, many of the latter being newly built by the Government. The explosive social and political problems created by these urban Africans are the chief focuses of race tensions in the Republic.

TABLE 38

Percentage of population living in the urban areas of South Africa (1960)

	percentage
Total	49
Europeans	84
Asiatics	83
Coloureds	68
Africans	32

SOURCE: Republic of South Africa, *Statistical Yearbook*, 1965, p. A34.

THE LAND AND ITS RESOURCES

As anyone knows who reads the travel posters or the labels at the

fruiterers, South Africa is a land of sunshine as well as race tensions. Although much of the north and west is too dry for arable farming, the country has a great deal of good agricultural land, abundant mineral resources, no tsetse fly (except in part of northern Natal) and a climate over most of the country which is generally regarded as invigorating for human activity.

The two main regions of commercial arable farming are those which have more than 20 inches of rainfall as well as a temperate climate. They are the area around Cape Town and the High Veld (most of Orange Free State and Southern Transvaal) and contain the chief concentrations of white farmers. A third region of commercial arable farming is the coastal strip of Natal, specializing in sugar cane and to a lesser extent bananas and other tropical fruits.

The Western Cape region, having a Mediterranean type of climate with good winter rain and hot dry summers, specializes in wheat, vines (both for dessert and wine making) and in temperate fruits like apples, pears and peaches. Fruit in particular has found a ready market in the northern hemisphere, where it appears in the off-season for home-grown fruit. This off-season peak in marketing in Europe probably accounts for the material (as distinct from propaganda) failure of the boycott of March 1960 in Britain. In many shops it would be a case of buying South African or going without.

The western Cape region of winter rain merges gradually along the coast into the summer rainfall region of the eastern half of the country. Animal husbandry as well as arable farming becomes important, and there is some citrus fruit growing, especially in the irrigated areas north of Port Elizabeth.

The High Veld at an elevation of from 4,000 to 6,000 ft lies to the west of the Drakensberg mountains. It is naturally a region of rolling grassy plain – the *platteland* (flat land) home of the Afrikaner nation. At the centre of the region is the so-called 'maize triangle', containing some three quarters of the Republic's cultivated area. Although this is the centre of maize growing in the Republic it is by no means confined to this area, nor is the region entirely dominated by the cultivation of maize. It is essentially a land of mixed arable and pastoral farming. To the north, in the lower-lying and warmer Bush Veld of the central and

northern Transvaal, tobacco and citrus fruits become important.

In over half of South Africa 'the spectre that haunts the farmer most frequently is drought. Some 53 per cent of the Union has an average rainfall of less than 20 inches and the variability of this rainfall . . . tends to be proportionately greater as the mean amount decreases.'[10] In these drier areas, in the centre and west of the country, the dominant activity is cattle and even more sheep farming of an extensive kind – extensive in the sense that animals (and men) are scattered over a wide area of sparse pasture. The absence of the tsetse fly has aided this development. There are in South Africa over twelve million head of cattle and over forty-two million sheep, compared with some six million cattle and four million sheep in the whole of Rhodesia, Zambia, Malawi, S.W. Africa, Botswana and Moçambique combined. In 1964 wool came second to gold in South Africa's exports (£66 million). This underlines still further the difficulty of organizing a consumer boycott of South African goods. Fruit and wine may be fairly easy to identify: wool is not.

The conservation of available water supplies is important not only for agriculture but also for industry and the needs of a growing urban population moving rapidly towards Western standards of consumption. This is particularly significant on the Witwatersrand, which draws most of its water from wells and from the Vaal Dam at Vereeniging. In 1947, 67½ million gallons of water per day were used on the Rand (about half by industry and the mines) but by A.D. 2000 it is estimated that 953 million gallons will be required. More dams will certainly be needed to cope with this demand and with the needs of agriculture. The trouble is that the Republic's rivers, being shallow and irregular in flow, are not well suited for the construction of dams and irrigation schemes. The major irrigated areas and potential schemes are indicated on Map 26. Of these, the Orange River Project is the most ambitious. The project will take at least thirty years to complete and will cost over £250 million. When finished it will provide water, power and recreation over an area considerably larger than America's T.V.A. A tunnel joining the Orange and Fish rivers (51½ miles) was started in 1968 and should be finished in 1973. A canal linking the Fish and Sundays rivers was started in 1969.

South Africa lies at the southern end of

> ... the richest mineral belt so far discovered on the earth's surface, stretching from Katanga and the Northern Rhodesian Copperbelt in the north ... to the northern Cape Province.... No other area of comparable size can show so large and so continuous an output of gold, diamonds, copper, coal, iron, chrome, manganese, asbestos and ... uranium.[11]

Most of these the Republic has in abundance. It is particularly fortunate in having by far the largest reserves of bituminous coal in the whole of Africa. Whereas it has less opportunity than many other African countries for the development of hydro-electric power, it also has less need.*

The development of gold and diamond mining in the 1870s brought the first large-scale foreign investment to South Africa. It upset the quiet pastoral life of the Boer farmers but it also provided the basis of capital and labour for later economic growth. It was thought at one time that the problem of finding a sufficient number of workers able and willing to work in the mines of the Rand might be solved by bringing in Chinese labour, and there were in fact some 55,000 Chinese there in the early years of this century. However, these were all repatriated by 1910 and the mines have since had to rely on the recruitment of Africans over an extensive area of southern Africa. This migrant labour is housed in special compounds near the mines, and workers usually come under contract for a spell of fourteen months or so before returning to their homes elsewhere in the Republic or in neighbouring countries. The mine compounds are under the control of the Mining Companies and should not be confused with the shanty towns and 'locations' elsewhere on the Rand, which are under the control of the municipal authorities.

Iron and steel form the basis of modern manufacturing industry, and the beginnings were made in South Africa during the First World War. It was not until the formation of the South African Iron and Steel Corporation in 1928, however, that a firm basis was laid for the development of South Africa into a modern industrial state. The Corporation (I.S.C.O.R.) established a works at Pretoria in 1934, using local ore, but the most

*But there is no oil – a fact of some importance if an economic boycott of South Africa ever became a reality.

spectacular development came in the 1950s with the beginnings of operations at the new, fully integrated steelworks at Vanderbijl Park near Vereeniging. This works, which comprises coke ovens, blast furnaces, slab, strip, and rolling mills, and ancillary plants for by-products, came into operation in 1951 and now has an ingot capacity of over 3 million tons. What in 1948 was a piece of open veld now contains a township of over 50,000 people, besides all the industrial plant. Ore is obtained from Thabazimbi in the western Transvaal and also from Sishen in the north-western Cape. Coal comes from the Newcastle area of Natal and from Witbank. I.S.C.O.R., a Government-owned enterprise, produces about two thirds of South Africa's steel requirements.

TABLE 39
Growth of steel production in South Africa

	(in thousands of metric tons)
1948	596
1956	1605
1957	1737
1958	1832
1959	1895
1960	2113
1961	2475
1962	2634
1963	2834
1964	3107
1965	3293
1966	3285
1967	3651

SOURCE: *U.N. Statistical Yearbook 1965*, p. 306, and *1968*, p. 305.

THE GROWTH OF SECONDARY INDUSTRY

Investment in mining, the growth of an urban labour force, Government encouragement and protection and, especially, the stimulus given by the Second World War brought about an industrial revolution in the Republic, and the economy has

continued buoyant to the present time. Growth has taken place above all in the Southern Transvaal (Pretoria, Witwatersrand, Vereeniging), and to a lesser extent in the other major industrial centres of Durban, Port Elizabeth/Uitenhage, Cape Town, Bloemfontein, Pietermaritzburg, Kimberley and East London. The four largest conurbations – Southern Transvaal, Capetown, Durban/Pinetown and Port Elizabeth/Uitenhage – together account for over 82 per cent of the net industrial output, 75 per cent of the industrial labour force and some 60 per cent of the factories.

By 1960 63 per cent of the total population of South Africa was contained in the eight major urban areas listed above. About one third of the whites and one sixth of the Africans were concentrated in the southern Transvaal alone.

In the Cape Town area the main industries are clothing and textiles, canning and food processing, distilling, printing, and leather working. Port Elizabeth is the centre of the Republic's footwear industry and also has plants for car assembly, tyres, batteries and food canning and processing. Durban concentrates on chemicals, paints, paper, hardware, clothing and domestic appliances, while the southern Transvaal is the centre of the country's metal-working and engineering industries, among others.

This industrial growth has been accompanied by an influx of workers – both white and non-white – from the countryside. It has affected the balance between town and country and also between the various racial groups in different areas. Africans have left the reserves in larger numbers than ever before but Whites too have left their traditional strongholds. 'The migration of Whites is proportionately greater than any group except for the Asiatics.'[12] Huge areas of the Republic have far smaller white populations today than they had forty years ago. Not only in the countryside has this shrinkage of white South Africa been apparent. In 1960 Cape Town and Pretoria were the only towns in which Whites outnumbered Africans, while nowhere are the Whites more numerous than all other groups combined.

Industrialization has not only brought the different racial groups into greater geographical proximity, but has had the effect of breaking down barriers within industry. Gone are the

days of the 1920s when the first Hertzog Government introduced discriminatory legislation to protect the interests of poor white workers. The industrial expansion has brought about a shortage of labour and as a result Bantu have been moving into the skilled and semi-skilled jobs. As early as 1946 nearly half the semi-skilled jobs were being done by Africans. If there are not enough white men to do the jobs available, black men will be asked to do them. By 1948 the process of industrial growth had not brought greater social and political rights for Africans, but it had improved their purchasing power as well as enhanced their importance in the economy of the country. It had, above all, centralized social and political pressures in the key industrial areas, particularly the southern Transvaal. Left unchecked it might well have brought about closer integration of the various racial groups. It was this possibility that the Nationalist Government, coming to power in 1948, at once tried to prevent from happening.

They argued that there were two courses open to South Africa. Either the process of integration could be allowed to continue, in which case eventual cultural and social equality would lead to complete racial assimilation: or, as this is too horrible to contemplate for them, the races must be kept apart in all spheres. To this end they have passed, and put into effect, a whole complex of legislation designed to prevent any sort of contact whatever (except the master–servant relationship) between the different racial groups.

THE GEOGRAPHY OF APARTHEID

The Bantu are to have political and other rights of citizenship only in the Bantu areas, i.e. in the present native reserves. In the White areas they are allowed to work, but not to have permanent homes. In these areas they have to live in segregated townships and within these townships each person is classified according to his tribal origin so that he will be made to feel that his first loyalty is to the tribe and not to the urban community. Above all, an attempt is being made to decentralize industrial growth so that expansion in the four main nuclei can be slowed down and industries started on the fringes of the reserves. To

encourage fewer Bantu to leave the reserves, economic development will be encouraged within the Bantu areas themselves. The blueprint for this geographical apartheid is known as the *Tomlinson Report* and was issued in the form of an extended summary in 1955.[13]

The present Bantu areas consist of rather less than 13 per cent of the total area of South Africa, situated in the form of a horseshoe around the Transvaal and Orange Free State. They are excessively fragmented. (See Map 29.)

The horseshoe shape of the Bantu areas and to some extent their fragmentation into many separate blocks can be explained by the historical geography.... The Europeans who first moved eastwards along the coast clashed with a southward moving stream of Bantu in the region of the present Ciskei. As a result of these clashes and other circumstances, a very broken up Ciskei was produced, while a large northward movement of Europeans occurred which took the form of the Great Trek... the Europeans found little difficulty in establishing themselves on the grassy plains of the Orange Free State and the Transvaal.[14]

The Bantu were already settled in the warmer bushveld areas. The reserves in the south-east are well watered and have a relatively high density of population (80 per sq. ml.). Those in the west are semi-desert areas with a much lower density of population (25–35 per sq. ml.), while those in the north are well watered tropical and sub-tropical areas with a density of about 60 to the square mile. Apart from the cities of the White areas, the reserves in the north and south-east are the most densely populated parts of the country.

All the Bantu areas are run-down rural areas of subsistence agriculture, concentrating on the cultivation of 'mealies' (maize) and 'kaffircorn' (sorghum). There are no industries, nor any towns or cities. The whole of the population lives in villages of varying size. Even the larger settlements (such as Umtata in the Transkei) do not have the range of services and amenities associated with towns in the real sense of the word. In general, the main lines of communication have left them on one side. A place like Port St Johns, which figures prominently on atlas maps, was described by Tomlinson as 'unfortunately silted up to such an extent ... as to become unusable'.[15] Soil erosion is widespread. In the Transkei, for example, 30 per cent of the land

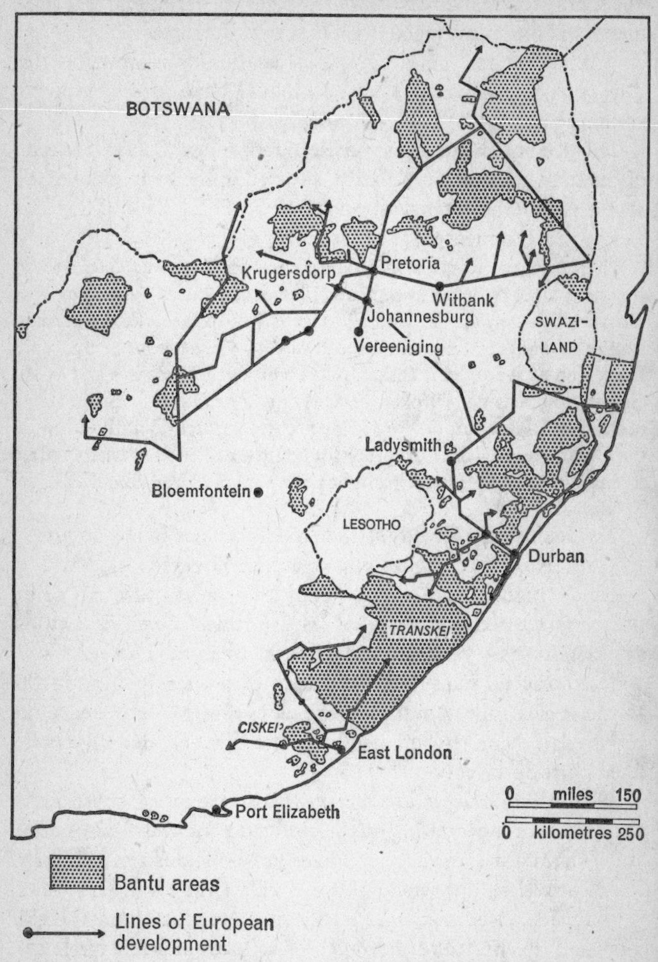

MAP 29. Lines of European development in relation to the Bantu areas as proposed by the Tomlinson Commission

is badly eroded, 44 per cent moderately so, while only 26 per cent is free from erosion (but may be too hilly for cultivation). In consequence of this and of primitive farming methods, pro-

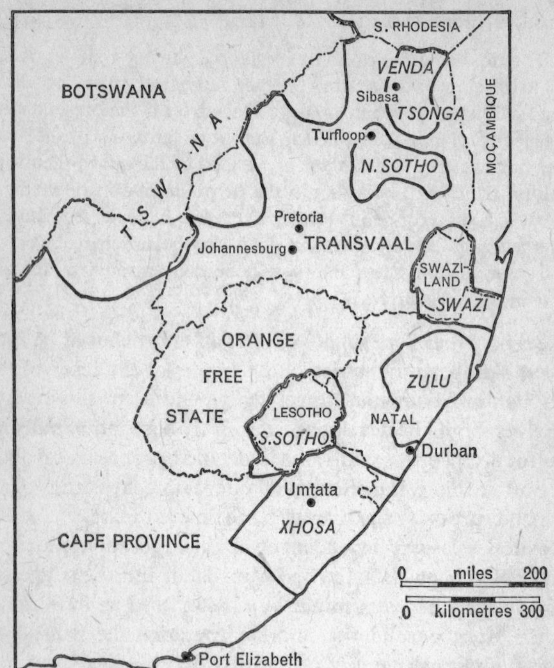

MAP 30. Possible consolidation of the Bantu areas as proposed by the Tomlinson Commission

ductivity is extremely low. In short, the reserves are completely underdeveloped backward areas within the boundaries of what is, in some parts, a modern industrial state.

At present some 40 per cent[16] of the Bantu live in the reserves, and the density of population has certainly reached beyond the upper limits of their capacity without extensive development. The Tomlinson Report suggests that by the year 2000 the racial balance of South Africa's population will be as follows:

Whites	4,588,000
Bantu	21,361,000
Coloureds	3,917,000
Asiatics	1,382,000

It argues, moreover, that

> If the tempo of urbanization experienced during 1946–51 is continued to the close of the century . . . then more than 10,000,000 Bantu will be established in urban areas. . . . Moreover if the present absorbent capacity of the Bantu areas, European farms and other rural areas is not raised . . . more than 15,000,000 of the above-mentioned 21 million Bantu will be living in the urban areas outside the Bantu areas. . . . Unless economic development can be diverted from its present geographical concentration . . . it may be anticipated also that the vast majority of these Bantu will be concentrated at the four existing industrial complexes . . .[17]

The report therefore suggested that an effort should be made to divert European industries to the fringes of the reserves,[18] to which Bantu labour can travel daily, and that the reserves themselves should be developed extensively both industrially and agriculturally. To this end it made detailed proposals involving among other things the creation of a development authority and the expenditure of £104 millions in the first ten years.

The proposals were dependent on the incorporation into South Africa of Botswana, Lesotho and Swaziland, and the suggestion was made that the areas might be consolidated as indicated in Map 30. After consolidation and incorporation the Bantu areas would amount to 47 per cent of 'Greater South Africa'.

If sufficient money is spent and if further territory were acquired (however remote this possibility may be) then the report suggests that the Bantu areas could support a population of 8 million together with 1½ million dependent on work in White industries outside the reserves. If migratory labourers are added this would amount to a '*de jure* population' of about 10 millions – about the same *proportion* as are at present supported in the reserves. In other words, even in its most generous and optimistic form, apartheid could not make racial separation any more effective than at present.

So far, only a few steps have been taken to implement the proposals of the Tomlinson Commission. Two five-year plans have increased investment in the 'homelands'. The Bantu Self Government Act of 1959 envisaged the establishment of the seven national units but with no suggestion of consolidation. 'University' colleges have been set up for Zulu, Xhosa and

Sotho – the latter at Turfloop, visited by Mr Macmillan in his 1960 tour. And there is now a 'Government' in the Transkei.

Meanwhile the growth of the urban African population continues. Between 1951 and 1960 the African population of Johannesburg, Durban, Pretoria, Vanderbijl Park, Vereeniging and Port Elizabeth increased by a total of 397,578 as opposed to a White increase of 180,047.[19] Moreover the list of new industrial enterprises still shows a heavy concentration in the four main areas. Much of South Africa's private industry is still financed by foreign capital. The Tomlinson Commission and to a lesser extent the Government may be willing to subordinate economic to doctrinal interests. Private investors and especially foreign investors are not.

In the long run, industrial development based on a segregated labour force is bound to be inefficient even if it provides cheap labour in the short run. Overheads are greater for one thing – the provision and maintenance of two, three or even four washing, eating and lavatory facilities for workpeople can be an expensive business. Not to be able to promote according to ability and to have to keep job segregation enforced will also become increasingly inefficient as more Africans become used to industrial processes. Finally, the proposals of the Tomlinson Commission for overall economic planning based on apartheid will cut across the economic interests of the country, which need to be developed as a whole, not piecemeal. Mineral resources and possibilities for irrigation in northern Transvaal, for example, overlap both White and Bantu areas. To develop them in the most efficient way would tend towards integration, not apartheid.

The reliance on private, and especially foreign capital is, therefore, most important when considering the practicability of geographical apartheid. Investors will usually look for greatest profitability rather than bow to purely political considerations. Taken together with the need to incorporate Botswana, Lesotho and Swaziland, the large amount of investment involved, and the incomplete nature of the proposed separation (even at its most optimistic), the conclusion is inescapable that geographical apartheid is unworkable, although this does not seem to have weakened the determination to make it work in some form or

other. Perhaps one day the South African Government will face up to the minority report of Mr Bisschop, a member of the Tomlinson Commission. 'If in due course, it is found unpractical,' he said, 'and I greatly fear that it will be found to be so, progressive integration with its economic and political consequences will have to be accepted.'[20]

Notes on Chapter 12

1. About twenty still exist in the Cape Province. The estimated total number still alive is about 55,000, scattered over Botswana, S.W. Africa and Angola, with a few in the Rhodesias and the Republic. Most of them – about 30,000 – live in Botswana.
2. Note on racial terminology in South Africa:
   (a) 'Whites' and 'Europeans' are usually synonymous. However, some use 'Europeans' for English-speakers to distinguish them from 'Boers'. It is probably best to stick to 'Whites'.
   (b) People of negroid racial origin are referred to officially as 'Bantu'. This is now used in preference to 'Native', as the latter implies that the Whites have less right to be in the country. To call black South Africans 'Africans' is to stamp the speaker or writer as a 'liberal'. Afrikaans-speaking Whites, particularly, object to this as they now refer to themselves, not as Boers, but as 'Afrikaners' – which in English means 'Africans'.
   (c) Coloured – people of mixed racial origins.
   (d) Asiatics – mainly Indians.
3. About 50 per cent of Dutch origin.
   27 per cent of German origin.
   18 per cent of French origin.
   5 per cent of others. (Mainly Huguenots, Protestant refugees from Catholic France.)
4. Ian Laing, 'Tragic South Africa', *Sunday Times*, 5 Jan. 1958.
5. *State of the Union. Year Book for South Africa 1958*, p. 59.
6. The Afrikaners' share in business 1957:
   Commerce 25 per cent, finance 11 per cent, industry 6 per cent, mining only 5 per cent, ibid., p. 59.
   J. H. Wellington, *Southern Africa*, Vol. II, 1955.

7. 5 Europeans to Natives
6 Europeans to Asians
80 Europeans to Coloured
100 Coloured to Asians
566 Coloured to Natives

8. Geo. Findlay, *Miscegenation*, 1936.
9. Western Cape. Durban/Pinetown. Southern Transvaal and Port Elizabeth.
10. J. H. Wellington, op. cit., Vol. I, p. 42.
11. ibid., Vol. II, pp. xvii–xviii.
12. H. C. Brookfield, 'Some Geographical Implications of the Apartheid and Partnership Policies in Southern Africa'. Article in the Institute of British Geographers' *Transactions and Papers*, 1957, p. 232. See also R. J. Davies, 'The South African Urban Hierarchy', in *South African Geographical Journal*, 1967.
13. *Summary of the Report of the Commission for the Socio-Economic Development of the Bantu Areas within the Union of South Africa* (the Tomlinson Commission), U.G. 61/1955.
14. *Tomlinson Report*, p. 47.
15. *Tomlinson Report*, p. 51.
16. Between 4 and 5 million people – 2·6 per cent less than ten years ago.
17. *Tomlinson Report*, p. 29.
18. See lines of European development on Map 29.
19. Both natural increase and migration.
20. *Tomlinson Report*, p. 108.

13 Namibia, Botswana, Lesotho and Swaziland

NAMIBIA (SOUTH WEST AFRICA)*

Namibia is not important for what it is but for what it symbolizes to the outside world. It is a vast country nearly as big as Nigeria and almost eight times the size of England and Wales, but most of it is desert (the Namib) or semi-desert (the Kalahari) and at present supports only about half a million people.

To the outside world it symbolizes the struggle between black and white in South Africa. Ruled by South Africa since 1918, its international status is in dispute between the U.N.O. and the South African Government. After the First World War, the country was handed over to South Africa to be administered as a League of Nations Mandate. It was, however, a different type of mandated territory from any other in that it was allowed to be administered as an integral portion of the administering power.

In 1946 South Africa asked the U.N. to be allowed to incorporate S.W. Africa. This request was refused and South Africa was asked to place the territory under the U.N. Trusteeship system. The U.N. claims to be the legal heir of the League. South Africa claims that the League has no legal successor and, therefore, that it has no obligation to place S.W. Africa under Trusteeship. Deadlock between the U.N. and South Africa over the status of S.W. Africa continues down to the present time.

The coastal Namib Desert is one of the most truly arid regions of the world. Known to the early explorers as the 'skeleton coast' and the 'coast of death', it would today be almost entirely uninhabited were it not for the rich diamond deposits found there which now produce the chief revenue of the country. The diamonds are found in easily worked surface deposits.

*The name declared official by resolution of the U.N. General Assembly on 12 June 1968. This change of name is not recognized by South Africa, which continues to administer the territory as part of the Republic.

The eastern half of the country, bordering on Botswana, is also largely uninhabited, although the Kalahari is not such a forbidding area as the Namib and does support a small population of Bushman hunters, who wander over large areas in search of game.

The chief areas of population coincide with the areas of highest rainfall. In the north, still under a system of indirect rule, are the tribal areas of the Ovambo and others. In the central highlands are the chief areas of white settlement and social conflict.

The northern tribal territories are some of the most backward and untouched in the whole of Africa. Here live about two thirds of the African population and over half the total population. Theirs is still a life of subsistence agriculture and cattle farming with no exports save that of labour to the south. The area contains some of the best-watered country in the whole of S.W. Africa, but it is malarial and tsetse-infested, and little money has been spent on it. There are certainly possibilities for future development.

The central highlands, lying between 5,000 and 8,000 feet, have a fairly low rainfall and are unsuitable for crop cultivation. However, they contain some of the finest ranching country in the whole of southern Africa, country famous for its production of Karakul pelts (for 'Persian lamb' coats); it is this which has attracted the European settlers. Today most of them are Afrikaners, with some Germans and a smaller number of English-speaking South Africans.

South West Africa was a German colony from 1890 until after the First World War. Before the coming of the Germans the native tribes of the central highlands appear to have been fairly prosperous cattle farmers. The chief groups were the Hottentots and the Hereros, a Bantu tribe. The early explorers spoke of 'countless herds of horned cattle'[1] and when the territory was annexed by Germany 'the Herero people must have possessed over 150,000 head of cattle'.[2]

This prosperity was soon destroyed. In just over ten years a tribe of over 80,000 people had been reduced to less than 15,000 impoverished refugees,[3] mainly by the ruthless and bloody suppression of the Herero revolt of 1904. As a German Colonial Office official put it, writing in 1890:

> The decision to colonize in South-West Africa could after all mean nothing else but this: namely that the native tribes would have to give up their land in order that the white man might have the land . . .
>
> When this attitude is questioned from the moral law standpoint, the answer is that for nations of the *Kultur* position of the South Africa natives, the loss of their free national barbarism and their development into a class of labourers in service of and dependent on the white people, is primarily a law of existence in the highest degree.[4]

Those who did not accept this doctrine had, quite naturally, to be suppressed.

During the inter-war years, S.W. Africa was an almost forgotten land. Annual reports were submitted to the League of Nations and although there was criticism of racial policies and lack of progress towards self-government, both reports and criticisms soon collected dust on the shelves of governments and publicists alike.

Since 1950 the South African government has unilaterally incorporated S.W. Africa into South Africa. S.W. African M.P.s sit in the South African Parliament and, as far as the central and southern areas are concerned, the territory is to all intents and purposes part of South Africa.

The U.N./South African dispute over the territory has grown more angry since 1946, but little progress has been made towards resolving it. The only suggestion for a compromise solution came from the 1958 U.N. Good Offices Committee under the chairmanship of Sir Charles Arden-Clarke. This suggestion was that the *status quo* should, in effect, be recognized and that the territory should be partitioned. The central and southern areas would become part of South Africa and the northern tribal areas made a separate territory and placed under U.N. Trusteeship. In 1964 the South African government accepted the Odendaal Commission Report. This recommends the establishment of ten 'Bantustans' and a White area – i.e. complete geographical apartheid.

This suggestion for partition did not find much support in the Councils of the U.N. By this time the status of Africa had come to symbolize the whole quarrel between South Africa and most of the outside world over apartheid. Partition looked too much like a form of apartheid. In addition, the continued exis-

tence of the dispute provides the international opponents of apartheid with a legal weapon with which to fight South Africa. South Africa's racial policies are considered by some to be an 'internal affair' with which the U.N. is not competent to deal. Namibia is an 'international' dispute and may, therefore, be used to provide a means of criticizing apartheid at the U.N. and, perhaps, acting against it as well. It is thus a far more significant country than its population, resources and state of development alone would warrant. However, the 1966 ruling of the International Court of Justice that Liberia and Ethiopia had 'no legal right or interest' in the dispute between South Africa and the U.N. was a setback for those who believed that legal processes might be used to fight apartheid on the international stage. In 1971, however, the Court ruled that South Africa's presence in Namibia is illegal and called on South Africa to withdraw its administration.

BOTSWANA, LESOTHO AND SWAZILAND

These three countries were formerly known as the High Commission Territories, administered through a High Commission responsible to the Commonwealth Relations Office. The fact that the High Commissioner was also the Ambassador to South Africa emphasizes the close links the three countries have always had with the Republic (formerly the Union) of South Africa. They still have a customs union with South Africa.

Under the South Africa Act of 1909, which brought the Union into being, it was envisaged that the three territories might at some future date be incorporated into South Africa.[5] However, in spite of constant pressure from South Africa, Britain honoured the pledge given in 1909, and renewed in 1959, that no transfer to South Africa would take place until the inhabitants had been consulted. In 1962, South Africa stated that she was no longer interested in incorporation as independence for the territories was in line with her own policy of self-rule for the Bantu 'Homelands'. Both Botswana (formerly Bechuanaland) and Lesotho (formerly Basutoland) gained their independence in 1966. Swaziland is still a British responsibility.

Botswana is dependent economically on South Africa and its

administrative headquarters was at Mafeking inside the Republic until recently. However, a new capital has now been developed at Gaberones.

It is a large country, some three times the size of the United Kingdom but supporting only 543,000 people. Like S.W. Africa it is an arid land with a rainfall which varies from 12 inches in the west to 19 inches in the east.

The country can be divided into three natural regions: the Kalahari 'desert', better described as sand veld, for it provides some good seasonal grazing which could be extended; the Okovango Basin; and the relatively fertile and developed eastern strip near the railway line.

The Okovango Basin has been the subject of several inquiries and surveys. There are clearly large reserves of untapped water there, but the area is tsetse-infested and malarial. It is probable that the Okovango Basin itself could be developed for agriculture and surplus water made available by canal for areas to the east.[6]

The eastern strip, near the railway, was the area which first interested Britain and contains about 80 per cent of the population. At the time a Protectorate was proclaimed (1895) it was regarded simply as a 'road into the interior',[7] a convenient by-pass for Rhodes' pioneers which would avoid the Transvaal and provide a clear line of expansion for the British empire in central Africa. Some of this eastern strip has been alienated to European farmers and there is a small area of European farming at Ghanzi, near the border of S.W. Africa.

Cattle farming is the most important economic activity and provides 90 per cent (1967) of total exports. The chief markets are in South Africa, Congo and Rhodesia, but in 1958 some meat was, for the first time, exported overseas. Up until 1954 all cattle were exported on the hoof, but in that year an abattoir was established at Lobatsi and exports are now largely of carcasses and processed meat products.

Following on the publication of the 1963 F.A.O. survey (*The Beef Cattle and Meat Industry of the Bechuanaland Protectorate*), measures were put in hand for stock and pasture improvement, bore holes, transport facilities and the expansion of the Lobatsi abattoir. A target of 2 million head of cattle (against about 1½

million in 1965) is planned.[8] Together with improved communication to western areas, this could provide a firmer basis than at present on which future economic growth can rest.

Botswana has workable coal reserves near the railway which could be used for power stations for the development of industry, and as an export to neighbouring countries. The development of copper and nickel mining at Pikwe-Selibe is planned by Botswana Roan Selection Trust, and of diamonds at Letlhakane and Orapa by de Beers. There is presently a small export trade in manganese.

Lesotho is entirely surrounded by South Africa and is the poorest of the three countries. About two thirds of the country consists of high mountains rising to 11,000 ft and most of the population of about 900,000 is concentrated in the western lowlands.

The economy is almost entirely devoted to subsistence agriculture and the density of population in the more fertile areas has been accompanied by serious soil erosion. At present the only significant export is labour. No less than 43 per cent of the adult male population is away at work in South Africa at any one time.[9] There is also some trade in wool, livestock, diamonds and mohair. About half the total revenue comes from U.K. government grants.

Lesotho's most urgent needs at present are an extension of the soil conservation programme and the development of its only other available resource – water. The 1960 Economic Survey Mission recommended a hydrological survey as 'an urgent necessity'.[10] It suggested that Lesotho ought to be able to sell both water and hydro-electric power to the neighbouring areas of South Africa.

Swaziland is smaller than the other two Territories and potentially the richest of the three. It is about the size of Wales and contains some 363,000 people of whom about 9,000 are Europeans. It is unlike the other two countries in that there are considerable areas of land in European ownership and that the economy is increasingly based on the exploitation of minerals and on commercial agriculture. About 45 per cent of the land area is in European ownership.

The climate and soils are much more favourable for agricul-

ture than in the other two territories and a variety of crops are grown. There is a considerable export of sugar, canned fruit, citrus, meat and meat products, and wood pulp (16·5 per cent in 1967). The latter comes from plantations, established after the Second World War in parts of the high veld; here the rate of growth of pines and gums (eucalyptus) is one of the highest in the world. Pulpwood can be grown on a 15-year rotation compared with a 40 to 50 year rotation in Germany and Scandinavia.[11]

For many years asbestos was the country's chief export (14 per cent in 1967) but has now been overtaken by iron ore (27·1 per cent in 1967). Mined in the north-west at Bomvu, the ore has an iron content of 64 per cent and is transported by a new railway for export to Japan through Lourenço Marques. This railway development also makes possible the exploitation of extensive coal deposits.

All three countries are close and dependent neighbours of South Africa. In the past they have suffered from neglect just as the African areas of the Republic have suffered, and little money has been spent on them. The appointment of the 1960 Economic Survey Mission was the first sign that the Government intended to help to improve this state of affairs.

The Mission approached its task 'with the question whether there are any development projects which could be started promptly and carried through within the next decade or so – projects which could carry each Territory well on the way to becoming a viable economic unit'. The Mission's recommendations would, if adopted, 'make the attainment of this goal a near certainty in the case of Swaziland, a reasonable probability in the case of the Bechuanaland Protectorate and a possibility in the case of Basutoland ...'[12]

Successful development of the countries as envisaged by the Mission depends on two essentials: money made available by Britain and other countries, and cooperation with South Africa.

Already the three countries are economically dependent on South Africa. To develop them successfully would mean that their economic relations with South Africa 'must become more numerous and complex.'[13] The political implications of this – on all sides – have yet to be worked out. There is certainly a continuing need for financial and other support from Britain.

Notes on Chapter 13

1. Van Renan and Brandt, *Eighteenth Century Explorers*, quoted by Michael Scott in *Shadow over Africa*, 1950, p. 4.
2. *The Native Tribes of South West Africa and their Treatment by Germany*, H.M.S.O., 1918, quoted ibid., p. 4.
3. C. Arden-Clarke, 'South-West Africa, the Union and the United Nations', in *African Affairs*, Jan. 1960, p. 27.
4. Paul Rohrbach, quoted by M. Scott, op. cit., p. 5.
5. The Act empowered the King in Council, on address from both Houses of the Union Parliament, to transfer the territories to the Union subject to certain conditions designed for the protection of native rights.
6. See Chapter 15, *Basutoland, Bechuanaland and Swaziland: Report of an Economic Survey Mission*, H.M.S.O., 1960.
7. ibid., p. 53.
8. A. Storey, 'The Botswana Livestock Industry', in *Geography*, Vol. 53, 1968, pp. 87–9.
9. See note 6, p. 226.
10. ibid., p. 255.
11. G. W. Sneesby, 'Economic Development in Swaziland', in *Geography*, Vol. 53, 1968, pp. 186–9.
12. *Basutoland, Bechuanaland and Swaziland. Report of an Economic Survey Mission*, H.M.S.O., 1960, p. 12, note 6.
13. ibid., p. 12.

See also:

M. Cole, *South Africa*, 1961.
Republic of South Africa, *South West Africa Survey*, 1967.
D. Barker, *Swaziland*, 1965.
A. Coates, *Basutoland*, 1966.
B. A. Young, *Bechuanaland*, 1966.

Conclusion

There has been an enormous upsurge of interest in Africa in the last ten years, even though some of it may prove to be transient and perhaps fickle. Since this book was first contemplated (1960) the amount of genuine expertise – and the number of 'experts' of all kinds – has grown out of all recognition. So too, has the temptation to generalize about Africa. But we have now seen enough of the variety of the continent to realize that generalizations can be dangerous. Differences in climate, resources, racial types, social systems, economic development, and the rate and type of political progress are greater than we should find in Europe. There is no *one* Africa and no widespread sense of the need for African unity, except among intellectuals and at the highest political level, as seen in the formation of the Organization of African Unity, on which *all* of independent Africa is represented. There are local loyalties and local problems, only some of which exist throughout the continent.

It is a truism to say that Africa is changing, but the picture of a uniform 'wind of change' was always a false one. The pace of change varies as much as the scenery, and is producing even greater contrasts than before in some areas: the contrasts of modern chain stores and tin-roofed one-man shops, of university education and illiteracy, of prosperous farms and run-down subsistence holdings or of 'one man, one vote' and continuing dictatorship.

Everyone wants freedom these days and everyone has a vaguely defined desire for a better life. The two are not always complementary, however; nor do they always mean the same things. In South Africa the black Africans are certainly not 'free' but many are materially better off than they would be if they lived in any other part of the continent. In Rhodesia, Europeans have seized freedom from Whitehall and Africans

would like freedom from white political control. In Uganda, some Africans want freedom from Asian 'economic domination' as much as they wanted political independence. Pan-Africanists want not only independence but freedom from the boundaries of the colonial past.

It seems, then, that for a long time to come Africa will be divided in all sorts of ways, as indeed we might expect any other thirty or forty independent states to be. And yet, on reflection, it seems extraordinary that such a statement needs to be made at all. The countries of Europe have had contact and some understanding for centuries and are only now groping towards a wider unity. Why should we expect to find similarities rather than differences in a vast continent whose peoples are only now beginning to have close contact with each other?

The statement needs to be made, I think, because we all tend to be over-sensitive about skin colour and to feel that there must be something in common between men because they are black even more than because they are human. It leads us to be surprised at the differences and to be constantly in danger of falling back into the trap of assuming that they do not exist.

In spite of differences, however, there will still be the uniting themes which have been forced on Africa by Europe – those of anti-racialism, anti-colonialism and poverty. These will present a continuing challenge to Europeans and to Europe as long as they exist anywhere in Africa. The first theme of racialism needs no emphasis but it may, perhaps, be profitable to look more closely at colonialism and poverty.

Colonialism, you will say, is on the way out. As was described in 1961,

> European administrators are packing their bags. They are having a last look around the compounds with the whitewashed stones and the tropical flowers, the orderly district offices, the cool and old-fashioned bungalows. . . . History, having irrevocably left its mark on a changing African scene, has taken a new turn . . .*

Two things need to be said about this sort of view. First, there are still many parts of Africa where colonial-type rule is strongly entrenched. Second, and perhaps more important, the

*D. Apter, *The Political Kingdom in Uganda*, 1961, p. 3.

suspicion of some form of 'neo-colonialism' is likely to endure for longer than the continuance of colonial rule itself. This implies a hyper-sensitivity on the part of newly emergent states about the good intentions of European countries. It may make even well-intentioned policies misunderstood. In particular, Europeans need to be wary of making their own definitions of 'independence'.

It was suggested in the House of Lords as late as 1961 that Britain must 'ensure' African independence by teaching Africans not to be communists. 'We can reasonably conclude,' said Lord Twining, 'that the great majority of Africans are not enamoured with communist ideology; but they are susceptible to communist methods, and may find themselves unwittingly entrapped by them.'* Those who go to Africa to teach *against* any '-ism' rather than *for* and *with* Africa will find an increasing resentment against the continuance of paternalism and quite possibly end up with the situation they most wanted to avoid.

Racialism and colonialism are largely challenges to Europe. Poverty is a joint challenge to Europe and Africa alike.

It was the experience of European rule which 'opened up' Africa and made the people of this continent of isolation and difficulty aware of both the possibility and the desirability of material progress. Self-interest and morality alike dictate that the interest of Europe in the elimination of poverty should not end with European rule. Self-interest dictates it, not because of the Cold War, but because there can be no peace in a world where the gap between the rich countries and the poor countries is increasing rather than decreasing and where the aspirations of the poor are becoming increasingly greater than the possibility of their fulfilment. Morality dictates it for those who believe that a common humanity implies a common responsibility.

For Europe this means a willingness to provide the trained men and the money necessary to help promote economic growth, and to do so on a scale large enough to narrow the gap between aspiration and fulfilment. Already in some countries there is just no margin to spare for further economic progress

*Speech in House of Lords, 8 November 1961. Reported by British Information Service, Kampala, 10 November 1961.

unless help comes from outside or standards are further depressed for the sake of future generations. The report of the Commission on International Development* set a target growth-rate for the developing countries of 6 per cent per annum (currently 3 per cent in most of Africa); to achieve this would require that aid from the richer countries should rise to 1 per cent of their Gross National Products – a modest enough goal given that it includes private investment.

> Specifically, official development assistance should be raised to 0·70 per cent of donor G.N.P. by 1975, and in no case later than 1980. This compares with average flows of 0·39 per cent in 1968.†

The challenge to Africa is no less important. It means a willingness to change cherished ways and institutions, a willingness to experiment, to learn, and to wait for results. Above all it means a willingness to cooperate both within and between countries. Such cooperation might yet overcome the limitations of boundaries imposed by European rule and produce a much more real sense of 'Africa' than at present exists.

*Lester B. Pearson (Chairman), *Partners in Development*, 1969.
†ibid., p. 18.

Index